D1015834

MARGOT MERTZ
TAKES IT DOWN

MARGOT MERTZ TAKES IT DOWN

CARRIE McCROSSEN & IAN McWETHY

PHILOMEL BOOKS

CONTENT WARNING: sexual harassment and revenge porn

PHILOMEL BOOKS
An imprint of Penguin Random House LLC, New York

First published in the United States of America by Philomel Books,
an imprint of Penguin Random House LLC, 2021

Copyright © 2021 by Temple Hill Publishing, Carrie McCrossen, and Ian McWethy

Philomel Books is a registered trademark of Penguin Random House LLC.

Visit us online at penguinrandomhouse.com.

Library of Congress Cataloging-in-Publication Data is available.

Printed in the USA

Hardcover ISBN 9780593205259
Export ISBN 9780593464007

10 9 8 7 6 5 4 3 2 1

LSCH

Edited by Kelsey Murphy

Design by Monique Sterling

Text set in Mercury Text G1

This book is a work of fiction. Any references to historical events, real people, or real places are used fictitiously. Other names, characters, places, and events are products of the author's imagination, and any resemblance to actual events or places or persons, living or dead, is entirely coincidental.

The publisher does not have any control over and does not assume any responsibility for author or third-party websites or their content.

MARGOT MERTZ
TAKES IT DOWN

February 18, 1:44 p.m.

MARGOT: B, you were right. the internet is a dark and disgusting place

1

WHEN TEACHERS CRY

"I mean . . . he was in such incredible shape. There wasn't an ounce of body fat on him. His shoulders, his arms, you should have seen his—"

"Mrs. Blye—" I interrupted, hoping to steer this conversation away from . . . wherever it was going.

"Sorry. I was just trying to give you context but . . . you're right. That's not important. Nor does it excuse what I did. Or the damage it could do if it got out! Margot . . ."

Mrs. Blye looked down at her drink, as if her gin and tonic were somehow going to save her. Clearly she was embarrassed and a little confused. This must have been weird for her. The random brunette she had once given a B+[1] suddenly had a lot of power over her.

---

1. She gave me a B+ for using the colloquial name for a sugar solution on the final, instead of using the chemical formula. Which is BS because she knows I was doing A-level work. (Not that I hold a grudge.)

"Josh was one night. It was just sex. Great sex, yes, but—"

"Mrs. Blye, again, I really, *really* don't need to know—"

"I still love my husband. Sure, we have our problems. I can be distant. And he's gotten very into role-playing board games." She cringed. "But that doesn't excuse what I did! And I don't want one stupid, drunken night to . . ." She started to tear up. "I believe we can make this marriage work if you can just, please, help me."

And that's when she really lost it. We're talking heaving, loud, ugly crying. Normally, Mrs. Blye was pretty attractive. For a teacher. Her white skin was a little too tanned, especially for winter. But she dressed okay and knew her way around a Sephora. If you passed her on the street you wouldn't be like, "Daaammn." But if you had to stare at her for forty-one minutes while she described oxidation-reduction reactions, you might find yourself thinking, "Huh, she's kinda pretty." But right now? She looked like wet garbage. And she was starting to attract attention.

"You okay over here?" The ancient cocktail waitress, who I assumed was named Rhonda or Nancy, had appeared beside our booth.

"We're okay, thanks," I answered confidently for both of us. Rhonda/Nancy hobbled back to the bar.

I never worried about being carded at Petey O'Taverns. Petey's was a seedy bar for serious drinkers who didn't require ambiance or natural light. The floors were sticky, there was a cigarette machine (?!) by the bathroom, and behind the bar hung a poster for a movie from the '80s called *Ski School*. (This exceptionally misogynistic poster features a giant pair of bikini-clad boobs with two tiny "cool guys" skiing down the cleavage. The tagline: "Curves ahead *and* behind." I feel like this movie hasn't aged well.[2])

Anyway, I wasn't there to score booze. The only drink I ever ordered was a club soda with lime. I just needed a place to bring clients. Petey's was gross, sure, but it allowed my adult clients to be anonymous, order a drink, and forget that they were about to Venmo a teenager thousands of dollars.

"Look, it's always a mistake to sleep with a man named Josh," I said, trying to lighten the mood. It wasn't clear if she found this funny. "But . . . I might be able to help."

Mrs. Blye looked up at me, searching my pale, pale (so pale) white face for a glimmer of hope.

Over the past two years, I had sat across from teachers, students, parents, and one time a state legislator. I listened to the details of their affairs, their embarrassing tweets, their shameful videos—and then I'd make it all go away. That was the job. For the right fee, I would go to the ends of the internet to clean up their mistakes.

In this case, Mrs. Blye, a tenured chemistry teacher at Roosevelt High, cheated on her husband with Josh Frange, a chemistry teacher at Brighton High. (Brighton is our school's rival. If you care about high school rivalries, which I don't.) Josh had kind of a rep. He was a teacher-slut who slept with most of the district's STEM departments. I've seen his Instagram account, and I have to say I don't quite get it. In my opinion, he's an average-looking forty-year-old with a very punchable face. But to each their own, I guess.

---

2. And it begs so many questions. Why is she wearing a bikini to ski? Did the men shrink or is she a giant? What did female moviegoers do in the '80s?

This is how it went down. Last weekend, Mrs. Blye's husband left town to visit his sick mother (oof!), and Mrs. Blye got hammered at a "Teachers and Administrators Bonding Night of Rockin' Karaoke!!!" [Shudder.] There was off-key singing, there were premixed margaritas, and there were a lot of pictures taken. By Josh. Pics of Mrs. Blye singing. Pics of Mrs. Blye and Josh dueting "Under Pressure." (Thus causing both Freddie Mercury and David Bowie to die again.) And . . . pics of Mrs. Blye and Josh kissing.

Mrs. Blye was now freaking out because one of those photos had shown up on Josh's Instagram feed. It was one of their tamer "duet" pics, but it contradicted her alibi that she "went bowling with Sheila." Mrs. Blye worried that it was only a matter of time before more pictures showed up on his feed. Or before her husband saw it and started asking questions. She'd tried texting Josh to see if he would take it down, but so far, he hadn't responded.

"Well?" Mrs. Blye asked after telling me her sordid tale. She was dying for a response.

I know this may sound like an easy gig. I mean, all Josh did was post one picture, right? But it was never that simple. You never knew how many pictures or tweets or emails there were, or who had downloaded them. You never knew where they were stored. On just one phone? Uploaded to the cloud? Backed up on a laptop? And you never knew what your target's intentions were. What was Josh planning? If he was just a careless dum-dum who didn't realize he was putting Mrs. Blye at risk, then erasing the pics might be easy enough. But if he was purposely trying to break up Mrs. Blye's marriage? Well, that could get ugly real fast.

My gut told me Josh Frange was going to be a pain in my ass. And that Mrs. Blye probably hadn't told me the whole story. Which could mean tons of billable hours for one stupid picture.

"I have to think about it."

Mrs. Blye wrinkled her UV-kissed brow. "I have to think about it" wasn't the answer she was expecting. Suddenly, she was a pissed-off teacher who would not accept your forged doctor's note. "What is there to think about? My life is falling apart, and I'm willing to pay you. What the hell else do you have going on? Studying? Extracurriculars? An awkward hand job? You're a high schooler!"

High schooler? That pissed me off. The label "high schooler" completely trivializes what I am. Labels I prefer? Entrepreneur. Tech-curious. Lone wolf. Daughter. Misanthrope. Possible witch. (Okay, I'm not a witch at all, but Greg Mayes called me that once in a study hall, and I have to admit, I kind of liked it. Even though the witchiest thing I've ever done is burn palo santo in my room.) Point is, call me any of those things! But when you say "high schooler," it sounds like I'm some dud who doesn't know who she is. And I know who I am. I'm Margot Goddamned Mertz.

And besides, Mrs. Blye needed *my* help! Did she think her "I'll send you to the principal" voice would really scare me? She just told me she'd had an affair! I had the upper hand!

But of course I didn't say any of that or even show the slightest bit of resentment. Because I'm a professional. I simply responded, "It's gonna cost you."

Baller move, if you ask me. Like I said before, I didn't need this job.

Mrs. Blye didn't care about the price. Nobody cares. Once they think you'll fix a life-destroying mistake for them, teachers, teenagers, local weathermen . . . they always agree to my terms. What choice do they have?

"Thank you. Thank you, Margot. Whatever it costs! Just make this go away!"

Mrs. Blye reached into her big teacher tote bag and gave me $200 as a down payment. I told her I'd be in touch with further details regarding her case. And then I got the hell out of there. Petey O'Taverns smelled like failure, and I had a lot of work to do.

2

THE DICK PIC THAT
STARTED IT ALL

At this point you're probably wondering several things. Like: What's it like to watch a teacher cry? What's palo santo? And probably most pressing . . . how exactly did you *get* this job?

To answer your questions: 1) It's weird. 2) A stick you burn. And 3) I ask myself that all the time. And honestly, I'm not sure. Most days, it feels like a random accident.

But, when I really dig deep, I think it was two things. Two particularly shitty, kick-you-in-your-braces life lessons that both hardened me *and* railroaded me to where I am now . . .

SHITTY LIFE LESSON #1: BEST FRIENDS ARE NOT FOREVER

Friends have never been easy for me. In elementary school I had "friends" (in that I was invited to birthday parties and swapped fruit snacks with Megan Mills). But when middle school started,

I was relegated to a life of loneliness. I guess making a passionate speech against the electoral college on my first day of school . . . turned some people off. For the majority of sixth grade I did a lot of things by myself, like: Eating! Riding the bus! Even, believe it or not, group projects! (It can be done if no one likes you!) My parents thought I was depressed. But I don't think I was, like, "officially" depressed. I just wasn't used to being hated . . . for no reason at all.

But then I met Bethany. And things got better. We randomly sat next to each other one day in the library and we bonded over our shared love of dumplings and Sonia Sotomayor.[3] We discovered that we both lived in apartments and not houses (like most of our classmates). And we hadn't grown up with nannies or au pairs; our families relied on overcrowded day cares or overwhelmed grandparents. Soon, we were hanging out after school, binging *The Office* together, talking about boys, and laughing so hard that a little pee came out. Sure, my classmates were still being cruel. Like when Megan Mills, no longer my fruit-snack friend, "joked" that my new haircut made me look like a [homophobic slur that I will not repeat because let's be better than Megan Mills]. But with Beth, I was at least surviving. It's my belief that you can get through anything in life, even middle school, if you have one really, *really* good friend. And I had the best one.

But then we went to high school. And everything went to shit.

Beth and I had high hopes for ninth grade. The lockers were bigger, the teachers were smarter. And everybody got slightly less

---

3. She's a hero! Imagine going to work every day with Clarence Thomas and Brett Kavanaugh! It must suck, but she is *making it work*!

awkward. Plus, for the first time since . . . ever?, we were getting attention from boys. Attention that we pretended we didn't want because we were "above" such trivial and patriarchal things (but secretly we wanted it). And no one's attention was more coveted than that of Chris Heinz.

Chris Heinz was unrealistically handsome for high school. He had pouty lips, shaggy brown hair, and warm ivory skin. Even as a sophomore he had the six-pack of a twenty-eight-year-old and the sinewy hands of a longshoreman.[4] Neither Beth nor I had any classes with him. But, like everyone in school, we knew him. We'd see him and his friends rocking the vending machine, trying to get free snacks. Or hear teachers in the hallway saying, "Mr. Heinz, where are you supposed to be right now?" He was our go-to hot-guy crush, so removed from our actual lives that Beth and I could project whatever personality we wanted onto him. So it was pretty momentous when he asked Bethany out on a date. A real, in-person, not-at-all-imaginary date with the hottest and best cod-smelling boy in the school!

If only we had known how fucking gross Chris was. The "date" consisted of Chris repeatedly offering Beth alcohol she didn't want, followed by Chris groping her and sticking his tongue down her throat like all the porn stars he had watched on a loop for the past three years. When she stopped him, Chris got mad and told her to leave. Then, the next day, he spread rumors that Bethany had given him a "toothy blow job" and gave

---

4. Look, I have a thing for longshoremen. Ever since my dad made me watch *On the Waterfront*. And I swear, Chris smelled like salt water, cod, and the quiet dignity of a man who works with his hands.

her the nickname "Blow-job Beth" (clever!). People started tagging Beth on anything having to do with BJ's (BJ's Wholesale, BJ's Brewhouse, etc.) and flooding her with DMs of porn GIFs. And then a week later . . . Bethany tried to kill herself.

The thing about Beth, which I didn't really understand at the time, was that she struggled with depression. I thought she was depressed in the way that I was in sixth grade, but apparently it was more serious than that. A lot more serious. And around the time she went on a date with Chris, Beth was really struggling. It turned out to be a very bad week to get sexually assaulted then slut-shamed.

Beth spent the remainder of the year in a psych ward, then moved to Colorado to be closer to her grandparents. And I guess it was all too painful for her, because when she left, she cut herself off from any connections she had in North Webster. Even from me.

Well, not entirely. I made a vow to text her at least once a week so she'd know what was going on in my life. This friendship wouldn't die just because Chris Heinz sucks. She hasn't texted me back yet, and that's okay. She will when she's ready.

SHITTY LIFE LESSON #2: MY PARENTS ARE BAD AT MATH

I have wanted to go to Stanford University since I was eight years old. That was when I mistakenly received a brochure meant for my upstairs neighbor, one "James McCarthy," who I've never met. When I opened the brochure, I was smitten. I don't know if it was the photos of the campus, or the industrious alumni like

Sergey Brin and Larry Page and Sandra Day O'Connor.[5] It was the first college I remember being aware of. As a thing. It seemed like this glorious place where intellects would be challenged. Where work ethics would be celebrated. And where I would be, like, normal. From then on, I was obsessed. While other girls were daydreaming about which teen pop star they'd lose their virginity to, I was daydreaming about Stanford. I mean, if I could, I'd lose it to Stanford. (That's right. I'd have sex with a college. I apologize for nothing.)

So it was pretty devastating when, just a few months after Beth moved away, my parents sat me down and said the always-ominous phrase, "We need to talk." (I thought it was going to be a sex talk, which, in retrospect, would have been less awkward.) They informed me they weren't going to be able to pay for college. So if I wanted to go, I was on my own. And look, I wasn't expecting a free ride or anything. My dad owns a dry cleaners, and my mom is a nurse. It's not like we're rolling in it. But still, my parents knew how much it meant to me. They had promised they'd pay for it. They said they had a plan.

Unfortunately, it was not a good plan. Basically, they invested their life savings/my college fund into a *second* dry cleaning business. The first location was thriving and they figured, why not start a second? Which made sense. But then they thought, why not let Margot's idiot uncle Richard run it? He just got fired from ShopRite and he's going through a divorce, so he seems like the kind of guy you could TRUST WITH MARGOT'S COLLEGE

5. And . . . Elizabeth Holmes. They're not *all* winners.

FUND. So yeah, the second dry cleaners did not go well. And in the span of six months, Richard tanked the business, and my college fund evaporated.

SO THIS WAS WHERE THINGS STOOD WHEN I ENTERED ROOSEVELT High sophomore year. No friends and no money and no future. Basically, I was screwed.

But then, as I sat down in Ms. Okado's homeroom, I heard muttering. A sad, dull muttering, coming from the prepubescent white boy seated next to me. It was Kevin Beane, aka my very first client.

Kevin is an extremely anxious young man. He chews his nails, grinds his teeth, and has a penchant for impromptu, anxiety-induced public vomiting. He threw up at the third-grade talent show, the fifth-grade spelling bee, and *every Wednesday* in seventh grade. One time in chorus, he puked so hard it was rumored he had Ebola, but actually he was just very, very nervous about singing "Shenandoah."

"I'm screwed. I'm so screwed. Oh . . ." Kevin muttered, eyes bulging at the ground.

I immediately went into vomit-prevention mode. Did I have a tarp? No. Did Ms. Okado? Doubtful, she seemed like she forgot to brush her teeth most mornings. Could I use my backpack as a shield? Not good enough.

"Kevin, are you okay?" I said in my "hostage negotiator" voice. Sympathetic yet firm.

"My dick's going to be everywhere."

My dick's going to be everywhere. It was not even eight o'clock in the morning!

"Okay, I'm not sure I'm the right person to talk to about this," I said, to no avail.

"It . . . it wasn't my fault. It was an accident. I really wasn't trying to do a dick pic," he said, eyes glued to his desk.

Look, let me be clear. If a boy sends you a picture of his dick and you didn't ask for it, you should crucify him. Seriously. Fuck him. Would he show you his dick in real life? Probably not. That would be creepy. And illegal. So why is he showing you his digital one?

But when Kevin told me that it was a pic he never intended to send, one he took solely because he was worried he might have a malignant tumor, one that his older brother Trevor then sent to several girls in our grade as a "joke" after stealing Kevin's phone, well . . . I believed him. Because "sexual dick pic predator" doesn't really fit Kevin's delicate "I once threw up because it rained" persona.

I didn't know what I was supposed to do, other than kill time until the bell rang. But then Kevin got that look. That "I have to sing in public" look, and vomit was sure to be on its way. I. Had. To. Act. Because. I. Don't. Do. Vomit.

"So your digital dick is on a few phones. That's true of most guys since like . . . 2012! Including many that hold public office," I said, subtly moving my desk six inches away from him.

"But I can't . . . what if it gets out? Or goes viral?"

"Your dick's not going viral, Kevin."

"What if my mom sees it?! What if I can't get into college

because—" He retched. Then retched again. Oh god.

"Then I'll stop it from spreading! Okay? I'll fix it."

I'm not sure what gave me the confidence to say that. I think I just wanted him to calm down. Or maybe the image of a college admissions officer looking at Kevin Beane's penis and evaluating it next to his SAT scores was so absurd it short-circuited my brain. For whatever reason, the words "I'll fix it" shot out of my mouth. And I guess he believed me, because Kevin stopped talking and actually looked me in the eyes for the first time.

"You will? How?"

And then . . . I'm not sure what I said after that. Knowing me, I talked confidently out of my butt and said something like, "Every application has safeguards," or "It's probably a malware issue," or "Time is a flat circle." A whole lot of nonsense that Kevin believed because A) I wrinkle my brow a lot, and if you wrinkle your brow when you talk, people tend to believe you, and B) he was desperate. He wanted to believe miracles could happen, and that his penis could go back in his pants where it belonged.

He started manically digging in his backpack, searching for his iPhone, which he quickly found. "I have a hundred fifty dollars in my Venmo bank right now, and I could bring in another three hundred in cash tomorrow. I just had a birthday, and my Grammy gives cash. Will that be enough?"

Holy shit. He was going to pay *money* for this. *Serious* money. *Bribe-your-way-onto-a-crew-team* money. Jesus. I guess I shouldn't have been surprised. A recent, much-debated rezoning of our district had put trash like me into the same high school as ultrarich kids like Kevin. And I was not above capitalizing on that.

He sent me the $150, then quickly ran to first period. I mumbled "thanks" with the understanding that I would somehow collect all his dick pics and make sure they never saw the light of day. (Which within a few weeks, I did.)

And before I knew it, I was bombarded with new clients, all in need of my services. All willing to *pay*. I realized if I put my head down and didn't get sidetracked by all the usual high school bullshit (parties, cliques, boyfriends, or just . . . friends in general), that I just might make enough to get my lower middle-class ass to Stanford. All I had to do was figure out how to make more people's filth go away. Which was going to involve a lot more hacking know-how than I currently had.

Luckily I knew of exactly one computer nerd who was more in need of money than I was. Enter: Sammi Santos.

3

ANOTHER EFFING JOB

MARGOT: Ugh took another gig. Interested in more work?

SAMMI: sure

MARGOT: Great! Heading back to school now. Left my laptop in my locker. Woof! Are you in lab? I'll come find you.

MARGOT: And I know I said I wasn't going to take on more work but she was desperate. And she's paying. Premium rate.

MARGOT: So it'll be worth it. For both of us.

SAMMI: i didn't say anything

MARGOT: Anyway I like my work.

SAMMI: k.

MARGOT: Don't say "K." Admit it. I'm at my best when I'm working.

SAMMI: k.

MARGOT: Now your trying to annoy me. I'm not gonna bite.

MARGOT: *you're

MARGOT: Fine. Don't say anything. I'm taking your silence to mean you agree with me.

MARGOT: The job is for Mrs. Blye. She was your chem teacher freshman year, yeah?

SAMMI: no

MARGOT: Yes she was.

SAMMI: she wasn't

MARGOT: Yes she was. I remember it was weird you were taking chem as a fresh. Remember? Because your mom made you take summer school before fresh year so you could be two years ahead and I was like, "Geez, Mrs. S, chill the F out."

SAMMI: I had mr. pasquale i didn't have mrs. blye

MARGOT: No. I would've remembered that. Mr. Pasquale is super tall.

> **MARGOT:** He's like 6'5".

> **MARGOT:** I would've remembered.

> **MARGOT:** I always remember tall people. I'm afraid they're going to hit their heads!

> **SAMMI:** . . . .

> **MARGOT:** Aha. The dot dots. Are you thinking? Are you looking at your freshman year class schedule because you know I'm right? Because I tend to be right when it comes to almost everything?

> **SAMMI:** ur exhausting

> **MARGOT:** *you're

> **MARGOT:** SO I WAS RIGHT!

> **SAMMI:** no

> **MARGOT:** Would you at least check your class sched freshman year?

> **SAMMI:** ill be at lab.

When Sammi said "I'll be at lab," I knew I wasn't going to eke out another sentence from him. So I figured I might as well wait until I saw him face-to-face. I shoved my phone in my pocket and walked back to school.

Mrs. Blye had insisted on meeting me during seventh period,

since apparently she didn't have any classes after sixth and was desperate to get her misdeeds off her chest. Wiggling out of seventh and eighth periods was always a little hazardous. Those are notorious class-skipping periods, and Principal Palmer loved catching ditchers as they returned to school to catch their buses home.

I walked up to the main entrance just as the bell was about to ring. And sure enough, there was Raymond Palmer, standing by the front door. Button-up shirt. L.L.Bean khakis. And whistle. Always a whistle, which, as far as I could tell, he never actually used?

"Mertz. Well, well, well. What brings you *back* to school at 2:35 p.m., when you should be in class?" he smugly asked. The smuggy smug idiot.

"It's the only time my chiropractor could see me," I replied, continuing to walk in his direction. "And believe me, I hate missing health class. But given that my chiropractor is a health care provider . . . I feel like it all evens out." I didn't even bother delivering this with a fake smile. I just kind of stared him down, simultaneously producing a signed "chiropractor's note" from my back pocket. Then I kept walking. "Great tie, by the way."

And then, as if on cue, the bell rang. Students flooded the halls. Principal Palmer read over my doctor's note, furrowing his pasty white brow and slumping his shoulders with all the disappointment of a forty-five-year-old man who was regretting his life choices.

I ducked and weaved my way to Stairwell C, where I almost

tripped over two freshman girls who seemed to be crying into each other's phones. I tried to give them some privacy by not staring as I made my way to the school basement, where only the weirdest and nerdiest of clubs meet. Shop, computer lab, technical theater, and nerdiest of all . . . robot club. I think the official purpose of robot club is to learn about automation and participate in statewide competitions, but any time I stopped by it was just Sammi and a few random freshmen who hadn't discovered deodorant yet.

When I arrived, Sammi was building what could only be described as a robot with knives for hands.

"Sammmi," I said in a kind of singsong as I leaned into the doorway.

"Maaaargot," he replied, completing our weird little "name game" that we'd been doing for years, which was never actually funny.

"So! At my rather depressing post-lunch seltzer with Mrs. Blye—are you wearing a Yankees hat?" I interrupted myself. This was shocking. Sammi had had the same haircut (short and curly on top with a medium fade) and fashion sense (jeans, graphic tee, black Nikes) since the sixth grade. And every day he used exactly two dollops of aftershave on his boyish, brown-skinned face. He loved his routine, and he never wavered in his outward appearance. Even when encouraged by an attractive girl to . . . mix it up a little, he was steadfast. And the Yankees? He knew as much about sports as I knew about . . . well, sports.

"I'm trying something different," Sammi said, his dark brown eyes now hyper-focused on his knife-robot.

"Trying something different? You've been eating seventeen Frosted Mini-Wheats for breakfast ever since elementary school. Remember that one morning you came over and my mom gave you fifteen and you freaked out?"

"When I was ten? You know I'm seventeen now, right?"

"Sammi, I just don't know if I can live in a world where you wear hats. I think we really need to unpack this."

"Are you going to fixate on my hat for the next two hours? Or are you going to tell me about Mrs. Blye?" Sammi interjected.

I didn't really want to let this whole *hat* thing go unanswered, but I needed to get home and get to work. So I gave him the lowdown on Mrs. Blye.

"Cool. Should be easy." He shrugged. "Not like you need me to make phony HTTPS certificates again. That sucked."

Sammi had a number of qualities that made him an ideal associate.[6] Whenever we worked on a job together, Sammi would do all the high-level tech stuff that I had no interest in. And I would do everything else. From the unsexy (filing taxes for my LLC) to the mildly sexy (impersonating lawyers, meeting with clients, coercing creeps to delete their nudes, etc.). We played to our strengths. I was good at manipulating people. And Sammi was practically a computer.

I mean, I write Python and can hack a Windows box, but Sammi is next-level. One time he commandeered a botnet to brute-force a state senator's email password, but the really impressive part is that he commandeered *someone else's* botnet to

---

6. His actual title is "Chief Technology Officer and Coding Czar." But he refuses to call himself this.

do it. He hacked some hackers to do his hacking. (God willing, this will be the last time I throw around jargon like botnet and brute-force, because it is exhausting.)

I asked him to poke around Josh Frange's social and said I might need more help if I got behind. He shrugged with a look that meant, "I know you're going to get behind and need more help . . . but I'll wait till you ask for it." Which was infuriating. But in kind of a good way. The way my parents can sometimes push each other's buttons, but also call each other on their bullshit.

"Name one Yankee. Past or present," I pestered him, sure there was more to this hat business than he was letting on.

"No."

"Babe Ruth was a Yankee! Sammi, you should know something about the team you're advertising. The only graphic tee I've ever worn had Eleanor Roosevelt on it. But that's because I support the Universal Declaration of Human Rights!"

He rolled his eyes at me. He rolled his eyes at me a lot.

Sammi and I had a long history. I'd known him since I was in the third grade (and he was in fourth). That's when he and his mom moved into the same apartment complex as me. (Trinity Towers represent!) Sammi's parents were both born in the Dominican Republic. They met in Washington Heights, fell in love, and moved to North Webster. I think they were pretty happy. But then Sammi's dad died of a heart attack, and Sammi's mom sold their house. When they first moved in, I couldn't get Sammi to speak more than two words to me. (Those first few playdates were very awkward!) But eventually we realized we had a lot in common. We both liked computers a lot. And had a closeted appreciation for K-pop.

Most importantly, Sammi was loyal. Maybe the most loyal person I'd ever met (next to Beth). He was always up for taking a job, no matter how tedious or technical (or illegal), and he always, always answered his phone when I called. So yeah, that was just the kind of associate I needed as MCYF was taking off. (MCYF stands for Mertz Cleans Your Filth, LLC. And yes, I really did incorporate. I like everything I do to be legit. Especially MCYF.[7])

"Margot, someday you're going to try on a hat. Or get highlights or something. And when you do, I'll be there to give you shit about it."

"Are you coming?" I asked as I slung my backpack over my shoulder. "Or do you need some alone time with your sex robot here?"

"His name is Magnus." He pressed a button, and Magnus waved his knife-hand at me.

Terrifying. Sammi grabbed his bag and followed me to the door.

After a few more questions about that *hat*, Sammi and I fell into our usual walking-home routine: he says I walk too fast, I walk faster to annoy him, he stops walking until I slow down and circle back to him. We have fun. But then it started to rain, so we both started to haul ass. And since I refuse to wear galoshes

---

7. Yes, I've been told that Mertz Cleans Your Filth is a bad name. And yes, I've thrice been asked to clean houses. But I have a thousand business cards already, so let's all deal.

because they make my feet sweat, my high-tops were starting to fill up with water.

That's when I noticed a Tesla slowly following us. My fight-or-flight goose bumps popped up at the back of my neck. I put my keys into my fist (something I saw in a self-defense video on YouTube). I wasn't going to count on Sammi to defend me. He once let a fifth-grade girl beat him up and take his phone . . . when he was in seventh grade.[8]

I'd seen this car before, but I couldn't place where, which made me all the more uneasy. (Plus Teslas are creepy. Anything having to do with Elon Musk is creepy.[9]) My suspicions were confirmed when the car pulled over, and Avery Green popped his creepily handsome head out of the window. Avery had light brown skin, a Hollywood smile, and perfect coils somehow unaffected by the humidity. (But, like, how? My own hair was frizzy as hell.)

"Hey, Margot. Hey, Sammi. You guys want a ride home?"

Sammi was about to answer when I shrieked out "No!" a little too forcefully. Avery seemed taken aback. But not enough to stop smiling. Avery always looked like Instagram come to life.

"Uh . . . you sure? There's plenty of room!" Avery said, casually gesturing to his roomy back seat. And that's when the sky opened up and biblical rain poured down. The smiting kind that soaks your clothes in a matter of seconds.

"Nah! We're good!"

---

8. In fairness to Sammi, Rebecca Gupp had a really early growth spurt and was actually pretty scary.

9. Except Stanford. He did go there. I already said, they're not *all* winners!

"*Are* we, Margot?" Sammi asked, looking at me like I was deranged. I get it. Most people like Avery. He was the unofficial mayor of Roosevelt, the biracial homecoming king voted "Nicest Guy in School" two years running.[10] But the guy creeps me out.

To me, there's normal nice, e.g., holding the door open for someone, or saying thank you. And then there's *Avery nice.* Which is too much. He's just one of those obnoxious, overly earnest people who seems to get along with everyone. On four separate occasions, he's invited me to join one of the fifteen clubs he participates in. Plus he makes eye contact when he gives you a high five (bleh). In my opinion, Avery is . . . *serial-killer nice.* (Watch a few documentaries on Ted Bundy and tell me I'm wrong.)

"Thanks, but I think we'd rather walk. It's not that bad," I said as lightning literally zigzagged across the sky, followed by a one-Mississippi *boom*! It was like God was undercutting my argument. Avery shrugged "okay," rolled up his window, and drove away.

"What the hell, Margot?" Sammi whined as we walked into the street to avoid a four-sidewalk-square puddle.

"Sammi, you know my stance on Avery Green," I said, speeding up my pace again.

"But we're wet. And his Tesla is dry. Plus I think the back seat is one big massage chair."

I shot him a look that said "you realize that's probably a dumb rumor, and I'm disappointed you believe it."

A Tesla. That's another thing I didn't like about him. Avery was rich af. His dad owns several car dealerships and a brewery

---

10. According to the Roosevelt High School yearbook. He also won "Best Shoes" last year. God, I hate superlatives.

downtown, plus he hosts a weekly radio show called *Drive My Car* that is apparently very popular. I wouldn't know. I take the bus.

His mom (who sounds way cooler, in my opinion) graduated top of her class at Howard and is now president of Atlas Health, a group of for-profit hospitals. They say the Green money really comes from her. Which is impressive considering their home is rumored to have a screening room, an entire fridge dedicated to LaCroix, and not one, but two infinity pools. (While Trinity Towers has a sketchy hot tub that once gave me a rash!)

"Do you really think he's creepy? Or are you just doing that thing where you pretend to hate the person, but really you have a crush on them?" Sammi asked, suddenly avoiding eye contact with me.

I stopped in my tracks. What a truly insane thing to say.

"Avery? Avery Green?"

"What? Kelsey Chugg said he looks like 'if Michael B. Jordan and Harry Styles had a hot baby.' "

"A baby who would seduce you then skin you alive. Why would you ever say that, *crazy*?" I sniped.

"I dunno, he's had like twenty girlfriends . . . Girls like him . . ." he muttered apologetically to his shoes, which made me feel bad for calling him crazy. I think it was kind of a trigger for him. A lot of people wrote Sammi off as "crazy" or "weird" or "other." Spending all his time in robot club and having the biggest collection of Yu-Gi-Oh! cards in the school may not have helped his reputation. But still, I should've known better than to use the C-word. I tried to apologize.

"Sorry, I—"

"I just wish we were home already," Sammi interrupted. Confrontation, be it physical or emotional, wasn't really Sammi's bag. So we both moved on.

"Listen, you're going to thank me when your head doesn't end up in the trunk of his car. 'Cause he was definitely going to murder us just now."

Sammi stifled a smile.

"And if I ever do get murdered, it won't be because I did something dumb. Like got into a Tesla. The only way I'm getting murdered is in a fit of passion. Maybe a love triangle between two oil tycoons? Ooh! Or in a proper duel between tormented half brothers . . ."

I could tell Sammi was tuning me out. He did this when I went on and on. But that was another thing I liked about Sammi. He let me talk.

1.3 SOGGY MILES LATER, WE GOT TO TRINITY TOWERS AND WENT our separate ways. I live on the fourth floor, while Sammi and his mom are on the ground floor next to the "gym/common room" nobody uses. I brushed my teeth, wrote up an invoice to send to Mrs. Blye, started a background file on Mr. Frange, and accessed Roosevelt's remote database to see if Mrs. Blye was in fact Sammi's chemistry teacher. (She wasn't. Damn it! What the hell was I thinking?) I was on track to be in bed by two if I really hunkered down and had an unfortunate-but-sometimes-necessary fourth cup of coffee. But that's when a familiar *knock-knock-knock* came upon my door.

"Who's ready for some Faaaaaamily Tiiiiiiiiime!" my dad mock-shouted in his favorite "late '90s announcer" voice.

Crap. Family Time. I forgot it was Tuesday. I was gonna be up all night.

My parents mostly left me alone because, I mean, what was there to parent? I got straight As. And if I didn't get straight As, I would argue with my teacher until they saw my point of view. But once I started MERTZ CYF, my free time became nonexistent. And my parents, while not fully understanding what I did, could tell that the grind was starting to wear on me. So they insisted I do one of two things: either spend one night a week "just hanging with friends," or spend two nights a week partaking in "Family Time." I think they were hoping the threat of forced family time would motivate me to make friends outside of Sammi, but I chose family time instead. Why do I need more friends? Everyone at my school is lazy, or self-absorbed, or thinks crop tops give them a personality. My parents, on the other hand, are fun, considerate, and almost never wear crop tops.[11]

I mean, sure, they blew my college fund. And there are other things they're weird about: My mom is a low-key hoarder who has saved every *New Yorker* magazine since 2009. And my dad is way too passionate about movies.[12] But other than that, they've been great parents. They took me to museums, signed me up for camps, and bought me a bunch of boring, educational toys that were less fun than, say, a Nerf gun. I have love and attention and

---

11. My dad has one "muscle shirt" that I swear is a crop top. He wears it to wash the car.

12. Or, as he insists on calling them, "films." Pretentious.

no other siblings to take said love and attention away from me. I cannot complain.[13]

"Family Time! Family Time! Fam-ily-Tiiiiiime!" My dad grabbed my shoulders and marched me out of my bedroom in a two-person conga line. He always makes such a production of "Family Time." At work, as far as I can tell, he's all business. His four employees are even a little afraid of him I think. But at home, boy, he's real weird.

"Oh no! Did I just miss a conga?" my mom said, bringing a bowl of popcorn to the couch, where my dad had plopped us down. "Next time, call me! I love a conga." My mom wiggled her hips back and forth with the grace you'd expect from a suburban woman who's pushing forty. "You know, I think my hips are getting more flexible from all the Salsarobics."[14]

I glared at them as I dug my hand into the popcorn bowl. My dad with his pale skin and light hair that receded into a weird little patch on the top of his head; my mom, her dark eyes matching her olive undertones that she somehow didn't pass on to me (like, not even a little bit). I knew they did stuff like this to rankle me. Not gonna work!

"So! Margot. How was school? Anybody do anything illegal?" My mom plopped her flexible hips down next to me.

"How's the love life? Any guys . . . or girls you're into these days?" my dad chimed in. I could tell they so desperately wanted me to be a "normal" high schooler. They would have loved it if I

---

13. I do, though.

14. My mom did whatever proprietary fitness dance was the current fad. (DanceLetics, Barre Rhythm, Park-CORE and, before that, Zumba.)

had a group of friends or went out on dates to the movies. Or if I came home crying because someone broke my heart. But I refuse. Dating in high school is a waste of time. Seventeen-year-old boys are immature, weak, and, I suspect, very bad at sex. I had explained this to my parents several times.

"Nope." Silence. "Still saving myself for Stanford."

They looked at each other. Then gave up trying to *engage* me.

"Okay! For your viewing pleasure, I have chosen *Dog Day Afternoon*. Classic '70s movie with a killer Pacino performance."

"Nuh-uh. Not your night, Dad," I interjected, before he got even more excited about whatever weird cinematic "masterpiece" he was trying to push on us. "You picked the movie two times ago. And Mom picked *British Bake Off* last Sunday. Which means it's my turn. And I say we are watching a TED Talk with Indra Nooyi. Former CEO of Pepsi and number two on *Forbes*'s Most Powerful Women in Business."

My dad collapsed into the couch. This was not his idea of a fun evening.

But my mom shot him a look that said, "Shut up and show some interest in Margot's thing." *Thank you, Mom.* Dad still glared at me, because he knew that I had already seen Indra Nooyi's TED Talk five times and that I was only forcing this edutainment as punishment for making me do Family Time.

"You don't even like Pepsi!"

"Indra Nooyi has like six masters degrees, was in an all-girl rock band in college, and is on the board of an organization that supports environmental causes! We all could learn something from her!"

My dad gave up. What was he really going to say?

Forty-five dry yet inspirational minutes later, I retreated to my room. If I really focused, I could get some work done on Mrs. Blye's case and then bang out the homework I owed for AP Stat. Maybe. Hopefully. Probably not, but what choice did I have?

And that's when Sammi texted me again.

SAMMI: how was family time?

MARGOT: Fine. Watched a TED Talk by Indra Nooyi.

SAMMI: I'm more of a fanta man myself.

MARGOT: And I'm more of a water girl. I was just trying to bore my parents.

MARGOT: Anyway, now I'm way behind. Probably won't sleep much tonight.

MARGOT: Thanks, Mrs. Blye!

SAMMI: yea I could tell u looked stressed today u had scary eyes

MARGOT: Thanks!

SAMMI: check ur email it might help

MARGOT: Help how? What are you talking about?

SAMMI: check email

> **MARGOT:** You cryptic bastard.

Waiting in my inbox was exactly one new email from Sammi. Subject: You're Welcome. In it were the answers to my AP Stat homework (he took AP Stat last year). And Josh Frange's Instagram password.

See. He's the best.

February 24, 11:15 p.m.

MARGOT: B, sorry I haven't texted in a while things are crazy busy.

MARGOT: got a new case. so much to tell you. i'll fill you in this weekend!

MARGOT: miss you!

4

YET ANOTHER EFFING JOB

The next morning, I woke to the sound of my mom in the shower. This was a bad sign. She usually wakes up a full hour after me. I rolled over and sure enough, the clock said 7:03. Shit. Now I was going to be late.

Well, not really *late*. Just late for me. I like to get to school twenty minutes early so I can beat the morning rush. My periods one through four are *technically* independent study, Latin, gym, and lunch. But I've turned that block of time into my unofficial MCYF office hours. Latin is free because I did a quick pro bono job for Ms. Gushman. (She had no idea how to change her Twitter password.) And gym is free because I paid a freshman to skip her lunch every day and go in my place.

I barged into the bathroom to brush my teeth.

"Why the hell didn't you wake me up?" I whined to my mom, mouth full of toothpaste.

"I figured you were sleeping in on purpose!" It was 100

percent not her fault that I was late. But that didn't mean I couldn't take it out on her. I rinsed, spat, and ran back to my room, pulling on jeans.

I grabbed a banana because there was nothing good. (We usually have muffins as long as my dad's not being cheap and/or on a diet.) Then I half jogged the 1.3 miles to school and made up a little time, arriving at 7:40. Which is exactly when *everyone else arrives* (gross).

Normally when I get there, the halls would be empty. School without other students is like a museum. Sure, it's a second-rate museum that's in need of a grant. But at least it's quiet.

But coming to school *on time*? I don't know how other people do it. The bumping of bodies. The lockers slamming. The sneaker squeaks. The morning breath. The cell phone pings. The bedhead. The acne. The girl crying into her iced coffee. The newly-in-love couple showing way too much PDA. The aggro guys shouting to draw attention to themselves. The girl crying into her compact. (Why were so many girls crying?)

And then, just as I reached my locker, I felt the sweaty, unwelcome arm of one such aggro guy around my shoulders. It was Peter Bukowski, aka P-Boy, tall and skinny with wavy black hair, your typical loud, entitled white boy. As far as these types go, Peter was pretty harmless. He's mostly known for getting drunk at parties and peeing on house plants. (That was his "move," according to Instagram.)

I cringed. And suddenly my ears felt hot. Before I could do anything, he shouted, "Check it out! Me and Mertz are dating!"

Most people at this school had learned to leave me the F

alone. The popular girls thought I was an alien. To the jocks, I was invisible. The socially awkward boys were too intimidated to dare speak to me. The nerdy, unconfident girls worshipped me from afar. The drama kids found me to be an interesting character study. And the teachers treated me as if I had tenure.

But then there was a certain subgroup of boys, the "entitled, lazy, but popular" group, who would attempt to mess with me from time to time. They catcalled me in the hallway. Or they'd do this hilarious bit where they acted like we were hooking up. Hahahaha. (It's funny because the idea of dating me is disgusting! LOL!)

I tried to wiggle a little to get P-Boy off me, but he had a firm grip. He was a pretty big dude, actually, which made it all the more uncomfortable to have him towering over me. Down the hall, I could see his friends laughing at the whole thing. P-Boy's friend Kyle was even making a video on his phone, egged on by their informal ringleader, Chris "Assaulted My Best Friend" Heinz (what a prince). I felt trapped and not in control of my body. Which I hated. It made me hyperaware of everyone in the hallway. Harold Ming and a bunch of other do-gooder Christian types were just . . . watching and not intervening. And some members of the Trees for Frees club,[15] Claire Jubell and Josh Halloway, were standing there waiting to see how I'd react. Will she tell P-Boy to shut up? Will she laugh and pretend it's all a joke? Will she cry?

I decided to employ a survival technique for drowning that

---

15. Trees for Frees is a club that plants trees in parks, schools, even at your house if you register, for free. Not frees. Because "frees" doesn't make any sense, no matter how much it rhymes.

I learned at swim camp at the YMCA when I was in the third grade: go limp. Don't ask me how that's supposed to help you when you're drowning in the ocean. I guess it's so you don't tire yourself out flailing around? I don't know. I'm not a lifeguard. But I thought it would work on P-Boy. So I went fully limp, slowly collapsing to the ground in kind of a puddle. His grip loosened. He looked super confused. And once I made it down to the floor, I stayed there for four seconds, before rolling away from him, getting up, and walking down the hall like nothing ever happened.

P-Boy stood there with the same dead-eyed look he gets when he tries to do long division. He had no idea how to respond. And I was free to proceed without a mouth breather attached to my shoulder. My drowning technique worked.

Thirty-three uneventful seconds later, I got to homeroom. I checked in, mumbled the pledge, and then made my way to the library to start my day. Sammi had given me a head start on Mrs. Blye's case, but I had to make a ton of content in the next twenty-four hours to bury Mrs. Blye's pic with Mr. Frange. (The pic would still be on his Instagram, of course, and I would have to tackle that eventually. But I knew if I sufficiently buried it, there was no way Toby Blye would find it unless he really went sleuthing.) I had just signed into Medium when over the top of the nearest bookcase, I noticed a nest of big red, curly hair slowly making its way toward me. This could only be Shannon Finke, a senior whose hair and pink freckled skin, combined with her perpetually wide-eyed expression, made her seem like a Muppet come to life.

"Margot!" Shannon shrieked. There was a nervous energy in

her eyes. Almost like she had been practicing this conversation in the mirror all night and really needed it to go well. "Could we talk? Or, I was wondering if I could—"

"Actually, I'm a little busy today."

"Oh. Okay. Right. I know you're busy. But, uh, I have a . . . problem. And you know how you're like Sweden at this school?"

"Do you mean Switzerland?" I asked politely.

"I don't know. You're, like, neutral? Nobody messes with you?"

"You mean Switzerland." It was true. Outside of the occasional taunt from the P-Boy set, nobody messed with me. Nor did they invite me to their parties. (Though I'm not even sure Switzerland is the right way to describe it. What's a self-isolating country that doesn't take shit from anybody and will aggressively defend itself if threatened? Oh my god. I might be North Korea. Gonna have to unpack that later.)

"Okay. Well, I think you're the only person I can talk to about this. Tracy Alverson told me you, uh, you have a company where you . . . um . . . help people if someone has something online that . . . is bad . . ."

Oh god. Another job? There was a time when I worried about getting enough clients to pay for a single semester at Stanford. But now I was swimming in work. I should really franchise.

"Unfortunately, I just took on a big case and I'm not sure I have time to help you."

"Oh. So you're, like . . . okay."

I had turned people down before. Usually they were disappointed, or desperate enough to make a splashy counteroffer. But

Shannon looked beyond crushed. Like I'd just told her she could never have a dog because she's allergic to dogs. And also I just killed the dog she wanted.

"Look, in my experience, whatever's online, it's not as bad as you think," I reassured her. "I can give you some pointers on how to manage your—"

"It's bad. It's as bad as it gets. It's . . ." Now tears were starting to roll down her face. Right in the middle of the library. And not just tears: she was hugging herself tightly. Whatever was online had gotten into her muscles, her bones, her whole body. It was hurting her. "It's just that . . . I'm on Roosevelt Bitches."

Roosevelt Bitches. I had no idea what that meant, but I knew that I hated it. I hate the B-word. And I hated that it made Shannon seem out of control. Like the way I felt when P-Boy put his arm around me, but, by the looks of her, a thousand times worse. Whatever had happened to her, whatever she was going to ask, I knew right then that I couldn't say no. Which meant I was about to take on my second case in two days.

The rest of junior year was going to suck.

5

HOW ONE ACTUALLY GOES ABOUT CLEANING YOUR FILTH

I made a plan to meet Shannon at Greenbaum's Bakery after school. She was overjoyed, like I had brought her dog back to life. People are always so dazzled by this job. I snap my fingers and their lives go back to normal.

But, like, Margot, how are you doing this? Like . . . how? Because it seems impossible to keep anything on the internet from spreading, let alone to make it go away entirely, right? So . . . how?

Over the years, I've honed a kind of method for cleaning people's filth. It's not a science. It's not even a consistent set of rules. But this is the best way I know to explain it.

Okay. This is how I do what I do.

STEP 1: ASSESS THE DAMAGE

The first thing I do when I get a job is try to get a sense of what

I'm dealing with. Sometimes clients will say they know of only two people who have an embarrassing video of them, when in reality it's something like seventeen. (Karen Mercer told me there was only one video of her flashing a gang sign at Six Flags, but there were a lot more. Twenty-five, to be exact. And Karen is not in a gang. Unless you count her folk-dancing club.) So I've got to track down all the pics/vids/etc., figure out who posted them, and note the platforms on which they appear. (All this is done without hacking. I simply comb through every SM[16] feed at our school and do a little background work via brief personal interviews.) As I said, it's not an exact science, but after a few hours, I usually have a rough idea of the damage and how long it'll take me to clean it up. (Three days, in Karen's case. And only because some of the videos on the teacups were too blurry to prove conclusively that it was her.)

STEP 2: CREATE A BUTTLOAD OF CONTENT TO BURY THE EMBARRASSING THING ONLINE

This is the most tedious step, but also probably the most important. Especially in the first few days of a job. If somebody has something embarrassing floating around online, the last thing they want is for someone of real importance to see said embarrassing thing. And the best way to ensure this doesn't happen is to bury it, so that it won't appear on the first five pages of any Google search. How? Content. I build some dummy websites,

---

16. When I say SM, I mean social media and not sadomasochism, like my mom once thought.

self-publish some "news" articles about the person, and then I flood their SM with lots of @s and mentions. (Last time I checked, I had sixty-two fake Medium accounts with hundreds of fake articles for the sole purpose of burying clients. The sad thing? People actually read them. And comment! I wrote a dumbass article about how Ms. Corman really liked tomatoes: "Local Teacher Won't Eat Salad without a Fresh Tomato." And it got 30,000 claps. WHY?)

Anyway, pretty soon you can only see the offending post if you know where to look for it. And the client can breathe a little easier until I get my hands on the leaked pics/vids and delete them.

STEP 3: ROLE-PLAY

At some point in any job, I'll have to pretend to be someone I'm not. I often don't want a target to know I'm seventeen years old and living with my parents. Therefore, fake personas are a must.

Over the past two years, I've pretended to be a job recruiter, debt collector, police officer, principal, and many, many lawyers. Sometimes I just say I'm the *secretary* of a lawyer, which is even easier. But being a fake lawyer is always useful. A random phone call or a "cease and desist" email from a lawyer will scare the crap out of most people and is a great motivator for getting them to delete their illegally obtained . . . whatevers. I usually go by *Melanie P. Strutt, Attorney-at-Law.* She's based out of Rochester, passed the bar in '08, and is on track to be made partner at the mythical law firm of Warren, Phillips, and McKenzie.

When you interact with someone as a fake person, it's almost always done over the phone, or with email and DMs. Only once has a person asked to meet me IRL. I had to pay a local actor to pretend to be Melanie Strutt. She didn't memorize her lines or do the improv exercises I recommended, and the whole thing was kind of a disaster.

Things you'll need to create a fake character: a backstory/bio, a distinct speaking voice (different from your own), fake stationery with legal office letterhead, and a burner cell phone.

STEP 4: HAVE ELITE HACKER ASSOCIATE HACK MAIN TARGET'S COMPUTER AND/OR PHONE

Look, I'm a big fan of privacy. I was as creeped out as the next person when I heard that Google and Facebook and the NSA monitor our keystrokes like . . . all the time. But in cases where a person is posting photos without consent . . . then I kinda feel fine invading their privacy. They started it. I know, I know, all this feels like a moral gray area, but what can you do . . . it's the internet! Plus there's only one way to be absolutely, 100 percent positive that the pic/vid I'm looking for has been erased and won't be used again. And that's by looking at the offending party's hard drive, phone, and cloud. Which Sammi will gleefully do for me, at a fair price.

STEP 5: CLEAN OUTSIDE THE BOX

So once I do steps 1–5, which could take me as long as a few weeks or as short as two days, depending on the nature of the job (and how much a client is willing to pay me) . . . it's time to get creative! In my experience, every job is different and may require different additional steps from here on out. In fact, it might be easier to just give some examples of previous jobs to show what I mean.

For instance, MCYF job #00006, Shontae Williams. In April of my sophomore year, senior Jordy Fence, a gangly white guy, asked sophomore Shontae Williams to prom, believing that a sophomore should be honored to be asked by a senior (even one with chronic tuna breath). Shontae was a cute, well-liked theater person with dark brown skin and big curly hair who was, quite frankly, way out of Jordy's league. She declined. Jordy was so enraged by the rejection that he threatened to send a mass email with questionable photos of Shontae to everyone in his contacts. The pictures were from the cast party of that year's spring musical, *Cabaret*. Apparently, Shontae was on a real high from being called "ebullient" in the *Roosevelt Gazette*'s review. So after downing three Diet Cokes (remember, it was a theater party), Shontae got a little overzealous and did a weird striptease for several of the cast members. For this case, all that was needed was a call from "Police Officer McKellan." Jordy was so thoroughly freaked out, he deleted his photos of Shontae and quit Instagram. He then informed his friends via group chat that anyone who had copies of Shontae's photos should delete them immediately (which, as far as Sammi's backdoor snooping could tell, they did). Success.

Sometimes jobs are easy. Take MCYF job #00011. Amelia Lopez, a Mexican American junior with light brown skin and a nose ring, was concerned that a picture of her vomiting on a cat at Brendan Buckler's Halloween party would go viral and get her rejected by the ASPCA, where she planned to do her senior volunteer hours. The picture was posted on a dummy Instagram account, and Amelia had no idea who was behind it. Luckily, this account had only three followers, none of whom seemed interested in reposting the photo (or maybe they just never saw it). This job required no threatening phone calls or lawyer impersonations. The only real problem was figuring out who owned the dummy account, which Sammi was able to do by using a password-cracking program he created called Fuzzword.[17] The owner of the threatening account turned out to be . . . Amelia herself (a twist!). Apparently she created the dummy account and posted it herself when she was drunk (like, very, very drunk). That case was wrapped up in about two days.

And then there are jobs that are *very* complicated and thoroughly test my in-person social hacking skills.

MCYF job #00019. Reggie Storm, a corn-fed, white Norman Rockwell painting come to life, was one of my very first adult clients. Reggie was a weatherman (I know, and his last name was Storm. I looked it up. It's on his birth certificate. I don't know what to tell you.) and on track for a big promotion. But then, he accidentally emailed a dick pic (intended for his boyfriend) to his boss, Channel 4 news anchor Chuck Gravely. Chuck was on a meditation retreat at the time and had no access to phone or email. (Which sounded like true hell to me, but to each their own.) Reggie hired me to get the picture back before the retreat

---

17. You can go online and see a list of the one hundred most-used passwords. They're as obvious as you'd think: password1, 1234567, etc. Sammi's program automatically tries the top twenty thousand. I know. Computers are fast.

ended. Sammi thought he'd be able to hack his account pretty easily, but Chuck had hired a private security firm to digitally lock his shit down. Thus hijinks ensued. I had to sneak into his office, pretending to be his niece, and erase the email at his desk. It was honestly thrilling. I ran into a co-worker on the way out who said, "I didn't know Chuck had a niece." I pretended to be hurt that he'd never mentioned me, and the co-worker apologized. Then she acted like maybe he *had* mentioned me to spare my feelings. Then she gave me $20 and offered to write me a recommendation for Ithaca (she was an alum), if I wanted to go there (I did not!). I got out of there without being detected and Reggie is now the *senior* meteorologist at Channel 4.

So . . . THAT'S WHAT I DO. LET ME BE CLEAR, I'M NOT A MIRACLE worker. I can't close Pandora's box or reverse global warming. If you're a Kardashian or Taylor Swift or Jennifer Lawrence, I cannot make your nude pics or sex videos go away. That shit is viral and way above my pay grade.

But for a random high schooler or local resident of North Webster, chances are your messes are a lot easier to contain. So for once, be grateful that you don't have two million followers on Instagram.

Anyway, that's how I do it: I bury, I hack, I lie, I improvise. And with two years and twenty plus jobs' worth of experience, I felt like I could handle whatever Shannon was going to throw at me.

I was wrong.

6

THE RISE AND FALL OF
SHANNON AND KYLE

Greenbaum's Bakery is my Petey's for clients my age. They let you sit there as long as you want, and there is never anyone under eighty-five in the whole place, so you don't have to worry about running into someone you know. Plus they have rugelach.

When I showed up around three fifteen, Shannon was already there, breaking apart the pieces of a giant chocolate chip cookie and not eating them. I set down my bags and ordered coffee and rugelach, but I didn't end up touching them. The moment I sat down, Shannon unloaded.

"I just want you to know, I don't normally do things like that! We were just having fun, and he kept asking for them, and I was trying to be sex-positive." She started scrunching her hair over and over. "I didn't want to go to college not having experienced, like, anything."

I nodded and was about to ask her what the hell she was talking about, but she kept going.

"And he *seemed* nice. I thought we were both having fun. But, you know, like, respecting each other."

"Right. Why don't you start from the beginning?" I prompted. Hoping if she did, she'd start making a little more sense.

She smiled a little. Then she took a deep breath and told me about her summer dating Kyle Kirkland. Kyle, whose social circle boasted the likes of Chris and P-Boy, was a gregarious blond with an offensive lineman's build. Not my type really, but it was very much Shannon's. She'd been smitten. She talked about how cute he had been when he asked her out. (He wore his Supreme sweatshirt.) She talked about how they had this game where any time they saw a Dunkin' Donuts they had to take a picture of it and DM it to the other person and how she commented every time he posted to @TheKirkOut (the IG he reserved solely for his workouts). She talked about how he brought spiked seltzer to all the summer parties for her because she didn't like the taste of alcohol but still wanted to get buzzed. Kyle and Shannon had been a thing for most of the summer. But she explained that it was never serious—for either of them. Shannon was set to have a crazy busy senior year, and she didn't know if she could handle a "real boyfriend commitment." And Kyle was still kinda tortured by his last girlfriend, Tamara Something, who went to Brighton. So he wasn't ready for anything too serious either. But they had their fun, flirting, hooking up, and eventually having sex.

It was Shannon's first time. She didn't know if it was Kyle's or not, but he didn't act like he was a pro or anything. He was nice, and he stuck around afterward and even brought her a stuffed dog the next day. (Which, let's be honest, is a gift you would give a small child recovering from a broken leg, not someone you just had sex with. But that's just my opinion. Shannon liked it. She thought the dog was [raise vocal register three octaves] *"So cuuute."*)

"Okay. So just to be clear, every time you had sex, it was consensual, right?"

Her eyes widened. "Yeah. Totally. I mean, at the time, I wanted to. I'm sorry."

"Why are you apologizing for having sex?"

"I don't know." She put her head in her hands. "It's just a reflex. Apologizing."

"It's fine. I just want you to know, you've done nothing wrong." I tried to be reassuring. I've learned the hard way that if clients think you're judging them, they won't tell you the whole story. And I needed to know everything.

Finally she gulped and went on, "And then, after we had sex, we started sexting. And . . . uh . . . I was the one that actually sent him the first sext. Does that mean I'm, like, guilty? Or . . ."

"Guilty of what?" I asked.

"I don't know. Like, maybe I brought this on myself?" The quiet tears that had been rolling down her face for the past few minutes were now replaced by audible sobbing. I looked around, grateful that the Greenbaum's ladies were in the back chopping baklava into triangles.

Using my mom's calming nurse voice, I said, "Keep going. What happened with the sexting?" I was really trying to keep her focused on her story. In my experience, once people start crying, they can really go off the rails. We're talking intense therapy levels of confession. For example, when I met with Mrs. Blye, she told me that she's "never been as successful as her sister" and that she's "run over three cats with her car" and that she's "always had a thing for guys with thick glasses." And that her "uncle Charlie had thick glasses, and she doesn't know what that means." Which is all fascinating/horrifying, but wasn't really helpful. Luckily, this didn't happen with Shannon.

"So. I sent him the first one the night after we had sex. It was a picture of . . . my chest." If she scrunched her hair any harder she might have ripped it out. "And it was kinda dark, so it wasn't like you could see everything. Sorry."

"Shannon—"

"Right, I know. Stop apologizing." She looked down at her wreck of a cookie.

"What was Kyle's response?" I asked.

"Um. This." Shannon took out her phone and showed me a text with a bunch of asinine emojis. Fire, fire, peach, peach, etc. Then finally, some words: DAMN GIRL U HOT.

"This is so embarrassing," Shannon said, taking the phone back.

"A lot of people sext. So *do not* punish yourself." Shannon nodded, a little more comfortable knowing I wasn't gonna slut-shame her. "Just remember, Kyle's the asshole here for sharing them. Not you. Okay?"

"Thanks," Shannon said, now biting a nail. "It just sucks. Everyone I know trades nudes all the time, and nothing bad ever happens."

Well, not *everyone*. I don't. But I'm a bit of a control freak. And to me, sexting is like handing someone your Social Security number or your credit card. You're giving that person way too much power.

Also, no one's ever asked me for a sext, which makes abstaining *way easier*.

"So what happened next?"

"He asked for more."

She showed me more texts. Kyle would text late at night asking for pics. She would sometimes write back and say no. Then he'd keep texting, trying to persuade her, and eventually she'd give in and send another pic. Then a few days would go by, and there'd be little to no interaction. Then Kyle would start in again asking for another pic. This happened for a while, until she'd sent about six or seven pics. As far as I could tell, Kyle never sent any back.

"Were you ever upset that he didn't reciprocate?"

"What do you mean?"

"That he never sent you any pictures back?"

"No. I guess I never thought about it." She got quiet again, and I felt bad. I could tell that question embarrassed her. Luckily, she moved on without any prodding.

"And then—you know, *RB*."

"Roosevelt Bitches?" I asked, meeting her more than halfway.

"Yeah." She nodded.

"Okay," I continued. "And . . . what is that?"

She exhaled deliberately. "Um. Okay. Well, I mean, have you been on it?"

"No."

"Okay, well. It's a website," she offered, ratcheting up her nail-biting. "Maybe it's easier if I just show you."

She handed her phone over discreetly, making sure the Greenbaum's ladies didn't see. And I soon saw why. Apparently, Roosevelt Bitches was a password-protected revenge porn site. It featured seminude to X-rated pictures of girls at our school. All of which had been posted without permission. Girls would send sexts to someone, and then those pictures would appear on RB. Sometimes it was the result of a pissed-off ex-bf. Sometimes, like in the case of Kyle and Shannon, the person wasn't mad at all, he just wanted to add to the ever-growing catalog of near-naked underage girls.

Wakefield High, a school in neighboring Yates County, had a sexting scandal like this two summers ago. (My cousin Arya went to Wakefield and relished telling us all about it at Thanksgiving.) A group of boys were sharing private sexts, and then one of them started an Instagram account that was quickly discovered and reported.

But this was one million times worse. Someone had taken the trouble to make an actual site. One that was password protected. Shannon only learned about it because someone anonymously sent her a link. I exhaled and pushed my thumb into the ridge on my forehead.

"There's like twenty girls on it," she said as I scrolled through the site. I couldn't help thinking she must be exaggerating. Twenty girls? Really?

"And no one knows who made it?" I asked.

"No. As far as I know. I mean, a lot of people have added to it. But no one knows who operates it. Or who made it in the first place."

At that point, the whole conversation got a little blurry. It was infuriating. Seeing all these smart, capable, amazing women who had been turned into unwitting sex objects. Girls in my homeroom. Girls who did the morning announcements. Girls I did Girl Scouts with (a lifetime ago). Not girls, young women. Human beings. I was pissed. Like, really pissed. I thought blood was going to come out of my ears, that's how fucking furious I was.

"Doesn't that hurt?" Shannon asked, a worried look in her eyes.

I had broken a plastic coffee stirrer into tiny shards, and one of them was stuck into my palm. I couldn't even feel it.

I took the shard out of my palm, gave Shannon a reassuring look that said, "I'm not crazy," and tried again to study the site. How many people knew about this? And for how long? What kind of fucked-up bro code kept a thing like this running, in secret, for months now? And how did *I* not know about it?

I took a deep breath and shook my whole body and head for a few seconds to calm myself (a trick I learned at theater camp in sixth grade. Thanks, YMCA All-Stars!). Then I gave it a closer look.

To my horror, the site mostly worked. It was, dare I say, well-designed. It wasn't glitchy, loaded quickly, and was encrypted. It even had search.

And this somehow made me even angrier. It just didn't

compute. How could this cesspool of male shittiness have a better-functioning website than my dad's dry cleaning business? I don't exactly remember what I said to Shannon after that. I remember her telling me to be quiet because I must've started talking loudly. I remember wanting to punch Kyle in the face and wondering if I could make it all the way to his wrestling practice and then get on the mat with him and then just punch him in the face as hard as I could with my rings out before Coach Swanson intervened. But instead of saying any of this, I'm pretty sure I just muttered something about taking on Shannon's case. Yes, I would do it. No, I wouldn't charge her full price. And yes, she could trust me. Her trust had been violated again and again by nearly every boy at the school, and I wanted her to know that wouldn't happen with me. I would right this wrong. I would make the horny fuckbois pay.

I left the coffee, the rugelach, the shards of stirrer, and a stunned Shannon sitting at the bakery and walked quickly home. This was a big job, and I had to get started.

7

ROOSEVELT BITCHES

When I got home, my parents were out. I rifled through the pantry and pulled out a bag of emergency Cheetos, which I hate-ate in under a minute. Then I went straight to my room and signed on to RB again. The password Shannon had given me, "DISTEDDYFUX," worked with no problem. (DISTEDDYFUX roughly translates to "This Teddy Fucks." Roosevelt's mascot is Teddy! A bear version of Teddy Roosevelt. *Clever!*)[18]

I couldn't concentrate on the site. It was too much. All these young women displayed and categorized without their permission. With charming tags and comments like "big tits" and "hot mouth" and "decent body but fug face." With how many asshole guys looking at them, judging them, and probably jerking off to

---

18. If you're going to make Teddy Roosevelt a dirty password, it seems like a real missed opportunity not to do something with "Rough Rider" or "Carry a big stick," but . . . I wasn't consulted.

them? As if it were their right? I remembered all the girls I'd seen crying in the Roosevelt hallways lately. Could this have been the reason?

I thought about Kyle. He needed a pig's-blood moment. I could go after his car. Kyle loved his Ford Escape more than anything. He named it "REO Weedwagon," I guess because he liked weed and '80s music? But maybe there was an even better way of humiliating Kyle . . . Could I somehow get naked pictures of him and put them somewhere? There's a billboard by Costco that seemed like a proportional response.

But then I realized it wasn't enough to just take down Kyle. Multiple people deserved my righteous anger. First, I had to brutally punish whoever built the site. Maybe I could tar and feather them? Or arrange some kind of old-school stockade? I wanted to ruin lives so that these assholes couldn't sit on the Supreme Court someday.

But what about the average, run-of-the-shitty-mill guy who had just *visited* the site? They didn't deserve to be physically harmed, but some sort of punishment seemed apt. Kicked off the football team? Could I give them *all* a really bad case of athlete's foot?

Suddenly it seemed insane to me that all these guys had a password to RB, and yet *no one* knew who made it. I called Kevin Beane. Ever since sophomore year, he had been unflaggingly loyal. I also scared the shit out of him.

He answered within seconds.

"Have you been on Roosevelt Bitches?"

"I, uh—"

"Kevin, can we skip the part where you stammer and lie, and just tell me? I'm not judging. I just need to know." Lie. I was judging him real hard.

"I, uh, yeah. Kind of. A few times. But I haven't gone in a month. Jess Lind is on it, and she's a really good friend of mine so . . . I stopped."

The "it finally affected someone I know" argument. Whatever. Punishment was for another time.

"How did you get the password?"

"Justin gave it to me."

"And where did Justin get it?"

"I don't know, I think he found it on a subreddit or something."

"Who made it? The site? Who's running it?"

"I don't know."

"Now's not the time to lie, Kevin. Or cover your friends' asses. Who made it?"

"I really don't know! I don't! And if I did, I would tell you. Seriously. I feel terrible I ever went on it, it . . . it was a moment of weakness. I've been really stressed out because of SATs and . . ." He made a retching sound. Then another. So I hung up. Clearly, I had taken this as far as it could go.

I did this three more times with boys I knew were scared of me and wouldn't lie. Two had been to the site. But neither knew who made it. They'd all gotten the password from a friend or a mysterious Reddit post, which apparently no longer existed. I went on Reddit anyway to see if I could find it. Then Shannon called.

"Hi. Sorry to ask you to do more. But Tyra Michaels is also on Roosevelt Bitches. Do you think you could . . . take her pictures down, too? Also, Sara Nguyen has a pic on it. She thinks her phone got hacked and—"

"Shannon, did you think I was just going to take down *your* pictures? This whole site is disgusting. I'm going to burn it to the ground."

"Oh. Okay. Cool," she said sheepishly. "I'll tell them. We, uh, we have a group on WhatsApp."

"Who's *we*?"

"Like, the victims. The other girls. It was just Tyra, Sara, and me, but then we added some of the others."

"So you can all talk privately? Makes sense."

"Maybe I could add you to it? And you could, like, tell everyone what you're gonna do?"

"Uh, sure," I said, not that eager to be added to any group thread. "I guess?"

"Thank you. That's really going to help. It's been . . . hard."

I could imagine.

She went on, "You know, it's stressful enough having your nipples flung all over the internet. And then the guys make it so much worse."

"What do you mean?"

"It's like you can tell who's been on it and who hasn't. 'Cause once a guy's been on RB, he starts getting, like . . . aggressive. Like he'll message you and ask for pics. Or he'll just assume that you're, like, down to do stuff."

"Gross." Guys continued to disappoint me. I wished I had

some kind of religious background so I could become a nun or something. Cloisters sounded pretty appealing.

"We've all noticed. All the girls," she said, for once sounding sure of herself. "It's like a direct result of RB."

"No, it's a direct result of men *not listening to a woman when she fucking says no.*"

Shannon was quiet for a second. Then she just quietly said, "Yeah."

"Sorry, I didn't mean to yell. It's all just so infuriating."

"No. It's fine. It's nice to hear someone say it. I've been screaming into my pillow every night for the last month. My pillow might need therapy now." The more I talked to Shannon, the more she surprised me. Spearheading the WhatsApp and hiring me? She was a lot more proactive than I gave her credit for. Made me want to earn my $300.

"Just add me to the group. I'll keep everyone updated on my progress. And trust me. I will get Roosevelt Bitches taken down as fast as I can."

"Thank you. You're amazing. Everything people say about you is true."

"Oh. Good," I said, trying to act as if I didn't care, but with a tone that clearly meant, "What the hell are people saying about me?"

"It's all good stuff!" Shannon continued, "I was just talking to Sara about how you're, like . . . intimidating."

I gave her an "uh-huh," hoping she'd just leave it at that and hang up.

"Everyone who's ever hired you said you were really good.

Like, surprisingly funny and easy to talk to. And that was just, like, unexpected because in the halls you're—"

"An asshole?"

"Haha, no! Oh my god, no! You're . . . independent."

"Right." I got the feeling that "independent" meant "heartless bitch."

"I mean, obviously it's working for you, your whole Sweden thing!"

I let it go that time.

"And maybe it's good that you don't *fit in* because it means you can take on shit like this. Right?"

Right. That's what I always told myself. (Although I admit, it doesn't sound great coming from another person. Do people think I really don't fit in *at all*? That I don't have friends? They know it's *by choice*, right?)

"What I'm trying to say is . . . you're great, Margot. Thank you."

I really wish she had just said thank you and not told me I had Resting Mean Face, but what can you do?

After she hung up, I sat there for a few minutes. I was trying to make sense of all the information racing around my brain. Never mind that I had the reputation of being an outcast, and, I guess, a neutral European democracy. I was now about to join a WhatsApp with clients (and probably become their de facto trauma counselor, which I was *not* qualified to do!). I still had no idea who made the site, where it was being hosted, or how I was going to brutally punish the person/people behind it. I mean, what these guys were doing was violating and immoral and illegal and—

Illegal. Right. That brought everything into focus. A quick search told me that RB had broken at least a few laws. It contained pornographic images of minors, and thanks to a new law, "the non-consenting sharing of intimate images is a class-A misdemeanor" with fines and up to a year in jail as a punishment.[19] Jackpot.

I called Shannon back. She answered after half a ring.

"Shannon. I think this is easier than I was making it out to be. Posting pictures of you without your consent is illegal. And you're a minor, which technically makes it even more illegal. I'm pretty sure I could take the site down and hopefully destroy as many of the original pics as possible. But that still doesn't *punish* the guys who made this horrible thing. And they have to be punished! I don't usually like to get the authorities involved, but if we take Roosevelt Bitches to the police—"

All I could hear on the other end of the phone was shallow breathing. Shannon was hyperventilating. "Please," she finally gasped. "*Please! Don't!* You can't, Margot! *Please!*"

Shit. Maybe I had sprung this on her too quickly. I tried to explain. "Shannon—"

"If you go to the authorities—my parents will know, and they'll kill me!" she pleaded. "My mom—she's—It'll be on the news, Margot."

Shannon's mom, Eliza Finke, was a judge. Specifically, a county court justice for the seventh district. Which was kind of a big deal, I guess. She had to run for office and everything. I could imagine the headlines from our terrible local news: "Local

19. Law S.1719-C was passed on February 28, 2019, in the New York State Senate. About damn time.

Judge's Daughter Victim of Revenge Porn." "Judge's Daughter Drops Robe in Porn Scandal." "Disorder in the Court: Revenge Porn Scandal Hits Home!" I understood Shannon's concern.

"But what if you told them before you went to the police? After the initial shock, I'm sure they'd come around and—"

"What good do you think that will do?" she said, trying to keep a lid on her anger. "I play soccer with a bunch of girls from Wakefield. They went to the police."

Right. My cousin had told me about the fallout from the sexting scandal there. Only a few of the perpetrators were suspended. But in a real fuck-you to women everywhere, *all the girls* were forced to take a class organized by the Yates Police Department called "Privacy and Body Awareness." And apparently some of them were suspended, too. For "sharing lewd and graphic images." Because according to Wakefield . . . I guess this was all their fault?

"The police did basically nothing to the guys. And everybody, *everybody* found out about it after that."

She had a point. If she did press charges, everyone would know about it. Even if the authorities tried to "respect her anonymity," word would get out. It always does. It would be the story of her senior year.

"I came to you because I wanted you to clean this up quietly. I just want to move on with my life," Shannon said, her voice trembling.

I tried to think of another option, but I couldn't. It's not like I could take this to Palmer. Beth went to him after she was assaulted, and his response was that because the incident didn't happen on school grounds, there was "nothing he could do."

So it looked like I was back to plan A. Somehow take down the secret porn site myself, and do it quickly and secretively so that no one ever found out about it.

The only problem was this didn't address my issue of "righteously punishing the dickheads who made this site," but . . . one thing at a time.

"Okay," I said. "I hear you. Sammi and I can do it ourselves. It won't be easy—"

"Sammi Santos?"

"Yeah."

"No. I'm sorry. No, no, no. You can't tell anyone. Especially a guy." And then she started crying even harder. Part of me was kind of annoyed. This was going to be an enormous job, and doing it without Sammi was like taking away my thumbs. Doable, sure. But it's so much harder to hit the spacebar without them.

"Okay. Okay, I'll do it myself," I interjected between sobs. Her weeping immediately stopped.

"Thank you, Margot."

I hung up the phone. I had no idea what I was going to do, but I felt like it was important to give Shannon a little peace of mind. I thought of a stopgap. Something that probably wouldn't work to take the site down permanently, but was worth a try.

I could see that Roosevelt Bitches was running on Amazon Web Services[20] in total violation of the platform's content agreement. (Hello! It's revenge porn!) So I flagged it. They were pretty good about responding to flags and taking down sites that

---

20. AWS is the world's biggest cloud computing service. It's estimated to be worth $500 billion. Amazon didn't get rich off you ordering Funko Pops!

violated their terms. Hopefully RB would be down by morning.

Still, it felt like a temporary solution. All the files, all the pictures and videos, still existed. Someone could easily pop them up on a new site whenever they wanted. If even one picture made its way onto Pornhub or XX-nudey.whatever, I'd never forgive myself. And that's when my thoughts started to spiral. My heartbeat quickened, my eyes watered.

Shit. Not this again.

Back in middle school, I used to get these weird, mini panic attack things when I was stressed about a test, or when Jessie Belcher said my skirt looked "slutty." They freaked me out because once they started, I didn't know how to make them stop. Luckily, Beth was around back then, and she could usually make me feel better. She'd just talk to me quietly and hold my hand till I could think clearly again.

I tried to relax. I tried to calm down. But none of my old tricks worked. Damn it.

I got into bed, curling up into a ball and squeezing my pillow like it was a supportive but silent Chris Hemsworth. I knew that Shannon and the other women were counting on me. But I wasn't going to solve this tonight.

February 25, 11:47 p.m.

MARGOT: hey.

MARGOT: i mis you.

MARGOT: *miss. Jesus!

8

THE "IN"

After a sleepless night of tossing and turning, which not even Chris Hemspillow could relieve, I decided to get up early and start my day. I checked RB and sure enough, it was reading Page Not Found. My flag had worked, and the site was down. At least for a while. I also noticed a new message on WhatsApp, inviting me to a group called "Fury," which I assumed was Shannon's group for RB victims. I knew I should respond to that soon. So I decided to get to school extra, extra early.

When I got there at five thirty a.m., all the doors were, understandably, locked. So I had to go around from entrance to entrance until I remembered that the robotics lab has its own keypad-protected entry. Which Sammi had the code for.

> **MARGOT:** Wakey wakey. I need the code to the robotics lab STAT.

> **MARGOT:** And sorry to text so early. I suck I know.

At least five minutes went by while I chilled in the loading dock, freezing my butt off. And then finally—

> **SAMMI:** u woke me up

> **MARGOT:** I said sorry. Code please?

> **SAMMI:** ur ridiculous

> **MARGOT:** I'll make it up to you. I'll take you to a Yankees game sometime!

> **MARGOT:** lol?

> **SAMMI:** what do u need it for?

> **MARGOT:** Trying to get into school. Have a big case.

> **SAMMI:** what case? u mean mrs. blye? Or another one?

Shit. It hadn't even been twenty-four hours, and I'd almost told Sammi about the new case. Keeping him in the dark was going to be tricky. I haven't *not* employed Sammi on a job since Kevin Beane. But a promise was a promise, so I did something else I really didn't like doing. I lied to Sammi.

> **MARGOT:** Yeah. It's for Mrs. Blye. I'll fill you in later.

While I was great at lying to other people, I was pretty bad at lying to Sammi, as one could tell from a follow-up lie-text I started drafting: "Very intense case! Mrs. Blye now wants me to surveil her husband! She thinks he hired Josh Frange to seduce her so he could divorce her and maybe KILL her and—" But before I could send this text (which was a rambling lie and also the plot of Alfred Hitchcock's *Dial M for Murder*), Sammi responded.

SAMMI: 47926.

MARGOT: Thank you!

I'm sure he could tell I was hiding something, but he wasn't going to push me. He would never say, "Margot, you're lying to me, and it makes me sad." He just couldn't talk about his feelings in that way. Which, in this instance, worked in my favor. Still, I could already sense it was making things weird between us. And I hated that.

The code worked. I made my way to the library and plopped down at my usual desk. I sent Sammi a fun GIF of a dog sniffing a Blue Apron box and hoped it would cheer him up. Then I got to work. I opened up the Register.

I had a job earlier this year that required me to put everyone in the school on a spreadsheet. It took me forever, as I included way too much detail about each student, their interests, and their grades. But it resulted in a comprehensive list I use often. Sammi and I call it "the Register." It dehumanizes my fellow classmates in a way I find *very* helpful. It's much easier to hack a person's computer when they are #173 and not . . . you know, Kate Fu, a senior with asthma and the right to privacy.

So the first thing I did was run through that list looking for students with the, let's say, "moral flexibility" to make a site like RB. That's people who have cheated on tests or on their SigOths, known liars, and bullies. (Also known misogynists, the porn-obsessed, and guys with goatees.) Then I cross-referenced my results to see how many of those people had the necessary tech skills to make a site like RB. This quickly got me down to a list of three. Because it turns out many of my "usual suspects," like porn enthusiasts Cory Sayles and Ray Evans, didn't have the computer skills to make a site like RB. Which is a nice way of saying . . . they're dumb.

The Register had already broken two cases for me. So I trusted my results. Now it was time to dig deeper.

MARGOT'S LIST OF TECH-SAVVY ASSHOLES WHO ALSO HATE WOMEN

SUSPECT #1: HAROLD MING

Harold was the first person I thought of. A phony, upbeat senior, he was known primarily for three things:

1. Being second chair flutist in jazz band. (Who will never rise above second chair because he can't compete with Greg Mayes.)
2. Being the avid and vocal leader of Support Group, a school-sanctioned club that officially celebrates "support,

love, and fellowship," but which is, in reality, a Christian youth group that in no way should be allowed to function in a public school.

3. And finally, Harold was also known for a sexting scandal. Seems that the good Christian and so-so wind instrumentalist had a thing for sending aggressive, anonymous sexts to girls. They came via group chats, DMs, and private texts, without warning or consent. Apparently he was targeting young women within the ranks of Support Group, and was eventually confronted by SG's adult chaperone (and youth minister), Todd Gent. Lucky for Harold, the scandal was handled within the Willow Brook Evangelical Church. The school decided not to get involved.

But . . . did he have the ability to make a site like RB? Oh yeah. Because Harold was also the president of CODERS club, where he routinely built Christian-themed apps (including one for Support Group). I didn't particularly like the content of the SG app, which was loaded with Leviticus[21] quotes. But there was no denying it was professionally made.

So yeah. A repressed pervert with a knack for coding? Harold was my number one suspect. But still, it's good to cast a wide net and track down a few other possible leads.

SUSPECT #2: **DANNY PASTERNAK**

Danny definitely had the tech wherewithal to pull off something

---

21. There's a lot of nice, uplifting stuff in the Bible. But Leviticus is not that. It advocates for homophobia, witch burning, and slavery. Read it at your peril.

like this. Danny spent his free time maintaining websites for various local businesses in the area. (He wasn't getting a fat allowance check like some of our classmates. He had to work for his gas money.) He was considering forgoing college to develop an app he'd been working on. According to Danny's science fair presentation, MeetPup would "revolutionize the way dogs interact and fall in love online." Which . . . seems problematic, but apparently there was already something called Tindog.[22] So what the hell do I know?[23]

But where did Danny fall on the aggressive-sexually-maladjusted-man scale? Well, he didn't have a history of online harassment, and as far as I could tell, his porn habits were on par with most boys his age (so . . . too much, but not a lethal amount of porn). But everyone seemed to notice one very odd thing about Danny. He liked to put pictures of girls up in his locker. And not like . . . hot movie stars or random influencers he didn't know. They were pictures of girls from our school. *Cut out* from the yearbook and *taped* to his locker like they were . . . I don't know, his celebrity crushes? And these were not girls he was personally friends with either. He had no connection to them at all. It was the kind of thing that you only noticed the third time you passed his locker. And then you'd find yourself having conversations with random people, being like, "Does Danny Pasternak have a picture of Tina Hernandez in his locker? Are they friends?

---

22. Tindog was launched in 2015 as an app that allows dogs and their owners to connect. "Tindog: Meet and talk for free with dogs in your neighborhood."

23. According to Danny, Tindog is garbage and "not at all what a dog dating app should be."

And why is it a picture of her doing a gymnastics routine?"

Now, I had never actually spoken to Danny. But he had a rep for being a decent guy, locker thing aside. He did Meals on Wheels and reposted a lot of Sunrise Movement stuff.

But still, the locker thing is weird, right? So for now, he was on the list.

SUSPECT #3: JENJI HOPP

A woman! I know. Look at the strides we've made! Sure, we make eighty cents to the dollar[24] of what men are paid, but at least we can still be suspected of creating an illegal porn site! The future is female!

To be clear, I wasn't as hot on Jenji as I was on Danny or the most-likely-guilty Harold. But Jenji did have a couple of things going for her. For one, Jenji had a taste for digital bullying and loved a good screenshot. Jenji'd been known to blackmail, slut-shame, and repost DMs if it meant she could get . . . whatever she wanted at the moment. She once outed a girl who didn't come to her pool party. She broke up a couple on their anniversary because the guy lied to Jenji about knowing Shawn Mendes. And she instigated a cycle of Thespian Society infighting that was so epic Ms. Corman, the drama teacher, threatened to cancel the spring one-act festival. Apparently not getting cast in Ms. Corman's self-written one-act adaptation of *Dear Evan Hansen* really set Jenji off. (Though if you ask me, she dodged a bullet.)

24. Or worse, if you happen to not be white. U-S-A! U-S-A!

Some of the DMs she posted were clearly between her and the person she was targeting. But some were not, which led me to believe she had hacked people's phones or computers.

I saw several girls on RB who had tangled with Jenji in the past, including both Kelsey Chugg and Sara Nguyen, but would she really go so far as to make a site like Roosevelt Bitches just to spite her enemies?

THE BELL RANG FOR A SECOND TIME. SHIT, I WAS GONNA BE LATE for fifth period. I stuffed my laptop into my bag and booked it. I really wanted to catch Sammi before the final bell rang. I needed him to take on even more of the Mrs. Blye case. Plus I wanted to smooth things over in case he still thought I had lied to him (which I had).

I sped past the cafeteria, bypassing the always-overcrowded stairwell by the front door, and opted instead to take the one by Palmer's office. I passed the group of awkward freshmen who were always playing Tails of Time (a "card game" that looked like a knockoff *Lord of the Rings* starring sexy cats). But there was no time for Tails today. Instead they were hunched over their phones, nudging each other and whispering. Were they looking at RB? I couldn't help but wonder.

Could one of these awkward weirdos be the mastermind who created RB? Was there anyone else I was leaving off my list? Could it possibly be someone from another school? Or an adult? The only other person I could think of was Sammi. Which was laughable. Aside from the fact he's not a scumbag, he lets me use his login all the time, which he wouldn't do if he had stuff to hide on his computer. And yes, I've snooped his hard drive. (I'm a snooper. And I have to live with that!) But I'm happy to report he has better things to do than make porn websites!

"God damn it! This piece of shit!"

As I stepped out of the stairwell, an iPhone whizzed past my head and hit a locker, its screen cracking as it hit the ground. The phone belonged to Chris Heinz. He has a lot of trouble with his phone because . . . I hacked it. Earlier this year, Sammi and I were hired to make an app for spirit week called TeddyFace. It was a basic photo filter that made you look like our school mascot, Captain Teddy![25] But Sammi added an exploit that gave us remote access to any iPhone that downloaded the app. It got over a hundred downloads by our classmates, teachers, and even some of the more helicopter-y parents. Mostly I respect people's privacy . . .

But with Chris, it was just too tempting. I never do anything too crazy, but every once in a while I lock him out of his phone or randomly delete his photos. The kind of problem that would cause a rational/calm person to go to the Apple Store, where it could easily be fixed. But Chris wasn't known for his patience, so when his phone stopped responding or the screen froze, well . . . smashy smashy. I'd watched him go through at least six phones, and it was incredibly satisfying.

"Hey, Margot!"

---

25. Captain Teddy, our school mascot, is a bear, with the glasses and mustache of President Theodore "Teddy" Roosevelt. He's also wearing a pirate's hat. It truly makes no sense, but I try not to think about mascots. They're all equally pointless to me.

I turned around to see . . . one of the Kelseys. I wasn't sure which.

"Heyyy . . ." I said, buying myself a few seconds so I could place her. There were two freshman Kelseys at Roosevelt, and they were best friends. They both worshipped me and followed me around when they saw me in the halls. To make matters worse, they also looked alike. Like . . . a lot alike. Same light brown hair, same pinkish, indoor-kid skin. They even had the same helix piercing on their right ear. If someone told you they were fraternal twins, you'd believe it. Most people simply re-ferred to them as Straight Kelsey (that's Chugg) and Gay Kelsey (that's Hoffman). This seemed reductive and not fair to either of them, especially Hoffman, who had just come out two months ago. So I do my best to call them by their last names and remember which is which.

But it's not always easy. Especially when they pop up next to me like out of a horror movie. It's at times like these that I resort to a very roundabout mnemonic device. *Chugga-chugga choo choo! Chew, chew. Chugg always chews gum.*[26]

". . . Chugg! What's up?!" I said, I think saving face?

"First of all, really cool kicks. I mean, shoes. I like your shoes. Is what I'm trying to say." Normally, Chugg's nervous stammer was flattering. But at this particular moment, it was unwanted. I refused to slow my pace as I said, "Kelsey, I really don't have time to talk—"

"Right. Totally. I'm sure. I mean, I heard you're taking down

---

26. I said it was roundabout! Leave me alone!

RB. Which is like, wow! So freaking cool. That site ruined my life. I only have one picture on it, but—"

"The site's down. I checked it this morning. So sleep easy," I said without breaking stride.

"Oh, great! Wow. Thanks so much, Margot . . ." She started to trail off as she checked her phone. While she lagged behind, I made a clean break for it, hoping to catch Sammi before trig.

But a moment later, Kelsey reappeared, now blocking my path. "Um, not to, like, contradict you or whatever, but . . . I don't think it is." And she flashed her phone at me, displaying the RB site, up and running again.

"God damn it," I said aloud, coming to a full stop in the hallway. "What the hell, Jeff Bezos? You can't be putting sites back up after they get flagged for kiddie porn!"

"S-sorry," Kelsey stammered, as though she were in some way responsible. "It's on a new site now. That's what I was trying to tell you. The old one went down but now it's on . . . Onion, whatever that means. You can't search for it. But if you install the Onion browser and type in the address, it's still up."

She showed me her phone and sure enough, RB was going strong. Now at rooseveltbitches_69.onion. Great. The site was now on Tor, which made it way harder to take down—maybe impossible.

"Is this, like, the 'dark web'?" she asked, wide-eyed.

"There's no such thing as the dark web. The web is the web. It's all pretty dark," I replied. "But yes, this is what people mean when they say that."

"Oh my god." She whimpered.

I inhaled deeply. "Trust me. I will take care of this. I'm on it."

I pulled away, leaving Kelsey rambling on about how great I was as I scuttled toward Sammi's classroom.

The site was moved to Tor overnight? Who the hell was running this thing? Tor servers are hidden and indirect, so a back door wasn't going to work. I'd need to get on the controlling laptop directly. Which was going to be a verrrrrry annoying test of my social hacking skills.

I looked up from my phone in time to narrowly avoid a phalanx of cheerleaders walking arm in arm. I was almost to Sammi's classroom and had broken out some cute pit stains in the process. Never mind. I had bigger problems.

I didn't know if it was Danny, Jenji, or Harold, so I'd need to check all three of their computers . . . Woof. The easiest way to do this would be to get invited to their houses, ideally during a party. While everyone else was bein' all cool vapin' and drinkin' and awkwardly gropin' each other, I could find my way to their rooms and hack their computers in person. The only problem was . . . I didn't really know them. (And with good reason! A pervy flutist? A screenshotting psycho? Whatever it is Danny does to his locker? No thank you!) So it's not like I could just show up at their houses and be like, "Heeeeey . . . friend!" They'd slam the door in my face. No, in order for me to hack their computers IRL, I was going to need an "in" with each of them. Three separate accomplices who could get me invited to each of their hangs. I was going to have to make "friends." Woof again. If only there were *one* person flexible and basic enough to be friends with *all* of them, it could save me a lot of time. But did Roosevelt really have a unicorn like that?

It was at that moment that I slammed into the surprisingly muscular torso of Avery Green. Hard. The force of impact should have caused us both to stumble backward, but instead he barely moved, while I fell flat on my ass.

"Oh, man! Margot, I'm so sorry." Avery helped me up with the ease of a guy who spends way too much time on a Peloton. Not even a hint of struggle as he lifted me back on my feet with one arm. A serial killer with core strength? Terrifying.

"You sure you're okay? That was quite a spill," he said, sounding, as always, like a dad.

One of my shoes had come off, and I grabbed his arm to steady myself as I slipped it back on. His sweater felt like money, and he smelled like the beach. Eye roll. I was ready to chew him out. ("Watch where you're going, you rich dad!") But then it dawned on me in this very clichéd meet-cute moment: *I had found my unicorn.*

Of course! Avery Green! He's in every club! He's seemingly friends with everyone! Sure, I found Avery's boring personality and unnecessary muscles ridiculous, but to everyone else he was the "nicest" guy in school.[27] He was invited to every party and had a toe in almost every social group.

If I could date him for a few weeks (and he always had a new girlfriend, so why not me?) I could be his plus-one to all sorts of hangs and parties and get closer to my suspects. Nobody would ever question Avery Green's girlfriend—it would be a free pass.

Avery would be my in.

---

27. Don't forget best shoes.

9

IT'S ABOUT TO GET REAL

I decided to take the rest of the day off. I hadn't ditched English since October, but I knew for a fact they were just reading *The Scarlet Letter* out loud. I've already read *The Scarlet Letter*, and it is a terrible book. (My main issue with it, besides the prose being horrible and boring—Nathaniel Hawthorne never says in five words what could be said in five hundred—is that Hester isn't really the main character. She has no arc. She's just a "good woman" from beginning to end. Albeit one who made a mistake. Hawthorne spends most of his time on the minister character, the guy who—spoiler—knocked her up. Anyway, it's boring and bad and told through the male gaze.) So anyway, it seemed like a good day to skip and get a jump on "Operation: Oatmeal Avery." I needed him to fall madly in love with me. Or at least like me enough to be bf/gf for as long as this case would take.

When I reached the main entrance, I could see Palmer stalking back and forth between the doors and the office, I guess trying to catch people skipping again. Didn't that guy have anything better to do?

Luckily, I spotted a group of students with the "Career and Technical Education" program.[28] Every day, they left school to go learn skills like welding, auto body repair, or phlebotomy at a separate campus. I tucked myself among them and used them as cover to exit the building. But I wasn't sure that was enough to get Palmer off my back, so I got some insurance.

John Pfeiffer, phlebotomist in training (please, God, don't ever let him near my veins!), was walking in front of me. John was Korean and Scottish, with a stocky build and a shaved, stubbly head. He had a carabiner hooked to his backpack with keys, a Wellmans Shoppers Club card, and a lighter. I reached over quickly and unhooked the carabiner, sending the keys jangling to the floor.

"Wait," Palmer shouted as he bent down to retrieve them. But as he went to hand them back to John, he noticed the lighter on the keyring.

"What is this? *Contraband?*"

John had already reached for his keys, so he couldn't deny anything. "I need it for CTE."

"Lighters are not allowed in school. Please remain behind, Mr. Pfeiffer. The rest of you may go." Palmer launched into a stern lecture, taking a moment to wave goodbye to the rest of us.

And because I couldn't resist, I waved back.

---

28. Called CTE for short. Which is an unfortunate acronym, because CTE also stands for chronic traumatic encephalopathy, the brain injury many football players have.

I sent a text to Sammi on my way home so he wouldn't wait for me after school.

> **MARGOT:** Not feeling great. Heading home early. Will call later to touch base on Blye.

Now, since Avery already kinda knew who I was, and presumably was not attracted to me, I was going to have to really wow him in order to get his attention. That meant I needed to be prepared with a full psychological profile on Avery to figure out what he desired. *And then*, I needed to become it.

But what type of girl would a creepy bland-o like Avery actually like? I started with what I knew about him. Avery was . . .

1. Boring.

2. Maybe a serial killer.

3. Rich af.

4. In an insane amount of clubs. Too many. And they were so all over the place that it was impossible to tell what he was actually passionate about. Habitat for Humanity! Black Student Union! Soccer! Marching band! Cheerleading! Photography Club! Jazz band! Trees for Frees! He even started a club called Magic 4 Kids.[29] In my opinion, colleges will look at his application and assume it is fake.

5. His dating history was also all over the place. Since eighth grade, he'd dated Rebecca Fujita (a soccer jock), Keisha Phillips (a vapey girl with several bird tattoos), Tiffany

---

29. Was it a club that *performed* magic for kids or a club that *taught* magic to kids? And what kids? I'd never seen him perform a magic trick, but Avery was very good at making my desire to talk to him disappear, so hey, that's something!

Sparks (head cheerleader and self-proclaimed "it girl"), and Claire Jubell (a pretty, 4.0-GPA smarty). As a freshman, he dated Cora Murkowski, who was a senior. And this year, as a junior, he dated Amanda Tupper, who is a freshman. That was followed by a brief tryst with Sophia Triassi (an animal lover/future vet who had once helped a horse give birth). This is not a complete list.

But his type? I was stumped. If he had just dated jocks, I could've boned up on whatever sports team he was into and, like, bought a foam finger. If he loved theater, I could've memorized the cast album of his favorite musical. If he were into horse births, there were some terrifying YouTube videos I could show him. But there was no *trend*. Maybe I could just talk to him about rich people stuff like . . . butlers and dressage? But for some reason, I didn't think that was really going to work.

I scoured his Instagram for almost an hour, looking at basic, smiling pictures of basic, smiling Avery with his various friends, girlfriends, and teammates, all basic and smiling and too numerous to count. I was tempted to message him so I typed—

> **MARGOT:** Hey Avery. Funny bumping into you. Literally!

A dad joke for the guy who inexplicably always sounded like a dad. But as soon as I typed it, I deleted it. I just couldn't. I wasn't getting anywhere on Instagram. If I was going to figure out Avery's type, I was going to need his Netflix.

I had a theory that if you want to know what a person *really, truly* desires, all you need to do is check out their streaming history. Not YouTube; I don't care who gives you bad makeup tips or racist video game advice. No, it's Netflix, Amazon Prime, Hulu, HBO Max, etc. That's where you go if you want to look into someone's soul. Have you watched all 201 episodes of *The Office* twice and seen the episode "Casino Night" in particular thirty-three times? Then your ideal man is Jim Halpert. Funny, tall, loyal, and surprisingly approachable, thanks to a terrible haircut. Streaming reveals all.

My own Netflix history is mostly documentaries about women in business and repeat viewings of my favorite movie ever, *Misery*.[30] I'll let others judge what that says about me.

Rich boy Avery seemed to have all the streaming accounts, but luckily they were easy to hack. I didn't even have to use Fuzzword, Sammi's password cracking app. I just tried "Averypassword" as a joke and it worked on all of them. (Jesus, Avery.) And what it revealed was . . . pretty disappointing. The vast majority of his viewing was . . . reality. And not the classy kind like *Queer Eye*. Just the awful, garbage, drunk-screaming kind. You know, the ones that feature "contests" where the (admittedly very hot) dregs of humanity compete for money or love or free drinks. I'm talking *The Fortress* and *One and Done* and *Sex Condo: Beach Edition*. He seemed to be a particular fan of *Cheat Retreat*, which is about a bunch of bros who spend a month at the "Cheat Retreat" to see if they can be tempted to cheat on their fiancées by a bunch of class acts with names like "Lexie" and

---

30. *Misery* is about a frumpy lady who kidnaps a famous writer and ties him to her bed . . . then smashes his legs with a sledgehammer. (Sorry, *spoiler*, but the movie is like thirty years old now.) Yes, it's violent. Yes, you're supposed to be rooting for the writer. *But* . . . there is something very satisfying about watching a woman, even a very disturbed woman, wield her power.

"Ambyr" and "Chauffeur." If the guys don't cheat, they get $5,000 and a free honeymoon. The women . . . get nothing. They're just there to drink and, in Lexie's own words, "tempt some D, y'all!" It sets feminism back at least a decade, and it looked like Avery had seen every episode of *Cheat Retreat* . . . twice. All five seasons.[31] Two times.

While these results were disappointing, they were at least something I could work with. If a giggly drrrnk blonde with a busting D-cup was what Avery desired, then I would give him my best brunette C-cup version. I'd laugh at his jokes. And then after I was done laughing, just to make sure he really got it, I would touch his arm and say, "You are *so* funny!"

Avery's latest post was about a fundraising car wash he was spearheading for the varsity soccer team. Apparently they needed better shin guards or something? What better place to unveil my new persona than at an event stereotypically known for impromptu wet T-shirt contests?

I PIECED TOGETHER AN OUTFIT FROM MY CLOSET THAT LOOKED like a cross between "going clubbing" and "high-end prostitute." I practiced my enthusiastic upspeak? By the time the weekend rolled around, I was ready to unleash my new persona, "The Real Margot of Roosevelt High."

When I arrived at the car wash, I saw a group of mostly dudes and a few of their girlfriends[32] lazing about the parking

---

31. They do twenty-eight-episode seasons. That's too much cheating!
32. Or WAGs, I guess.

lot. Some were holding poorly drawn and poorly worded signs, which read, "Help us score our GOAL of raising money!" and "SOC-CAR WASH!" etc. A few guys were attempting to actually wash the cars, most likely doing some mild topical damage to their friends' moms' Lexuses.

This was already a strange experience (I did not do school fundraisers), made all the stranger by the attention I was getting. My chest was like a magnet, and I could feel everyone's eyes tracking me as I walked across the parking lot. Traydon Reed took out his phone, and I immediately worried he'd try to take my picture, though I think he was just texting someone. But still, it made me wonder: was my cleavage enough to get me on RB? What if they zoomed in on my butt? What if they sprayed me with water, and my shirt became see-through? For a second, I got a mini-glimpse into what this site was doing to all my classmates' psyches. Our bodies suddenly sport for anyone with a smartphone. I did not like it.

I shook off the icky feeling and spotted Avery, who was earnestly attempting to clean a car. He was flanked by Ray Evans and Cory Sayles, who stood by and watched, limply holding hoses. Ready or not, it was go time. So push-up bra pushing and with a fake smile so big it killed my soul, I made my way over to them. Cory, pink and perpetually sunburned with a medium build, and Ray, lanky with a dark brown complexion and a high-top fade, looked together like a teenage Bert and Ernie. But, you know, with legs. And with no interest in teaching you your ABCs.

"Guys? I'm sorry I'm late? I had a crazy night. Uh! I'm so hungover but . . . I'm here. Do you need a girl for anything?" I vocal-fried while making sure to touch both Ray's and Cory's arms. I thought I might get more pushback as to why I was there at all, but Cory and Ray looked so happy that a girl was talking to them, they didn't question it.

"Uh, well, Avery's doing a lot of the scrubbing and detailing and stuff. Then we spray it down with a hose when he's done," Ray mumbled.

"HOSE CREW!" Cory added, spraying Ray in the face. They were not much help.

"Oh my god! You guys! That's so funny!" Big laugh. Arm touch. Arm touch. I could see Cory's and Ray's eyes light up. They were not used to this kind of attention and were both excited and terrified by the power they suddenly seemed to have. But Avery . . . seemed not to notice. Hmmm.

A soccer ball appeared out of nowhere. Cory stopped it on his chest and kicked it to Ray. Then he and Ray began volleying the ball back and forth in an attempt, I think, to prove their soccer superiority to me. It had a very cavemen-fighting-for-dominance feel to it.

"You have some bubbles in your hair," I said, pointing to Avery's coils.

"If you really want to help, there are sponges over there and we have a line of cars, so—" Avery said, trying to gauge if I'd be more helpful than CorRay.

"Yes! Totally! I'd love to!" I skipped to Avery, twirling my hair. "But, like, just so you know, I'm soooo bad at this. I tried to wash my dad's BMW the other day, and he got so pissed 'cause I used the wrong soap or something? But I was like, Dad, it's body wash. It smells so good. See?" I thrust my wrist under his nose, encouraging him to smell the "vanilla sugar."

"Uh . . . nice," Avery said, pulling away. Then, to the next driver in a line of cars, "You can go ahead and pull forward."

Was he shy or something? I grabbed the sponge out of his hand. "Okay, now . . . what am I supposed to do?" Hoping he would get the hint that he needed to guide my hand himself. I needed a lesson from a big, strong, car-washing man like him if I was ever going to learn. But when I looked in his eyes, I didn't get even a hint of satisfaction or arousal. It was more confusion. Or pity. Or worse . . . disappointment?

"Yeah, that's how you wash a car," he said, confused. "Are you okay? You're being weird."

How would he know I was being weird? Since freshman year, we'd said all of ten words to each other.

A car honked. The line was growing. Avery waved to the drivers, turned back to me, and said, "You know what, maybe you should just stick to hose detail. We're starting to get a rush and I don't think I have time to . . . teach you. Sorry."

Avery went back to scrubbing and I went back to hose island. My new reality-bimbo persona didn't seem to be working. Well, it was working great on CorRay. They were more than happy to show me "good spraying techniques" and "how to get the kinks out of a hose." I thought blatantly kicking a soccer ball over to Avery might do the trick, but every time I did, he simply kicked it back. Missing the fact that this was clearly a "flirt ball." Shoot.

After a couple of hours, my jaw started to hurt from all the fake laughing, and my boobs needed a break from the underwire that was now fusing with my body. I excused myself, changed out of my fuck-island costume, and headed for the bus to go home. If Avery wasn't going to be my in, I'd have to think of a different way to get to Harold's, Danny's, and Jenji's computers.

I booked it past the parking lot, hoping I could still catch the 4:10 bus back to Trinity Towers. I was about to cross the street when a Pontiac Grand Am with a loose muffler sped by and nearly hit me. "*Hey!* You piece of shit! Slow your ass down!"

The car came to an abrupt stop. Some bleary-eyed forty-year-old popped his head out. "What did you say to me!?!"

"I will cripple your hard drive and put you on an FBI watch list! You know how easily I can find you? WYZ-6615! Slow! Down!"

He nodded, realizing that I was clearly capable of the threats I'd just yelled at him.

"Sorry, I'll—sorry," he mumbled, before slowly driving away, making sure to use a turn signal before making a left onto Jefferson Road.

I exhaled. Some people! I turned around and noticed that the entire soccer team was now looking at me. Apparently my feelings about motor vehicle safety were now known to them as well. Cory, Ray, and Avery, in particular, looked perplexed. *What happened to you, Margot? Why so serious?*

I barely gave them a shrug as I turned and made my way onto the bus. My attempt to seduce Avery was a failure, so there was no need to explain to them why I was suddenly acting like a completely different person. I just needed to get home and come up with a new plan.

March 7, 3:07 p.m.

MARGOT: my middle toenail finally fell off- the one I hurt on the diving board. it's as gross as you think. bodies! amirite?

10

You'll Never Walk Alone

Since the car wash was a complete failure,[33] I went to school on Monday resolved to work harder. I had tried to keep my messages on the Fury WhatsApp to a minimum, figuring it was best for the victims to talk amongst themselves. But at least once a day, someone would ask me how the case was going. I always responded with some variation of "I'm working on it." But I understood their anxiety and I felt it, too. Every day that site was up, it was steadily growing. In two days, four more victims had been added to RB: Tatiana Alvarez, Michelle Flood, Ashley Heart, and Kelsey Hoffman, aka the other Kelsey.

I had to be smarter and find some other way to get close to my suspects. One that didn't involve Avery Green. Both the Kelseys were really active on the WhatsApp and kept offering their services to me. But I couldn't think of a way for two freshman girls

---

33. Except that it raised $1,600 for the soccer team.

to help. They weren't friends with my three suspects. They just weren't popular enough. It was looking like I'd have to befriend my suspects on an individual basis, feigning interest in flutes or yearbooks or whatever. It would take longer, but what choice did I have? RB was a plantar wart, and I had to dig it out before it spread any further.[34]

I had just settled into my office hours in the library when Sammi came up to me, his laptop in hand.

"I hit a snag with Mrs. Blye. Apparently Mr. Frange—"

"Shh! Sammi, you know how goddamned gossipy the librarians are." I looked around to see if anyone had heard us. Sammi was never as discreet as I would've liked.

"Okay, I'll talk quieter."

Over Sammi's shoulder, I could see Michelle Flood sitting at the AV desk, biting her nails. Thanks to her sudden appearance on RB, she looked like hell. Like she stayed up all night crying. Just because she got drunk one time at a party. Michelle was cool. A senior. Early decision at Brown. I hated this. It was erasing what little patience I had for Mrs. Blye's case.

"Did you get into Frange's phone? Can we delete Mrs. Blye's pics and be done with it?" I asked sternly.

"I phished him into opening an attachment, so I can remote access his home computer. I can take the pic off his feed whenever you want. But the original still exists on his phone. And . . . his phone is gonna be a problem. It's an off-brand Android, and it looks like he has a custom ROM."

---

34. Obviously I've had a plantar wart. And yes, I dug it out before it spread. And yes, it was the grossest thing I've ever done. Blech.

Woof. Androids were already tough. Not because they were necessarily more secure, but because there are so many different versions of Android on so many different devices. Like millions. So the same hacks don't work on all of them. And a custom ROM? Forget it.

"So I'll have to get to it in person," I said, resigned.

It looked like a field trip to Brighton was in my near future.

"Or, I don't know," Sammi continued. "Could you just send him a cease and desist? Like you did to Jordy Fence—"

"No. I don't like doing that with adults."

Sammi nodded. My forgeries were good, but not *that* good. "Sorry, M. I tried—"

He could tell I was annoyed. But I wasn't annoyed at him, just at, like, the world.

"It's fine. You did good, Sammi. Want some of this muffin?"

"A muffin? *No*," he said, affronted. (Sammi doesn't eat muffins. He thinks they're boring cupcakes.)

"Sorry. That was thoughtless of me," I said with mock penitence. "It won't happen again."

He might be wearing hats now, but it was comforting to know that underneath it all, Sammi hadn't changed that much. If he started liking muffins, I don't know what I would do.

"Good," he said, picking up his laptop and shoving it in his backpack. "See ya later, Maaaargot."

"Saaaammi." I nodded, with a little less vigor than usual. As I dove back into my computer, I saw Sammi leaving the library out of the corner of my eye. He reached into his bag and pulled out his hat, securing it on his head as he disappeared from my view.

Brrrrrnnng. The bell rang. I'd wasted first period.

Damn it.

Luckily, my next period was Latin, so I still had more "office hours." Unfortunately, Miss Watt and her freshman humanities class had reserved the entire library for second period. Miss Watt was one of those teachers who tried to make every class *engaging* and was always taking her students out of the classroom. Which was great for her students, but annoying for me, as she was kicking me out of my office. I had a couple other haunts at Roosevelt where I could usually get work done. But one was, by far, my favorite: the tech booth above the theater.

In ninth grade, I had worked on the stage crew of *Seven Brides for Seven Brothers,* a heinously problematic musical that actually features a gleeful, up-tempo ditty about the Rape of the Sabine Women.[35] (I thought, *Maybe they'll cut that song.* But they didn't. It always amazes me what parents are cool with when it comes in musical form.) Ms. Corman had trusted me to lock up the tech booth after each show. So I knew the six-digit code. I just hoped it was empty, and not occupied with awkward techies playing spin-the-Playbill.

As long as they're not rehearsing a show onstage, the booth is a great place to work. There's a rickety table (an old set piece from *The Producers*), which I use as my desk. And against the back wall, there's a little couch (*Damn Yankees*) I once napped on after staying up all night with Beth.

---

35. The Rape of the Sabine Women is this famous event that took place in the early Roman Empire. The Romans abducted a bunch of women from neighboring tribes and basically forced them into marriage. Google the song "Sobbin' Women" from *Seven Brides* and tell me it's in good taste. I dare you.

I climbed in, blew the dust off the table, and put down my laptop. I was ready to resume MCYF work when I was interrupted by a middle-aged man screaming into his phone.

"One! One! Speak to an associate!"

I looked down from my perch to see the shiny, bald head of Mr. Lumley strutting and fretting upon the stage. Mr. Lumley was short, with deep brown skin and glasses. He spoke pointedly to his phone, simmering with impotent rage. "SPEAK TO AN ASSOCIATE." "SPEAK TO AN ASSOCIATE!"

This wasn't going to fly.

"Phil?" My voice echoed throughout the theater.

He looked up, confused. I spoke into the God mic again. "Phil? Can you do this someplace else?"

Finally, he squinted and saw me in the booth. He gave a little apologetic bow and tiptoed out the back. I'd done a little job for Mr. Lumley last year. (And by little, I mean I covered up his gambling habit so he could get a small business loan.)

"How do you do that?"

Now it was my turn to be shocked. The voice was coming from *inside the booth*. I spun around to see the broad shoulders of Avery Green, who was standing just inside the door.

"Sorry. Didn't mean to sneak up on you," he said in response to my pure terror. (Which had less to do with being surprised and more to do with my suspicion that he was secretly a murderer.)

"It's fine. I just—wasn't expecting anybody," I lied, shutting my laptop. "What are you doing here? No one's ever here."

"I'm not really here! I'm late for AP Stat. Just dropping this off." He gestured to a binder in his hand. Then, as if realizing he needed more context, explained, "I'm running the light board for *Carousel*."[36]

My god. Were there any extracurriculars this guy didn't do?

"So . . . how do you do that?"

"Do what?" I asked.

"Talk to adults like you're their boss? I'd get in-school for talking to a teacher like that. But when you do it . . . it's like you have immunity." He was looking at me in awe. Like I was an eclipse or that TikTok where the guy jumps over elephants. "I once saw you chew out Ms. Gushman in the hall. And last week, I saw Mrs. Blye talking to you like you were friends or something. Or like you were her therapist. I was like, what is Margot's deal?"

Okay, stalker. I grabbed the pointiest pen in my bag.

He placed his binder down on the soundboard, but instead of leaving as I hoped he would, he plopped down on the couch and rested his too-white Nikes on a cushion. Rude. After the car wash, I had abandoned any hope of using Avery for my work. So talking to him now was pointless.

"I really can't talk about my clients. Sorry."

A smile crept across his face, revealing a lone dimple on his left side. "Oh, right! You have that weird job! Shontae told me about it. You're like a fixer."

"I guess. Yeah."

He nodded knowingly. "'Margot Mertz Cleans Your Filth.' That's your company, right? That's so cool."

He was still sitting there. And I know I'm usually pretty

---

36. Another problematic musical. Such beautiful music. Such a toxic take on domestic abuse.

smart, but it took me until that moment to realize that Avery was *trying to flirt with me.* What in holy hell?

Obviously, I should have been trying to *flirt back*. But how? He didn't seem to love car wash Margot, which, according to Netflix, *was his type.* Could he really be into *me*? Like actual me? Wearing a stained hoodie and giving off "please leave me alone" vibes? I wasn't sure how to act.

When I didn't respond, Avery continued, "It's too bad you won't talk about clients. Because I would love to know what Mr. Lumley is like outside of school. I want to believe he's in a fight club or something. Something about that guy is seriously repressed."

"No comment." I wasn't giving him anything. Though Avery was right. Very repressed.

He stood up, straightening his shirt ('cause god forbid it had a wrinkle). "Okay . . . but you do, like, clean up people's mistakes? That's your job, right?"

"I . . . that's one aspect of my company. Yes."

"Okay. That is insane!" He took a step toward me, and I could *feel* his tallness. "You're like . . . Trudy Keene or something."

Trudy Keene is the protagonist of *Trudy Keene Is on the Job!*, a series of books everyone read in middle school. If you're not familiar, Trudy is a Nancy Drew or Hardy Boys type. But instead of solving crimes, Trudy is a fixer. So if you got a D on your report card, or got suspended for smoking, you hired Trudy and she would fix your problems. The books are . . . unrealistic and very dated. And after the first two, the series was clearly written by a team of (mostly male) ghostwriters. A few of the later books are extremely problematic. In one, she "fixes" her uncle's drinking problem by locking him in the bathroom for three hours! Three hours? That's not how alcoholism works! Needless to say, I didn't appreciate the reference.

"That's not—I really wish people would stop comparing me to Trudy Keene."

"Right. I mean, for one thing, you're not perpetually thirteen. And I'm guessing you never saved a prize cow at the state fair."

"Nooo." I smirked. Avery was a little funnier than I expected, but I wasn't going to give him the satisfaction.

He finally walked toward the door, and I relaxed a little, hoping to soon be rid of him.

"Maybe I should hire you sometime," he said, turning back. "Get you to erase all the bad pictures of me on Instagram. You know, before I figured out my hair."

Avery never had bad hair. I didn't know what he was talking about.

"You can do that, right? Take pictures off Instagram?"

He cocked his head to meet my eyeline and hit me with his big brown girlfriend-magnets. He was so obviously flirting. Fine, Oatmeal Avery. You want to get to know me? Let's do this.

"Sure. I could take your pictures down. But usually my cases are a little more complicated than . . . you."

"Oh, yeah?"

I wasn't even trying to impress him. My cases really *are* complicated. "Now, if you needed me to hack someone's phone? Or if stuff got reposted by a vengeful ex and you wanted me to get rid of it? That would be more typical. But something tells me you don't need that."

"Why wouldn't I need that?"

"Because I don't think you have any bad pictures on Instagram."

He smiled, and I realized he thought this was a *compliment*. Like I would tell him to his face that he was hot! I just meant that his social seemed carefully curated, filtered, and *possibly* Photoshopped.

"I mean not Clean Your Filth bad. And I don't think you have any enemies. You seem to get along with everyone. Even your ex-girlfriends. And there are a lot of them . . ."

He smiled. "Hey! I don't have *that* many. Or . . . I don't know, what's a lot?"

"More than ten is a lot."

Avery did some quick girlfriend math in his head. The answer was thirteen, but I let him come to it on his own. Finally, he said, "Yeah, so I guess I've dated a few people."

"And yet, they have nothing bad to say about you. For some reason, everyone at this school seems to think you're, I don't know . . . swell. Nice." I leaned back a little in my cabaret chair, and that cocky bastard came over and leaned against the desk right in front of me!

"And you don't?"

"Honestly, I kind of think you're a serial killer."

Oof. Was that too honest?

Avery laughed, then stood. "Wow. Okay. Well . . . I guess I understand why you jumped when I came in here."

He turned to leave, and I felt a surprising urge to stop him. But then he stopped, whipped back to face me, closed one eye, and pulled his head back to make a huge double chin. He stuck out his tongue, snapped a selfie, and started typing on his phone.

"There," he said. "I have a picture I need removed from Instagram." He shoved his phone under my nose to show me.

"That is objectively terrible," I said. "But sadly, I still cannot take on this job."

He nodded. "Oh, well. Guess this will just have to live on the internet forever." He sighed. "So what was with you the other day? Was that for a job?"

"What are you talking about?"

"At the car wash? You were acting so different. It must have been for a cleanup job, right? Am I right?" He squinted at me, I guess hoping to read my expressionless face.

When I made my persona to seduce Avery, I assumed he did not know anything about the real me. Guess that was a miscalculation. Now I was going to have to lie to his face. "No. Why would you think that?"

"Come on. You're normally Margot Mertz. Serious, intense. Like Batman! Without the weird voice."

I honestly didn't mind that description.

"But Saturday . . . was not normal you," he went on.

Obviously I was there for a job. And weirdly, I felt like *telling* him that. But I came to my senses before divulging anything. "I really can't talk about it," I said, and looked back to my computer.

"Damn. That's cold, Mertz! But I respect it." He was *still standing* in the damn doorway.

I could tell that shutting him down like this was making him all the more interested in me. Which was odd. People usually prefer a fake-Margot persona. The real me is a little blunt.

"Okay . . . good talk, but I have work to do. Bye-bye," I said as I walked over to close the door. He was beaming. How was this working?

"Oh. Okay. I guess I'm leaving," he said, a little flustered. "Filth doesn't clean itself. But look, if you're ever not working, even though it seems like you always are . . . But, if you're ever *not* and you want to, I don't know, hang out . . . well . . . I've been known to do that. Especially on weekends. Even, possibly, this Friday night?"

I closed the door on him completely as I said, "Sure," so nonchalantly you'd think I was dead.

Huh. My in was into me. Well, well, Avery. Game. On.

11

JENJI HOPP

I smelled pancakes. Which meant my dad was in an especially good mood. I was hoping this meant he was finally out of debt, or that he'd reached his "New Year's resolution weight," but instead it was for a much simpler reason.

"My new sneakers are arriving today!" he exclaimed happily as I poured myself a coffee. Just so you know, these weren't the kind of cool sneakers they have release parties for. It was a pair of classic Reeboks that he had bought over and over again, in the same size and color, since the 1990s.

"Pancake for my little pancake?" he offered.

"Why am I a pancake?"

"I don't know. Because you're . . . sweet and . . . buttery?"

"Okay . . ." I rolled my eyes with extra vigor and started eating.

"Before I forget," my mom said as she joined me at the table, "Friday night is your uncle Richard's birthday. So that's going to be our family time this week."

"Sorry, Mom. Friday's no good."

"Margot," she intoned in her "you're about to be in trouble" mom voice.

"Mom," I intoned right back.

"I know you have issues with Uncle Richard—"

"You mean because he ruined my life?"

"He's not a bad person, Margot. He's . . . a little lost." "Lost" is a nice person's way of saying "self-destructive" or "bad at life." My mom is an incredibly nice person.

"Uh-huh."

"He's not perfect, but he's family, and he's trying to . . . make amends. So I think he deserves another shot." God. Another shot at what? We don't have any more savings for him to lose.

"Mom, I just . . . I actually cannot go. I have this . . . thing."

"That sounds made-up." My mom was right. It did sound made-up. But it actually wasn't.

"Well, it isn't, and I have to go. Seriously."

She crossed her arms. And I could tell she was about to transition from "annoyed" to "real mad." So I had to come up with a really good, legit excuse. Which is why I panicked and told her the truth.

"I have a date."

My mom's arms uncrossed real quick, and a flash of joy spread across her face. A look usually reserved for 70-percent-off sales or whenever she sees Jon Hamm on TV. Finally, her weird little entrepreneur daughter was going on a date.

"Oh. I—okay. Okay. A date." She was trying not to giggle. She was failing. My mom has no chill.

"A date," my dad repeated, having no chill either.

"Mom, Dad," I intoned with my own "you're about to be in trouble" voice.

"Does he have a name?"

"Or she?" my dad added.

"It's not Sammi, is it?"

"Guys!" I snapped. This was making them way too happy. "We are not going to talk about this."

"Okay. So you're not coming to Richard's party," my dad said with a goofy look on his face, the kind he saves for grilled meats or whenever he sees Rachel McAdams in movies.

Until this whole thing was over, they were going to be unbearable. I stuffed a pancake in my face and ate the rest of the meal in silence.

Avery and I still hadn't agreed on what to do Friday night. I was trying to think of something safely unromantic so I didn't have to get too close to him. Then he texted me:

> **AVERY:** We don't have to do this, but HAH is having a party with free pizza. We could stop by then hang after?

> **MARGOT:** Yes and yes. Please.

Ah-HAH. Already this "relationship" was paying dividends.

HAH stood for High Schoolers Against Homelessness. (Here's some free advice. Don't have your charity acronym sound like "Ha!"[37]) Avery had been a member of HAH since freshman

---

37. Though it's certainly better than CTE.

year. Usually the club consisted of volunteering at soup kitchens and running donation drives for the local homeless shelter. Admirable. But I was more interested in their new president, Jenji Hopp . . . suspect number female.

Jenji joined HAH in January and was trying to make it more of a social scene, suggesting parties and trying to raise the club's profile in the school. She quickly usurped Kara Michaels as president and became more aggressive in her new leadership role. Jenji's parents had bankrolled Friday night's pizza party. Where anyone present could vote on the future mission of HAH. (Must be nice to have your parents buy you a bunch of votes via pizza.) Clearly, Jenji was up to something with HAH. The only thing I knew for sure was that she was not just doing it out of the kindness of her heart. Jenji wasn't kind.

I needed a chance to get close to Jenji's computer, and this seemed like a great one. Thanks, Avery. I texted him back, and we made plans to arrive at the Eastman Park multipurpose room at six thirty. Avery offered to drive, but I told him I preferred the bus as it was a way to "rub elbows with the common man and experience humanity at its most raw." I was trying to keep some distance from him. I wanted things to go slowly, so I could use him to get close to the people on my list before things ever got "serious." I was worried kissy/handsy stuff with Avery might engage my gag reflex. (I don't know everything about boys, but I do know that if you gag or vomit after kissing them, it's kind of a turnoff.[38])

---

38. Just ask my fifth-grade boyfriend, David Ruttura. Sorry, Davey!

But then Avery showed up at my bus stop. Which I'm sure most girls would find charming, but which had me clutching for my keys.

"This isn't your Tesla, silly. This is a bus! With regular people! And air-conditioning that smells like body odor!" I said when he sat down on the bench next to me.

"Wow. That is very insulting," he said, stretching his back. "You don't go on a lot of dates, do you, Mertz?"

No. I do not. "Sorry. I . . . it was nice of you to take the bus to . . . meet me."

"I actually had to take three buses. So . . ."

Well, this plan really backfired. Not only had I made him feel bad, I was now going to spend even more time with Avery than if I just let him drive. Crap. Luckily, the bus was so crowded from rush hour we had to sit in separate seats. Well, I sat. Avery kept giving up his seat to pregnant women, the elderly, and a couple of guys his own age who I don't think really needed the seat. Jesus, was he really this nice? It was exhausting.

Eventually I gave up my seat too (out of guilt) and was forced to spend the last ten blocks gripping a pole and trying to keep from pummeling into Avery every time we took a left turn. He did not seem bothered.

"So . . . what do you want to do after this?" Avery asked during our body-bumper-car ride.

My brain scrolled through all the potential date-type things we could do and decided that the least awful plan would be one that involved dessert. "Let's get pie," I said definitively.

"Sweet." He nodded, catching me before I slammed into his

chest. And then he rattled off seven places you can get pie, three of which were legitimately good.

WHEN WE ARRIVED AT THE PARTY, JENJI AND HER LAPTOP WERE sitting at a folding table by the door. She was marking down attendance and handing people ballots. A diminutive white girl with poker-straight black hair inexplicably wearing a blazer, Jenji looked more like a thirty-year-old pharmaceutical rep than a high schooler. She seemed intently focused on her task, which meant I'd need to distract her in order to access the laptop. I had brought a small NVMe flash drive in my bag. If I could get it plugged into her laptop, it would take about ten minutes to copy what I needed from her hard drive.

"Oh my god, I'm so happy you're here. We're crazy behind," Jenji said to Avery, leaving her laptop to personally greet us. "Can you help with the pizza? We need to get rid of the empty boxes." The pizza tables were currently unsupervised and therefore a shitshow.

"We're on it," Avery said for both of us. I guess I was on pizza box detail.

"I'm just so happy you're here! Both of you!" Jenji said with a forced, desperate-looking smile.

Something about her seemed off. The Jenji I knew was judgy and acerbic. Dead-eyed in a Billie Eilish kind of way. This Jenji seemed upbeat, eager to please. It was strange.

"Margot, it's so cool of you to come to this. Maybe I could get your contact info if you're going to come to more HAH events?" she said, motioning to a sign-in sheet.

"And have you screenshot all my conversations? No thank you!" I said like John Mulaney, emphasizing the "no thank you" as if it were my catchphrase. I was hoping that my delivery would sand off the edges of what I actually said.

Nope! All conversation came to a halt. There might as well have been a record scratch. Everyone nearby, including Avery, looked horrified. I tried to save myself by mumbling . . .

"I, uh . . . I don't like . . . to be blackmailed. So . . ." This did not dig me out of the hole.

Jenji just nodded, biting her lip so hard I thought she was going to give herself a new piercing. Her eyes even welled up a little.

"Right. Well, if you put down your email, you'll at least be on the email blast. I think you're pretty safe if you just . . . do that." She took a deep breath, then addressed Avery. "Okay! Thanks for doing pizza. Don't forget to vote!"

Avery looked at me like I had killed a kitten. "You don't pull punches, do you? Like, ever?"

I really needed to cool it. I felt bad and I didn't know how to respond. Luckily, Avery filled the void with "Well, I'm gonna start on pizzas. Join me after you vote?"

I looked for the first time at the ballot in my hand. It read, "What would you like to see High Schoolers Against Homelessness do next? Circle: Abused animals. Global warming. Gun control." What did those things have to do with homelessness? Something was definitely going on here. With the club, with Jenji. Something.

I followed Avery over to a stack of pizzas and helped him consolidate boxes.

"This is Jenji, right? Jenji Hopp? The same person who got the entire JV soccer team disqualified from state by reposting a group chat she wasn't even in?"

"Yeah. But, Margot, she hasn't done that stuff in a while. I think she's really trying to—"

"What?" I asked, not sure why he was defending Jenji.

"Be better, I guess. Why do you think she joined HAH in the first place?"

"I assume she has ulterior motives. Didn't she force out Kara Michaels as president?"

"No," Avery said, genuinely confused. "We all kicked Kara out of HAH because she never came to meetings. Jenji's really tried to expand what we do here. She's been a good president."

Avery, now finished with the boxes, finally took a break and helped himself to a slice. He took a moment before saying, "People can change, you know."

I nodded as though I was really considering what he was saying. But of course I wasn't. Only someone as rich and popular as Avery could think people were inherently good and that someone like Jenji could change. I'd seen what people did when they were online. When they thought they were anonymous. And as far as I could tell, when people changed, it wasn't for the better.

For the rest of the evening, I kept my head down and didn't make any more clever/mean comments to Jenji or anyone else. I helped people help themselves to pizza, I cleaned up soda spills. I tried to be useful. I did this all while keeping a side-eye on

Jenji's laptop, which she was now using to record all the votes. She never let it out of her sight. A couple of times she caught me eyeing it, which seemed to make her even more attached to it. The evening was looking like a bust.

Later, as people were starting to leave, I was off to the side, wiping up tables with a few random sophomores who seemed too afraid to talk to me. My phone pinged with a text from Mrs. Blye and I snuck into the bathroom to text her back.

> **BLYE:** Any updates? The karaoke pic is still up and I'm worried someone will show Toby.

> **MARGOT:** Sorry we're having some trouble with his cell phone. Hopefully we'll crack it soon. Just want to make sure we have all copies of the pic before we delete it.

> **BLYE:** But it's out there! What if someone sees it!

I didn't want Avery to start wondering where I was. But Mrs. Blye was being so needy. I had already explained to her in a lengthy email that Josh Frange had exactly ten followers on Instagram, and that we'd buried him under a mountain of fake pages and misdirects if anyone were to google him.[39] No one was going to find that photo unless they just stumbled on it in his grid. Mrs. Blye was safe until I could get the original down. But she clearly hadn't read my email. I was about to resend it when I heard—

---

39. I discovered there's a magician named Josh Frange who lives in Tucson, Arizona. He was not very popular, but thanks to my unsolicited promotion and tags, he is now the most-searched Josh Frange on the web.

"Did someone hire you?" I looked up and saw Jenji in the bathroom mirror. Wide-eyed, panicked. Clutching her backpack like it was a stuffed bear.

"Hire me?"

"Amelia Lopez told me about you. She said you're a hacker for hire. And that you got Craig Layton's dad thrown in jail."

Amelia, what are you telling people? Craig Layton's dad went to jail for his third DUI. I didn't have anything to do with that!

Jenji looked freaked out, so I just said, "I don't really like to talk about my work."

"Right, she said you'd say that, too. Who hired you?"

"I don't know what you're talking about, Jenji. Nobody hired me."

Before I could respond, she shoved her backpack into my chest. I didn't realize until this moment how nervous she was.

"I don't screenshot people anymore. Or blackmail, or do any of the other petty shit I used to," she said, holding her arms for comfort. "So here's my computer and phone. Go ahead. It'll save you the trouble of hacking it, I guess."

I took her Lululemon[40] bag tentatively.

"Are you okay, Jenji?"

"I'm fine. I've just—had a bad year . . ."

I was going to say something about how bad it was for the people she screenshotted. But for once this evening, I used self-control.

"I know what people think of me. I've done some really bad

---

40. Did you know they make bags? They do! (For rich people.)

things, but . . . I'm really trying not to be that person anymore."

"Which is why you're doing HAH?"

She nodded yes.

"That's good. I see you're trying to expand HAH to include global warming and puppies and—"

Sensing that I was critical, she blurted out, "Look, I don't know what I'm doing, okay?" And then she started crying. She had thick lines of black eyeliner above her eyes that remained intact despite the waterworks. "I thought if I did more good things, it might cancel out all the bad things I've done! I don't know if that makes any sense or not, but . . . I'm trying."

I nodded. Fair enough. Then Jenji abruptly excused herself to the multipurpose room, where she continued to spearhead cleanup. I had a feeling she'd be the last one to leave.

Well, that was unexpected! I had never had a suspect literally give me their computer before. Sometimes you get a freebie. Weird.

I suddenly felt like getting the hell out of there. Part of it was the excitement of seeing what was on Jenji's laptop, and, presumably, crossing her off my list. But there was also a part of me that felt . . . bad for Jenji? Which didn't make any sense, because she'd done terrible things! Far worse than my mild insults at her pizza party. But still . . . I didn't like that my snark seemed to hurt her.

So I shot Avery a text saying I wasn't feeling great and slipped out. He responded right away with:

AVERY: Want me to call you a ride?

> **MARGOT:** Nah I'm good.

I had boarded the W22 bus when I saw his second text.

> **AVERY:** Too bad. I was really looking forward to some pie.

Oh right. Pie. Not only had I ditched him, but I'd completely blown off our pie plan with my Irish goodbye. Shit. It was starting to become clear to me why I'd never had a boyfriend.

I sent him a couple apology texts assuring him that I was actually sick. And going into far too much detail about my digestive tract. He responded with a meme of a dog shrugging. Soooooo . . . he didn't seem mad? I don't think? I really didn't want him to break up with me before I got to Harold and Danny. I was going to have to do better on our next date and, like . . . actually go on it.

When I got home, I fired up Jenji's phone and laptop, and it was just as she'd said. Clean. Full of nothing but homework, newsletters for HAH, and lots of emails. I also found a running diary she seemed to be keeping. It looked like an assignment from a therapist or something. It was very raw and personal, full of random thoughts, notes, even a few poems. And something called an "apology tour" with a list of twenty-seven names. Ten were crossed off, presumably because she'd successfully apologized to them. Under the list was the quote, "Apologize today. Because tomorrow is already here." Oof. Sounds like a cat poster. And what does that even mean? Was she going to apologize to everyone on that list? I couldn't imagine saying sorry to that many people. But, I also couldn't imagine ruining that many people's lives, so . . .

From what I could piece together, Jenji had thrown herself some kind of splashy sweet sixteen party, and nobody came. It was a wake-up call. She wanted friends. She didn't want to be an asshole anymore. She was trying to turn things around. After reading a few entries, I x-ed out of it. They seemed private, and I didn't want to pry for no reason. Whether she had really changed or not, only Jenji knew. Personally, I'm not sure anyone can ever really change who they are deep down. But it was clear she was trying. Avery was right.

Weird.

I shot a message to the Fury group.

> **MARGOT:** Narrowing down suspects. GETTING CLOSER

Which was met with a cascade of indecipherable emojis and one cogent text from Hoffman.

> **HOFFMAN:** Tell us if we can help. I'm willing to commit B&E! And possible manslaughter. Under the right circumstances!

Good to know. But I guess you don't have to commit breaking and entering if your suspect just hands you their computer.

I turned off Jenji's laptop and crossed her off my list.

March 13, 12:31 a.m.

MARGOT: I had olive pizza tonight. Remember how I said olives were disgusting and I would never like olives because they're an abomination? Well I had a piece. By accident. It was fine.

12

TURN DOWN FOR PUTT

At seven a.m. the next morning, I was awoken by a series of texts.

> **BLYE:** Just wanted to see if there were any updates

> **BLYE:** Got your email, wondering if you could take the instagram pic down anyway

> **BLYE:** would feel better if it was down, even if the other ones are still out there

> **BLYE:** Can you confirm your getting these texts

> **BLYE:** Please Confirm

> **BLYE:** Please Confirm

My god, woman! We went over this! How many times did I have to explain that it was in her best interest that I leave the Instagram pic up for now? If I took it down, Mr. Frange might realize someone had hacked his computer and take additional steps to safeguard his stuff. Then we'd never be able to get to any remaining pictures.

> **MARGOT:** I promise you, this is the safest way to ensure we delete all the photos. Let's schedule a call later today so I can go over the plan in detail.

I sent the text and rolled over, hoping to go back to sleep. But my mind was racing. I had an AP Gov paper to write, a tedious Blye phone call to make, and thirty-seven missed messages on Fury. Reading and responding to the chat was draining. People weren't sleeping. Their grades were dropping. I sat up in bed and started scrolling. Eve Brunswick and Keisha Hill had just been added and were freaking out. The other girls were sending a flood of supportive GIFs and messages. I figured I should, too.

> **MARGOT:** I'm getting closer. I know it's hard that the site is still up. But trust me, if you want it down for good, I need a little more time to find out who's behind it. I'm going to destroy it, the right way, so that these pictures will not continue to haunt you.

And then, because I was beginning to understand my audience, I sent a GIF of Laura Dern kicking someone in the face.

I noticed that Shannon was notably absent from the group. In general, I try to update my clients every week with a progress report. The hope is that by proactively updating, it stops them from DMing me with every worry or question (like what Mrs. Blye was currently doing). But Shannon was proving to be a way easier client than most. After every report, she'd respond with a cheery "Thanks so much for the updates!" or "You are so professional!" It was remarkable how upbeat she was, considering she was the victim of a heinous cybercrime. But my guess was that Shannon was one of those people who always stayed friendly and *used lots of exclamation points in her emails to prove how nice she was!!!*

I texted Shannon and typed up a quick email to Mrs. Blye, then decided to get out of the house. I figured I might as well knock out my AP Gov paper while I was up but only half awake. Mr. Thames preferred papers that were regurgitations of the textbook. He was a classic busywork kind of teacher, so I was in the right headspace at 7:05 to write such drivel.

I texted Sammi.

> **MARGOT:** Wanna get a coffee? I feel like getting out of my room.

> **SAMMI:** sure meet ya in 20

> **MARGOT:** Great! Anywhere but the Jefferson Road Starbucks please!

Sammi always insisted that we go to the Starbucks in the sad strip mall on Jefferson Road. He knows I don't like Starbucks coffee. He knows it's idiotic to go to a Starbucks that is half a mile farther than the Starbucks near Trinity Towers. But he says there's "something about Jefferson Road that's just . . . special." (While rubbing his fingers together, just to get a rise out of me.)

> **SAMMI:** but Jefferson rd is so gooood

> **MARGOT:** Sammi. No.

> **SAMMI:** it's got that special something

> **MARGOT:** It doesn't! There's nothing special about it!

If I could just not react and pretend I didn't care, this pointless game would end and we could finally go somewhere else. With more room. And better coffee.

Anyway, after a few minutes he responded with:

> **SAMMI:** ha ha. see you at Jefferson road Starby's on me!

He is so annoying.

We had to sit outside on the patio because, as usual, there were no open tables. Sammi got a cold brew even though he was freezing. (He only drinks cold brew.) I ordered a banana, because even Starbucks can't ruin a banana.

"You look a little cold there." I smirked at him.

"I'm not," Sammi said, pulling his hoodie tighter.

"Well, I'm just glad you're suffering. As you know, the cold doesn't bother me because I have the constitution of a tough pioneer woman."

"Yeah, yeah, yeah."

From my seat on the patio, I could see down the stretch of mostly vacant strip mall that connected to Starbucks. There was a Sally Beauty, a vape outlet, and a Beacon's Closet second-hand store, with many empty storefronts in between. I watched a woman struggling just inside the door with a stroller and a cup of hot coffee. I debated going to help her, but then I saw someone else reach for the door. He waited patiently as she wedged her stroller out of the Starbucks, then he turned toward us for a moment, and I saw his face. It was Chris Heinz.

There was something so icky and weird about seeing him outside of school. In school, I knew where he was at all times, and there were limits to what either of us could do. But the idea of running into him in the real world . . . I don't know, it was so uncontrolled. It made me both furious and nauseous.

Chris went in, ordered a stupid double-whip creamy mocha whatever,[41] and was about to leave when he spotted us. He took a step toward us, almost like he was going to say hello. He even opened his mouth, but then, thinking better of it, turned and walked to his car.

"That was weird."

"Huh?" Sammi said, not even bothering to look up from his computer.

"That dickhead Chris Heinz looked like he was gonna come over here."

"Huh."

---

41. The kind of drink a fourth grader would order.

"Sammi, what are you doing? Playing that gross sex tentacles game?"

"No. I stopped playing SQIGGLE." Sammi turned his computer to show me, "This is Grimlex. It's an indie game out of South Korea. You're a baby named Grimlex and you go around finding adults who are either secretly sex predators or deadbeat dads who don't pay child support. Then you either kill them or you report them to the IRS. It's still in beta, but it's pretty cool."

I know. That was a very weird and disturbing description. Unfortunately, this is very typical for Sammi and the games he plays. Can you imagine if I didn't give him jobs? This would be his life.

I gave up talking to Sammi and went on Avery's Instagram. His latest post was a picture of a stack of pizza boxes that said, "Carbs for a good cause."

Creative.

Before that was a post of the car wash. Caption: "Bros before hose." I don't even know what he was going for with that one.

He had some admittedly cute pictures with a gorgeous woman I assumed was either his mom or a Kerry Washington impersonator. And then a couple with a white man who appeared to have stepped out of a Lands' End catalog. His dad, I assumed. Then all three together. On a hike! Playing a board game! Wearing sweaters at the beach! They were having lots of very grammable quality time.

On his story was a picture of him with Claire Jubell holding a spicy-looking pepper. And it said, **@clairejuby dared me to eat**

this so . . . pray for me. Then he posted a brief video of him chewing and crying.

Shit. Had I messed this up? Was he hanging out with Claire because I'd blown it last night? Claire was one of his exes, and in my opinion, the prettiest. They'd been together an epic (for Avery) three months. Did he still have feelings for her? My stomach sank. I still needed him to get to Danny and Harold.

I thought about texting him, but everything I started to type screamed "boom box over head." After forty-five drafts, the best I came up with was . . .

> **MARGOT:** So did you take the bus home?

. . . when I got a DM.

> **AVERY:** Last night was kinda weird, huh. Wanna try again tonight?

> **AVERY:** mini golf maybe?

Okay! Guess Claire wasn't a thing, because he was asking me out again. This was good! Right? I mean, sure, yes, this meant I had to spend my Saturday going on a date with Avery to the most autofill of teenage dates . . . putt-putt. Which I would not call "good." But if this was what I had to do to get to Danny and Harold, then fine.

> **MARGOT:** Hell yeah. I must warn you, I'm very good.

I'm not especially good at golf, mini or otherwise, but that didn't mean I couldn't trash-talk. In my experience, if you were planning to trash-talk, the best time to do it was early and often.

He texted back.

> **AVERY:** That's sweet. But I will destroy you. I'm the LeBron James of mini golf.

I know who LeBron James[42] is. But still I texted,

> **MARGOT:** Who?

> **AVERY:** Fine. The Michael Jordan of mini golf.

> **MARGOT:** ???

> **AVERY:** TIGER WOODS THEN.

> **MARGOT:** That can't be a real person.

At this point our *hilarious* bit was interrupted by Sammi.

"All right. I admit it. I'm cold and miserable. I'm going home," he said, slamming his laptop shut. "You want to hang out later tonight?"

Oh, man. I'd much rather hang with Sammi. We could put on a terrible movie, and his mom might even make us breakfast for dinner. I have *dreams* about Mrs. Santos's mangu.[43] Damn it all.

"No. Sorry. I can't tonight."

---

42. He started a public charter school in Akron, Ohio! Oh, and basketball.

43. The italics are meant to illustrate that these are *borderline* sex dreams. Yes, I'm turned on by Stanford and plantains! Don't kink shame me!

"Oh. Family Night?"

I figured I should just tell him about Avery. Word would get out sooner or later we were a thing. Better that Sammi hear it from me.

"Actually, no. I'm going to play mini golf with Avery Green. So . . ." I didn't know what was more absurd, the idea of me golfing or Avery Green-ing. I expected a lot of razzing after the shit I gave him about his hat. Or maybe he'd see through it and know it was for a job.

But I just got a "Oh. Okay. Well . . . Maaargot." He left, giving me an awkward wave goodbye. Hm. Weird. But I guess that's Sammi, he's inscrutable when he wants to be. I closed out Instagram. I was determined to get my stupid paper regurgitated before I had to go to Jenji's. She'd asked me to return her computer before some HAH event she was hosting.

After a smelly bus ride and fifteen awkward minutes of small talk, I left Jenji's and headed home to get ready for my "date." Avery insisted on picking me up at my house. And my parents insisted on meeting him. I told my parents things with Avery were not serious and that they didn't need to meet him. But they insisted. Everybody was insisting. It was obnoxious.

"Hi, Ms. Mertz. Mr. Mertz," Avery said, going in for handshakes. My parents were visibly stunned by the sight of him. This handsome leading man was not the awkward weirdo with concave biceps they expected me to be dating.

"You must be Avery," my mom managed to say through her gleeful smile.

"What a firm shake!" my dad exclaimed with a glint in his

eye that said, "Maybe I'll finally have someone to talk sports with! Oh, please, please, please!!!!"

"Yes, yes, well. We're gonna get out of here," I said, urging Avery back the way he came.

"Have a pop before you go! Would you like a pop, Avery?" my mom asked.

"Absolutely! I brought these cookies." And only then did I realize he was carrying a box of fancy little macarons. Of course he was. If Avery were a cookie, he'd be a macaron.

"Ooh, macarons!" My dad squealed, overdoing the French accent on *mac-a-run*.

"Sorry! No time for a pop or pretentious cookies! We gotta go!"

"Hey." My mom smiled. "Don't worry about your curfew tonight. It's Saturday."

"Really? No curfew? You aren't worried about . . . midnight murderers?"

"Meh." My mom shrugged.

God, Mom. She was so desperate.

"Nice to meet you guys," Avery said as I dragged him away by the arm. "But it looks like I have an appointment to crush your daughter in mini golf."

My parents laughed. What a card.

"Haha. Let's go!"

As we walked to his car I nudged him. "Well, aren't you just so great with parents."

He shrugged. "When you don't have any siblings, you kind of . . . have to learn to speak adult."

"I'm an only child and I can't charm adults," I replied, remembering the many times my aunt asked my mom, "Is she always like this?"

He cocked his head at me, squinting as he smiled. "I don't believe that."

"I can't!"

"You have clients that are adults, don't you? So you must be able to talk adult, too."

I squinted back. He may have been partially right about that. I could turn on the "adult voice" when I wanted to.

"But I know you can't talk about your business, so . . ." He shrugged before *opening the passenger door for me*. I was about to go off: What was this, *Pride and Prejudice*? Was he also going to ask for my dowry? But then I looked at him, with his happy grin, and I just let him do it. Because, I don't know, it was kind of nice? Sure, the act of opening a door for a woman is probably baked in a bunch of patriarchal bullshit that goes back centuries (I vowed to research it when I got home). But . . . it also shows that someone is making an effort? And is making an effort such a bad thing? I was getting the slightest (*slight-est*) glimpse as to why Avery had had so many girlfriends.

As I buckled up, I reminded myself that I had to up my game this time. I was kind of an asshole at the HAH fundraiser, and I needed to keep our faux relationship going. I tried to find a common interest. I went back to Netflix.

"Well, I hope you're ready to get your ass handed to you,

because like Chauffeur says, 'I play to get paid. And win,'" I said in my best Chauffeur impression.

Avery looked so confused. "What? What's Chauffeur? Is that a person's name?"

"Yeah, from *Cheat Retreat*!" I knew he'd seen it. Why would he lie? Was he embarrassed by his streaming habits?

Avery shook his head. "Uh. That's not really my thing. My mom watches it, though."

"Your mom?"

"She loves all that stuff. She watches it all the time. And she forgets to sign out of my Netflix, which is . . . very annoying. I keep getting recommendations for a show called *Sex Condo*. And I'm like, 'I'm pretty sure I won't like *Sex Condo*, Netflix.'"[44]

"Oh," I said. Hm. Might have to reconsider my "streaming is the way to a person's soul" theory.

"I've set up her own account, but she just doesn't get how streaming works. Neither does my dad."

"Well, if I ever meet your mom, we'll have to talk about it. Because last season was . . . crazy."

"Yeah. She'd love that." Avery smiled, but I could tell it was forced. *He did not want me to meet his parents.* Ouch. Too soon? I made a mental note not to bring them up again. "You cold?" he asked as we pulled out of the Trinity Towers parking lot. "You can adjust the temp there." Again with the chivalry.

"I'm freezing, actually," I said involuntarily, adjusting the knob. At the next red light, he took off his reversible down jacket

---

44. The show's full title is *Sex Condo: Beach Edition*, but I didn't bother correcting him because I've never cared less about anything in my life.

and tossed it to me. I hate down jackets because they're so puffy-ugly. But I put it on to be polite, and honestly, it felt like being in a marshmallow. It was divine.

We arrived at Gulf of Golf, North Webster's second most popular mini golf destination (and there are only two), in which every hole is made to look like a famous gulf. So hole one is the Gulf of Mexico. Hole two is the Persian Gulf. And so on. I know. What does the Gulf of Mexico even look like? Exactly. Avery insisted we go to Gulf of Golf and not the far more popular Mini Golf Max! because it was never crowded (true!) and the designs of each hole were, according to him, "superior" (can't be true!).

We got our clubs and balls and that weird little pencil and scorecard. Avery insisted on paying because "he already felt guilty for beating me by so much." I said I would take the first shot to "show him how it was done."

If it hadn't been clear before that my boasting was baseless, it was pretty clear after my first shot. It was a par-three hole and I got a seven, which we decided was the most we'd ever give a hole. So essentially, I could've eaten the golf ball and gotten the same score. I narrowed my eyes at Avery. I wasn't about to stop my trash talk now. "Just warming up." I smiled.

It was Avery's turn. And in a fun reveal, Avery turned out to be at or *below* my skill level. He managed to hit into the water hazard three times in a row before we marked him down for a seven as well.

"What a game," he said. Before hitting the ball into the water for a fourth time. (The hole was over, he just wanted to take one more shot to prove he could keep his ball on the grass if he wanted to. He did not prove this.)

The second hole was the kind where you have to chip the ball up over a hill with just the right amount of pressure, or risk it coming back down again. We couldn't. We both got sevens again.

I lost my ball on the third hole when it rolled into the parking lot. Avery lost his on the sixth hole when he somehow got it wedged between some stalks of bamboo in the Gulf of Tonkin. The guy working the ball desk hated us. We were causing a bottleneck of golfers, and twice we had to let families of four play through.

The worse we golfed, the better we bragged. "Here's how you want to do it," I instructed as I squared my legs to take a swing. "Make sure to swing your body like a pendulum. That's what you're doing wrong." I hit the ball against the edge, and it bounced off into a gutter.

"A lot of golf is in your head," Avery explained with a patronizing smirk. "If your head's not in a good place, you're not going to sink the ball." His ball lost steam and rolled back into the Gulf of Panama.

I had to give Avery some credit, he could keep up with the trash spewing from my mouth.

By the eighteenth hole he was up, or rather down, by two strokes. Which, in golf's truly stupid way of keeping score, means he was winning. I needed a miracle on turf. He went first and sank his ball in four strokes. The best hole he had played by far, which didn't make things any easier for me.

As I set up to take my first swing, he said, "Look, Margot,

don't feel bad about losing. You have lots of other nice qualities."

That smug jerk. I wanted to club him. Instead I lined up my swing. Then I lifted my head so I could look him straight in the eye. "If I sink this, will you take off all your clothes and jump into the Gulf of Gibraltar?"

"A hole in one? Yes. Sure. Not only will I do that, I'll also—"

I didn't even let him finish the sentence. I just cocked my club and swung it without even looking where it was going. Because who cared?

And then I sunk. A hole. In one. *One!*

"ONE! ONE, DAMN YOU! HOLE IN ONE!" I screamed, running after my ball. "I WIN! I WIN! I WIN!"

A family of six looked up, concerned. I was getting a little loud.

"Holy shit," he said, dumbfounded. "That is . . . impossible! How the . . . there's no way!"

"There's always a way when you're as good at golf as I am." I flexed. "Now get your naked ass in that gulf! Now!"

The family of six decided to leave early. Clearly, we had ruined their night. But I didn't care. When was I ever going to get a hole in one again? Never, because I was never going to play putt-putt again, because it's a terrible game. But . . . damn . . . it did feel good! And to be able to rub it in Avery's face. Mwah! What a sweet delight!

As we walked back to the ball window, Avery pored over the scorecard. "Are you sure you only got a five on hole seven?"

"Honestly? I've already forgotten everything except my hole in one." I shrugged.

"I think I have to demand a rematch," he said in a very undemanding voice.

I put my finger to his lips. "Less talk. More skinny-dipping." I pointed to Gibraltar.

"Are you serious? I thought we were joking. The water is, like, Kool-Aid blue. I think it's toxic."

"So you're saying you're a loser and also a liar?"

Avery squinted, his face saying, "How dare you, madam." And then he pulled up his shirt, revealing four of his I'm sure, like, twenty-four abs. There was a group of middle school girls on the fifteenth hole looking on, mouths agape, becoming women right in front of us.

"All right. That's enough. Put your shirt back on, Peloton." I grabbed his shirt and pulled it down.

"You called me a liar!" he said, threatening to yank it up again.

"Just . . . buy me an ice cream sandwich or something. Okay? And live in shame for the rest of your life."

"You got it," he said, leaning in and snapping a selfie of us holding the scorecard.

"What are you doing?" I asked.

"Letting the world know that I've been beaten and humiliated by Margot Mertz. May the gods of Instagram be merciful!" He showed me before posting, mostly for filter approval. And it was . . . kind of surreal to look at. I almost didn't recognize myself. I had this huge grin on my face. So big it was almost grotesque. Was this what my life could've been if my parents hadn't blown my college fund? Was I just deep undercover, or did I actually enjoy it?

Also, it was our second date, and he was already posting pics of us together? It was almost like this made us *official* or something. Though we'd definitely never talked about that. The hearts came flooding in immediately. Huh.

We turned in our clubs, and the man at the ball window informed me that because I made a hole in one on eighteen (which, not to brag, is apparently the hardest Gulf on the course), I was entitled to a free game.

I actually, truly wanted to play it so that I could beat Avery again. Why not? The whole point of this night was to patch things up with Avery and convince him I should be his girlfriend. Wouldn't another game do that?

"Avery? Hey!?" I looked over and saw a foursome walking toward us from the parking lot. Cheryl Graham, Greg Mayes, a twiggy blonde girl I didn't know, and trailing behind, eyes awkwardly glued to his phone . . . Danny Pasternak. Suspect #2. Coming right at me.

My free game would have to wait.

13

DANNY PASTERNAK

Danny Pasternak and Greg Mayes were on an awkward double date with Cheryl Graham and this blonde who went to Brighton. They all looked surprised to see me with Avery. Everyone had the same look. *"Him?* With *her? What? How?"* Fortunately, this look/moment didn't last long. Out of respect for Avery (or fear of me), everyone just kind of accepted us and moved on.

We began an awkward "What are you doing at Gulf of Golf?" conversation, during which I quickly sized up their situation. Danny, an aggressively average white dude, was clearly in love with Cheryl and stared at her whenever she spoke. Cheryl, tall, ivory-skinned, and intimidatingly good-looking, seemed like she did not want to be there at all. She mostly spoke to Brighton Girl, who seemed to be on a mission to drink. A lot. Brighton Girl's breath smelled like the cheap vodka and lemonade that she sipped out of a Wendy's cup. And several times she offered me her drink and said, "It's actually vodka!" in a way-too-loud whisper.

Greg was a short, light-skinned Black nerd obsessed with music, online poker, and also, I think, Avery? At least that's what it seemed like from his stalkerish asides. "Dude! That jacket is amazing. I just commented on your gram. Where did you get it? Would you care if I bought one?" He went on, kissing Avery's ass with perfect jazz band embouchure.

This was not a fun group.

After a few minutes of mindless chatter, during which Greg said, "You guys wanna make this a sixsome?!" at least three times, Avery shot me a look that said, "You want to get out of here so we don't get stuck with them?" And I had to catch myself, because I almost said, "Yes! Please! *Please!*" I did not want to add our twosome to this awkward foursome. That sounded like a root canal.

But then I looked into the steel-gray eyes of Danny Pasternak. He was either a quiet dud with weird locker decor or the ruthless mastermind behind RB. And if he was the latter, I needed to find out and crucify him. I couldn't just play mini golf. I couldn't just be a regular teenager. Not when the Fury group was regularly blowing up my phone with the most maddening updates. Every ping a visceral reminder that they had their regular teenagerness taken from them. They were counting on me.

And so, I unfortunately responded to Greg's offer with "Yeah! That sounds fun! Let's sixsome it up!"

Avery seemed a little confused. And maybe a little hurt. But he didn't push back.

We played a very uneventful eighteen holes. Danny said

almost nothing the entire time, except for occasional monosyllabic responses to someone else's questions. I tried to engage him by asking about his app, but all he said was "Yeah" and "It's good" and "MeetPup." I would have found it funny if it hadn't been so frustrating. He was comically quiet.

Was he always this quiet? Was he just shy? Or did his reserve mask something darker? Like a secret hatred of women? I couldn't get much from his face, which said as little as his non-words. He didn't smile, but he didn't frown. His eyes were not expressive. There was nothing to *read*. It was like looking at a sphinx.[45]

Why had I never heard about how *silent* this guy was? Probably because Danny was tall and despite not being rich, he dressed pretty well. He seemed "cool." So he got a pass. If a girl were ever that quiet, she'd be labeled a bitch.

In the Gulf of Aden, Danny tried to correct Cheryl's swing by putting his arms around her. She did not seem into it, so he quickly backed off. Was that a sign of male aggression? Or just a guy who read some signals wrong? I wasn't sure what to make of it.

Avery and I remained terrible golfers, and the rest of the gang was no better—except for Greg Mayes, who beat us all by twelve strokes. When it was over, Greg said, "Let's keep this party going!" And someone (me) suggested we go back to Danny's house.

Danny seemed surprised. He hadn't intended to steer the party to his house. But rejecting that plan would've meant explaining why, which would've meant he'd have to *talk*. So instead he just shrugged and said, "Okay."

---

45. Minus the animal body.

Avery shot me another, more severe look. Like, "Why would we keep hanging out with them? This group is terrible!" But I pretended I didn't see him.

Greg was on board as soon as Avery said yes. It was just the matter of convincing the girls. Thankfully, Danny spoke up, uttering the longest sentence he'd spoken all evening.

"My parents are out of town."

Thank you, Danny! This immediately made Danny's house *very* appealing to Brighton Girl.

"No parents? Yesssss. What's their liquor cabinet sitch?" she asked, and took another sip, ever on-brand.

Cheryl, the last domino, looked at Danny and shrugged. "I don't really care where we go." Thank you for your contribution to the evening, Cheryl. You're a real fun girl.

It was settled. Avery and I got in his car and followed the foursome in Danny's Toyota.

"Well, Mertz, you keep surprising me," Avery said without taking his eyes off the road. "Wouldn't have guessed this was your scene."

"I'm having fun."

"Liar!" Avery pounced, pointing a finger at me. "What do you find appealing about this? Danny clearly likes Cheryl, and Cheryl clearly doesn't like him. Or anyone, maybe. Greg's potentially stalking me. And that girl from Brighton is only going to get drunker and louder." He made a left on Sycamore, following Danny.

I desperately tried to concoct an explanation. But Avery was onto me and quickly followed up with "Is this about a cleanup job?"

He was getting a decent nose for my bullshit. But before I could be impressed with him, he ruined it by being too damn impressed with himself.

"I'm right, aren't I? It's a JOB! Holy shit!" He honked the horn a couple times.

"Oh my god, please stop."

"Filth is about to be CLEANED!" Honk.

He was going to be insufferable, so I figured I might as well tell him. "All right! Yes. This is for a job. But I'm not giving you any details."

"I KNEW IT! Oh my god! This is so exciting! OH MY GOD!" I had thought Avery would be offended that I'd sidetracked our date. But he was the happiest I had seen him all night. What a weirdo. Wait, was I dating a groupie?

"Stop saying 'oh my god.' It's just a job."

"Just a job. A super-secret hacker spy job. And I'm your getaway driver! Or am I your muscle? I have a green belt in tae kwon do . . . from the fourth grade. But I don't think it expires."

"Okay, haha. Just act normal when we get to Danny's, okay?"

"Absolutely. I will be the *most* normal." He was grinning ear to ear.

"Great," I said, regretting everything.

"Maybe I'm your Moneypenny."

"I don't know what that is, but sure. Be whoever you want. But the second we leave this car, you have to calm down and be normal." I couldn't tell if it was sinking in, so I went on, "I can't tell you any of the specifics, but, there could be some stuff on Danny's computer that could cause a lot of harm to my client.

Some . . . really fucked-up, blackmailing shit. So I need you to take this seriously."

Avery straightened up. Nodded. "Blackmail. Right. Wow. You deal with a lot of dark stuff, huh?"

"Unfortunately, yes," I said.

We shared a brief but intense look, and I knew he was finally taking me seriously. "I'll be myself," he said. "And if you need me to do anything else, just let me know."

We parked in Danny's driveway, and as promised, Avery was as fun and easygoing as ever. Not a trace of playacting or nervousness. He was surprisingly . . . reliable.

My plan was to install a RAT onto Danny's computer. A remote access tool, once installed, would allow me to access Danny's computer from anywhere on the internet. RATs can be found and removed, so it was a risk. But I didn't have an external hard drive on me. It would have to work. I just had to find a reason to be in Danny's room by myself to get it installed.

Once Danny led us inside, I realized another reason Danny didn't want us to go back to his place. It was a little *Lord of the Flies*–ish. There were dishes piled in the sink, and he'd left socks and underwear strewn across the kitchen floor. Clearly, Danny hadn't been cleaning up after himself while his parents were gone. When he offered us something to drink (two words: "Margot? Drink?"), he realized all his cups were dirty (one word: "Huh.") and started cleaning them by hand. I had a sip of water that tasted like soap and politely spit it back into my cup.

Danny led us into the living room, which contained more of his dirty laundry and a pizza box I prayed was only a day old.

"Sweet poster," Avery said in reference to a framed poster of some football player for "the Chiefs" wearing the number 15. I guess he was good because Avery seemed impressed. "Did he really sign it?"

"Yeah" was all the response Danny gave. Great story, Danny!

Everyone settled on the couch. Danny tried too hard to sit next to Cheryl, who was on her phone watching TikToks. Brighton Girl had helped herself to a beer from the fridge and was trying to impress Greg by telling him how much she *loooved* IPAs. And Greg was showing Avery memes so that Avery could tell him whether they were funny or not.

Avery looked at me expectantly. His look said, "Soooo . . . when does the cool spy stuff start?" How did I tell him? It had already started. And it wasn't cool. It was tedious.

I knew I'd never get to Danny's laptop if all we did was sit on the sofa all night. So I made a move.

"Why don't we play a game?"

Brighton Girl shouted, "Ooh, yes! Let's play quarters." Jesus, Brighton Girl, read the room! Avery and Danny were each nursing a beer. And the rest of us weren't drinking. No one wanted to play a drinking game.

"What about running charades?" I said, ignoring her and getting up to my feet. The response was only marginally better than the response to quarters. But running charades, I knew from experience, was actually fun. The only problem with it is getting over the "let me explain the rules" hump. It's a little complicated.

"It's basically charades, but in teams. We each make a list of ten clues. Then we divide into two teams. Each team has a home base, and the list-giver is in a separate room. Did I say there was a list-giver? They read the clues. And we run in between! Does this make sense?" It didn't. The more I explained, the more they retreated to their phones.

Avery looked at me and literally winked (which is *not* acting normal, btw. But thankfully, no one noticed). Then he stepped in. "Come on. Everyone up. After the first round, it'll make sense. Margot, Cheryl, and Danny, you're on a team. Then it's me, Greg, and Angelica. (Brighton Girl had a name?! How the hell did Avery know that?) "Margot, you be the first list-giver." And then everyone stood and got into teams. How come when I explained the rules they looked at their phones, but when Avery said basically the same thing, they then suddenly all wanted to play? It was like they were hypnotized by his alpha-ness.

"Help me clear a path into the kitchen," Avery said, moving a chair and ottoman out of the way. Danny helped by picking up his damn laundry. Once clear running lanes were established, we started to play. And, because I am a genius, I suggested the list-giver be stationed in Danny's bedroom,[46] which would give me time alone with his computer. Avery quickly echoed his support of this idea, and the game was afoot.

I stationed myself in Danny's room, unfurled my list of clues, and gave the first one to Avery and Cheryl. The moment they left the room (to go charade it to their teams), I turned to Danny's laptop, which was open on his bed.

---

46. If you've ever played running charades, you know this is a terrible idea, because the list-giver should be stationed in a central place. But I was full of terrible ideas that night.

I attempted to turn it on, but it was out of power. Also, like everything in his house, it was filthy, like really gross. Each button was sticky and smelled like beans. *You can wash your hands later, Margot, don't let the germs stop you!* I said to myself. Once plugged in, the computer turned on. His screen was password protected. I plugged in my phone and used Fuzzword, but it came up empty. Apparently his password was not one of the 20,000 most obvious passwords you could use. Then I got an assist from his filthy keyboard. The letters *m*, *p*, *t*, *e*, and *u* were all slightly less dirty. They looked worn and oily instead of smudged with "beans" like his other keys. His password had to be some combination of those letters. "Muppet"? No. "temptU"? Damn it. I thought about his file, and everything I knew about him. Quiet. Locker. Made an app. Wait! His awful dog dating app! I tried "MeetPup" with a variety of numbers after it, then remembered the football poster Avery was drooling over. "MeetPup . . . 15." Yahtzee! His desktop appeared, and I was in! Thank you, me, for doing your homework!

I quickly opened up a new private browser to link with an external IP. But before I could download the RAT, I heard someone bounding up the stairs.

I instinctively jerked my hand away from his computer just as Brighton Girl popped into the room.

"Okay, I'm ready for my next thing!" she slurred, leaning into the door frame.

I couldn't fathom how she'd guessed the first clue already. Avery must've been really good at acting it out. I gave her the next clue,

"George McGovern." (All my clues were purposely very hard so that I'd get more time with Danny's computer.)

Brighton Girl nodded. But she didn't leave.

"Yes?" I said impatiently. She was wasting valuable RAT-ing time.

"Are you and Avery, like . . . a couple? Because if you're not . . . I don't know . . . he's, like, very . . ." She made a pinching motion with her forefinger and thumb, which I guess was her way of saying she liked Avery.

"We're together. Sorry," I said sternly, and she wobbled away. I was surprised by how good it felt to say that. Obviously I was just happy to stick it to Brighton Girl. *Now get the hell out of here, you drunk idiot, and don't fall down the stairs!* I thought and definitely didn't say out loud as she wobbled away.

I hadn't heard anything from downstairs. Usually there was a big "YES!" when a team guessed a charade, which meant someone would be up for another prompt. So I still had time. I opened Chrome and accessed my personal Dropbox. (I always keep a link open with useful programs I might need in a hurry.) I started downloading DarkComet, my preferred RAT. Then I looked up to see *Danny standing in the doorway.* Eep.

I was caught red-handed. How could he have gotten up the stairs so silently? And why was he here?

"Danny, I—"

"Sorry," he said, apologizing to me? Then he started rummaging through the clothes at the foot of the bed, barely registering that I was there at all, let alone hacking his computer.

"Danny, what are you doing?" I asked.

"Uh . . . Cheryl's cold," he muttered in a complete ga-ga-for-Cheryl fog.

I looked at the screen. It was still downloading. I decided to let it.

Danny found a hoodie on the floor. Smelled it, and was about to leave. But I couldn't, I just couldn't.

"Danny. Bit of advice," I said. He stopped by the door.

"Yeah?"

"If you're going to give a girl a shirt because she's cold, give her a clean shirt. One you know has been washed. Don't . . . pick one off the floor."

He nodded. Yep. Good advice. He picked out a different sweatshirt from his dresser.

"Thanks," he said, and smiled for the first time all night. Then he hesitated. "I—I don't know what I'm doing."

I didn't know what he was doing either. This was the most he'd spoken all night.

"I've liked Cheryl since eighth grade."

I couldn't help but feel some compassion for him. Even though Cheryl was very blah in my book. "Maybe just try talking to her more? Let her know how you feel? Or just . . . talk. More."

He nodded, seemed to really be taking it in. "Yeah. I . . . yeah." Then without another word, he left. Maybe he wasn't taking it in?

The RAT was running. I reset a few security settings, cleared his DNS cache, and closed the incognito window. Then I set his computer down. My work was done. All I needed to do now was win at charades.

Two hours later, my team had lost. By a lot. Avery was eerily good at running charades. It was like he went to mime camp or something (which, knowing Avery, was possible).

But he was surprisingly chill about his victory, so much so that I almost felt bad about trash-talking him at golf. That was, until I got into his car. The second the door shut, he turned to me to say, "Hey. Just so you know, you shouldn't feel bad that my team won by *so much*. I'm just freakishly gifted at running charades." He was so excited to brag, he didn't even bother starting the car and I was c-c-cold. "Sometimes I think it's a curse, because it would've been nice to let you get *close*. I mean, you were trying so hard to win."

"You must have been cheating!" I charged, fully taking his bait. "How did Brighton Girl guess your clues so quickly? I couldn't get her to bring me a seltzer from the fridge, let alone guess *A Midsummer Night's Dream*."

"Well, my mom drinks too much at parties so . . . I have some experience playing with the imbibed." Eek. That got a little dark. I was more comfortable with the trash-talking.

"I'm sorry. That sounds . . . tricky."

"Yeah. Tricky." He fidgeted with the wheel and gritted his teeth. "I'm sorry about earlier, by the way. When you said you wanted to meet my parents and I was like . . . weird."

"Oh. That's okay. I'm not exactly parent material . . . Compared to all your exes I'd be a huge letdown!" I joked, thinking how much they probably loved Claire Jubell.

"What? No. My parents have never met anyone I've dated. They're not exactly . . ." He was searching for the right words.

"I know everyone thinks we're like this perfect family. Like we're the Obamas of North Webster or something. Except my dad's white. And he's never been president. And we don't have a dog . . ." He trailed off. Then, turning serious, "But that's not us."

"Oh. So . . . what are you?"

He winced, and I immediately regretted asking. He clearly did not want to talk about it.

"I don't know . . . They just don't, like, *talk*. They care way more about their careers than about each other. I guess the easiest way to explain it is that my parents probably should've gotten divorced a while ago. Like . . . at least since I was born? But they haven't. And it makes being around them . . ."

"Tricky?" I said.

"I was gonna say a nightmare. Whenever I'm home, I spend most of my time trying to keep the peace. So I try not to be home." *Hence all the clubs*, I thought.

He stared ahead silently for a few moments, his dimple nowhere in sight. His eyes betraying something dark or sad. But then he did a quick tap-a-tap-tap on the steering wheel, which seemed to change his mood. "Anyway, sorry! How did your secret mission go? Did you get the . . . nanobyte from the . . . processor?"

"I did, actually." I smiled. It was honestly nice to share some of this. The whole RB experience had been so lonely, since I couldn't even tell Sammi about it. "And you actually created a pretty good diversion by getting the game going."

"I knew it! I helped! I'm such a good Moneypenny!"[47]

---

47. Apparently Moneypenny is a character in the James Bond franchise. I don't watch James Bond.

We laughed, both energized by a job well done. Then it got deadly silent. He had started the car, but it was still in park and barely making a sound (Teslas are eerily silent!). My mind started to spiral with thoughts like, *Why aren't we moving?* And, *Why is it so quiet?* And, *Why did time get so slow?* And, *Why are my palms sweating?* And, *Jesus, is he going to kiss me? It would probably be good if he kissed me, for the sake of the case.* And, *OH GOD HE'S LEANING! IT'S VERY SUBTLE BUT I BELIEVE HE'S SHIFTED HIS WEIGHT AND—ABORT! ABORT!*

"*Hey!* I wanted to ask you—" I blurted out, not sure I knew how to finish my sentence. He looked at me, a little thrown. "At the house. I was talking to Brighton Girl—"

"Angelica. Her name is Angelica."

"Thank you, but I prefer Brighton Girl. And . . . she . . . asked me if we were together. And . . . I said we were. Mostly to protect you from her vodka breath . . . so . . ."

I trailed off. And Avery let me sweat a minute before finally saying, "So we should probably make it official."

I smiled.

"If only to keep Brighton Girl off my back." He smiled back.

Then he held my hand as he drove me home. Which was honestly fine, because my hand was kinda cold.

March 16, 8:15 a.m.

MARGOT: i had a . . . wait for it . . . sex dream. I fell asleep watching The Office and then . . . i had a sex dream about jim halpert.

March 16, 8:15 a.m.

MARGOT: i know i know. he's not even one of my five!

March 16, 8:17 a.m.

MARGOT: yeah i was standing across from him in the gym and it was prom. (maybe he was my date?) and even though there were people around us, we just started making out. like aggressively. and then we started like . . . taking off all our clothes. and even though we were in a room full of people, we were in an invisible bubble so no one could see us. so I didn't mind being naked. but then he stopped and he was like "sorry, do I have your consent?" because, like, of course Jim Halpert would ask for consent. And then . . . I woke up!

March 16, 8:18 a.m.

MARGOT: So I guess it wasn't even a sex dream it was an almost sex dream. maybe it's for the best. Jim's kind of a marry, you know?

14

YOU FRANGE?

Danny's laptop was clean. Except for some *bracingly* earnest "poetry" he wrote about Cheryl Graham.[48] So I woke up Sunday morning and went all in on my third suspect, Harold. I devoured his Instagram, Twitter, and TikTok. All pretty boring. I was about to go deeper when I heard the doorbell ring, followed by my mom's "You have a visitor," which meant only one thing, a visit from Sammi. He had been texting me about the Mrs. Blye case.

"Saaam—" I started to singsong, but then I stopped myself. Sammi was not standing in the doorway to my room. Mrs. Blye was. Huh-boy.

"It's Mrs. Blye!" my mom exclaimed, positive but confused.

"It is!" I exclaimed back, trying to act like this was all

---

48. Let's just say he's no Amanda Gorman.

supposed to happen. Mrs. Blye, on the other hand, looked frazzled. She was literally wringing her hands.

My mom followed up with "You didn't tell me you were interested in applying to the Annover Science competition?" I didn't know if there even was such a thing as the "Annover Science competition." But I went with it.

"Mom, I told you about this. It started in January. It's why I couldn't go to that concert with Dad, because it's the third Thursday of every month," I said without hesitation. I knew that there was no way my mom would remember what I had done every third Thursday for the last two months.

"Right. Of course. It's just . . . hard to keep up," my mom said, a shade embarrassed. "She's doing so much these days."

I didn't like lying to my parents. And mostly I didn't. They knew I had a company. They knew the purpose of it was to help people when they had something online they wanted erased. However, I purposely kept them in the dark about how I did that. The illegal-ish hackings and whatnot. And I also hadn't told them about any of my adult clients. But the longer Mrs. Blye stayed in my room, the more my mom would realize how strange it was for her to be here at all.

"Well, shall we get going?" I said, zipping up a hoodie as I led Mrs. Blye out the door. "We've got a lot of work to do before the finals in April, and I do my best work over coffee and eggs. You want anything from Nick's, Mom?"

"My treat! Of course," Mrs. Blye interjected. And then, unfortunately, she continued, "I know this is highly unusual, but there was a very unexpected emergency. The science fair's student president contracted . . . Legionnaires' disease."

Oh dear lord. Mrs. Blye was lying to my mom, a nurse, about a medical issue. Mayday! Mayday!

"Oh my goodness! Do they know how she was exposed? Have there been any other cases?" I could tell my mom had a million follow-ups.

"Not yet, but . . . Sue Feldman isn't very hygienic," I said, yanking Mrs. Blye out the front door. "I saw her lick a doorknob on a dare once. Good at science. But low self-esteem. You know the type. I'll be back at two." I slammed the door.

Mrs. Blye immediately turned to me. "You have not been returning my calls!"

I shoved my finger in her face. "Not. Here." My anger seemed to outweigh Mrs. Blye's, and she snapped her trap once I shoved my pointer at her. I think it suddenly occurred to her how crazy she was for showing up at my doorstep. We didn't speak again till we were eating.

HALFWAY THROUGH A GIANT GREASY PLATE OF EGGS, CHEESE, BIS-cuits, sausage, and "Nick Sauce" (which is creamy, red, and a complete, delicious mystery to me), I explained to Mrs. Blye, again, why she shouldn't be worried about her husband finding Josh Frange's Instagram account. That I (well, Sammi and I) had spent fifty hours making fake content on social media and posting articles to bury any mention of Josh Frange. I even created thirty-one different IG accounts with names like @JoshFrange,

@J.Frange, and @frangejosh.[49] And since Toby barely knew Josh Frange, there was no way he'd know which @josh.frange variant was correct.

"Whenever I bury a picture, it stays buried. I have never, ever had anyone find the bad pic or video I wanted hidden," I said, pointing a forkful of eggs at her before shoving it in my mouth.

"But you said you would get rid of it entirely. Off all his platforms. And it's there! It's just in his feed staring at me!"

She had a point. Usually I would've gotten to this pic by now. It had been two and a half weeks since our meeting in Petey O'Taverns. If I let Blye's job go on any longer, she was likely to show up at my house again. Except this time . . . I don't know, in my shower?

"Well, I'm planning on wrapping up your job this week. All the pictures of you with Mr. Frange will be erased by Friday. I promise."

Mrs. Blye gave a big sigh. It wasn't what she wanted to hear. She wasn't going to feel better until this was over with. But for now, she had to accept it. I thought we were done when she said, "I'm really working on things with Toby." She started to tear up. I ripped off a scratchy napkin from the dispenser and handed it to her.

"It'll be over soon. I promise," I said. She nodded. Reassured because I can sound really reassuring when I need to.

• • •

49. Each of these accounts posted all the same photos on his actual feed. Except for the Mrs. Blye pic. I'm not even sure Josh Frange could tell which was the real Josh Frange.

So despite the fact that I had fifty-eight new messages on the Fury chat, I now had to take Mrs. Blye's case off the back burner and put it onto the . . . front burner? Which meant I'd have to get my butt over to Brighton. I did some more research on Mr. Frange. His feed was mostly school-related: experiments with students, a video of a skit he was involved in at Brighton's pep rally, a pic of his fantasy football trophy, etc. And then he posted a new video from class. It was a pretty basic experiment in which he used a D-cell battery, a copper wire, and a nail to create an electromagnet. This must have been his remedial class. I noticed a 45-volt Alpha Scientific electromagnet on display. I guess to show the class what a high-voltage electromagnet could do. Science teachers love their toys.

I also discovered on my tour of Mr. Frange's SM feeds that he was in charge of the prom committee. At Roosevelt, the student government was in charge of all things prom-related. It was kind of their only job: to find a venue and make sure enough funds were raised to pay for it. Apparently Brighton had a separate committee just for prom, which made me wonder what the hell student government did over there.

Regardless, this seemed like a good way to get to Mr. Frange. The committee met on Wednesday. I could drop in and pretend to be a student. Mr. Frange didn't seem like the type of teacher who would remember students' names. At least, that's the vibe I got.

I skipped seventh and eighth on Wednesday to make sure I had extra time to get to Brighton. After looking at the school's yearbook, I decided I'd attend the prom committee meeting as

Elysse Brown. Elysse was a Brighton senior whose interests appeared to be volleyball and poetry. But more importantly, we looked enough alike[50] that I could pass, especially if I wore some chunky glasses.

Elysse was not on the prom committee, nor had she ever had Frange as a teacher. But I figured this was a good thing. Hopefully he would just accept that I was Elysse. I didn't have time to create a well-researched backstory, but I wagered the loose resemblance would be enough.

I was feeling pretty good about my plan as I made my way into the building. I had done a few jobs at Brighton. I even went to their homecoming one year so that I could hack their mascot's computer. So I was pretty familiar with the layout. But I was surprised to see a newly installed security guard stationed by the front entrance. He was one of those police officers that they use to scare away potential shooters, and, you know, to make school feel a little more like jail? He had white hair and a friendly enough face, which squinted when he saw me. He didn't recognize me. Because I didn't belong there! I figured it was too late to turn back, so I doubled down and turned on the charm.

I skipped right over to him. The nameplate on his desk said OFFICER J. HARRIS. But I didn't know if I should call him Officer Harris, or if students called him Officer J-something. So instead I hopped up on his desk and said loudly, "Are you even going to say anything about my haircut?"

He looked flummoxed. He had never seen me or my hair

---

50. Except for her eyebrows and very white teeth, which I would kill for.

before. But he was definitely of that generation where it was a crime not to notice and compliment a woman's hairdo or dress. He scrambled for something to say, like a married man who forgot his anniversary.

"It's . . . it's very fetching."

I now saw a flash of concern over poor Officer J. Harris's face as he wondered if "fetching" could be considered offensive and could land him in some kind of Me Too hot water.

"I just mean that it looks good for spring!" he added, backing his chair about three feet away from his own desk.

"*Thank you for noticing*," I said, walking away, still "upset" that he hadn't mentioned it without my asking.

I entered Frange's room just as the prom committee meeting was about to start. I was hoping to slip in the back, unnoticed. But I was immediately greeted with "Elysse! What are you doing here?"

Damn it. Mr. Frange knew Elysse. Although apparently not well enough to know that she wasn't actually me.

"Sorry, I know I haven't been to the past few meetings, but I thought I could still participate."

"I mean, you can. But . . . don't you have mono?"

This is what happens when you rush a job, folks. You don't do enough research and you show up to your rival school as "mono girl." Everyone knows mono girl. She's the lucky bastard who doesn't have to go to school for two months. I chose the one person everyone was at least vaguely aware of.

"Nope!" I said flippantly, and made my way to the back table, hoping my blasé attitude would calm any suspicions. "Turns out it was just a weird mix of allergies and bronchitis. Plus I have a UTI, which doesn't act like mono but . . . is quite uncomfortable." A few of the students giggled. Mr. Frange's eyes widened. I had a feeling that would make him want to change the subject real quick.

"Okay. Well . . . good to have you back!"

Seeing him in person for the first time, I have to say . . . I still didn't get it. His sand-dollar skin highlighted his dyed-brown mustache and short hair, which upon closer look I was sure was actually hair plugs. This is who you have an affair with?

I took a seat next to a girl with severe bangs and bad posture. She was looking at me suspiciously. "Did you pluck your eyebrows?"

"Uh-huh. I had a lot of downtime."

Bad Posture shrugged. "They look good." This was a lie. Elysse's eyebrows were superior to mine. Bad Posture Girl could not be trusted.

Mr. Frange tried to get ahold of the room. "Okay, everyone, before we can get to fun prom stuff, they're making me do a new thing. I'm supposed to collect everyone's phones in this box, and I can't give them back till dismissal."

Mr. Frange held up a tub.

"Mr. Frange! We're allowed to have phones after school!" said a petulant little whiner from the third row.

"Not on school property. Apparently," he went on, picking up a paper and reading from it, " 'Students are no longer permitted to use phones during after-school sessions while on school property. Phones are to be collected at the beginning of each session and will be returned at dismissal.' "

The class groaned as Mr. Frange passed out his plastic tub, handing in their phones like prisoners turning in contraband.

"It's not coming from me. You know I don't give a shit if you text during my classes," Frange said. He was one of those teachers who cursed to sound cool and irreverent.

As the *thump, thump* of glass and plastic made its way around the room, I realized I had an opportunity. I started to type out a text with my right hand as I raised my left to be called on.

"Today's the day we vote on a prom theme . . ." Frange turned to the board, not noticing my hand.

"Mr. Frange?" I asked, locking eyes with him as he turned around. "Don't you think it's a little hypocritical that you're allowed to keep your phone while we have to surrender ours?"

On my phone I typed out **Call Josh Frange! Now!** to Mrs. Blye. Whenever I texted, she responded right away. She had been glued to her phone ever since she hired me. She wrote back immediately.

> **BLYE:** What? Why would I do that?

"It is. But you're sixteen, and I'm . . . older, so I've earned the right to have a phone whenever I want. Plus, unlike your generation, I don't get distracted by my damn phone." He smirked back. OK boomer.

"So you're saying if your cell phone was a distraction, then you would put it in the tub?"

"Sure." He shrugged, unimpressed with my threat. "But until I do, put your phone in."

The tub was a row away from me.

Mrs. Blye texted back.

> **BLYE:** The whole point of hiring you was so I wouldn't have to talk to him! What if my husband sees the call history?!

> **MARGOT:** Just delete it after you call him!

> **BLYE:** I don't know how to do that!

Jesus Christ, adults could be infuriating. You don't know how to delete calls from your call history?! How?! Mrs. Blye probably spends fifteen minutes every day getting into arguments with Alexa.

> **MARGOT:** I'll do it for you! but I really really need you to call him. It's vital. Call him and then tell him you called by accident.

The tub had arrived at my desk. I texted as fast as my fingers could type. Mr. Frange looked annoyed.

"Elysse. Come on. Be cool. Put the phone in," Mr. Frange commanded. With every keystroke, he was getting madder, but trying not to show it. He started to walk toward me.

> **MARGOT:** Do it! NOW NOW NOW!

I threw my phone into the tub just as Frange got to me.

"Sorry, I just . . . had to tell my mom where I was. Sorry," I said, holding my hands up like my phone was a hot potato. Mr. Frange exhaled.

And then, his phone rang with "Under Pressure." Could he have a special ring just for Mrs. Blye? Gross.

He froze. I could see the wheels turning. *Do I take a call from a woman I slept with a month ago who might sleep with me again if I answer it? Or . . . do I ignore it, thus proving Elysse wrong and keeping my authority over the class?* Of course, like most men, he chose sex (or in this case, the faint possibility of sex).

"I . . . I'm sorry, I need to answer this," Frange muttered, looking at the number.

"Really," I shot back. And then it was blood in the water. Everyone started taunting, "I thought you didn't get distracted!" or "What?!" or "That's not fair!" A symphony of indignation.

"I'm sorry, this is . . . very important, but fine! When I get back, my phone'll go in the tub, too! Okay?!" He practically ran out of the room.

I leaned back in my chair and stretched because, damn, that felt good. I checked in with Bad Posture Bangs, who was maybe now my best friend.

"I love it when teachers have to eat their own bullshit," Bad Posture said.

"That's a gross image, but yeah, I know what you mean," I said back. Then I leaned in slightly, "What's Mr. Frange's deal? You think he's a good guy?"

BPB squinted at me like I was seven-point font. She had clearly never thought of her teachers as "good" or "bad" or anything in between.

"I don't know." She shrugged. "He teaches chemistry."

Very insightful. Maybe we weren't going to be best friends.

After a few minutes Mr. Frange reentered, seemingly flustered by talking to his one-time booty call and getting rejected so quickly. "Sorry, everyone, as I said before . . . that was important, so . . ."

The class didn't care, as you could tell by their chants of "Phone in the tub! Phone in the tub!"

"Okay, okay. Here! Happy?" Mr. Frange put his creepy rooted phone in the tub, then put the tub in a drawer in his desk. My plan was in full swing. Now came the hard part.

FOR THE NEXT TWENTY MINUTES OF PROM COMMITTEE, A GIRL with a pierced tongue I'm calling Rebel and a girl with braids I'm calling Blonde Anne of Green Gables were arguing about which theme was better. Rebel wanted "Brighton to the Future," a take on *Back to the Future,* while Anne of Blonde Gables wanted the theme "Bachelor," which I guess meant confessionals and the prom king handing out roses? Gables pointed out that "Brighton to the Future" was rather forced and inelegant. Rebel said "Bachelor" was demeaning to women and "If you want a misogynist prom, why don't we just make the theme 'Roosevelt'?"

A bunch of the students laughed and said things like "Oh shit" and "Epic drag."

I leaned over to Bad Posture Bangs. "What does that mean? Aside from the fact that Roosevelt sucks! Obviously!" I said, maybe laying on my "Brighton spirit" a little thick.

"You haven't heard? They have a whole revenge porn site over there. It's so fucked. And now Michelle Bruckner is on it."

Why did that name sound familiar? . . . Because Michelle's picture was right next to Elysse Brown in the Brighton yearbook.

I put my forehead on the desk. I tasted metal in the back of my mouth. RB had expanded to *Brighton*? Had it reached other schools as well? Other counties? States? I felt gross. I needed to check the site every day from now on.

Toward the front of the room, some freckled boy put forward the idea of a no-theme prom, which was very polarizing. I used the resulting argument as cover to excuse myself to the bathroom, where I called Sammi on my burner. After one and a half rings, he picked up.

"What's up?"

"I'm doing it. Now. I'm gonna brick Frange's phone."

"Sweet. Finally," he said. As though I'd been taking my sweet time.

"I need you to delete the pictures from his hard drive and cloud as soon as I kill the phone."

He paused. "Okay, but I'm not home right now." What the hell? It was Wednesday. Sammi was always home after school on Wednesdays. And literally every other day.

"Are you kidding?" I asked.

"I can be home in ten, Margot. We're fine."

"I wish you'd told me you weren't going to be home."

"Yeah, well, I wish you told me you were gonna brick the phone today!" He was right. I probably should've. But in the past, he'd just always been around. I never needed to clear my schedule with him.

"I'll be ready in ten. Text me when you do it."

"'Kay."

In order for this plan to work, Sammi would need to get into Frange's Instagram to delete the picture at the same time I bricked his phone. It wasn't worth the effort of Sammi deleting it if Frange could just reupload it. Our plan would make it seem like the picture got lost when his phone died, probably due to some kind of bug. Which meant Frange would never know there were contract hackers out to get him.

It was go time. Instead of going back to Frange's classroom, I went out the back doors to the Brighton parking lot, where a couple of heavily pierced kids were hanging around the bike racks. I paid them $20 to pull the fire alarm. Five minutes later, that horrible *"Rrrr! Rrr! Rrr!"* was ringing through the halls.

Various students from various club meetings started to file out of the classrooms. The drama kids in their partial costumes, the Model UN kids with their policy binders, etc. I took an alternate route to get back to Frange's now-empty room. I beelined to the back and grabbed the electromagnet from the previous day's experiment.

Next I ran to Frange's desk, which he stupidly left unlocked. I grabbed his phone from the tub of phones. I could have just smashed it there, but I had a way better (and significantly more complicated) plan. And I wanted to kill it without it looking like someone murdered it. An electromagnet would do just that.

I put Frange's phone on top of the magnet's coil and flipped it on. In five to ten minutes, it would be toast. Bye-bye, pictures of Mrs. Blye (and everything else). Meanwhile, the outside of the phone would remain pristine. It would be impossible to know that anyone had tampered with it. It was the perfect crime.

I made sure the tub of other phones was four feet away from the magnet and started a timer. A crackle came over the loudspeaker,

"Okay, everyone, it appears this was a false alarm. All after-school activities and clubs may return to the building."

Crap. Crap, crap, crap. I checked my timer. Only two minutes had gone by. I looked outside. Everyone was filing back into the school. I was out of time. I turned off the magnet and picked up his phone.

I pressed the power button. Dead. I tried to reboot it. Dead. I tried again. Dead, dead, dead.

Voices from down the hall wafted into the room. Had to move. I unplugged the magnet, threw Frange's phone into the tub, and dumped the tub into the bottom drawer of the desk. I slammed it shut and whipped my head up to see . . .

Bad Posture Bangs. Standing at the doorway. Her deadpan poker face revealing nothing. Was she silently judging? About to narc on me to Frange?

We just kind of looked at each other. She looked at the phone drawer then back at me. Then she gave a little nod and walked silently to her desk. We were cool. I walked out of the classroom, through a tide of students reentering the building, then I kept walking.

On my way to the bus stop, I texted Sammi.

> **MARGOT:** Operation Death Magnet a success! Brick achieved.

MARGOT: Ball in your court. Or your diamond. Since you love baseball.

SAMMI: sometimes your plans are needlessly complicated. why didn't you just smash his phone.

MARGOT: Because I'm a genius. This way he thinks it died on its own. Hence no suspicion of foul play.

After a few . . .

SAMMI: still seems complicated. i would've smashed it.

MARGOT: Just delete the pic please.

And a minute later . . .

SAMMI: done.

I texted Mrs. Blye to let her know her job was done and that she could pay me the remainder of my fee. Phew. Success. Stress lifting.

I had reached the bus stop. In fifteen to forty-five minutes, I would be home. I'd eat whatever my mom left for me to reheat and then I'd veg out on true crime podcasts until I passed out in bed. I checked Roosevelt Bitches one more time. Aside from Michelle Bruckner, there were no new victims. Okay.

My phone pinged with a text from Avery.

> **AVERY:** Missed you today. Want a ride to school tomorrow?

> **MARGOT:** Sure.

I was all set to type a pithy response when I got another text from Sammi.

> **SAMMI:** let me know when the next job comes in.

My heart sank. I wanted so badly to say, "Actually I took the biggest job of my life, and it's killing me, and I need you to hack Harold Ming's computer!" but obviously I couldn't. A promise is a promise is a promise. So instead, I just said . . .

> **MARGOT:** Of course.

I put my phone on airplane mode. I was done for the night.

15

IN A DARK, DARK ROOM
WITH HAROLD MING

I woke up at six a.m. able to breathe out of only one nostril. My head was pounding, my throat scratchy. All the adrenaline from the Frange hit had worn off, and now my body was hosting some kind of a cold/flu that was making everything hurt. I needed to stay home from school, order pho from the above-average Vietnamese place down the street, and enter Mrs. Blye's case into QuickBooks. (One of the very annoying things about owning a small business is that you have to balance your books. It's like a homework assignment that never ends.)

I was about to shoot a text to Avery to let him know I wouldn't need a ride, but he beat me to it.

> **AVERY:** I forgot I have photography club today. Can we hang saturday?

My instinct was to write "Sure," crawl into bed, and not return for three days . . . but I had a sinking feeling. A "God damn it, this is going to ruin my sick day" feeling that Photography Club was important for some reason. I dragged my sick ass to my desk and pulled up Harold's file. Yep. Harold was in Photography Club, too.

Avery and Harold didn't have a lot of overlapping interests. Despite belonging to almost every club, Avery had politely avoided Support Group. He told me he'd gone once and found the experience a little . . . forced. Which I took to mean creepy. Also, the youth minister played his acoustic guitar for three hours straight. Which is about two hours and fifty-seven minutes too long.

Anyway, Avery and Harold were far from besties. There was no guarantee they'd be hanging anytime soon, so Photography Club was definitely my best chance. And since it met only once a month, I knew I had better go. I wrote Avery back.

> **MARGOT:** Can I crash?

> **AVERY:** You mean you want to come to pc?

> **MARGOT:** Yeah. I'm kinda into photography. Might join next year or something.

> **AVERY:** Cool okay.

Avery picked me up at seven. It was raining, and even though I had a raincoat, I got completely soaked on the walk from my building's entrance to his car. I meant to thank Avery for the ride, but instead I just had a coughing fit and caught some snot trying to sneak out of my nose.

Avery looked concerned.

"Are you okay?"

Crap. I needed to do a better job of covering my symptoms, or I'd be sent home before fourth period.

"Yeah. Sorry, it's just . . . allergies." I smiled, trying and failing to look like a healthy, normal person.

"Allergies? You sure?" He frowned.

"Look, I can't miss school today. I have a bunch of tests, and besides, it's really important that I go to Photography Club because your Instagram is amazing and mine's just pictures of my feet and . . . I want to get better at taking pictures." I guess another symptom of this cold was "barely coherent stream-of-consciousness ranting." I closed my eyes and decided not to open them for the rest of the trip because that seemed like *so much work*.

"Is your seat a good temp?" Avery asked, and I realized my butt was warm. Had I just peed? How sick was I? No, it was a seat-warmer. Of course his fancy-pants car had fancy-pants seat-warmers.

"Sure. I mean, us plebes over at Trinity Towers don't see too many butt-warmers. So this is a treat."

I heard no laugh. No witty comeback. I opened one eye and saw Avery staring ahead at the road. He did not seem charmed by my crisp observations of our wealth disparity. Oops.

We parked in the student lot and sat there for a bit. I expected Avery to get out and open the door for me, due to his

Regency manners. But he didn't, and instead said, "Well. I had a whole plan this morning. I was going to escort you to the front door with this . . . giant, executive umbrella my dad uses. But . . . I forgot to bring it." He made a little fart sound with his lips.

"That would've been very gentlemanly of you."

"I know!"

"Should we run for it?" I asked. I didn't have an umbrella either.

"You're sick. I could just drop you off by the front."

"No. I'm good." I wasn't. I was so sick. "Want to race?" What is wrong with me?

"Okay . . . but I should warn you . . . I'm, like . . . really fast," he said, making a big show of stretching his triceps. So arrogant.

It was about fifty yards to the entrance. Avery was wearing a no doubt very expensive wool sweater.

"Yeah, well, I play dirty." Before he could say anything else, I grabbed his keys, threw them in the back seat, and sprinted to the entrance.

I could hear him behind me, shrieking like a little kid when he splashed his "best shoes" in the puddles. "Shit! *Shit!*"

I couldn't help but laugh. I got to the door first (I *won*) and turned to say, "FIRST," as I yanked open the door . . . but the door didn't yank. It was still locked.

"What are you doing to me, Mertz? Open the door!" he cried.

"It must still be locked!" I yelled over the rain.

"That's because only crazy people would get to school this early!"

We were completely exposed. I took pity on him, took off

my raincoat, and draped it over both our heads like a tarp.

"Come on, the door by the main office is usually open." We took a couple of steps, awkwardly sharing the tiny raincoat. It was kind of like a three-legged race where if you didn't stay in sync you got pelted with water. Avery grabbed my waist with one hand and used the other to hold up the raincoat. I'm shorter than him, so the water kept dripping down on my side. Which made him hold me even closer. I might have guessed that he "forgot" his umbrella on purpose. But I honestly don't think he was capable of that kind of manipulation. Which made me feel a smidge bad that I was.

We reached the main entrance door, completely soaked, hair matted to our faces. We both looked awful. And then, for some reason, we started laughing. It was kind of a sweet moment until I sneezed in his face.

ASIDE FROM MY POUNDING HEADACHE AND TAKING NAPS through fourth and fifth period, the rest of the school day passed uneventfully. Well, except for when Mandy Tillman let out the world's biggest fart in the middle of AP Gov and then cried. Mandy was the type of stick-up-her-butt debutante who would rather die than fart in public, and this huge, noxious fart was so obviously hers. I'm not usually one to wallow in someone's misery, but this was fantastic. Everyone laughed. I feel like we'll remember it for the rest of our lives.

Otherwise, though, uneventful.

The last bell rang, and I quickly googled some famous

photographers. I realized I should have something interesting to say about Avery's photos (e.g., "They've got the pensive vibe of Stieglitz, but with the cheekiness of Annie Leibovitz").[51] At 2:35, I met Avery in front of the photography lab. He was carrying two cups of nondescript liquid, one piping hot, one cold.

"Chug the cold one first. Then the hot one slowly. It won't help you right now, but by tomorrow . . . you'll be golden," he said, putting both cups in my hands.

My mom was a nurse, so I knew that the only thing to do for a cold was sleep and watch a season of TV I had already seen. But since we were "dating" and all, I played along. I chugged the cold cup, or at least attempted to, because it was wretched.

"This tastes like death. Why?"

"Don't be such a baby—and chug it, or it won't work. It's basically kale and zinc."

"You're not an anti-vaxxer, are you?" Rich people often were.

"Drink!" he teased. So I did. Each gulp was worse than the last.

I walked in holding my less-disgusting cup (tea) and sat next to Avery. Coach Powell was the random teacher on photography duty that day. A middle-aged white guy with a belly and his basketball days long behind him, he didn't look up from his book for even a moment. He was reading Toni Morrison, though. Respect.

"What are you doing here, Margot?" asked Tara, a girl I vaguely remembered from freshman year geometry. Oh, right, it was super weird to just visit a club you didn't belong to.

---

51. The rule for spelling photographers' names is *i* before *e*, OR *e* before *i*, go fuck yourself.

I pivoted. "Did you get your braces off? Your teeth look amazing!" If you ever don't want to answer someone's question, respond with a compliment. They'll immediately forget what they asked you. People, in general, are very vain and love to talk about themselves.

On cue, Tara's eyes lit up. She was about to dive into a monologue about her "braces story"[52] when we were interrupted by "Margot Mertz! What a fun surprise!"

I spun around to see a camera fixed on me. And behind it, the hulking frame of Harold Ming. Harold was tall and bulked-up from wrestling (and/or possibly steroids?) with sandy beige skin and hair overloaded with product. He stopped himself.

"Oh, sorry. Do I have your consent to take your picture?"

"Actually, I'd rather you didn't. I'm kinda sick," I said. I caught a half second of resentment from Harold before his phony salesman smile appeared. He lowered his camera.

"Cool. No problem. We want everyone to feel safe and supported. So psyched you're here, Margot!" He put his fist out for me to bump, which I begrudgingly did. I didn't want to seem like a total dick who hated him (also, I was hoping he would catch my cold).

Harold turned his attention to the rest of the Photography Club. "Okay, so today we're going to be developing Tara, Avery, and Bella's photographs and giving feedback on their work. Coach Powell, would you like to supervise us in the darkroom?"

---

52. Everyone who has had braces has a "braces story," and it is always exactly the same. They had braces. For longer than they anticipated. They hurt. Then they got them off. Fin.

"Nah, Ming. You got this," Coach Powell said as he turned the page in his book. Then he muttered to himself, "You *are* your best thing," while underlining the quote with a pen.

"Wonderful. Well . . . let's get to it!" Harold exclaimed with the upbeat cheer of a Sunday school teacher. I got halfway out of my seat when Harold said, "Oooh. Sorry, Margot. I'm not sure you can go in the darkroom. Not until you've gone through the health and safety seminar we all did at the beginning of the year." His face looked like he had just given me a cancer diagnosis. Every word that came out of his mouth was so overwrought.

Avery countered, "Harold, she just wants to watch. If she has goggles—"

"*Actually* . . ." Harold cut him off, and I could tell he was about to launch into an annoying mansplanation of safety procedure.

So I interjected with "No worries, Hal. I'll stay here. I don't want to break any Photo Club rules."

Harold nodded with a smug, pained grimace. "You get it. It just wouldn't be fair to the other PC-ers who attended the seminar." I gave him two thumbs up. *No problem, ya dope. I'll just stay right here and copy your hard drive.*

Harold led the group into the darkroom. Avery lingered behind for a moment.

"Are you sure you don't want to just . . . go home? It might be a while."

"Nah, I'm good," I said, holding back snot.

Avery narrowed his eyes. Almost like he knew something was up. "Okay. So . . . do whatever you need to do, and I'll be back in a bit."

"Great. I can't wait to see your pictures so I can give them a scathing critique!"

"Ooh! Feedback! I love it!" He smiled as he caboosed his way into the darkroom.

I smiled back until the second he was out of sight, then I got to work. I grabbed my bag and moved to Harold's table. I put my stuff directly next to his. Then I took off my hoodie and threw it over the laptop.

As I plugged my external hard drive into his laptop, a weariness washed over me. I was sick of tracking down hard drives and finding various ways to scour them. I was sick of doing all that work and turning up nothing. And now I was *literally sick*. I hoped Harold's would be my last. I wanted this to be over. I popped open his laptop, and lucky for me, Harold hadn't shut down his computer since last period. He was the kind of overly confident prick who didn't bother protecting his devices with a password. I wouldn't be surprised if he didn't lock his locker. Hubris!

I had a program called FAST-D[53] which could copy a hard drive in thirty minutes. I knew nothing about developing photos, but I had seen movies where photographs were developed in darkrooms. You put the photo in a tub of chemicals. Then you move it to another tub. Then you hang it for a long time. Seemed like a process that would take at least an hour or more, which would be plenty of time. I checked in with Coach Powell, still engrossed in the superior prose of Ms. Morrison. I looked at the

---

53. Do yourself a favor and don't google this. It's also a category of porn that I now can't unsee.

clock. I checked the download time. Nine minutes remaining. I considered putting my head down to rest for a few minutes. I knew that was a bad idea, but the table seemed . . . so nice. And my head was . . . so heavy. So . . . very . . .

I HEARD THE DOOR. MY EYES POPPED OPEN TO SEE AVERY BOUND- ing out from the darkroom. He was holding two photos he had just developed and practically shouted, "Hey, Margot! We're done. Critique me up!" Harold followed close behind. My waking-up brain was starting to play catch-up. *You fell asleep, Margot! And your hard drive is still connected to Harold's laptop! Do something!*

I stood up. "Back already! Nice! That was quick!" I said with way too much enthusiasm as I sniffed snot back up my nose.

"We were in there for over an hour," Harold responded.

"Yeah?" I said, feeling insane. I was sure I had a fever. I looked at the wall clock. Yep, it was 3:50. Harold and Avery were now standing in front of me and my hoodie, which was still covering Harold's laptop.

"Why did you switch seats?" Harold asked.

"Uh . . ." I responded. Was I sweating? Did he know? Did everyone know? "I just uh . . . wanted a more comfortable seat." Harold's eyebrows furrowed, because I had moved from one metal chair to another identical metal chair. *Must lie better, Margot!*

I saw his mouth purse, his right hand lurch forward. He was going to rip my hoodie off his computer and expose my hard drive. He'd call me a thief and a liar and probably get me expelled if I didn't turn things around right *now*.

"CAN I JUST SAY SOMETHING!" I shouted, slamming my left hand on the table (while reaching my right hand under my hoodie to yank the USB from Harold's computer).

Everyone froze. Harold included. I had their attention. But I had nothing to say.

"I've been here for over an hour, waiting patiently for you to return with your photos, and not once! Not one! Time!" I shouted, while in one fluid moment lifting my hoodie off of Harold's computer with my external hard drive hidden in its sleeve.

"Has anyone . . . told Tara . . . how good she looks without her braces?"

Everyone looked to Tara, who was now blushing (but not unappreciative of the attention).

"You people have no idea what it's like to have braces! How insecure you feel! And how much your mouth hurts. Tara suffered for three years with braces—"

"Actually, it was only two . . ." Tara meekly interjected.

"Two years! But it felt like three! With the adjustments! And the name-calling! The, the . . ." I snapped two times, then pointed at Harold. Hoping he would finish my sentence.

"The pain?"

"The pain! Yes! Yes! And the least we can do is, is . . . see her. I mean, isn't this Photography Club? Isn't it the mission of photographers to notice . . . you know . . . life?"

Everyone began to mutter. Some agreed with me. Others apologized to Tara, who assured them she was okay. Tara then gave me a grateful look and mouthed, "Thank you." Which I truly didn't deserve.

I felt dizzy. I steadied myself on a table. I looked around the room. Even Coach Powell had taken a break from his book to see what the crazy girl would say next.

"Okay, well, let's all try a little harder. To . . . see . . ." I then turned to Avery. "And I will *see* you . . . by your nice fancy butt-warming car. Good day."

And with that, I turned, head held high, and marched out of the photography room.

TEN MINUTES LATER, I MET AVERY BY HIS CAR. WE GOT IN, AND for a moment didn't say anything. I was half asleep, using all my willpower to keep my head erect. I knew I owed him an apology, or at the very least an explanation. But then he said, "So did it work? Did you get what you needed from Harold's laptop?"

I opened my eyes. Avery didn't look mad, just curious. I was too tired to feign innocence. "I copied his drive. So we'll see." Then, "How did you know?"

"I've had girlfriends come to soccer games and school concerts. But never once has a girl wanted to come to Photography Club. I mean, I know I'm cool, but I'm not that cool." Fair point.

"Sorry. I should've told you I just . . ." I trailed off into a mumble.

"No worries, Mertz. Happy to be your muscle," he said, starting the car. "You know . . . if you give me a heads-up next time, I could help even more . . ."

"More?"

"I stalled Harold! I even messed up a photo on purpose, which meant I got a Harold Ming lecture on 'chemical bath protocol,' and it was *very* condescending. I hope it was worth it."

"It was. Thank you." I smiled earnestly.

Avery started messing with his Tesla's touchscreen and looked nervous for maybe the first time since I'd met him. "Can I . . . I wanted to ask you something."

"Oh, I see how it is. You helped me out, so now I owe you?"

"Not at all! No." He paused. "I just wanted to ask you . . . something, a favor, I guess? But you totally don't have to do it. But . . . uh . . ."

"Jesus. What is it?" I asked, actually starting to worry he needed a kidney or something.

"Okay. My mom's hospital—my mom works at a hospital, did I ever tell you that?"

"Everyone knows who your parents are, Avery."

"Ah. Okay." He nodded, looking uncomfortable. "Well, her hospital won something called a NOVA. Which is this award for . . . I don't know, like, being a nice hospital or something. Anyway, my mom is accepting it at this . . . gala thing."

"Okay . . ."

"And I have to go. So . . . would you go with me?" He was literally holding his breath. "Full disclosure: it's going to be very boring and not fun."

"I'm sorry. You're asking me to a ball?" Maybe I really was in a Jane Austen novel.

"Not a ball. It's a gala," he corrected. (I looked it up later.

There is no difference.) "And I can't stress enough, it will fully suck." He looked uncomfortable just thinking about it.

"Can't you just skip it? Why is your mom making you go?"

"Fun fact. My mom does not care if I go. My *dad* is the one who really wants me there."

Seeing my look of confusion, he went on, "My dad never misses an opportunity to mingle at these things. I guess don't tell anyone this, but he's thinking about running for office someday."

"Whoa. That's crazy."

"And because he's a white guy running as a progressive, he loves to trot out his overachieving Black son for photo ops. As I said, it will not be fun. But hopefully we could peace early and do something . . . that *is* fun."

None of his other girlfriends had met his parents. But he wanted me to meet them? At, like, a . . . swanky rich person's gala? Words were failing me. And I could see Avery panic with every passing second.

"You know what. It's too terrible. I'm sorry. I can't subject you to—"

"No, no, no!" I said, trying to save face. "Sorry, I was just surprised. And honestly, worried that I might not have anything to wear. But, yeah, if you want me to go. I'll go. Of course. Sounds . . . well, not fun. But educational." I mean, we were "dating." It couldn't all be clandestine Mertz CYF jobs. And doing this really seemed to make him happy, as I could tell by the big, goofy smile he was now wearing.

"Oh, man. You're the best, Margot. Seriously, I can't tell you how much I hate these things and I really—"

"Happy to do it," I said, looking at his big, joyful eyes. He drummed on the steering wheel, but didn't put the car into drive. And it got quiet again. Just like after Danny's. My stomach knotted and I panic-said, "Your photos!"

Avery looked around, not sure if I was talking in code or just had a stroke. I clarified,

"Sorry. I just . . . I would actually like to see what you developed, if you're willing to share?" He nodded, then reached into the back seat for his messenger bag and pulled out his photos. The first was an artsy shot of the sign for Trinity Towers, this beige wood sign with knockoff nouveau-type lettering that said "Trinity Towers Apartments, Come Home?" (Don't get me started on the grammar.)

"Trinity Towers is a rent-stabilized monstrosity. Why would you want a picture of that?" I asked.

After biting his lip, he said, "Honestly? I was going to take a picture of you. But I knew if I did, you'd think it was clichéd or cringey or, you know, the patriarchy. So I figured I had to try a little harder if I was going to impress the great Margot Mertz and . . . this is all I came up with. Your apartment. In black and white. Sorry."

Jesus. He really nailed me. I absolutely would have crucified him if he took a picture of me. And I probably would have said something snarky and cutting. And the fact that he knew that about me was so . . .

I grabbed his face. I don't know if I was on a high from getting Harold's laptop or loopy from the cocktail of Tylenol and DayQuil I took or just regular ol' horny, but I felt like I had to do something. So I grabbed his face. His beautiful, stupidly angular face. And got right up in his business and said, "Thank you for not taking a picture of me. And thank you for knowing I would hate it. If I weren't a gross, infectious mess, I'd kiss you."

And then *he* kissed *me*, sealing his fate as the next cold victim. With a puffy face and snot dripping from my nose, he went for it. *And it was* . . . surprisingly . . . not bad. His breath smelled like nothing, which was infinitely better than smelling like something. And he held my shoulders with just the right amount of pressure. Which is why, even though I couldn't breathe through one nostril, I kissed him back. I'm not sure how long it lasted—it could've been three seconds or three minutes. I was in this kind of haze (I'm sure due to my being patient zero). Then he pulled back, and we just looked at each other. Before I killed the moment by saying, "You're an idiot. You're gonna get sick now."

He shifted into drive, left dimple on full display. "Don't worry about it. I have an incredible immune system. I haven't missed a day of school since the second grade." Hubris!

WHEN I GOT HOME, ALL I WANTED TO DO WAS CRAWL INTO BED and stay there until my nose stopped being a fountain of gross. But I was so desperate to see what Harold's laptop contained. Finally, the dates with Avery and sleepless nights researching Harold would pay off. Once I knew for sure that that smarmy fucknut was behind RB, I could finally take him—and the site—down. I drafted out a text to the Fury chat, complete with Harold's creepy senior photo and an invitation for them to deface it as they saw fit. But I practiced some self-control and waited to send it until I was sure.

I fired up his hard drive. Upon initial inspection, his desktop seemed clean. Most of his folders were devoted to homework. His Support Group folder was packed with schedules, email blasts, and all the raw code and beta versions for his app. Harold was smart. I had a feeling he had gone through and changed the file extension on everything he didn't want someone to find. Which meant I had to unzip and grep through every directory.

It took me a couple of hours, but eventually, in his "Freshman Homework Folder," I found a 7-Zip archive titled "Battle of the Bulge" (vomit). I hit the mother lode. Copies of all the anonymous sexts and dick pics he had sent to girls. Kept and stored so he could admire them later. And then there was his porn stash. So much porn. In the age of streaming porn, it always amazes me that some guys feel the need to actually download anything. But Harold clearly considered himself a connoisseur. The porn was categorized, cataloged, and dated, like he was hoping to open a museum one day.

I kept digging, eventually finding a file labeled "RB" and in it . . . pictures and videos. Pretty much all the content from the site . . . and nothing else. Huh? No project files, upload scripts, or anything that would show he actually designed the site. What? Where was it?!?

I knew it must be hidden or encrypted. I went deeper. I spent the rest of the night scouring every inch of Harold Ming's perverted hard drive, and couldn't find a morsel of code from RB. Which meant that Harold didn't make Roosevelt Bitches.

Mother. Fucker.

I washed my face, took two Tylenol, then buried myself under the covers. My cold had morphed into a full-blown flu . . . or plague? I curled up into a ball and tried to go to sleep. Tomorrow, I'd have to take a look at the Register. Again. The entire list. Everyone in the school.

Oof. The thought of starting over made me sick to my stomach. Or maybe it was the flu. Either way, I was about to throw up.

MARGOT: I'm siiiiiiiiickkkkkkk.

MARGOT: uuuuuuuuhhhhhhhhh. . . . .

MARGOT: booooooooooooooooooooooooooo!!!!!!!!

16

AND THEN THERE
WERE NONE

I spent three days in bed with a fever. I mainlined Netflix and podcasts about inspiring women. I checked Roosevelt Bitches religiously. So far, no new girls had been added. I felt relieved, but knew the reprieve wouldn't last long. I occasionally picked up my phone to see how many Fury messages I was missing and to assure Avery, numerous times, that I did not need his patented get-better tempeh-ginger soup. (If it was anything like that zinc juice!)

On the fourth day, my fever broke and I was ready to rejoin the living. But I told my mom I was still sick so I could miss an extra day of school and catch up on work. With Harold no longer a suspect, I had a lot to do.

First, I skimmed the RB WhatsApp. Sara Nguyen wasn't eating. The other girls were trying to cheer her up. And Michelle Bruckner and two other girls from Brighton had joined and were sharing their stories. I sent the group a quick update: my first three suspects were clean. I was extending my search. I was on it.

Likes started to pour in from pretty much everyone. Except Shannon. I was surprised to see, looking back at my previous updates, how Shannon's demeanor had changed. The cheery, exclamation-mark-laden texts had given way to "Sounds good" and thumbs-up emojis. She hadn't been on Fury in over a week. I messaged her to see if we could schedule a time to talk in person, just to make sure she was okay.

I collapsed onto my bed and closed my eyes. The stress of the case was getting to me. Sure, I told everyone I was "on it," but I had no leads. Not even a hint as to who it might be.

Then I remembered something I heard during my fever-induced podcast binge. I don't even know which empowering, women-in-business podcast it was. *Women Today, and Always*, maybe? Or *Push Up, Not Down*? I don't know. But just as I was drifting off to sleep, the show's guest, Kate Somebody, said something that stuck with me: *"Biases . . . exist in big data as much as they do in individual perceptions and experiences. Yet there is a problematic belief that bigger data is always better data and that correlation is as good as causation."*

God damn it, Kate Somebody,[54] whoever you are. If biases exist in data, then maybe my whole approach was wrong. Maybe the Register I made was biased.

I went back to the Register and scrolled through my list.

---

54. Once my fever cleared, I went back and realized I was listening to Kate Crawford, an expert in social change and media developments. No joke here. That's just her name.

What had I gotten wrong? What were my biases? Who had I crossed off who needed another look?

I opened my browser and typed in www.rooseveltbitches_69. onion. Every time I went on RB, I would scan the site for new victims, get pissed off, then slam my computer shut in a rage. Maybe I needed to give it a closer look. What could it tell me that I'd missed before? The landing page looked a lot like a generic yearbook page. With the masthead saying "Welcome to Roosevelt Bitches! Home of the hottest student bodies!" Besides the gross masthead and mean/graphic labels for every pic, it had a pretty sleek and coherent design. The layout was simple. There was a search engine with a filter and suggestions, and then there were boobs, boobs, boobs, butts, butts. I was ready to x out when I noticed the bottom of the page. Something was different, but I couldn't tell what.

I went back to Shannon's file and pulled up the screen grabs of RB she sent me the day we first met. The site looked the same, albeit with different "featured daily pics." But at the bottom of the page, in tiny writing that was almost impossible to read, was a bit of text. Text that had since been removed from the site. When I zoomed in, I saw that it read, "Gimme, Gimme, Gimme Productions."

This was some Zuckerberg shit. When the Zucks first created Facebook, every page said "A Mark Zuckerberg production." Because even at nineteen, he was a megalomaniac who needed the world to know he was special. "Gimme, Gimme, Gimme Productions" felt like that, a calling card. Maybe the site's creators realized what they were doing was illegal and decided to erase it. I wrote down "Gimme, Gimme, Gimme" in one of the many notebooks I keep at my desk.

Okay, so that was kind of a lead. But what did it mean? By far the biggest Google result for "Gimme, Gimme, Gimme" was the ABBA song "Gimme! Gimme! Gimme! (A Man After Midnight)," which came out in the '70s. Although the punctuation was different. ABBA! Used! Exclamation! Points! After! Each! Gimme! Because . . . ABBA.

I dug deeper. Apparently *Gimme Gimme Gimme* (no punctuation this time) was also the title of a BBC TV series that came out in 1999, a sandwich shop in Brewster, Massachusetts, and a dance popular in circuit parties in the '90s. I'd written "Gimme, Gimme" so many times in my notebook it looked like the journal of a psychopath.

But Gimme, Gimme, Gimme didn't point me toward anybody at Roosevelt. I went back to the Register and my list of known liars. Maybe one of them could point me back to Gimme, Gimme, Gimme? I dove into their socials and searched for "Gimme, Gimme, Gimme." Nothing. Joelle Cordello did a bizarre TikTok to an old Britney Spears song called "Gimme More." And Brendan Buckler visited Gimme, Gimme Records in Los Angeles on spring break his freshman year. That was not enough to go on.

I went back to the list again. This time I widened my search criteria. Forget liars and cheats. I wanted to know anyone at the school who was capable of coding. I got thirty-five names. One of which surprised me. Cory Sayles? What was he doing there? It seemed unlikely that half of that boob-drunk power couple

CorRay was capable of writing code. But when I looked more closely at the Register, I noted that Cory had designed the soccer team's website. And it wasn't the free Squarespace crap students usually come up with. God, how had I missed this!

I thought about how Cory never once acknowledged my presence as a living human until he saw me at the car wash dressed as "Reality Margot." The second there were boobs and short shorts, he transformed into Mr. "Hey, look at my soccer ball tricks!" I wrote him and Ray off as two harmless dummies. But maybe that's just my bias! Maybe Cory isn't that dumb! Maybe he's not that harmless! This felt promising.

I did a search of his socials (which took forever because he had like seven Instas). But finally, on his spinsta,[55] I got what I was looking for. A picture of him catching a soccer ball. And underneath the picture, a caption: **I went GIMME GIMME GIMME on that.**

I was ecstatic. A weight was lifting. I might have my man. I decided to treat myself to a shower to celebrate, which, after four days of sick hibernating, was both necessary and a relief.

Cory Sayles. How surprising. My reverie continued as I got out of the shower, wrapped a towel around myself, and made a pit stop in the kitchen. I hadn't eaten in like . . . six hours? Eight hours? I rummaged for a snack. My dad's diet appeared to be going strong, so there was nothing but disgusting low-fat crackers and carrot sticks. Thank god hummus is on his "healthy" list.

"You look better!" exclaimed my mom, popping in from the living room. "How do you feel?" She felt my forehead with her

---

55. "Sports Insta." Cory had an Instagram account entirely devoted to the sports he played. His followers were three of his teammates and no one else.

wrist. She still had on her scrubs, which always made her seem official.

"I'm better."

"Ninety-seven point nine!" she announced. My mom is convinced that she can tell temperature to the tenth of a degree just using her wrist.

"You're insane. You can't tell that," I told her.

"Oh, yeah? Where's your nursing certificate?"

Before I could retort, the doorbell rang. I looked down at my phone and saw several missed texts from Mrs. Blye. Dear lord! Was she back? What the hell was the matter with her? My mom moved toward the door, but I cut her off, hoping I could intercept Mrs. Blye and turn her away.

"I got it."

"You're in a towel!" my mom objected.

Good, I thought. *Let Mrs. Blye see me in a towel. Let her be thoroughly uncomfortable. And then maybe she'll stop bothering me at home.* "Don't be such a Puritan, Mom. I'm not naked."

I swung open the door to reveal . . . Sammi. Of course.

He immediately turned his eyes away from my towel and announced to our wall sconce that he had brought over my homework assignments.

"Thanks, bud," I replied.

"Is that Sammi?" my mom cried with joy, pulling him inside toward the kitchen. "Come have a snack while Margot gets dressed."

He tried to resist her, eyes fixed now on the carpet. "I can't stay, Mrs. M—"

"Yes, you can. I have oatmeal raisin cookies!"

I didn't know we had oatmeal raisin cookies!

"Give me five minutes," I said, heading to change. I knew Sammi was uncomfortable with parents, so I didn't want to leave him too long. I pulled on my Levi's, threw on a tee, and put my hair in a wet ponytail. When I returned to collect him, he was mid-cookie and trying to explain Reddit to my mom. He looked relieved. I brought him directly to my room.

As soon as I shut the door, Sammi took off his Yankees hat and shook out his hair.

"Does your head itch? That's because hats make your head sweaty and gross because they're awkward and pointless. Also, your hair looks terrible now."

He nodded, smiled. Then he firmly secured his very dumb hat back on his head as if to say, "This is me now. Suck it."

Sammi took out a pile of missed homework assignments from my classes. Then he looked at me, like he was expecting me to say something, but I couldn't figure out what.

Finally, he said, "Um . . . so . . . are you still going to pay me . . . for the Mrs. Blye job . . ."

Shit! I prided myself on paying Sammi no later than two days after a job was done. I didn't want to put him in this very awkward situation of having to ask me for money. I reached into my desk drawer and took out $200.

"Sammi, I'm so sorry. I got sick and—"

"It's fine. I figured since you missed school, you might be sick, and now . . ." He motioned to my bed and desk. My room was still littered with used Kleenexes. "I see that you were."

Then, suddenly eyeing my desk, he asked, "Whatcha working on?" I was sure he knew I had a case. It was so obvious. My laptop was out, notebooks all over the place. I had everything except the murder board with red twine connecting the dots.

"English project," I lied. Again, feeling terrible.

"Cool cool." He nodded. I wasn't sure if he bought it.

He turned to leave when I called out, "Hey. Does 'Gimme, Gimme, Gimme' mean anything to you?"

He snapped his head back to look at me.

"Is this for a job?" he said, his eyes squinting.

"No." Lie. Lie. "It's stupid. I'm doing a report on *Catcher in the Rye*. I thought at one point Holden said 'gimme, gimme,' but I can't find it. And now I'm thinking it's from another book, but I can't remember which one, and it's driving me nuts."

He bought it because this was very on-brand for me. Diving down weird rabbit holes that take up too much time.

"Isn't it an ABBA song?" he said, leaving my room. "You of all people should know that." Sammi knew I was raised by an unabashed ABBA superfan.[56]

On his way to the front door, I heard him say goodbye to my mom and get trapped inside what sounded like another hug. When I heard the door shut, I felt relief. Time to get back to work. Cory, whatcha got for me?

I stalked his social, then looked at his phone because Cory had, of course, downloaded my TeddyFace app. (He's got spirit, yes he does!) Nothing too incriminating. He had been on RB

---

56. Surprise! It's my dad! And not my mom. You just got gender-biased!!!!!

several times, but nothing in his texts or email led me to believe he had anything to do with it. In fact, he and Ray had several conversations that were basically:

> **RAY:** Who do you think made RB?

> **CORY:** I dunno. How about [INSERT RANDOM NAME]?

> **RAY:** No way! How about [ANOTHER RANDOM NAME]?

> **CORY:** No way! What about [THIRD EVEN MORE RANDOM NAME]?

They went on like that for a while. Which . . . wasn't really helping my case. If Cory had done it, wouldn't he have told Ray, his BFF?

No. No. No. Not another dead end. I wasn't ready to accept it. Maybe . . . this whole convo had been planted to throw me off the scent? That seemed far-fetched. But perhaps that was just my bias speaking again. *He created the soccer team website! Keep digging!*

THE NEXT MORNING, I RETURNED TO SCHOOL AFTER FOUR DAYS away. But instead of trying to catch up on classwork (something my teachers really would have appreciated), I spent most of the day following Abby Durbin.

Abby was Cory's longest-lasting girlfriend to date. They started dating last spring and made it all the way to October, when Cory dumped her. They were a weird couple. Abby, petite, pale, and with eyes that seem way too small for her head, is intensely introverted. Cory is . . . well, Cory. (Plus, I can't imagine how a relationship with Cory would work when he always seems attached to Ray. Maybe they were a thruple?) My thinking was, if anybody knew about Cory and his secret porn-site-making ability, it would be Abby. Or Ray, I guess. But I couldn't imagine Ray betraying their precious bro code.

But Abby was proving to be a tough interview. She was one of those intensely punctual weirdos who clutched their books to their chests and practically ran from class to class so they wouldn't be late. She was a moving target, hard to pin down. Which is why when I saw her dart into the counselor's office during fifth period, I skipped econ and hovered outside the door, waiting for her to emerge. She couldn't talk about her college applications forever!

My phone pinged. Two texts from Avery blooped up.

> **AVERY:** I know you're on a job or something cause your MIA

> **AVERY:** but if you wanna break? dinner tonight?

He was giving me space because he sensed I was busy. I appreciated it. But I knew I couldn't just ignore him forever.

"Margot!"

It was Claire Jubell. Walking at me with a big, friendly smile, flawless porcelain skin, and straight blonde hair; she looked like a nonthreatening Barbie doll come to life.[57] I was suddenly very aware that my shirt had a coffee stain on it.

"Hey, Claire," I said, meaning to sound friendlier, but refusing to take my eyes off the door to the counselor's office. "What's up?"

"Oh, well, I just wanted to invite you to a little birthday thing. April twenty-fifth. At Gaetano's."

"Cool. I love Gaetano's," I said. Still eyeing the door.

"Yay! That's so great!" She beamed. Aaaand she wasn't leaving.

After a few seconds of not getting my hint, Claire lowered her voice and said, "Also, I just . . . I want you to know that . . . Avery and I both agreed that we're way better as friends. And when I heard he was dating you . . . honestly, I kind of love that for him."

This pried my eyes away from the counselor's door. It sounded like frenemy bullshit. But when I looked at Claire's perfect sky-blue eyes, she seemed . . . genuine.

"You do?"

"Totally. Everyone Avery dated, and believe me, we all talk—" Oh, great. I had accidentally joined the Sisterhood of the Avery Exes. Woof. "We all agreed that dating him was like . . . being a satellite. For a while you were in Avery's orbit. It was fun, but he never really let you get too close, and then . . . he just let you drift away," she said, smiling in a sweet, detached kind of way. "But . . . I can't imagine someone like you just . . . rotating around planet

---

57. Liberal Arts Barbie?

Avery. For once in his life, he's going to have to rotate around someone else."

Shaky metaphor aside, I couldn't really argue with Claire's larger point. I barely had time to be his fake and mostly neglectful girlfriend.

"Yeah. I guess that's true. Thanks, Claire."

Abby shot out of the counselor's office like a wind-up toy, zipping down the hall so fast I almost lost sight of her. Damn it! How did her weak little legs move so fast?

"God damn it! I have to go! Thanks for the invite!" I yelled to Claire as I ran after Abby. "Abby!" I shouted, struggling to match her pace. How was I winded already? As soon as this was over, I vowed to get back on the rickety treadmill in the Trinity Towers "gym."

"I'm sorry. I'm going to be late!" Abby squeaked.

"No, you're not. You're never late."

"I'm sorry, Margot, I really can't talk."

"You have to. Principal Palmer asked me to investigate a matter on his behalf. One involving Cory Sayles."

This, finally, stopped Abby in her tracks. She was terrified of authority. "He asked *you* to investigate Cory?"

"It's an extension of peer mediation.[58] They want students to become more involved in disciplinary investigations." Abby,

---

58. The idea of peer mediation is that when students get into a dispute (often a bad one, like a fistfight), the school arranges for a "student mediator" to meet with the students and help them resolve their issues. Not an adult guidance counselor or a psychologist who like . . . went to college and knows what they're doing. A student who watched a thirty-minute video on how to be a peer mediator. I trained for it in sixth grade and participated in exactly two mediations. I solved nothing.

annoyed she wasn't asked to participate in "peer discipline," nevertheless nodded okay. I escorted her into an empty classroom and closed the door behind us. I pulled out my phone and showed her a screenshot from Roosevelt Bitches.

"I'm sure you're familiar with Roosevelt's underage smut site."

She nodded yes, but looked away from the screen.

"We have reason to believe Cory is behind Roosevelt Bitches."

Abby looked confused. "Cory? Cory Sayles?"

"Yes. You guys dated, right? For approximately six months?" I asked, doing my best impression of a TV lawyer.

"Yeah. We did. Do you . . . think that's why he put me on it?" Tears were now pooling around Abby's eyes. Oh fuck. Abby was on it? I checked the site this morning! God damn them! It was starting to feel like whoever made the site was messing with me. Waiting for me to sign off before adding a new person.

"I . . . I'm sorry. You're on it? Since when?"

"Trish texted me after second period. It's a picture of me in a thong. I don't . . . send pics like that, but Cory kept asking, and . . ." She was shaking.

"When we broke up, he told me he deleted it." She looked so ashamed. For anyone, this would be a nightmare, but Abby was so private and quiet. If it wasn't Cory, I was still going to staple his dick to the wall.

"But when I told you Cory was behind RB, you seemed surprised. You don't think it was him?"

"No. I guess . . . Cory barely knows how to use his phone. How would he make a site like that?"

"He made the soccer team's website."

"No," she said incredulously. "His dad made it. His dad used to work for Microsoft. Who told you Cory made it?"

"I . . . don't remember." Cory, probably? Shit.

"There's no way. If Cory Sayles ever builds a website, any website, I will *go out with him again*. Does that tell you anything?" Abby seethed. "Can I go now?"

"Uh. Yes. And just so you know, I've spent the past month trying to find the dirtbags behind Roosevelt Bitches. I will take the site down. I will stop this. It's just . . . proving harder than I thought."

Abby nodded. ~~Impressed with the leeway peer mediation~~ had these days.

"But if you hear anything . . . about Cory or anybody else, could you DM me?"

Abby nodded and wiped her face, then got up to leave. "Yeah."

"Oh, one last thing . . ." I said. Abby stopped at the door, hand on knob. "I know this is none of my business, but I'm glad you're not with Cory. You can do so much better." Abby nodded. Though I wasn't quite sure she believed it.

I plopped down in a random desk chair. My body suddenly felt like dead weight. I stared blankly at the dry-erase board ahead of me. It said, "Point Slope Form: $(y-y1) =$"

I had no idea what the answer was. I didn't know the answer to anything. Was I really back at square one again?

It clearly wasn't Cory, but what was more troubling was that I had convinced myself it was. How? And how had I convinced myself it was Harold and Danny and Jenji? Was I terrible at this? I had gotten to dead ends before in work, but nothing this demoralizing.

During English the next period, I went back to my list of the *entire student body* and started crossing off the people I knew were innocent. I crossed off myself. I crossed off the girls who appeared on the site. (Though I guess it was *possible* one of them were behind it, it was highly improbable. It would be some real Agatha Christie–level plotting if it turned out to be Shannon or something.) For everyone else, it was "guilty till proven innocent" time.

For the rest of the school day, I went full Woodward and Bernstein. I chatted up Martin DiCicco, Josh Halloway, and Traydon Reed in the hallway between classes. But nobody on the basketball team seemed to know anything. I talked to the Gersen twins in AP Gov. I waited outside of Gabby Alvarez's theater arts class. But the only thing she knew was that Shontae Williams got nodes. I spotted Imani Watkins by her locker. I plopped my bag lunch down at Tiffany Sparks's table during sixth period. I interviewed all four Melanies! Melanie Shultz, Melanie Hopkins, Melanie Shapiro, and Melanie Davis, *and* I even talked to the janitorial staff. Nothing.

Every day I didn't take down Roosevelt Bitches was another day it expanded. With Abby's unconsented addition, by my count, there were thirty girls on the site. Thirty. Who knows how many more were added while I was spinning my wheels, chatting up every random classmate in this godforsaken school? I desperately needed a break in the case. But then Avery texted again.

AVERY: So . . . dinner?

Why would I want dinner when it's only . . . 6:22. Right. That's when you eat dinner.

> **AVERY:** We can just study the whole time. you can do your work stuff. You don't even have to look at me.

> **AVERY:** I mean you have to eat, right?

I didn't want to stop. I didn't want to go on a date. As always, I had too much to do. But he was right, even Margot Mertz, cleaner of filth and defender of women, needs to eat.

We met up at Noodle Town, USA. A soulless chain that claims to make "Classic, delicious homemade noodle dishes from around the globe."[59] Not my first choice, but it was cheap and we did have plenty of table space to study, so I went along with it.

I had a boatload of trig and a Latin exam to study for. So for most of our hang, we actually did study in silence, occasionally slurping down lukewarm, luke-tasting ramen. But then, out of nowhere, Avery reached his arrogant man-hand over to my side of the table and closed my book.

"What the hell?" I said, ready to strangle him.

"I'm sorry!" He held up his hands. "I just thought you might want to take an actual break and, like . . . talk. It might clear your head."

"Everyone always says that. *Take a break, relax, clear your head and the solution will come to you.* Well, thanks for the

---

59. They were not delicious.

unsolicited advice, but that doesn't work with me. You know what works for me and women in general?"

"What?"

"Working insanely hard and never stopping."

He rolled his eyes and said, "Well . . . I'm glad you deigned to have dinner with me. I promise not to talk to you for the rest of the night."

"Thank you. Can we get back to work now?"

"Yes," Avery lied, before continuing to talk. "Except, one thing, sorry—"

"Avery! That didn't even last a minute."

"I know. Sorry! There's a bunch of annoying stuff I have to tell you about my mom's award thing. I have to put you on a list and you need to bring ID. And my mom is insisting she know what you're wearing so she can make sure to wear a different color? Or something. I don't really get it. Just a heads up, my mom *will* try to coerce you into liking her. She's on a mission. Oh, and do you have any allergies? They put shrimp in everything at these things."

"Oh god," I said out loud. This reinforced my personally held stereotype that rich people put shrimp in everything.

"It will be short. I promise. My dad wants me to introduce him, so I have to give a quick speech. But I think we can get out of there by ten or eleven at the latest." He stopped talking. Clearly my face was betraying my dread. "And . . . you look miserable. I'm sorry. You really don't have to go."

"No! I'm sorry. I'm just not looking forward to taking a picture next to your inarguably gorgeous mom. But I'm going. I said I'd go. I'm a person of my word. I will be there." And then I finger-gunned him. Which no one should ever do.

Avery nodded. "Well, I really appreciate it. Seriously. It means a lot." He was quiet for a moment before adding, "You're saving me."

Whatever was going on with his parents seemed to really bother him. The few times he hinted at it, the veneer of confidence that was Avery's trademark would vanish, and for a second I'd get a glimpse at something that was . . . sadder. And angrier. He must have been really good at compartmentalizing his emotions. Which, honestly, I can relate to. (And if I'm *really* being honest, is kind of a turn-on.)

When Avery looked up, his dimple was going strong. "Can I ask you one more thing? It's kinda serious."

"Sure," I said, surrendering any hope of finishing my work.

He held up his laminated place mat, which had an index of over one hundred noodle varieties. "I think we need to rate the noodles. All the noodles, from best to ziti."

I had already spent too much time talking. I didn't have time for games. But he was implying ziti was the "worst" noodle, which was heresy.

"Hold up. I love ziti."

"It's objectively the worst," he said dismissively. "But where do you rank the rest of them? Like pad see ew? Tortellini? And most importantly, what do you put in the number one slot? Angel hair or egg noodle?"

He'd said so many wrong things in such a short amount of time.

"Angel hair? Who gets angel hair on purpose?"

Avery grabbed my notebook and tore out a sheet to write down my list. "Start at the beginning," he instructed. He clicked his pen twice to really emphasize how serious he was. But then something stopped him. He turned his piece of paper over.

"Why did you write 'gimme, gimme, gimme' in the margins like . . . everywhere?" he asked, perhaps wondering if he was dating the Zodiac Killer.

"Oh, it's just . . . something for this job I'm on. It's nothing." I mean, it was everything, but I wasn't about to tell him that.

He shrugged, was about to move on, but clearly felt like he had to say, "You're not working for Chris Heinz, are you?"

What in the holy hell did that mean? Why would he ever say that? The ramen noodles I was slurping suddenly tasted like chalk. I spat them back into my bowl.

"Did you get a hair or something?" he asked.

I ignored the question. "What . . . uh . . . why . . ." I was really struggling to form a sentence. The thought of working for Chris Heinz had apparently given me a stroke. "Why . . . would you say that?"

"Well, look, I respect that you protect your clients' information and all, but if you're working for him—"

"I would rather jam these cheap plastic chopsticks in my eyes than work for Chris! I hate Chris!" I shouted. Our fellow noodlers all looked to our table.

"Okay, sorry. I didn't know. I just . . ."

"Does 'gimme, gimme' mean something to you?" I asked, my ears ringing.

"Well, that's like Chris's . . . thing. His catchphrase, kinda.

He says it all the time. I played soccer with him, and whenever he scored a goal he was all, 'Gimme, gimme, gimme, bitches.' Or when he did a keg stand at a party. Or when he, I don't know, ate a pizza by himself. Anything he did that he thought was cool, he'd say 'gimme, gimme, gimme' while, like, pretending to throw dollar bills in the air. And eventually, other guys on the team started saying it, too."

I closed my laptop and looked at my notebook. Gimme, gimme, gimme. It wasn't Cory's thing. And it wasn't an ABBA song. Or a record store. It was a catchphrase.

It was Chris Heinz. The whole time. He practically signed his name on every page.

I was gonna need a minute.

17

FFFFFFFF*#$*%$#*#!!!!!!!!!!

I T WAS CHRIS HEINZ! THE WHOLE TIME! THE RAPEY ASSHOLE WHO RUINED MY BEST FRIEND'S LIFE!! THAT ENTITLED, LOCKER-PUNCHING, IPHONE-SMASHING PIECE OF SHIT!!! THE GUY WHOSE INSTAGRAM IS MADE UP SOLELY OF #STRIPPERFAIL REPOSTS AND SHIRTLESS PICTURES OF HIMSELF!!!! HE'S BEHIND ROOSEVELT BITCHES!!! HE'S THE MAN BEHIND THE CURTAIN!!!! CHRIS?!?!?!?! HEINZ!?!?!?!?!!!!!!!! WHAAAAT!!!!!!!!!!

FUCK.

FUCK.

FFFFUUUUUUCKKKK.

Fuck.

MOTHERFUCKER!!!!!!!! GOD DAMN IT!!!!! FUUCK! FUCK FUCK FUCK FUCK FUCK FUCK!!!!! FUCK! YOU! GGGGGGAAAAAHHHHHHH!!!!!!

18

OF COURSE IT WAS

"Margot? Margot? Are you okay?"

Noodle Town, USA slowly came back into focus, and I realized Avery was staring at me.

"Yeah. I'm—I'm fine," I stammered.

I tried to take a bite of noodles to show him how fine I was. But as soon as the noodles hit my mouth, I retched, walked directly to the bathroom, and expelled everything I'd eaten all day.

I flushed, wiped my mouth, and looked in the spotty mirror. Chris had taken his brand of toxic male shittiness, the same entitlement that had allowed him to sexually assault my best friend with no repercussions, and spread it all over the internet like a disease. I was furious that someone as cruel as Chris existed in the world. Not only existed, but was thriving! He had friends, he was "popular." He was the type of guy who could flunk out of college, be terrible at his job, make all the women around him uncomfortable, yet somehow continue to fail up, skirting by on confidence and aggression. Chris Heinz: he'll either die of alcohol poisoning or be our next president.

I rinsed my mouth and brushed my teeth (I always carry a toothbrush in my bag) before leaving the Noodle Town, USA bathroom, which was about as clean as you'd expect. When I returned to the table, Avery stood up, napkins in hand, and asked me if I was okay. I said I was, that whatever I ate obviously didn't agree with me. He looked pained. My sudden nausea had turned Avery's savior complex up to eleven. He paid the bill and offered to drive me home.

We drove in silence for a bit. I got the sense Avery thought any sound or sudden movement might make me throw up again. Which, in all honesty, it might have. He often had surprisingly good instincts about when to leave me alone. My eyes closed, my seat reclined, and my tush amply warmed, I felt way better. Soon, I would be home. Soon, I would get to Chris and take down RB for good.

I opened one eye to spy on Avery. He noticed, and took the opportunity to say, "I'm sorry I made us go there."

"It's okay."

"No! I feel terrible. You just wanted to work tonight, and I made you eat Noodle Town noodles and they made you puke and—"

"It's really fine."

"I just feel bad and—"

"Avery. Don't feel bad. You did not make me sick. It is not your fault. Stop apologizing. Okay?" I sat up and punched him in the arm, now feeling like my stomach was more or less back to normal. He smiled. Nodded. Message received.

When we got to Trinity Towers, he parked and walked me up to the front door. Then he started kicking one of the paving stones that was loose.

"You want to apologize again, don't you?"

"Just one more time because it was literally my fault that you ate bad noodles. So can I one more time? Then I'll stop."

I rolled my eyes. "Fine. Weirdo."

"Sorry I made you take a break and you puked."

"Apology accepted." We stood there, smiling. Neither of us making the move to go our separate ways.

"Can I kiss you?" he asked.

"You do remember that I puked less than an hour ago?"

He reached up to touch the side of my face. "You're not puking now." What was I supposed to say to that? He waited, smiling.

"I mean, fine." Thank god I'd brushed my teeth.

We kissed, and this time there was 100 percent less snot. He had his hand at the side of my face, and I found myself reaching my hand to the back of his neck, feeling that rough bristle where his hair was buzzed short. I have to be fair to Avery, it was a pretty good kiss. He'd probably perfected his approach over the course of many girlfriends. But in that moment, I didn't care how he got good at it. I just closed my eyes and enjoyed.

"Can I ask you something?" I heard myself say. "Have you ever heard of Roosevelt Bitches?"

Avery seemed surprised by the question. And honestly, so was I. He took his hand away from my face.

"Yes."

Wrong answer, Avery.

"So you've, like, been to the site?" I asked, feeling myself getting queasy again.

Even if he hadn't made the site, visiting it made him culpable in a different way. There wouldn't be a Roosevelt Bitches if there weren't boys to gawk at it.

"I would never go on a site like that!" He looked mortified. "Cory and Ray showed it to me after practice one day."

"Yeah, okay." I wasn't buying it. "So you knew about it, but you never went—"

"I didn't. No. It's messed up. I told Cory and Ray they were assholes for looking at it." He was visibly upset.

I believed him. I don't know why. Actually, I do know why. I'd never seen Avery say or do anything dishonest. He just didn't lie.

I looked up at him. "So if I look at your browser history . . ."

"You will find porn. I look at porn! I'm not a saint." He put his hands up in his signature Avery "don't be mad at me" way. "But you will not find that site. Because that site is . . . bad."

"Well, thanks for being honest." I wanted to be angry with him for having seen RB. Also porn in general. But at least he knew the site was wrong. At least he had some kind of moral compass.

"I'll see you tomorrow, Margot."

"See you tomorrow, Avery."

He gave an awkward kind of half wave and turned away.

"And please rethink your relationship to ziti!" he shouted as he walked to his car.

I suddenly felt relieved. My stomach had settled. The

clamminess had gone away. It was still extremely troubling that Chris had created RB right under my nose, but at least now I could focus all my time and energy on taking him down. No more suspects and parties and dragging Avery on awkward triple dates.

No more dragging Avery on awkward triple dates. Huh. I hadn't really considered it until now, but I didn't need Avery anymore. At all. I'd never intended for it to go on this long in the first place. But now I realized I should probably Band-Aid-pull our fake relationship as soon as possible. Avery was a decent guy, and he didn't deserve to be jerked around. He wasn't the phony/possible serial killer I'd once pegged him to be.

I reached into my pocket to grab my apartment key and noticed two things. For one, my hand was kind of shaking. Weird. The last time I remembered my hand shaking like that was in my sixth grade YMCA All-Stars production of *Fiddler on the Roof*. (It was my first time being in a live musical, and even though I was only *Motel the Tailor's non-singing sister*, I was nervous!)

And second, my key was not in my pocket. Or my backpack. Or any other pocket. It wasn't anywhere.

Shit.

Both my parents work late on Thursday nights, so I knew no one would answer when I buzzed. (I still buzzed about ten times.) Then I buzzed Sammi's apartment. No one answered. I called his cell.

"Hello?" came Sammi's voice after one ring.

"Didn't you hear me buzz? Let me in, I forgot my key."

"You forgot your key?" Sammi replied, genuinely surprised.

I didn't forget things. My dad loses his keys all the time, and half the time they're in his pants pocket. I'm not one of those people. I know where everything is in the house and who last touched it and how long it's been there. It's kind of like having a photographic memory, but only for useless things like the Apple TV remote or the last bag of SunChips.

"Yeah, can you let me in?"

"Sorry. I just got out of a movie. I'm like twenty minutes away."

"A movie in a theater? Who *are you*?" It was already weird for him to be out. But it was even weirder for him to be at the movies when he normally just pirated whatever he wanted to see.

"Yes, Margot. I went to the movies."

I wanted to give him more shit about it, but I didn't have the energy. I was tired, cold, and suddenly hungry.

"Nah, don't worry about it. I'll buzz someone else. Have fun."

"Are you okay?" Sammi asked.

"I'll call you later," I said, and hung up. It had been a while since I'd talked to Sammi. I mean, I was sure one hang would bring me up to speed on his life: *"I got to level whatever in* [insert weird RPG about sexy elves]," or *"I just hacked a fast food chain's corporate database because I was bored,"* etc. But still, I missed him.

I buzzed my neighbor Miss Debra and she let me into the building. But I still couldn't get into our unit, so I settled myself in the building's foyer and brought out my computer. I knew my mom wouldn't get home until a little after nine, but I wasn't going to waste time when I could be working.

Five weeks had gone by since I'd taken on Shannon's case.

Five weeks of my fellow classmates' pictures being leered at without their consent—all while I had been dicking around, going on fake dates and hacking computers that were in no way affiliated with Roosevelt Bitches. But now that I knew it was Chris fucking Heinz, I needed to step it up. He'd keep adding, keep building his site, because he was a black hole. A void. One that could never be filled no matter how many people told him he was hot or good at soccer. Soccer! Right. Chris tore his ACL in the middle of the fall season and was now unable to play. Was he using all that extra free time to build his site?

~~Chris *building a site*?~~ I had a hard time picturing that. In some ways, it seemed so obvious now that Chris was behind Roosevelt Bitches. Morally, he'd have no problem administering a catalog of underage smut. But . . . could he code? How would he even begin to build a site like RB? Chris Heinz wouldn't know his PHP[60] from his ASS.[61] I couldn't even picture him at a computer. When I did, all I could think of was that meme of a labradoodle behind the wheel of a Prius. Plus, I had access to Chris's phone![62] How could he have pulled this off right under my nose!?

I opened up TeddyFace and scoured Chris's phone for traces of RB. I found only a few visits through his browser. He hadn't used his phone to build the site or anything like that. I started going through his texts. Again, nothing. Not one mention of Roosevelt Bitches. Was it possible Gimme, Gimme, Gimme Productions wasn't him? Had RB been built by a rabid ABBA fan all along?

---

60. PHP is a computer scripting language used by web developers.

61. ASS is a butt.

62. Thanks to an app that gives everyone a mustache and pince-nez.

I tried one more thing. I decided to DDoS (distributed denial of service) the RB site with so much traffic it would get overwhelmed and become inaccessible. This was a one-time play. Once they noticed the massive increase in traffic, they could get something like Cloudflare to block my botnet, and the site would come right back up. But the attack might get Chris to start texting. It took about fifteen minutes for the site to come down.

Soon after, Chris got a text from Kyle Kirkland.

KYLE: bitches is down again. sorry i can't fix

CHRIS: not here use the burner

KYLE: yeah yeah but can u call ur guy?

CHRIS: USE THE BURNER DICK!

Use the burner? Had Chris put so much thought into operating the site that he made his co-conspirators use burner phones? Was that even possible? I tried to think about Chris. I was so fixated on my hatred for him, I usually only thought of him at his worst: Entitled. Dumb. Attempted rapist. I couldn't imagine him being all those things and *also* a tech-savvy website designer, a leader, someone *capable*. Was he smarter than I thought? Had he ever shown initiative? There *was* a rumor going around Roosevelt that Chris was going to DJ the senior prom. Apparently he'd sweet-talked the prom committee chair into giving him the gig. That probably took a little effort. But RB-level effort?

I wasn't sure. Then I thought about prank week.

Each year, Roosevelt has an unofficial prank week right before winter break. Usually this is a time where friends do harmless pranks: filling your locker with shaving cream, jumping out of a trash can to scare you, etc. But Chris always took things way too far. One year he broke into the school at night and cemented five toilets in five different rooms: the gym, the front hallway, the chemistry lab, the cafeteria, and—most impressive—Palmer's office! I had initially written this off as Chris Heinz idiocy, but thinking about it now . . . that's a hard prank. Where'd he get the toilets? Or the cement? How did he get into Palmer's office without setting off the school's alarm? (I've done it! It's hard!) So maybe he *could* orchestrate a site like Roosevelt Bitches? But there was no way he built it himself. Clearly Kyle was working on it, based on the texts. (And that explained why Shannon, Kyle's ex, was one of the first to be featured on the site.) I suspected that P-Boy, their informal third stooge, was also involved. But did they know enough about coding to build a whole site?

"Forget your key?"

My mom appeared at the entrance in her scrubs with a bag full of grapefruits in one hand.

"Forget your . . . juicer?" They can't all be gems, folks.

"These," she said, holding up a grapefruit, "are from a patient! She has a time-share in Florida and she brought them for me because I . . ." My mom told me the woman's whole life story on our way up to our unit. (My parents don't believe in taking the elevator because stairs are "so good for you.") I was only half listening, my mind still fixated on Chris Heinz. Luckily, my mom has two types of stories from work: heartwarming or horrific. From her tone, this sounded heartwarming.

"That sounds great, Mom."

"Great? They had to amputate her leg!" Oops. Guess this was one of the horrific ones.

"Sorry, Mom. I'm tired. I've got a lot of . . . wait? Where are you going?"

My mom had changed out of her scrubs and into jeans and a sweater. She usually went straight from scrubs to her pajamas (also scrubs).

"Your dad wants to see the new Paul Thomas Anderson movie."

"You just got off a double."

"I know. I'm fried." She put on a little lipstick and grabbed her purse. "But your father really wanted to go the day it came out. No spoilers. You want to come?"

"No thanks. I still don't get why *you're* going."

"I don't know, Margot. I love him. And part of being in a re-lationship is doing things for the other person. It's why your dad pretends to be interested in tennis for me."

I rolled my eyes. I really do not get my parents. I could never spend time doing a thing I hated just to make my boyfriend or husband happy. But my parents aren't as ambitious as I am. They kind of settled. My mom got pregnant when she was twenty, and both she and my dad had to change their life courses drastically to support each other. My mom wanted to be a doctor and volunteer in a clinic in Malawi. And my dad was in his second year of film school, working at a laundromat part-time to pay his tuition.

But having me meant bye-bye to their dreams. They say they don't regret it, but I don't know if I really buy that. Just look how insane my dad is, dragging my mom to a movie on opening night. Does he wish it was a real premiere? For a movie he was directing? And my mom swears she's going to go to Africa once I'm out of college and settled. But will she?

"We should be home by midnight-ish. You can have Sammi over if you want, but no Avery. Yeah?"

"Okay, Mom." *Don't get too attached to the idea of me dating Avery.*

"Love you!"

After the door slammed behind her, I settled on the couch, nibbling on crackers. My hand was better, but every once in a while, I'd feel a little tremor. I googled "nerve damage," "blood clots," and "hand seizure," but got nothing helpful. Finally, I took out my laptop and checked in on Chris's phone again. Chris was texting, but this time he was sending DMs to a bunch of different groups—

> **CHRIS:** next saturday. offensive bd party. my house. wear something good but bad. invite everyone i give no fucks

It seemed Chris was having his now-annual "offensive costume birthday party." When he said, "Wear something good but bad," what he meant was, "Dress up as something that is really tasteless and shocking." I had heard about the previous year's party. Several people had dressed up as R. Kelly, others wore racist costumes ranging from "early 2000s microaggression" all the way to "1950s Strom Thurmond." P-Boy came as Jeffrey Epstein.

You get the idea. In a couple of months, people would hire me to delete pictures from this party. I just knew it.

I was obviously not excited about the party itself (gross). But I was excited about the opportunity it presented: a raucous, busy event at Chris's house, where Chris would hopefully be distracted and inebriated. I could slip in, steal everything on his laptop, and own his ass, then slip out quietly.

However, even though "everyone" was invited, people knew that I didn't go to parties and I didn't drink. Plus Chris knew that I loathed him. It might set off red flags if I showed up. It would have been so much easier to go with Avery. But we'd be broken up by then.

But did we need to be? It would be cruel to string him along for too much longer, but Avery was undeniably useful. I wouldn't have gotten into Photography Club without him. And at Danny's, his zeal for party games was a crucial distraction. Maybe he could do the same thing at Chris's?

I decided to postpone the breakup. At least until after Chris's party. I shot Avery a text, and we traded DMs for the next hour or so. He apologized a few more times. I told him all his apologies were making me nauseous, which just made him apologize again. Then we talked about things very important (climate change) and not at all important (how come people arm wrestle but don't foot wrestle?).

Before I knew it, it was two a.m. I said good night to Avery and was going to check WebMD one more time before I went to sleep, but my hand finally stopped shaking. Maybe it just happened because I vomited? I don't know.

The next morning, I was in a surprisingly great mood. Progress was finally being made in the case, my stomach felt better, and my dad must have broken his diet, because there was a twelve-pack of cider doughnuts from The Hole, my dad's favorite doughnut spot forty-five minutes away. (When my dad breaks a diet, he *breaks* a diet.)

But as soon as I entered the double doors of Roosevelt, my good mood went right to crap. Everyone was gathered in the east hall. Including Palmer and both assistant principals. They were surrounding a locker that a janitor was covering up with newspaper. Palmer implored everyone to go to class, trying to stop us from seeing what was written on the locker. But it clearly said SLUT.

Kelsey . . .[63] Hoffman appeared at my side.

"Did you see my locker?" she said, seething.

"That's your locker? Holy shit. Do you know who did it?"

"Probably Justin. My ex. He was the last guy I dated before I came out, and he took it personally. Like me being gay was a reflection on him or whatever. Ever since, he's been a real dick."

I didn't know Justin Spitzer all that well, but I made a mental note to write "small, spiteful turd" in his Register description.

"Are you getting any closer to taking this down? Stuff like this is starting to happen more often. Everyone on the group is freaking out."

I was aware of the other public displays of assholery. Someone had printed out a topless picture of Tyra Michaels and

---

63. This is the *short* Kelsey. A short actor is Dustin *Hoffman*. Hoffman! This is Kelsey Hoffman.

taped it to the windshield of her car. And Jess Lind's gym locker had been tagged with the ever-clever WHORE. And now this. I looked at the sea of people around me. Were we really going to accept this? Girls being bullied? Girls being slut-shamed? What kind of Nathaniel Hawthorne bullshit was this?

I muttered, "Sorry, but I gotta go," and broke away from the crowd of onlookers.

Fuck them. Fuck this school. Fuck RB. And fuck Chris Heinz. I kept picturing him behind a computer. Laughing as he uploaded pictures. Not caring about the chaos he was creating or the women he was hurting. I wanted to rip his fucking guts out. Inch by inch, and as slowly as possible.

I stewed to my locker, ears hot, where Avery was waiting for me. Nervously playing with a random lock, twisting the dial back and forth. I barely noticed him as he kissed me on the cheek and said, "Hey. I have to talk to you about next Saturday."

"Okay?" I said. Whatever his plan was, I had to steer him to Chris's party next Saturday. "About that—"

"I know we have my mom's thing," he continued, and it took me a second to remember that next Saturday was also the night of his mom's fancy gala thing. Shit. "And I'm really grateful you're going. But, I realized next Saturday is *also* our one-month anniversary."

Jesus. *Busy day.* "It is?" I asked, firmly believing that one-month anniversaries are for people new to sobriety, not relationships.

"And I *know* you probably think that's a stupid thing to celebrate. But before you lecture me on just how stupid it is, hear me out." He was flashing his smile and trying to be cute. But I was not having it. Not while SLUT and WHORE were being gleefully tagged on lockers. He went on,

"My parents' thing ends at eleven. I bet we could sneak out by ten thirty. And then . . . drumroll please . . ." He could tell from my look that I would not be making a drumroll sound, so he continued, "*Misery* is playing at the Palladium at ten forty-five. And we are going!" He presented his phone, showing two prepaid tickets to the revival screening.

"Really?"

"Are you impressed I found a screening of your favorite movie even though it's very old?"

I *was* kinda impressed. And it actually sounded fun. Who wouldn't love to see Kathy Bates break a man's legs with a sledgehammer on the big screen? For a fleeting moment, I considered postponing Chris's home invasion. But it didn't last. The site, the SLUT locker, the ever-growing Fury chat, it was coursing through my blood.

"Sure. But, Avery—"

"I'm almost positive I can get you home by one, but would your parents go for that? Do I need to sweeten the deal with some macarons? This is feeling like a macaron situation."

"Can I talk now?" I said with a little too much edge.

He seemed surprised by my tone. "Yeah! Sorry. What's up?"

"I can't go. To your mom's thing. I'm sorry."

He tried to smile, but couldn't hide what looked like a just-got-punched expression. "Oh. Okay. Did something come up?"

There was no good way to put it. "I have to go to Chris's party."

He looked wholly confused. "Chris's costume party? You don't even *like* Chris. You yelled at me yesterday because I asked if you were working for him."

"Yeah. Look, I feel bad about your mom's thing. But I'm sorry I can't—"

"Mertz, you are *so confusing*," he said, taking a step away from me. "I mean, most of the time that's okay, because I like you! I like that you're guarded and intense and a badass and way smarter than I am. I actually think that's pretty hot! But, I mean, this . . . this is kind of important. I thought you said you were a 'person of your word.'"

"Yeah—I know," I stammered, annoyed that he was using my own words against me. "Why don't you meet me at Chris's after your mom's thing?"

"Why can't *you* just come to my mom's thing first? I already told my parents. They put you on the list and—"

"Then take me off the list! Okay? Because I can't go!" I snapped. I probably seemed unhinged, but I couldn't help it. Real people with real trauma were counting on me. I needed to focus on getting Chris's computer, not eat shrimp with rich hospital people. The whole point of Avery, of this relationship, was to help me with RB. And now he was being so stubborn.

"Why are you yelling at me?" Avery asked in a condescendingly calm tone, which only made me want to throttle him more. "Is this for a job? Are you gonna hack Chris's computer or something?" He asked this loudly and several freshmen craned their heads to see who said it. I got that he was frustrated, but that was no excuse for being so sloppy with sensitive information.

"Can you lower your voice?" I pulled him aside, then whispered, "And what if it is?"

"Can't you do it another time? I know you love work. But . . . you promised . . ." He was clenching his jaw so much I thought he might crack his veneers.

"What do you want, Avery? A girlfriend who's obsessed with you? Who goes to your parents' boring parties? And your soccer games? And the spring musical to cheer you on while you run the lights?"

"No—" he shot back.

I slammed my locker door. "Because I have a lot of shit going on and I can't drop everything just because you can't stand to be alone with your parents!" That was unnecessary. I said it purely to get under his skin. And it worked.

"What's your problem? Why are you being so—" He was almost yelling now.

"I don't have a problem! And I think I'm being pretty clear about what I want!" I yelled over him. I really didn't want to do this now, but he was putting me in a corner and taking up time I didn't have. "Avery, I honestly don't care what you do. Because I am going to Chris's. With or without you." I couldn't look at him as I said this. It was so harsh. But I didn't see any other way. The truth was, I didn't need him anymore.

"Okay . . ." He replied, "Well, I don't know what to say to that. But if that's what you want . . ."

This was not what I really wanted. I wanted Avery to come with me to Chris's. I wanted him to distract Chris and then take me to see my favorite movie and then maybe go to Nick's for some pie.

But I didn't say this. I didn't even give a hint of remorse when I said, "Okay. Well, I'll see you around, then."

I turned to walk down the hall, pushing my hands so deep into my hoodie pockets, I thought they might rip through the fabric.

"Wait!" He took a few steps after me. "That's it? What about—"

"Jesus, Avery! Are you gonna make me say it?" My hand was going really nuts again, shaking in my hoodie pocket. Avery's jaw dropped. He finally realized I was breaking up with him.

"Wow. Okay." He shook his head and walked away, down the hallway to the gym, even though that's not where his first class was.

I looked down at my hand. It seemed okay from the outside, but inside it was numb and tingling again. I took a deep breath.

My fake relationship had come to a real end.

April 2, 8:15 p.m.

MARGOT: hey. i feel like i haven't been a very good friemd lately. my goal was alwyas to text you every week and ive been letting stuff get in the way of that so. not gonna do that anymore. hi.

April 2, 8:17 p.m.

MARGOT: question. have you ever broken up with anyone? I'm sure you've had a boyfriend or two since you moved away. or . . . more than two? you've probably had like 10! 10 skinny brown-haired boys who are a little bit shy but also worship you.

April 2, 8:23 p.m.

MARGOT: maybe you dated one redhead somewhere in there. Just to mix it up. And he was kind of a dick but in a hot way?

MARGOT: Clearly I've put too much thought into this.

MARGOT: did it suck breaking up with them? i mean, breakups are always awkward, right? or like weird. or sad.

April 2, 8:33 p.m.

MARGOT: night! Miss you!

19

ON THE OFFENSIVE

Since I no longer had a date, I decided my best option was to arrive at Chris Heinz's party at the halfway point. If I got there too early, everyone would notice me, wonder why I was there, and it would be harder to sneak into Chris's room. Too late, and only the hardcore stragglers would remain, and Chris would be passed out in his room. So I got there at ten thirty p.m., figuring that was the ideal, white cream center of this Oreo party.

There hadn't been a big, alcohol-fueled rager in a while, so everyone came out for it. Parties were a high school ritual I participated in only when I was working. I always felt like a zoologist, studying my classmates from afar, silently judging them.[64]

I opened the front door and slipped in. The scene was as

---

64. I don't know if zoologists "judge" animals, really, but maybe? "That penguin's kind of a dick," "That giraffe is a real Karen," etc.

expected: loud and sloppy. With any luck, I could go straight to Chris's room, copy his hard drive, and get the hell out of there undetected. But I was immediately met with: "MARGOT!!!"

Ray Evans and Cory Sayles, SOLO cups in hand, greeted me like I had just come home from war. Both buzzed and so excited to see the vapid, reality-show Margot they saw at the car wash! They talked over each other,

"So psyched you're here! You wanna drink?"

"Avery said you guys broke up! That sucks! Wanna drink?"

"There's a whole bar. I can get you a water, too, if that's all you want. No pressure."

"That costume is so funny!"

That caught my attention. I was not wearing a costume.

"Aren't you that hiker that got murdered by her gym teacher?" Jesus. Did I look like a murder victim? Disturbing. Regardless, I went along with it. Had to give them the fun, easygoing Margot they knew and loved.

"Yes!" I squealed. "Good eye!" Arm touch. Hair flip. Big laugh. "Not everyone has gotten that, but you guys so did!"

They bobbed their heads like trained seals.[65] I sent them off to make me a very complicated drink (one part Coke, one part Jäger, one part club soda, one part fresh-squeezed lime, one part iced coffee, fresh mint, bitters) that I had no intention of drinking. Then I made my way to the corner of the living room, grabbed an empty SOLO cup, and held it like I was drinking from it. I surveyed the scene: in the kitchen, people had gathered in three- to

---

65. "Those seals are so catty." Okay, I'll stop.

five-person clumps, loudly talking over the music. There was a group playing Switch on the living room TV. Outside, multiple beer pong tables were set up, and people were playing water volleyball in the heated pool.

I spotted Avery on the patio, in the middle of a game of Heads Up! that I was sure he'd spearheaded. He was with a bunch of randos, including Greg Mayes and Cheryl Graham (who . . . appeared to be a couple now? Sorry, Danny!) and Brighton Girl, wobbly as ever, and who, even from a distance, I could tell was throwing herself at Avery. I didn't think she'd be his type. But I guess I never figured out his type. I was sort of surprised he made it to the party at all. He must've left his mom's thing early. Whatever. Avery was now free to do what he wanted. I had more important things to think about.

I needed to find Chris's room, so I made my way up the crowded staircase to the second floor of the house. There was a landing at the top where couples lined up, many engaged in some heavy PDA. One of the couples at the back stopped making out long enough for me to ask, "Hey. What are you in line for?" They responded by laughing. The guy in front of them turned. (It was Isaac Oliver from my AP Gov class.) "Hookup room," he said before he and Craig Layton started furiously, and, I would argue, loudly, making out.

I made it to the landing and scoped out the scene below. Everyone seemed to be having fun, commenting on and debating their "offensive costumes." A lot of people went as Vanessa Black, that pop singer who checked herself into rehab last month and almost died. (Haha! That's what you get for having talent and a substance abuse problem!) This was also a popular choice because it gave everyone an excuse to dress up in Black's signature hot pants and halter top, i.e., *sexy clothes.* I spotted one group that was composed of five Vanessa Blacks all talking to someone dressed as the grim reaper, who looked a little like Sammi. Wait. Was it Sammi? Was that Sammi? Was Sammi at a party?! What in the what?! A hat was one thing, but I have never, ever known Sammi to go to any social gathering, unless you count his cousin's wedding, which his mom forced him to go to.

I almost walked back down the stairs to confront Sammi, but I shook it off. *You can interrogate Sammi later and make sure he hasn't been kidnapped. First do what you came to do!*

I made my way down the hallway, navigating around the couples patiently waiting to hook up in the privacy of either Chris's parents' or sister's room. There was a separate line of people waiting to use the bathroom. And at the front of it was John Pfeiffer, who had nominated himself the gatekeeper. "No hooking up in the bathroom! *People need somewhere to pee!*"

At the end of the hall, there was a mysterious fourth door with no line. This must have been Chris's room. The door was ajar, and despite the noisy chatter and thumping bass of the party below, I could hear voices coming from inside.

It sounded like an argument. Or a heated discussion. I walked forward gingerly, pushing the door open slightly so that I could peep in. And there they were: Chris, Kyle, and P-Boy. Kyle was at a computer, furiously typing while P-Boy watched over his shoulder. Chris was on the bed, shaking a Magic 8-Ball, then tossing it in the air like a baseball. I won't say what their costumes were, but they weren't "fun offensive." They were more "4chan offensive."

"Guys, what is taking so long?" Chris complained, "You said you could fix it, right?! Do I need to call—"

"No! I can do it," Kyle said as he kept typing. "It's just buggy. Ever since it went down, it's been like this."

I guess my DDoS attack was continuing to disrupt things.

"Let's just drink tonight and fix it on Monday?" P-Boy whined.

"*No!* You nutsacks! You see how much nakedness there is tonight?! All the Vanessa Blacks with their asses hanging out? We could increase our catalog by like . . . thirty percent!" In reality, every other word out of his mouth was "fuck," but I'm leaving that out because it makes it hard to read. "But no one's gonna upload anything if the site isn't up!" He whipped the 8-Ball at P-Boy's leg.

"Shit, dude! That hurt!" P-Boy hobbled around the room, walking off the pain. "You said this was going to be fun. But now it's like . . . a job. It's all we ever do."

"Yeah, we got pretty much all the hot girls," Kyle added. "I say we stop before we get caught."

Chris looked annoyed, like he might peg his two henchboiz with something else. But then he sat back in his desk chair.

"Look, I wasn't going to tell you this, but . . . my cousin Benny, from LA, he thinks we could actually sell this."

"Hold up. What?" Kyle sat up, his interest piqued.

"Yeah. For, like, *money*. He knows a guy that works for Porn Slash."

P-Boy smiled. Apparently the talk of cash had convinced them that it was worth getting pelted by Magic 8-Balls. As the three shared a barely coherent chant of "Yeah!" and "LA!" and "Money!" my stomach sank. This was bad. If RB got on a site like Porn Slash, it would be everywhere. And there would be nothing I could do.

Now newly motivated, Kyle tap-tap-tapped until he got the site up and running again. Then I heard them muttering about "getting back out there," so I hid in a nearby linen closet. As they walked out of Chris's room, I heard Chris say, "Hurry up. That girl from Brighton is here, and I wanna get to her before Avery does." The guys replied with "*Noice!*" and "*Sweet!*" before disappearing into the crowd.

She has a name, Chris! It's Angelica!

Soon my drunk and horny classmates would be rushing into Chris's room to hook up. I had to make my move. I slipped out of the linen closet and casually walked toward Chris's room. But as I put my goddamned hand on the goddamned doorknob I heard, "*Whoa.* Mertz. Where you going?" I didn't even have to turn around, I knew it was him, that cocky, chiseled asshole. *Chris.* I spun around and looked him right in his vapid blue eyes.

"Isn't this the hookup room?"

He eyed me suspiciously.

"And . . . who are you hooking up with?"

I could have lied. I could have said a name. Any name! Guy or girl! And I'm sure he would have allowed me to proceed into his room. But I didn't. I just stood there. And then my chest started to seize. My eyes got watery. God damn it. Not now.

"Yeah. That's what I thought. Mertz, this room is for couples only. Not for weirdo, lonely virgins like you."

A few people down the hall laughed. I wanted to rip his throat out. I wanted to push him off the balcony so he'd get impaled on the coat stand. But I didn't. Instead I just stood there, willing myself not to devolve into a full-blown panic attack as he put his bulky arm around me and escorted me down the hall.

"You just gotta loosen up, Mertz. It's a party." Then he grabbed my ass and squeezed really hard. Like, it hurt.

"*Stop!*" I pushed him away, and he immediately retreated playfully. Holding up his hands, making a big show for everyone waiting in line.

"Okay! Okay! Jesus! Don't Me Too me! I surrender!" He made mock prayer hands as he jogged down the stairs. More people laughed. Even some of the girls. The ones who didn't laugh just looked down at their shoes.

I went to the banister, breathing the way Beth taught me, and waited for it to pass.

This is how this shit happens. Chris grabs my ass. Then he says I'm a downer if I'm offended by what he just did. *Then*, for good measure, he throws in the Me Too movement and acts like a victim. The whole stunt was meant to make me feel like less of a person, while portraying him as just a fun, harmless guy. In less than a minute, he had prude-shamed me, gaslit me, and made a plea for misunderstood males everywhere. It was effective. And infuriating.

Luckily, I do some of my best work when I'm infuriated. Once my breathing returned to normal, I marched downstairs.

Fine. If I needed a hookup buddy to get into Chris's room, I'd get a hookup buddy.

I darted around looking for a mouth that was willing, then I spotted Sammi by the pool. Perfect. I'd feel safe making out with him, and there'd be no drama. I'd turned toward the back door when I bumped into . . . Avery. Of course I did. That stupid tree trunk of a torso was always getting in my way. He was there with Claire Jubell. I guess that made sense, since they're *"very good friends."* Something they both stressed to me multiple times. He was wearing a Planned Parenthood shirt and had his pockets turned inside out. She was dressed as a sexy elf, not sure why.

"You okay?" Avery asked.

"Yeah. Thanks," I said, keeping my eyes on Sammi. "Just . . . surprised to see you here."

"The gala ended early." He shrugged, and I could *almost* detect a tinge of resentment. But then he smiled, and he was back to his friendly, no-hard-feelings self.

Avery and I were due for a brief, awkward, exes-trying-to-act-cool run-in, and here it was. With the added bonus of an especially pretty Claire Jubell staring at me.

"Hey, Margot! Love that costume! It's so sad, though!" God. I must've really looked like that hiker.

"Yes . . . very sad . . . Well, nice to see you both," I said, turning to make my exit. "And great costumes. Sexy Elf and . . . the Defunding of Planned Parenthood?"

"Yup!" Avery smiled.

"That *is* pretty offensive," I said as I walked away.

Over my shoulder I could hear Claire say, "*That's* what you are?"

I went out to the patio. Sammi was on the other side of the pool, sipping a drink and watching beer pong. I whistled, then shouted, "Sammi!" waving him over to me. He waved back. I whistled again. He looked annoyed, but eventually walked over, his hands deep in his pockets.

"Yes?" he said curtly.

"What do you mean 'yes,' I need your help!" I whapped him on the arm, hoping to snap him out of it.

"Okay. Well, I'm on deck. Can I help you after I play?"

"Play what? What . . . beer pong?! You can't help me because you want to play beer pong!?" Someone sunk a ball, and everyone cheered.

"Yeah. That's why I was standing in the up-next circle. To play."

This was b-b-bonkers. Sammi didn't drink. He didn't play party games. And he didn't play party games where the point was to drink.

"I'm going to put a pin in how absurd that statement was, 'cause we have to go. We need to start making out. Like, now."

He suddenly got very quiet. "Okayyyy . . ."

"Great. This way!" I grabbed his hand, it felt tight and clammy. We made it back into the house, and I dragged him to the foyer, where he stopped suddenly.

"Wait," he said, now looking fully sober. He took off his hat, scratched his head. "Is this . . . what is this about? Are you just trying to get back at Avery?"

Avery was looking down on us from upstairs. Wait. *Was he in the hookup line? With Claire?* Okay. *Okay.* I guess I didn't need to pity Avery. He was doing *fine*.

I looked back to Sammi. Did I break down and finally tell him the truth about the job? Maybe now that I had been working on the case for a while, Shannon would loosen her "don't tell anyone else" rule. But . . . I couldn't just break it without talking to her first! I have a code. One that barely makes sense, especially since I'm the only one who knows about it. But codes are what separate us from the Chris Heinzes of the world. So I kept lying.

"Yes. I'm mad at Avery and I want to make him jealous," I said in a monotone, like I was reciting the state capitals. "But does it matter? Don't you want to make out with a girl before you go to college? Come on! It'll be fun!" He let go of my hand and stepped away.

"Naaaaah. That's okay," he said, slowly making his way back outside.

"Sammi! Come on! It's just . . ."

"Yeaaah . . . I don't want to do that . . . It's too weird. Sorry? Sorry."

He practically ran into the keg as he made his way back outside to his precious beer pong table. He kept looking back at me with a mix of horror and pity. And I guess I didn't blame him. Making out with Sammi would be like Frenching a cousin. Or a cherished childhood stuffed animal.[66]

---

66. I did it in fifth grade. To get some practice. It seemed harmless enough (albeit a bit fuzzy), but I could never look at Mr. Bear-Bottoms the same way.

Well, that backfired.

I scanned the living room. Sammi was out, but I still needed a mouth to drag into Chris's room. I spotted Cory and Ray, drunkenly shadowboxing by the refrigerator. I had spent enough time researching Cory (and, by extension, Ray) to know that even if they hadn't created RB, they still weren't top-shelf guys. I did not want to make out with either of them. But I forced myself to think of the greater good: Shannon, the Kelseys, Abby, Sara, Jess. They were all counting on me. And I was so close now. So I sucked it up and got ready to suck some mediocre face.

"Guys, guys, guys . . ." I stumbled over to them, making sure to use their big manly arms to steady myself. "I have a crazy idea. I have . . ." I pretended to lose my train of thought because I was sooooooo wasted.

"I got a number!" I shouted, 'cause drunk. "Whoever gets closest, we make out. Yeah? Yeah?" I punched them both. They both wobbled back, hitting the fridge before righting themselves. Cory burped, both eyes barely open. Yeesh.

"Okay, ready?"

"Ready!" Ray shouted. Cory just kind of stood there, willing himself not to fall over or puke.

"Okay, guess!"

"Twenty-five!" Ray declared, raising his hand (I guess to be called on?). I waited on Cory, who was trying very hard to respond.

"Allllll of themmmm . . ." Cory managed to get out.

"It was two! So Cory wins!" I figured Cory was the lesser of two evils. He'd probably pass out once he got into the room.

With Ray, I'd actually have to kiss his peach-flavored whiskey breath.

"But . . . wait! He didn't even . . ." Ray pleaded.

"He said all of them. Which is . . . you know . . . like, a good strategy," I said, taking Cory's arm and leading him away from Ray for maybe the first time tonight. Cory tripped at the top of the stairs. *Come on, buddy, make it to the bedroom, then you can go night-night.*

He eventually made it to his feet, and I used my body to support him as we walked down the hall to Chris's room. And suddenly his drunken hands were all over me. Feeling my waist, my butt, my boobs. He was breathing heavily down my neck. This is why I'd wanted Sammi. Behind every other guy, there was always this X factor you could never anticipate. Especially when drunk.

I grabbed his arms, and led him like a just-walking-infant down the hall. "Wait, wait, wait. All good boys who wait . . . get a little something at the gate!" Look, I'm bad at sexy talk. I know that sounded more like a nursery rhyme than a seductive come-on. But Cory seemed into it. He nodded. We cut the line and went straight for Chris's room.

John Pfeiffer was holding a baseball bat, which he was using to prod people in and out of the bathroom. As soon as we walked past him, he put his bat out like a parking gate, blocking us from entry.

"Whoa, whoa, whoa. Where are you two going?"

"To hook up! Duh! John, what are you doing? Why are you holding a baseball bat?"

"Chris made me the hookup monitor," he said proudly, flexing his bat. *The hookup monitor?* Where does Chris find these people? It was like all of Chris's friends were guards in the Stanford Prison Experiment.[67]

"Well, Chris said we could hook up in his room. So . . ." I lied, trying to push John aside. He didn't budge.

"Chris said that? About *you guys*?"

"He said we could cut the line because I did his math homework for him." Another lie.

"Come on, dude. Don't block a cock!" Cory added. Finally, an argument John found convincing. He moved the bat aside.

I led Cory into Chris's room and onto the bed. He plopped down with a thud. I couldn't bring myself to get on top of him, but I did play with his hair for a minute.

"I'm going to play some music," I said, and went over to Chris's computer. I'd hoped this would buy me enough time to rip off his hard drive using FAST-D.

"But . . . bed?" he said, sounding like a confused Frankenstein.

I plopped my butt into Chris's desk chair, linked up my external hard drive to his laptop. While I waited for it to download, I looked through Chris's desk for other evidence. But found only pens, a few loose vape cartridges, and an iPhone charger. Bust. When it was done, I unplugged my external, stuffed it in my shirt, and spun around to notice . . . silence. I was so focused on the task at hand that I hadn't noticed Cory had completely passed out in the bed. Hey, sometimes you catch a break.

---

67. Ahh, Stanford.

Then I jumped as a *bang! bang! bang!* reverberated through the room.

"You guys done!? 'Cause there's other people who wanna fuck out here!" It was John. Taking his duties as a sworn officer of hookups waaaaay too seriously.

The banging woke Cory. "What's—what's, uh . . ."

"Come on, Cory. Gotta go!" I said, hitting him with a pillow.

"Did we . . . uh?"

"Nope. No intercourse, you passed out drunk. And don't lie about it, because I recorded the whole thing on my phone," I lied.

"Wha? You did?" He got up slowly, then clutched his stomach, suddenly in pain. As I opened the door, Officer John was standing there, arms crossed. And that's when Cory bent over and threw up on Chris's rug.

Thank you, Cory, that was great. If you weren't so drunk and gross, I'd kiss you.

I exited quickly as John rushed in to deal with the situation. I ran down the stairs, shooting a text to my mom as I did. She said she'd be up all night if I needed a ride home.

When I got to the front door, I surveyed the party one last time. From my vantage, I had a clear view into the living room and kitchen. And I could see two distinct groups very clearly. The kitchen, where everyone was getting drunk slowly, enjoying each other's company and laughing. And the living room group, where everyone was getting drunk fast, hoping to join Cory in the puke club. In the kitchen I saw Avery, laughing, talking, pointing at a friend; and in the living room I saw Sammi, drinking from a SOLO cup, nodding his head. The past few months,

I'd spent more time with these two boys than I had with anyone else. Now . . . they were as distant as the rest of my classmates. Behind a glass for me to study.

When I left, neither of them even noticed.

April 11, 12:36 a.m.

MARGOT: you wont believe this but you will.

MARGOT: Chris Heinz groped my ass tonight.

MARGOT: Remember him?

MARGOT: Fucker.

MARGOT: I alwysy had this fantasy that if he ever dared try to touch me I'd like . . . punch him in the throat. Or tase his balls.

MARGOT: But I didn't. I just stood there. And then I almost had a panic attack. And then I did breathing thing you taught me so that I wouldn't. I dom't remember if it's supposed to be "in through your nose out through your nose" or "out through your mouth?" Since i cant' remember, I'm alternating every other breath. Good right? Take that, anxiety!

April 11, 12:42 a.m.

MARGOT: Sometimes I'm not as brave as I think I am.

20

Thank You, Godfather

By the time I got home, it was a little past one a.m. I was fried and in need of a shower, mainly to wash off whatever terrible cologne Cory was wearing. But I was desperate to look at Chris's hard drive. I hooked up my external, and it didn't take me long to find it: a file called "Ro-Bitches"[68] with all the different beta versions, pictures, scripts, code . . . everything I could ever want to prove Chris was behind the site. Success.

As I said, I'm not a master coder, but thankfully, this was in Python. And from what I could tell, it was pretty impressive. This was clean code, no Stack Overflow cut-and-pasting here—hell, it was even commented. Damn. Kyle and P-Boy had skills.

So now that the mystery of "who made the vile, woman-hating porn site" was solved, I moved on to the next phase, taking it down. Roosevelt Bitches could potentially be on three separate

---

68. Classy.

laptops (one each for Chris, Kyle, and P-Boy). Additionally, they could all be syncing to the server periodically. That meant to completely remove the site, I'd have to delete all three laptop copies and the server's copy *at the same time*. Otherwise, I'd just be Whac-A-Mole-ing the problem. This would be hard.[69] Like, explaining-TikTok-to-my-mom hard.

I heard garbage trucks coming down my street and I realized I'd stayed up literally all night. But I didn't feel tired. I felt amazing. It felt so good to finally get a break in this shit case and to be making actual progress. I had my hands around the neck of RB and soon, very soon, I would choke the life out of it.

According to WhatsApp, Shannon had not been active in fourteen days. So I texted to tell her I had a big update. She didn't respond. It made me realize I hadn't seen her in school in . . . a week? Or a month, possibly? Had she not been coming to school?

By text number five, she finally wrote back, and we made plans to meet up. Which was good, because aside from an update, I wanted to ask her again about bringing Sammi on board. I needed help and I thought I might have more luck if I asked her in person.

Shannon showed up at Greenbaum's around three thirty. She looked thinner, and her gorgeous naturally red hair was dyed brown. But it was her eyes that really worried me. They no longer had that scared, pleading, just-about-to-cry look. Now they looked empty. Like she wasn't really seeing me.

---

69. This doesn't even account for all the pictures that visitors have downloaded and have on their personal phones, computers, etc. But let's put a pin in that enormous clusterfuck for now.

I told her everything I'd learned so far. I thought she'd be happy. Instead she gave me "pretending to be happy." Head nods, forced smiles. Occasionally saying things like "Good."

"I have to ask you something," I said, picking at my rugelach. She nodded *okay*.

"The next phase of this job, it's going to be hard. I'm not even entirely sure how I'm going to do it. But it's going to require a lot of technical help. And I know you already said no, but—"

"No."

"Shannon, just—"

"No!"

"Sammi has been my trusted, loyal associate since I—"

"Margot! He's a guy!" she whisper-shouted, slamming her hand on the table. "You know how many random guys have texted me their junk? Or how many times I've heard 'Great tits, Shan!' in the halls? As if that's a totally normal thing to say *at school*? Men are fucking terrible. Okay?" Her eyes pooled with tears, then wandered away, and I wasn't sure if she was even still with me.

"I know this is upsetting. But I promise, Sammi is like a little brother. He—"

"So you think that means he doesn't look at porn? That he hasn't been to the site?"

I knew from having access to his hard drive that he *did* look at porn. But I also knew from said hard drive that he hadn't been on Roosevelt Bitches.

I sighed. The frustrating thing was I could hire Sammi, and Shannon would never even know. But *I* would know. And I couldn't break her trust. "Okay. I . . . I just had to ask. I'll . . . figure out another way."

She nodded. Looking down at the table, ripping up a napkin.

"How come I haven't seen you at school?" I asked, offering her a bite.

"I haven't really been going." She looked away. "It's kinda like, what's the point? I already got into college."

I nodded, but I wasn't really buying it. After a few seconds of napkin-fidgeting, she continued, "It's been hard, you know? I just don't really feel like being around people. Or talking to people. I quit social."

"I don't think you're missing much."

She smiled a little. "I can't wait to be done with this place."

I could sense she wanted to tell me more. Perhaps unburden herself. "Margot." She looked me in the eye for the first time that day. Then, with sincere concern, said, "Are *you* okay? I'm worried about you."

Was *I* okay? Shannon was the one with the sad eyes and the sad dye job! But then I caught a glimpse of myself in the cookie display glass and saw her point. I hadn't showered since before Chris's party. I still smelled like Cory's invasive cologne. Yeesh. Margot. You're a professional! Have some standards!

"I'm fine!" I assured her. "Just busy, that's all. This case has been . . . a lot." I grabbed my bag and stood. I had expected her to ask me for frequent updates now that the case had taken a turn. To encourage me to make Chris pay. But she just thanked me a couple times and quickly went out the side entrance.

When this case was over, and Chris and company were

thoroughly humiliated, I hoped that Shannon would return to her old self. Funny, outgoing, confident, silly. I hated seeing her so . . . withdrawn. Defeated. Like an adult who was jaded and let down by the world. I hoped this was something she could come back from.

It was spring break, so I didn't have to bother with school. And RB was thankfully quiet. The boys must have been busy on their fancy ski vacations. I sequestered myself in my room and made a nice little murder board that spanned an entire wall. I believed that once I made this big, elaborate map of the case, then, and only then, would I be able to figure out how to take down RB without Sammi's help. The murder board would reveal all!

But then . . . nothing. You see, the problem with my murder boards is that they never actually help. It's immensely satisfying to print out pictures, to tie string connecting those pictures. To look back at the whole, intricately designed mosaic and go "aha!" But that never happens. There's no "aha." Not once in two years. And this case was no exception.

Taking down the site wasn't going to be easy. Now that it was on Tor, it was untraceable. But I still had options. The easiest thing to do (which was not easy at all) was to figure out where the site was hosted (like GoDaddy or Wix or whatever) and call them, pretending to be Chris. I'd say, "Hi, it's me, the site's creator, and I'd like you to take my site down, thank you." Those places required like ten-step verification. I would need to know Chris's mom's maiden name and the last four digits of his social and his credit card and, probably, his childhood imaginary friend.

But if I successfully got GoDaddy or AWS or whoever to take down the site, there was still the matter of Chris and co.'s laptops. Those sync scripts would eventually run and reupload the site again. Anywhere. At any time. Which is why I needed to bring down the hosting account and laptops *at the same time*. And that's what I couldn't figure out how to do. Even with my useless murder board.

I spent the next seven days murder boarding and thinking and throwing pens at Mr. Bear-Bottoms. Occasionally I would take breaks to do exceedingly unimportant things, like doxing the crap out of Chris, Kyle, and P-Boy, signing them up for "Living with Erectile Dysfunction" support groups, and so on. But otherwise I was focused. I ignored all texts and calls, including two from the estranged men in my life: Sammi and Avery.

With Sammi, it was a no-brainer. I knew I owed him an apology for trying to make out with him. I just didn't really know what to say, and I was worried it might make things weird. So I figured I'd give him a little space, and he might forgive me on his own. He usually did.

With Avery . . . he hung up after one ring. I couldn't fathom why he called. Maybe he was still mad? Or maybe he was just being "nice" and seeing how I was doing? Or maybe he was pulling the "let's be friends, but really, let's get back together" reboot attempt?

I was ready to make a second murder board for that when he texted me back two minutes later:

> **AVERY:** Sorry. Butt dial.

Followed by a GIF of Sideshow Bob getting hit in the face with a rake.

ANYWAY, BY SATURDAY, I WAS NOT ANY CLOSER TO FIGURING OUT my "killing four birds with one stone" problem. I needed to think of an elegant solution, a silver bullet that would get at all those devices at once. But my stroke of genius kept eluding me. I was lying on the bed, my head hanging off the end so I could see my murder board upside down—you know, because then I'd solve it—when my mom pounded on my door. My parents had periodically knocked on my door throughout the week, usually at mealtimes, which I ignored. This time she shouted.

"*Margot!*"

"What?" I called back, my head a little foggy from being upside down for so long.

"It's Saturday Family Time!"

I had tried to hide the breakup with Avery from my parents. But they sniffed it out pretty quickly and reinstated Family Time with a vengeance.

"*Family night! Movie time!*" my mom squawked, opening the door and aggravating my growing headache.

"Can't, Mom. I got a, uh . . ." and then I pointed to the murder board. My mom looked at it, then me, unimpressed.

"You can take a break. Your psychology project will still be here tomorrow."

Normally, I'd offer more resistance. But this was getting pathetic. I mean what was I gonna do, redo my murder board for the seventh time?

Tonight's family-night-movie-time movie was *The Godfather*. It's one of my dad's all-time favorites, and ever since I can remember he's wanted to show it to me. So this was a big night for him.

The whole movie, he pointed out how "good" and "important" *The Godfather* was by saying things like, "Look at this scene!" "Look at the lighting in that shot!" "Ah! Classic!" This was followed by my mom either shushing him or asking, "Now, who's that again?" even though she has seen this movie herself at least five times. This is a pretty typical movie night at my house.

If you haven't seen *The Godfather*, it's this old movie from the '70s about a mafia family. Don Corleone, this old guy with jowls for days, is the head of the family.[70] It's super long and surprisingly violent. Brando was good, I guess, but I couldn't understand what the hell he was saying most of the time. He was doing this "voice" that sounded like my nana. The rest of the actors were good, and I liked the soundtrack a lot. But there were, like, no women in this movie. Well, scratch that, there were *three*. And one of them doesn't talk. *Ever!* So yeah, it didn't exactly pass the Bechdel test or anything. But it was fine. Not "the best movie ever made," as my dad kept proclaiming, but . . . fine.

But even I will admit, the end of the movie is great. There's

---

70. In a twist, Corleone is played by a now unrecognizable Marlon Brando (my longshoreman crush). I was sad to see that the years had not been kind.

this big, dramatic sequence where the main character, Michael, consolidates power by wiping out his competition. And the clever part is, he does it during his niece's christening. He's standing up on the altar with the priest, watching this little baby get baptized, meanwhile these goons he hired are brutally murdering people all over the city. One guy gets machine-gunned in bed. Another gets shot in the eye. *Bang! Bang! Bang!*

Bang! I stood up in the middle of the room.

"I need goons!" I cried aloud. Then I caught myself. My parents were staring at me like I was Fredo advocating for Moe Greene.[71]

So I said, "Great movie, Dad! Thanks for showing this to me!" My dad was so happy I liked his favorite movie that he forgot all about my "goons" outburst. I mean, I might never have to take out the trash again.

I sat back down, similarly happy. I finally had the answer. Goons! I needed my own Corleone-esque goons! I would close Chris's hosting account myself while hired goons crippled Kyle's, P-Boy's, and Chris's computers. *And we'd do it all at the exact same time.* Mafia style. In an instant, it would simply cease to exist. It wasn't elegant, it wasn't a silver bullet. It was scrappy. It was old school. Goons!

Shannon said I couldn't hire guys, but she didn't say anything about finding some willing *female* accomplices.[72] And I didn't think I'd have any problem finding some capable, trustworthy women who'd like to take an ax to those guys' computers.

---

71. *Godfather* reference. Basically, they thought I was nuts.

72. Female goons, or foons, if you will.

That night I slept better than I had in months, with only one single thought swirling around my brain:

Gotta get me some goooooooons . . .

April 18, 1:02 a.m.

MARGOT: Had a big break in the case!

MARGOT: Finally. Cracked it! RELIEF!

April 18, 1:07 a.m.

MARGOT: Sorry, I know you're probably with one of your ten boyfriends now doing something fun. I just needed to tell somebody. CAUSE I WAS REALLY STRESSING ABOUT IT! CAUSE I HAVE NO REAL LIFE JUST WORK!

MARGOT: RELIEF!

April 18, 10:00 a.m.

MARGOT: remember that time we went to church with your aunt and we started laughing at the priest guy? (deacon?) and the woman in front of us shushed us and you said, "i'm so sorry, jesus" to her? good times.

21

A Blye in the Ointment

Gooooooonnnnnsssss!

Monday morning, from my usual desk in the library, I was thinking about who I could recruit when my phone pinged. And I realized, why go on a goon hunt when I could just let the goons come to me?

> **CHUGG:** hey did you hear Tasha Ahmadi's bf broke up with her? He said he couldn't handle her being on RB. Dick.

The Kelseys. Of course. Sure, they were freshmen. But they were also energetic, smart, and fiercely loyal. Plus they were both victims of the site. I was certain they would be properly pissed off and motivated.

The bell rang. MCYF office hours were over. I texted the Kelseys back and asked if we could talk on the phone. They both sent the same meme of an old man stroking his chin, with the chyron INTRIGUED. Jesus, Kelseys, the same meme? Maybe they *were* the same person.

I scooped up my laptop and notebooks and shoved them into my bag. Then I made like Abby and practically ran to fifth period. I got seated in econ just before the bell rang. We were having a quiz I hadn't studied for, so I needed to cram in the five minutes Mr. Peletti used to take attendance and talk about his kid's basketball game. (You could almost always get Mr. Peletti off topic by talking about his kid. The one weakness of an otherwise excellent teacher.)

"Hey, Mr. Peletti! I heard Brighton got trounced in the game last night," I said, baiting him.

Mr. Peletti's eyes lit up. His daughter played for Penbrook, which had dominated Brighton's weak defense and won in a landslide, per Google. But before he could even start his recap, he was interrupted by, "Uh, Mr. Peletti? Principal Palmer needs to see Margot." I looked up. Sammi was standing at the door. Sheepishly pulling me from class for no doubt bogus reasons. We did this from time to time, but only for MCYF work, and only when it was really necessary. We didn't want to draw attention to the fact that we were skipping class and had a seemingly endless supply of hall passes.

If I left now, Mr. Peletti would make me take the quiz after school, and I didn't have time for that. I gave Sammi a very purposeful "not now" stink eye. He responded with a "too late, I already gave him the hall pass" shrug. If he was doing this just so we could talk about what happened at Chris's party, I was going to strangle him.

I pushed back again, this time actually speaking: "Are you sure Principal Palmer needs me *now*? And that this couldn't wait until after class?" Mr. Peletti raised an eyebrow. Sammi looked peeved. This was a surefire way to blow up our "forged hall pass" scheme.

"Nope. He said it has to be now. Sorry, Margot," he said with "just get your ass out here before we both get suspended" disdain. Mr. Peletti crossed his arms and sucked in his cheeks. I gave in.

"Okay. Mr. Peletti, I doubt this will take too long. So hopefully, I'll be able to come back and—"

"See you after school, Mertz."

I picked up my things and followed Sammi out of class, ready to lay into him about the importance of not abusing our forged hall passes. My lips pursed to make the "you" sound in "You can't just pull me out of class whenever you want!" But instead they said, "Bah!" As in "Bah, what the hell are you doing here, Mrs. Blye?!" Because she was standing right in front of me. Hugging herself. Eyes bulging.

"There's another picture!" she cried. Whisper-shouting in my face. "You didn't get them all. There's another one!"

"What are you talking about? You hired us to remove one picture of you and Mr. Frange, and that's what we did," I said, now defensive.

"But there's still—" She did a little circle around herself, throwing her hands up in the air. She was in full martyr mode.

"Mrs. Blye. Can you maybe calm down and explain to me what's going on?" I checked in with Sammi. He rolled his eyes.

Apparently whatever the issue was, it did not justify the drama Mrs. Blye was serving us.

"There is another picture on my computer! Somehow! If it's about money, you can charge me again. I don't care."

Justin Chen walked by. A freshman with big, thick glasses whose aura screamed "future middle management." We all stopped as he slowly passed us in the hall. Justin looked back, realizing we had stopped talking just for him. I think this made him nervous, yet his pace remained the same, taking him an eternity to walk to the end of the hall and out of sight.

"Okay. I don't understand. Where did this picture come from?"

Mrs. Blye took a big, annoyed breath and straightened her blazer before more calmly explaining the situation. "Last night my husband and I were playing Legends of Langloss. Which is . . . a very complicated and weird board game. But we're both making an effort to show interest in each other's hobbies."

"Okay," I said. Why was everyone doing that lately? Ugh. Marriage did not appeal to me.

"We were playing in the living room, and Toby had set up the Apple TV so that it showed pictures from his computer. Both our computers. I don't know how he does it, but it's like . . . random pictures of us all the time." I nodded yes, fully aware of what a screensaver was. "So we're playing his game, and right as I'm about to get a corset scepter, a picture pops up. On TV. Of Josh Frange's . . . genitals."

She took a break from her story to pace back and forth and wave her hands in the air. "On my TV! I screamed, Margot! Right in the middle of the game! Toby turned around and, thank god, the picture had changed, and all he saw was a selfie from our honeymoon! But still! I can't have that happening again."

I looked to Sammi, whose bored, blasé look meant the problem was what I thought it was. A very easy one to fix. "Mrs. Blye, let me just back up so I understand. Did Josh Frange at some point send you a dick pic? Recently, or—"

"It was from that karaoke night. I told him never to do it again. I hate those kinds of things . . ." She trailed off in disgust.

"Okay. But then, somehow, you saved it?"

"Apparently! I did! By accident. I thought I had deleted it, but—"

"Okay, hold on, we'll get to that," I said, trying to keep focus on the timeline of events. "So you saved it, by accident. Then it popped up on your Apple TV last night, as the screensaver was randomly slideshowing every photo in your iPhotos."

"Yes. I guess."

"Is it still there?"

"I don't know. I deleted it last night as soon as I got a chance. From My Photo Stream, my computer. I even checked Toby's computer."

"Then you're fine. The photo is deleted, and it won't show up on your TV again."

"But the photo could be *in* my TV!" she said way too loudly.

"No, it can't," I said. Sammi shrugged.

"It really can't, Miss Blye," he agreed. (Sammi was one of those boys who called every female teacher Miss Something.)

She tapped her foot nervously and looked around. She either

didn't believe us or thought we were being lazy. "I want you to look at the TV. And I want you to wipe it, just to be safe!"

I had a rule that I wouldn't ever bill clients for frivolous charges. Especially when it came to technical aspects of the job a client wouldn't understand. I could easily charge a computer-illiterate adult a "micro-processing digital scrubbing service outlet fee." Which is nonsense. But I wouldn't. Because we were running an ethical business, and it was paramount that our clients trusted us.

But Mrs. Blye was making it very hard not to break that rule.

"Mrs. Blye, it's really simple—"

"Look, I didn't hire you to give me a goddamned lecture. Are you going to fix this for me or not?"

You couldn't reason with her. Which meant Sammi and I were going to have to spend the rest of our day at Mrs. Blye's house pretending to fix her "TV problem" just so she'd leave us alone. I gave up and told her what she wanted to hear.

"Okay. We'll do it. It's possible that if the d-pic showed up on your TV, it has refragmented. Basically copying itself dozens of times, often in cloaked, phantom Zip drives that are very hard to find."

Mrs. Blye looked ashen. *It was worse than she'd imagined.* Sammi bit his lip at the pure drivel coming out of my mouth.

"So what are you saying? The pictures have . . . multiplied?"

"Possibly. If that's happened, we can find them all. Sammi is kind of an expert in phantom file detection. But it'll take time, and he'll have to use a special 'input defragmenting' program he developed himself."

Mrs. Blye nodded her head. Angry, but relieved that I gave her a complicated-sounding solution to her nonexistent problem.

Mrs. Blye signed us out of school. A reward, she told the secretary, for our excellence in this year's county science fair. Which was sort of true. Sammi's project on solar power earned him an honorable mention at this year's fair. And I supported Sammi emotionally in his efforts to create a solar panel. We followed Mrs. Blye to her car and sat silently through the ten-minute drive to her house, during which we texted each other in the back seat.

> **SAMMI:** how exactly am I going to find all these "cloaked phantom files" on Mrs. Blye's computer?

> **MARGOT:** I know

> **SAMMI:** broke ur own rule! this is such an easy fix! why are we going to her house?

> **MARGOT:** Because you need to infiltrate her computer's core rumbus to remove the phantoms!

We both stifled laughs. Mrs. Blye glared at us from the rear-view like we were two troublemakers on a field trip. Which, technically, we were. I shot off one more text before pocketing my phone.

> **MARGOT:** Just go into her desktop and mess around till you're bored.

She pulled up to a surprisingly palatial Tudor and let us

in the front door. Inside, it smelled and looked like a Williams Sonoma. Sammi and I looked at each other like, "Damn, what does Toby Blye do?"

Mrs. Blye prompted us to take off our shoes before looking down at the shoe caddy and gasping, "Oh my god. He's *home!*"

"Gosh, I hope *he's* not having an affair. Though that would be ironic," I replied out loud, and not in my head as I should have. Mrs. Blye looked furious. "Sorry. Bad joke. I was just trying to cut the tension."

Sure enough, we could hear the TV in the living room.

"I'll talk to Toby and keep him distracted while you bring Sammi to your computer so he can detrix the phantom files," I told her.

"But you said it was a two-person job!" I had said that. 'Cause I felt like messing with her.

"We don't have a choice now. Sammi, do you think you can do this on your own?"

"I did a detrixing job last week on a similar system. I can't promise anything, but I think with a little luck . . . I'll find your phantom files," Sammi said with the cheesy seriousness of an actor in a Lifetime movie. I was so close to laughing. It was a relief to see him playing along. Like maybe my awkward make-out attempt hadn't ruined things.

We were about to break when Toby Blye rounded the staircase and greeted us.

"I thought I heard you!" he said.

"Hey, babe," Mrs. Blye said, going in for a hug.

"No! No hugs!" he cried. "I'm super sick!"

That much was obvious to me. He was wearing pajamas and had a blanket draped over his shoulders.

"Sorry!" He sniffed. "You're home early."

"I'm taking two of my students out to lunch. They won the Annover prize[73] for chemistry at the science fair this year and I forgot my wallet. Have you seen it?" Toby looked around the living room.

"Uh. No. Sorry." He sneezed into his arm.

"Sorry. We both really need to use the bathroom!" I blurted.

Toby apologized and guided us to the half bath by the kitchen, which I darted into so that Sammi would have to go upstairs and use the other bathroom. Mrs. Blye followed Sammi upstairs to "look for her wallet." I fake-peed for a few minutes, then exited to find Toby still standing in the kitchen, waiting for a kettle to boil. I knew I had to keep him occupied, so I asked him about something that was sure to keep him gabbing. I had been around my fair share of nerds. Sammi was an über-nerd. Even *I* had dabbled in *GoT* fan fiction back in eighth grade. So I knew that if you asked a nerd even one question about their nerdy specialty, they would talk your ear off with no regard to your waning interest.

"So Mrs. Blye tells me you're really into role-playing board games?"

Toby looked surprised, then responded in a way that truly shocked me. "Wow. Karen told you that? Okay. Well . . . it is a passion of mine, but if you're not into gaming, most people find it a little . . ." He made a motion like he fell asleep.

---

73. I'm really killing it at Annover this year!

He wasn't taking the bait. What was his deal?

He went on. "So you won a science award? That's exciting."

"Yeah," I lied. "I enjoy science. I'll probably major in it in college."

"You know where you want to go?"

"Stanford," I answered a little too quickly/forcefully. I was a nerd for Stanford.

"Good school." He smiled, pouring some boiling water in his cup. "So what do you want to do? Research? Find the cure for cancer?"

"Computers, actually."

"Ah. So you're going to invent the next Facebook or something?"

"I would never create the next Facebook. It's undermining our democracy. Mark Zuckerberg is a sociopath."

"Right." He laughed, dunking his tea bag into his cup. "Well, maybe you could be more like, uh . . . Sheryl Sandberg?"

"If I didn't want to be Mark Zuckerberg, why would I want to be his employee?" I scoffed at him.

"I don't know! Didn't she do that whole 'lean in' thing?"

"Yeah. Great. But why didn't she lean in when Facebook started hosting white supremacist pages? Why didn't she lean in when Facebook started a genocide in Myanmar? Where's the leaning, Sheryl?" In case you can't tell, I hate Sheryl Sandberg.

"Okay! Okay! I surrender! I'm an orthodontist! I can barely email! I'm clearly out of my league!"

Toby was not what I expected. The way Mrs. Blye described him, he was an overbearing nerd who didn't listen to her. I also expected him to be kind of an uggo, but he wasn't. His hair was thinning, but he was cute, with boyish features, unblemished white skin (even while sick!), and piercing blue eyes. He seemed to be in moderately good shape. (All the married men I know give up and get dad bods.) But more than that, he seemed kind and was genuinely interested in what I was doing. It made me feel good about helping Mrs. Blye. She had been annoying, but if what I did helped them stay together . . . well, bully for me!

We talked easily about high school, Stanford (his ex-girlfriend went there), how baffled he was that teenagers still watched and liked *Friends*. (I was equally baffled. *Friends* is old and homophobic.) And before I knew it, Sammi and Mrs. Blye were back in the kitchen. She waved her wallet at us.

"Oh, good! You found it!" Toby smiled.

"Yes! It was behind my desk, I must have knocked it over or something."

"Great. And you found the bathroom okay?"

I realized that Sammi had been gone a while. "Sammi has to give a speech at the Annover award ceremony tomorrow. And when he's nervous he gets diarrhea, so . . ." I said, smiling. The "job" was done, so I could mess with him a little by giving him an unnecessarily gross lie.

Sammi gritted his teeth and responded with "Yes. Sorry. I had nervous diarrhea. So . . . that's where I was."

We all sat in the awkward silence till Toby mercifully said, "Hey. Happens to the best of us!"

After a few more minutes of polite chitchat (during which Sammi snuck away again and held his phone up to the TV like an ultrasound wand to "wipe de-matrixed photo files from the terminal"), we left. Mrs. Blye took us to Chipotle as a thank-you for our hard work.

Sammi and I skipped eighth and ate our burritos in the tech booth. For a moment my mind wandered to Avery. On his list of noodles, he put "rice" as number eight. He said it's technically a noodle, and I said that makes him technically the most ignorant man I've ever met.

Why was I thinking about Avery now? Our "relationship" was over, so why was he interfering with my enjoyment of rice? Or as he calls it, "a very short and compact noodle." Ugh. No. I pushed him to the back of my brain and shoved burrito into the back of my throat as Sammi told me about his time with Mrs. Blye. How he poked around her laptop and said things like, "The corrupted file is fragmented all over your computer!" while furiously pretending to zap the pictures one by one. Every once in a while, jobs were actually fun, and Sammi and I would spend all night after a case trading stories and laughing.

The final bell rang. We threw away our burrito wrappers, went down the ladder, and were about to part ways when I felt a tension. We hadn't actually talked since Chris's party, and I felt like I owed him an explanation.

"Sammi. Wait. About Chris's party. And, uh—"

"I guess you were upset about Avery and Claire, huh?"

No, I was not. At all. "Yeah. Kinda. It was just so soon and I—"

"I get it. That sucks," he said, seemingly fine now with our whole encounter. He smirked. "It's funny, I kinda thought you liked him that day he offered to give us a ride. So I wasn't surprised when I heard you were going out. But still . . . Avery's not who I ever pictured you with."

"Why? Because he's not my type at all and he's very bland and boring?" I offered.

"No, you just kinda hate rich people."

"I do not *hate* them. I think they're soft."

"Okay." After a pause, he added, "Maybe I don't actually know your type, anyway."

"I don't know if *I* know." In order to know your type I think you have to date a cross section of people over a period of time. And I had dated . . . no one. "But if anyone would know, it's you. You know me better than anyone."

Kids were racing out of classrooms. Desperate to go home or to their after-school activities. I was about to say bye and head over to Mr. Peletti's for my makeup quiz when Sammi took off his hat and scratched his head. It seemed like something was bothering him.

"You okay, Sammi?"

"No, I'm great. I just . . ." Sammi looked down at his feet when he said, "Do you . . . wanna go to prom? With me?"

22

The Ten Things I Need to Know About Chris

I'll admit. I was taken aback.

Sammi was asking me to prom? *My* Sammi? The guy who spent homecoming doing a WoW raid, even though he wasn't especially into WoW and considered it an "entry-level game."

Sammi knew my feelings about school dances. They are clichéd and pointless and rife with tackiness. The ill-fitting formalwear and the terrible food. The bumping and grinding, and the pit-stained tuxes. The bootlegged liquor and the teachers on chaperone duty wearing old bridesmaids' dresses. How could anyone seriously want to attend an event where Chris Heinz was going to be the GD DJ? (The rumors were true. They were letting that dipshit DJ.) No! Never. My ears were bleeding just thinking about it! Plus every idiot in school would be there.

Every idiot in school would be there.

Of course. In order to kill Roosevelt Bitches, I needed to

find a time when Chris, Kyle, and P-Boy would all be together, away from their computers and ideally distracted. I wasn't going to find a better time than prom, when they'd all be in the same place and hopefully very drunk. And if Chris was on DJ duty, that meant he'd have his computer with him! It was too perfect. Damn it. I realized, for the sake of the case, even though I'd hate it, I needed to go to prom!

But I couldn't just go to the senior prom by myself. I wasn't a senior. And if I showed up alone, I was sure to get comments like "I thought Margot hated dances" and "Why are you here?" and "You're not going to *Carrie* us, are you?" Going with Sammi would be the ultimate cover.

Still, it felt a little strange to be Sammi's "date." And maybe he sensed my hesitation, because Sammi blurted out, "Look. This was a bad idea. It's just that my mom wants me to go, and it would make her happy if I did something normal like this. And you seemed like someone who I could go with who wouldn't make a big deal about it, and maybe we'd even have fun, like the time we dressed up to go to Sbarro."

"Oh my god. I totally get it," I replied, relieved that the idea had originated with his mom and not, like . . . his own feelings. So I didn't need to feel any leading-him-on type guilt. "Yeah. I think it will be fun."

"Really?"

"Seriously. I'm in," I said, trying to sound as platonic as possible before punching him in the arm. "Let's get the bastards! Huh!"

I turned abruptly and walked away. Sammi looked like he

wasn't entirely sure what I meant by "Let's get the bastards!" And to be honest, I wasn't either. But I thought making a strong declaration was important so that he knew that I wasn't weirded out by his prom-asking. Which I mostly wasn't. I don't think.

Anyway, thanks to Sammi's impromptu promposal, I now had a time and a place where I would enact my RB-deleting plan: Prom. May 1. The date had a certain ring to it. Was May 1 a famous historical battle or something? Or was it Easter? Easter really gets around.

Next, I needed to enlist my goons. After Mr. Peletti's makeup test, which was drawn directly from the textbook and thus pretty easy, I called Kelsey Chugg. After swearing her to secrecy, I asked if she'd like to partake in a little subterfuge against the creators of RB. The answer was a resounding yes from *both* Kelseys (because Hoffman was at Chugg's house when I called, because . . . seriously, they're the same person).

I walked them through my plan to bring down the site, which for now I was calling OPERATION . . . REVERSE GENIUS BAR (I don't know. I'm still workshopping the name).

I would go to prom, disguised as a girl named Margot who was actually happy to be going to the prom. I'd wait for Chris to leave his laptop unattended while he . . . got drunk and hit on a chaperone or whatever, then I'd casually walk by his DJ booth and plug in an electromagnet to the booth power strip. This would render Chris's computer a three-pound aluminum brick, no longer capable of revenge porn or terrible playlists. I would then retreat to the bathroom, where I would delete RB from the cloud using my phone. (It turns out RB was still being hosted by AWS. Amazon took it down when I flagged it, but Chris got it back up on a Tor server at AWS using a different account. Using the same host again just seemed lazy! But whatever.)

"Really? You're just going to delete RB where it's hosted? Won't that be, like, hard?" Chugg asked.

Yes. Yes it would. Did I need to tell the Kelseys how hard it would be? No. No I didn't. But did I tell them anyway, because I wanted them to know how good I was? Yes. I did.

So I explained how I planned to delete RB from AWS, and how, in order to do that, I needed ten pieces of verification information. Ten. And I needed them all at once, because the whole process is timed. You only have four minutes to get to the end or it *locks you out*. If you answer incorrectly more than three times *total*, it *locks you out*. I know. It's all very *Mission Impossible*. Which brings us to . . .

THE TEN THINGS I NEED TO KNOW ABOUT CHRIS HEINZ BEFORE I CAN CANCEL CHRIS HEINZ . . .

1. His phone number
2. His email
3. His AWS password
4. His AWS Account ID
5. The last four digits of his social
6. The last four digits of the credit card he used to open the account

And the answers to four security questions:

7. What's your mother's maiden name?

8. What's the name of your childhood pet?

9. What elementary school did you attend?

10. Who was your first kiss?

"Jesus," said Hoffman.

"I know. It's very tedious. And personal!" I said. "*Your first kiss?* Why not just ask, *When's the first time you felt shame?* or *How many times have you cried in public?*"

"I can't believe you're going to do all that," Chugg fawned.

They were impressed. They should be. I'm very cool.

"We don't have to do all that to the other guys' computers, do we?" Chugg asked.

"Yeah . . . what exactly are we doing?" Hoffman added.

Right. I hadn't gotten to their part yet. "So I'm going to give you each a burner. Once I destroy Chris's computer and delete the site from AWS, I will text you. At that point, you will . . . somehow get access to both Kyle's and P-Boy's laptops and destroy them. I suggest a power drill, three quick holes should do it. But I'm open to other suggestions."

"And what about all the other pics? Like, when dudes visit the site, can't they download stuff? How do we get those?" Hoffman asked.

"I do have a tentative plan for those . . ." I didn't, but they didn't need to know that. "But what's important for now is that we cut off the snake's head. Then we'll worry about . . . rounding up all the snake babies and . . . killing them, too. The pictures. The pictures are snake babies and—"

"I get it," Hoffman said, mercifully cutting me off.

"We are so gonna nard those douchebags," Chugg added. "Seriously, thank you so much for letting us help you in all this. I feel so freaking . . . empowered!" She had recently discovered coffee.

"Glad to hear it," I said. "Honestly, I was worried you might be a little hesitant to, you know, commit a misdemeanor. But I'm glad to see that doesn't bother you."

"Nah. I just wish I could put the drill to their nuts, ya know?" Hoffman said so casually I really couldn't tell if she was joking. A little scary, but clearly I picked some good goons.

BY THE TIME I GOT OFF THE PHONE WITH THE KELSEYS, I HAD blown past dinner, which my parents didn't even bother to tell me about because they knew I was busy. I heated up a bowl of salty-and-bad-for-me-but-so-good-and-cheap mac 'n' cheese, brought it to my desk, and got to internet-ing. I had a lot of work to do if I was going to get the verification answers I needed. No day like tonight.

Some of the necessary info I had already, like Chris's email and phone number. Even the last four digits of his social. I was able to find his AWS password *and* Account ID because they had been saved in his computer's autofill. The last four digits of the credit card were a little tougher. But then I realized he only had one credit card. I found a paperless statement in his email that had the account number x-ed out. But lucky for me, the last four digits were not! I was getting more confident. I had six out of ten!

To find his elementary school, I went on Chris's mom's

Facebook page. Lucky for me, she was an avid Facebooker, so if you scrolled back long enough (and it was loooooong, she posted *a lot* of pics of herself drinking wine), you got to Chris in elementary school. It was named, and I'm not kidding, Walt Disney Elementary, which is a real name of a real school in our district. (Sadly, WD Elementary is not magical or fun. According to the PTA's Facebook page, it has a mold problem.)

For his mom's maiden name, I signed into Chris's AncestryDNA account. It's one of those DNA testing kits that's supposed to *help you connect with your roots*. Apparently everyone in the Heinz family got it for Christmas last year. His password and username was in an email from his mom, which went as follows.

MOM: Chris. Here's a link to the DNA service your father got us for xmas! You should really check it out, it's fascinating! I'm 22% dutch! Who knew? I set up your account for you. Username: ChrisHeinz Password: ChrisHeinzis#1!!! But feel free to change the password if you think that's too obvious or just don't like it!
CHRIS: K.

(Two months later)

MOM: Chris did you ever sign into the account! It's really interesting. Love you, hun! You're #1!

End of thread.

As far as I could tell, Chris never actually used his Ancestry-DNA account, *but I sure did!* From there, it was pretty easy to find that Chris's mom's maiden name was Powers. (Way better name than Heinz!) Also, he is 11 percent Coptic Egyptian!

It was getting late, and I knew that questions 8 and 10, the "first pet" and "first kiss," would require some recon with actual humans. So I dropped into bed, my brain asleep before I hit the mattress, hoping that four hours was all I needed to stay sharp for school the next day.

IT WASN'T. I WAS GROGGY AND HAD A HEADACHE AS I SPOTTED Shontae Williams during fourth-period lunch the next day.

Shontae was sitting with her normal crew, Theater Nerds 1, 2, and 3. (Shontae was their leader, I assumed because she was cast as Zoe in *Dear Evan*[74] while TNs 1, 2, and 3 were cast as "auxiliary offstage singers.")

I unceremoniously pulled up a seat, unwrapping my Lärabar next to their bag lunches mid-meal. "Shontae!" I said cheerily, as though I'd slept eight hours that night. "Also everyone else! How is everyone? How's your lunch?" The nerds all looked concerned. I had not, to the best of my knowledge, ever spoken to any of them.

Shontae responded cautiously with, "Hey, Margot. We're . . . good."

"Fantastic. I'm good, too. I'm so happy we're all good," I said,

---

74. *Dear Evan* is the official title of Ms. Corman's unofficial one-act adaptation of *Dear Evan Hansen*. Tickets are still available for all shows!

shoving the Lärabar in my mouth. "Well, now that we've got-ten the small talk out of the way, Shontae, would you mind if I asked you a random but hopefully not too personal question?" Shontae checked in with her nerds. They seemed concerned, but too polite to say anything, and instead stared at their multigrain sandwiches.

"I . . . guess . . . ?" Shontae ventured.

"Chris Heinz said he dated you in the sixth grade and that you were his first girlfriend. Is that true?"

"Uh . . . yeah. But you know, it was middle school. And it only lasted like a few weeks, and we barely saw each other." She was obviously embarrassed by the connection and trying to down-play it. Good for her.

"Totally! Middle-school boyfriends! There's nothing like them!" I said, clearly having never had a boyfriend in middle school or ever.[75] "And so, is it safe to assume that while dating Chris, you guys . . . kissed?"

Shontae responded with a barely audible "Uh . . ." before I barreled ahead with "Sorry, I know! This just keeps getting weirder and weirder! And, yes, I could explain why I'm asking you these questions, but why? It would only make this take lon-ger and no one wants that. Amirite?" I said, nudging Nerd #2, who did not appreciate the nudge. I was definitely riding high on my three cups of coffee (one cup for every hour of sleep I'd missed).

"So . . . if you could just answer my question, I'll leave you

---

75. Except Avery, I guess. Though that was for work. And Davey Ruttura, if you count fifth grade. (I don't.)

alone and we can all get back to our separate lives. At most nodding to each other as we pass in the halls."

"Yeah. We kissed. One time," she blurted out, hoping it would put an end to my blabbering.

"Great. So you were Chris's first kiss! That is all I needed to know! Thank you, Shontae!" I said, lifting my tush off the hard plastic seat.

"Oh. Well, no. Not technically," Shontae said. I let gravity bring my butt back down.

"What do you mean not technically?" I asked.

"It's just that . . . he told me the first girl he ever kissed was Melissa McNall. In the second grade. I mean, I don't know if this is true, but apparently a group of kids dared Chris to kiss Melissa. So eventually he did. And she was like, 'Yuck! Chris! You're so gross!' and she ran away. And everyone laughed. And then he started crying and, like . . . ran home."

"Chris told you that?" Nerd #3 asked, seemingly as surprised as I was that Chris was once a child and not a monster.

"Yeah. I know. But in sixth grade Chris wasn't . . . the way he is now. He was actually kinda sweet. It was before he got hot."

"I guess puberty did a number on him." All the nerds nodded, though I couldn't tell if they were thinking, *Yeah, he's such a dick now* or *Yeah, his body is so hot now.* It's kind of the same face.

"Well, thank you for your time!" I said, leaping out of my seat and spinning around a little too dramatically. I was nine-tenths of the way to my goal!

Next, I wanted to track down Charlotte Sheffield, who was Chris's next-door neighbor. I was hoping she could help me with the whole first pet thing. If I hurried, I could catch her on her way to fifth-period biology. I shuffled toward the back exit of the cafeteria, hoping to evade the hall monitor stationed at the front. But unfortunately, that meant I had to walk by the Trees for Frees club, which had commandeered the corner table by the door. And which included, of course, Claire Jubell and Avery Green.

By the time I realized, it was too late. There was no way to avoid them. I'd have to at least say hello.

"Hey, guys! What brings you to the cafeteria!?" I asked.

"Food. Mostly," Avery said. "But also ambiance. I don't know, I've always kind of loved the vinyl tile floors, the faint smell of old ketchup." He had erased the awkwardness of my question with his charm and good nature. Man, he *was* good at being an ex-boyfriend.

But then no one said anything. And *then* Claire and I did that regrettable thing where you both start talking at the same time, then apologize for talking at the same time, then try to talk again, and it feels like you're in a spiral of sputtering politeness that will go on forever.

"So are you—"

"Well, I should—"

"Oh! Sorry!"

"No, I'm sorry! You go!"

"No. You. Seriously. I'm so sorry."

This was followed by like five seconds of silence after which Claire bravely broke the cycle and said, "I was just going to say, I can't wait to see you this weekend! At Gaetano's!" She smiled.

Oh, right! Claire's birthday. I'd assumed I was disinvited after dumping Avery. But to Claire's credit, I wasn't. Classy. Still, I let her off the hook.

"Oh. Sorry. I can't. I forgot I have a . . . work obligation."

At the mention of work, Avery looked at me and almost, *almost*, scoffed. But he immediately turned it into a kind of sigh and then turned and waved to some other table.

"Oh, no!" she said, in a tone so sincere I couldn't tell if she was actually relieved (which she should've been! I would have made her birthday very awkward!).

"I know. It sucks. But thanks again for the invite. Really. It was very nice of you." It was. Claire, as far as I could scrutinize, was just a nice person. But as nice as she was, I had to extract myself from this thruple in the making before it got more uncomfortable. "Well, hopefully I'll see you guys around at . . . the cafeteria. Or in the halls. Or the prom."

"Oh! Cool! You're going!" Claire interjected, surprised but happy.

What had possessed me to say prom?

"Obviously, it's weird I'm going. But I am. Yes. I am going to the prom."

"Drop the 'the,'" Avery said. "Nobody under forty says *the* prom." Was I getting cool lessons from dad-talking Avery Green? Was the world *upside down*?

"Good advice. Gotta blend in with the youth! Aaaaand . . . I'll see you around, guys!"

And with that, I finally left their table.

"Great! And hopefully we'll see you at prom!" Claire said.

We'll see you at prom? Were they going together? I looked back at them. Their body language was unclear. They weren't holding hands, but they *were* sharing food. But good friends do that, right? I had worried that my dumping Avery would've been a blow, but clearly he was doing fine. And, if I'm being honest, Claire was the type of person Avery should be with anyway. Nice. Sociable. And very, annoyingly pretty. So it was all good. It. Was. All. Good.

I FINALLY CAUGHT UP WITH CHARLOTTE AS SHE WAS ENTERING biology. She didn't know Chris's first pet. But she had a lot of thoughts about her own dog, Rufus. Who was "empirically the best dog ever," and who I "*had* to follow on social." Charlotte seemed like a "cat person" kind of a dog person. Intense.

So it was a dead end. Annoying. But okay. I knew I'd get it soon enough.

In every case (or almost every case) I reach a sort of inevitable tipping point where I feel like all the work I've done, hours of research and random conversations and spreadsheets and hacking—it all starts to cascade and avalanche toward the finish line. It's exhilarating. And it justifies my whole approach and work ethic. This felt like that moment.

I took a deep breath and told myself to keep pushing. Because it would all be over soon. All I had to do was find the name of Chris's first pet.

23

THE DOG WHO MUST
NOT BE NAMED

Why can't I find the name of his goddamned pet?

W   Three days had gone by. And for three days I had done nothing but scour Chris's social, his mom's social, and his relatives' and friends' and acquaintances' socials to see if anyone mentioned his first dog.

Chris has had three dogs since he was five. I know his current pit bull's name is Roger, and that his golden retriever before that was named Kobe. But the first dog? The one that is in several pictures with Chris, including those taken at his sixth, seventh, and ninth birthday parties? *That dog has NO NAME APPARENTLY!* Why would no one just say his name? One time! One caption from Chris's mom literally reads: **There was a boy who had a dog and cutie-pie is his name-oh!** *No! Say his name-oh! Say his name-oh!*

This was infuriating. Prom was in two days, and if I didn't

figure this out, I could never hope for Operation Mertz's Three[76] to work. This stupid pet question was coming at the expense of everything else in my life. I needed to meet up with the Kelseys and go over the plan one last time. I needed to figure out a time for Sammi to pick me up, and I really needed to start sleeping more than four hours a night, because I felt crazy!

Why couldn't I find something as innocuous as his dog's name when I had already found his AWS Customer ID and the last four digits of his social? The more I thought about it, the more I doubted that his pet's name was anywhere to be found online. There is no First Pet Administration or Statewide Pet Bureau Database. (Though I kinda wish there were!)

"Ms. Mertz? Are you still with us?"

Mr. Thames was staring at me. And the rest of the class turned their heads back to look at me, too.

Shit.

I was in AP Government. And I was day-thinking again. I don't daydream,[77] but I do, from time to time, concentrate so hard on a job that I completely block out everything around me and kind of . . . forget where I am. Or how I got there. It's not great.

Mr. Thames had definitely asked me a question, and it was clear from my "Wait, where am I?" gaze that I hadn't been paying attention. My grade in his class had dropped seven points since I took on the RB case. His lips pursed into a Grinch smile that said, "Now I've got her." Like hell you do! I answered his patronizing

---

76. Like *Ocean's Eleven*. I don't know. Still workshopping.

77. Waste of time.

question with a bold, accusatory statement. "I disagree with the entire premise of what you just said!"

"You *disagree* that the Louisiana Purchase was good for our country?"

Now, I hadn't thought much about the Louisiana Purchase and whether or not it was a great idea. But Mr. Thames's empty rhetorical questions designed to entrap people? That's something that I do feel strongly about. So I pulled this out of my butt: "Did the Louisiana Purchase double the size of the country at three cents an acre? Yes, it did. But, we bought it from *Napoleon*. Why are we doing deals with an autocrat? It's undemocratic. Secondly, debt! This was more than the US could afford at the time, and we spent years in a financial deficit as a result. And third, I don't believe humans can really *own* land. So purchasing it runs counter to my ethics."

My argument was all over the place. I had vacillated between hippie communist and fiscal conservative in the same sentence. (I didn't even mention the mass displacement of Native Americans caused by our colonial expansion, which should've been my entire argument.) But at least I made it clear to Mr. Thames that I was, in fact, paying attention. (Even though I was, in fact, not.)

"Okay. Didn't realize you were such a deficit hawk, Ms. Mertz," he mumbled before turning his back to the class to drone on about Lewis and Clark.

I went back to my thought cave.

Maybe there was a simple solution to my Chris dog problem. Could I just ask Chris? *Hey, Chris, how are you today? Great shirt! Did you ever have a pet when you were a kid?* Maybe? But probably not. Our minimal exchanges were always colored by our mutual hatred. Maybe I could get someone else to ask Chris? Like a hot girl, so he wouldn't question it. No, I didn't want to send a girl anywhere near Chris.

Mr. Thames shoved a half sheet of paper onto my desk. Some kind of pop quiz. That man. I cracked my knuckles, willing myself to take a break and answer six puerile questions about manifest destiny (from a textbook written by 99 percent white people). But then I realized that the solution to my Chris problem was literally right under my nose.

I would draft a schoolwide survey to be given out during homeroom on half sheets like the one Mr. Thames just gave me. (We were often given surveys or simple assignments like this in homeroom. I guess because there was nothing else to do?) If I put stacks of questionnaires in teachers' mailboxes, claiming it was for student government or some other school club, they'd have to give it to their students.

When the period was over, I went to the computer lab to create my survey. I decided to say it was "a survey being conducted by the Roosevelt Honors Friendship Society." (There is no Friendship Society, but teachers never question anything with "honors" in front of it.) I came up with four pointless questions to mask my actual question:

1. How many Roosevelt sports events have you attended this year? Circle 0, 1–5, 5–10, 10–20, 20+

2. Do you have a close friend who is in a different grade level?

3. Skittles or M&M'S?

4. What was the name of your childhood pet?

5. Do you have any brothers or sisters?

I was pretty proud of the inanity of those questions. They seemed like the kind of thing the fictional Friendship Club would come up with.

I printed out five hundred half sheets of paper. I was worried if I just gave it to Mr. Lumley (Chris's homeroom teacher), he might find it suspicious. But if every teacher had it, they would write it off as just another club's annoying survey that nonetheless killed ten minutes.

As it was already the end of the school day, I decided to linger for another thirty minutes or so, until I was sure all but the most devoted teachers had left. I went to the "bookstore" (a repurposed janitorial closet where they sell candy, notebooks, and erasers) and bought a bag of Jolly Ranchers for $4.50. Then I waltzed into the main office and shoved my survey packets in all the senior homeroom teachers' mailboxes, and some of the juniors'. For Mr. Lumley, I included the bag of Jolly Ranchers and a note that instructed him to give candy to any student who completed the survey. (A little extra incentive couldn't hurt.) I would've included this for all the classes, but *one* bag was $4.50.

The next morning I got to school early and dropped off an empty file box labeled "Friendship Society Surveys" in the office. Then I waited for my results.

In between periods, I found myself walking by the office, looking through its glass windows to see how many packets had been turned in. And the box really started seeing some action, with teachers dropping off manila envelopes and pausing to chat with the secretary or refill their gross teacher coffees. It was kind of fun giving the teachers some busywork for a change. Felt like payback.

Finally, between fifth and sixth periods, I saw Mr. Lumley drop off his envelope. Just before the bell, I swooped in and collected the box. I walked straight to the tech booth so I could look through my results in private. I ripped open Lumley's folder and sifted through the surveys. Names, sporting events, Skittles, M&M'S. Finally, peeking out from the stack, I saw a survey with "Heinz" scribbled at the top. Yes. He'd done the survey. The dog's name was mine!

I grabbed the sheet. He didn't answer any of the questions. But across the entire page, in brutish, chicken-scratch pencil, he wrote, "Go Fuck Yourself."

I mean, we can talk about the audacity of writing something like this during school and then *signing your name to it*. This was not the behavior of someone who wanted a Jolly Rancher.[78] I was furious. All that work. Another day wasted, and I still wasn't any closer to finding out the stupid dog's name![79] I collapsed onto the gross tech booth couch, not caring that I likely now had body lice. I felt hopeless, but also furious. *This dog would not defeat me! Not now!*

I had one last move. One last, Hail Mary, not-great idea.

I took out my burner, and I called Chris's house.

After two rings, his mom answered. Chris's mom, Laura

---

78. I found out later that Mr. Lumley did not use the Jolly Ranchers for incentive, but instead ate them all himself.

79. I'm sorry. The dog is not stupid. Dogs are perfect. Chris is stupid.

Heinz, was well-known at Roosevelt. Mostly because she did all Chris's homework and frequently intervened on his behalf with the administration. Chris should've been a D student with several suspensions on his record. But thanks to Laura, who used her master's degree to drink wine and raise a monster, he's an A-.

"Hi. Is this . . . Laura Heinz?" I asked in my best telemarketer voice.

"Yes."

"I'm calling from Spectrum Internet. How are you doing today?"

"I'm okay . . ."

Laura was home alone all day. So I hoped she would be glad to have someone to talk to, even a telemarketer.

"Glad to hear it, glad to hear it." I went on, "TGIF, amirite?"

"Yes . . ." she said, now maybe regretting talking to me.

"Can I ask you some questions about your household's internet usage today, Ms. Heinz? We're conducting a brief survey to help us learn more about our customers. It's just three questions. And if you participate, we'll give you three free months of unlimited cable." (Incentive!)

"Um. Okay, that's fine. Go ahead."

"Thank you, Ms. Heinz. Now, before I begin the survey, I'll just need to verify that you are the account holder."

"Okay . . . but I have something at two."

"Absolutely. This should really take just two minutes of your time. Now, I have you residing at 741 Mosley Court. Is that correct?"

"Yes." She sounded annoyed. Like I was keeping her from an afternoon of drinking wine and watching *Cheat Retreat*.

"And your Spectrum ID is 782-42309."

"I . . . I don't know. I don't have it in front of me." She hesitated.

Trust me, it is, Ms. Heinz. I hacked your email. "Well, that's okay. I can see that this is the phone number associated with that account. And finally, I have a security question to ask you. One that you answered when you activated your account. What was the name of your first pet?"

"My first childhood pet? Ned."

"Ned! Great name for a dog, Ned!" I said, ecstatic.

"No. Ned was my rabbit. He was a birthday present when I turned seven." Right. *Her* first pet. This was going off the rails.

"Hmm . . . That's not what I have here. Maybe you entered the first pet you had in your current nuclear family?"

"Why would I do that?"

"Because . . . I don't know . . ." I said, clearly grasping—and clearly suffering from sleep deprivation. "That's what people do on these things. They don't think. They just answer. So can you please just answer the question? The dog's name. What was its name?" Uh-oh. My desperation was coming through, and my telemarketer voice was becoming a smidge aggressive.

"Excuse me?" she said, now pissed.

"Just tell me the name of your first dog! I'm trying to improve your cable and internet service! Okay? So tell me the dog's god-damned name!"

Aaaaand she rightfully hung up.

I took out my burner's SIM card and snapped it in two. And

then I actually started to cry a little bit. Which is rare. But I felt mad and helpless. And I was just so tired.

I aimlessly sifted through the survey packets. Skimming over the answers. Kelsey Chugg answered all the questions, except for #5, in which she just wrote, "What the hell is Friendship Club?" Apparently Jenji Hopp owns an iguana, whose name is The Future. (That's kinda cool.) And then I stumbled across Avery's.

His handwriting was so much better than mine. It was aggressively neat. And he answered every question succinctly and honestly. (He was probably hoping to *join* Friendship Club.)

1. School sporting events attended: **20+**

2. Friend in another grade level? **Yes** [and he wrote in "many"]

3. Skittles or M&M'S? **M&M'S**

4. First pet? **John (a labradoodle)**

5. Siblings? **I wish.**

Of course he had a labradoodle (rich-person dog). And John? Who names their dog John? What a weird, proper human name to—

John! Oh my god. *The story game!!!*

There was this challenge that went around everyone's Instagram stories a couple weeks ago. It was "Type Your Porn Name and Tag Three Friends." Avery had done it and tagged me. His porn name was John Haverhill, and I teased him because that sounds like a British colonialist and not a porn star. But what could he do? He had to follow the formula:

porn name = your childhood pet + the street you grew up on

Your childhood pet.

I felt so stupid, I must have blown past this game in a dozen different feeds and never connected the dots. I tossed Avery's survey to the side and went on Instagram. Chris didn't always do chains, but I was certain he did this one. I mean, he's a porn entrepreneur, how could he resist? But did he save it to his highlights? How funny did he think his name was?

Sure enough. It was there. On his story. Chris Heinz = *Cujo Swallow*

Cujo. His first dog was named Cujo. Never mind that only a true psychopath would name their family pet Cujo.[80] And I guess he lived on Swallow Court. Whatever. Finally, Chris had given me what I needed. I was ecstatic.

I ducked out of school a mite early and walked home. I had all the information I required to shut down Roosevelt Bitches for good. Now I just had to execute my plan.

WHEN I GOT HOME, I TEXTED THE KELSEYS. WE MADE A PLAN TO meet early in the morning so I could give them my dad's Dremel plus two burners, just in case. I had all the information I needed to close Chris's AWS account. *It. Was. All. Happening.* I even had a damn date. I'd never felt more ready. For Operation Sledgehammer.[81] For prom. For all of it.

• • • •

---

80. *Cujo* is a Stephen King book about a killer dog. Naming your dog Cujo was like naming your son It.

81. Do we like this? I think I like.

"CAN I SEE YOUR DRESS?" MY MOM ASKED AS SHE STUFFED Chipotle in her mouth.

Sorry, dress? Did she say dress? I was having another day-think, and I realized I had been zoning out for pretty much all of dinner, which was later than usual because my mom had worked a double.

My dad followed up with "Show us that dress! Fashion show! Fashion show!"

I did not *have* a dress. I had been busy covertly borrowing my dad's Dremel and unmasking Cujo. I had completely forgotten about regular prom stuff. Of course I needed a dress. And, like, shoes, probably?

"Right. Well, I have that one dress I wore to Grandpa Jay's funeral. That could work, right?"

My parents shared a look. Like a will-our-daughter-be-able-to-exist-in-the-world-one-day kind of look.

"Honey, you were in eighth grade when Grandpa Jay died. That dress isn't going to fit your grown-up tas [*sic*]. You need a dress or a suit if you're going to go to prom. It's a formal event," my mom said politely. "Tas" is what she calls boobs.

"Right. So . . . that dress is not an option?"

SEVEN MINUTES LATER, WE WERE IN THE CAR HEADING TO THE mall.

"This has to be a real speed-through," my mom said, prepping me. "The mall closes at nine. We're gonna start at Teru's. They have good stuff and they're not *too* pricey. But it might be a little mature for you."

"I don't care." I was literally ready to buy the first dress I saw that didn't have sequins. Or an asymmetrical neckline. Or tulle. Maybe I'm pickier than I thought.

We parked at the entrance by Chili's and got to Teru's at 8:05. I tried on three dresses and chose the least offensive of the three, a simple, sleeveless black sheath. With a boatneck. I could see that my mom was very tempted to tell the saleswoman all about this being my first big formal outing, and blah blah blah. But she bit her tongue because she knew I would snark the hell out of her. And anyway, we didn't have time.

Our next stop was Famous Footwear, where I ran in and bought a pair of size 8 black heels without even trying them on. They were not even on sale. (I never buy anything that's not on sale.) I . . . do not think they were very cool shoes. They had a closed toe, which I imagined was not what most people would be wearing. But I needed something I could work in. Something that wouldn't fall off in the event I had to run for my life from Chris. I also grabbed a large black clutch (which, thankfully, was on sale).

We were ready to go when my mom suggested we stop at one of those jewelry islands in the middle of the mall for a pair of earrings.

"You have earrings," I said. "Why can't I just borrow yours?"

"I think you should have a nice pair. For yourself. You can borrow mine any old time."

As my mom bought a pair of Swarovski studs for me ($63, also not on sale), I migrated toward the entrance, ready to go home. I just wanted to get some sleep. I was meeting the Kelseys early in the morning, and I had tons to do to get ready (including, apparently, "doing my hair" and "putting on makeup" and "showering").

I stared at my mom, willing her to complete her transaction and take me home. But she was being chatty and completely blocking out my stare. Ugh. I let my gaze pan over to the Chili's entrance, where a bunch of sad people were milling about waiting for their tables.

Most of them were just standing or leaning and carrying those disgusting beepers that inform you when your table is ready. And then there was one couple engaged in some fierce PDA (there's always one), which I would've almost found funny if they weren't so old and sleazy. The guy was copping a butt-feel, ensuring the poor woman would have a wedgie for the rest of the night. And the woman, who kinda looked like Mrs. Blye, but with shorter hair, giggled every time he grabbed her, then kissed him with a grotesque amount of tongue and—

Wait. Was that actually Mrs. Blye? With an ill-advised bob? And was the butt-grabber . . . was that *Josh Frange*? Were they— wait. *What?*

Perfidia!

I tried to double back. But by then, Mrs. Blye had spotted me. She was thrown for a moment herself, but then quickly walked over.

"Margot," she said, all smiles. "How nice to see you outside of school."

"Yeah . . ." I stammered as eloquently as Danny Pasternak.

"I'm so glad I ran into you becaaaaauuuse . . ." she elongated, rummaging through her purse. "I've been meaning to call you! I feel like we ended things kind of abruptly after our last . . . emergency session. But I really don't think it's right that you weren't compensated," she said, somehow smiling harder.

Behind her, Josh Frange stood for a minute and squinted, probably wondering why Mrs. Blye was talking to Elysse Brown.

"Oh. Well, you know . . ." I responded, as inarticulate as ever. I just couldn't fathom what was going on. She had hired me to make her infidelity go away. She'd cried and pleaded and swore to me that she was working on her marriage. She'd even dragged me out of class to erase the last trace of her relationship with Josh Frange . . . only to go out with Josh Frange again? At a Chili's? Where she could easily be seen?

It was infuriating. And reckless. And just so . . . gross! But before I could speak to any of this, she shoved $300 in my hand and clasped it shut.

"Here. For all the trouble I caused you. Because I know how professional and discreet you are." Her hand got tighter, forcing me to look into her eyes, which were both hyper-focused and wildly out of control.

I was about to rip my hand away when we were interrupted by my mom saying, "Hello, Karen." I guess they were on a first-name basis. I shoved the hush money in my pocket. I didn't want it. I had a code! But I couldn't give it back to her without my mom seeing. I was stuck. So I just stood there, stewing, listening to their pleasantries until I blurted out, "Well. Prom's tomorrow. We gotta go! Have fun, Mrs. Blye! Don't do anything I wouldn't do!" My mom and Mrs. Blye pretended to laugh, even though what I said wasn't funny. And then Mrs. Blye headed back to her super-sexy Chili's rendezvous.

On the way home, my mom noted that I was "a little rude to Mrs. Blye," reminding me that I wouldn't have gotten into the Annover Science competition if it weren't for her. This was technically true.[82] I looked out the window, too annoyed to respond.

When I got home, I retreated to my room and locked the door. I took out the $300 Mrs. Blye shoved into my palm and placed it on my desk. I felt icky. Like I was somehow complicit in her cheating. And I guess I was, on some level. I had covered it up for her. And now she could keep on lying to her husband without any consequences.

I leaned back in my chair, rubbing the ridge in my forehead as I thought about all the jobs I had taken. Over the past two years, I had become consumed and defined by this weird part-time-but-really-full-time job. I was doing it for the money, sure, but in my mind I was also providing a service. One that actually helped people. But was I? How many other cheaters and liars had I aided and abetted? How many dubious pasts had I scrubbed? I made it so people didn't have to face their mistakes. But maybe they should.

I put the money in my drawer. I'd have to think about my complicity in people's filth some other time. Maybe not all of my jobs were squeaky-clean, but the one I was doing tomorrow sure as hell was. And I could pull it off, if I could just get a few hours of sleep.

---

82. The Annover Science competition would not have existed without Mrs. Blye lying it into existence. There isn't even an Annover!

I checked in with RB (now part of my nightly routine) just to make sure nothing new had been added. The first thing I noticed was a new banner: "Happy Prom, Roosevelt! Don't forget to wear your birthday suit!" And on the front page was a heap of new girls: Kate Fu, Cheryl Graham, Amelia Lopez, and on and on. Freshmen. Seniors. Pics and videos. Girls I knew well, and some I didn't know at all (perhaps from Brighton?).

I was paralyzed by anger. Fifteen girls. All at once? I now knew the reason there hadn't been any new victims uploaded in weeks. Because he was saving them. For a big, disgusting, celebratory dump right before prom. It was like he was giving me the finger. Eventually, when the feeling returned to my extremities, I drafted a message to the group chat:

> **MARGOT:** So. 15 new victims have been added as of 11:33 p.m. Can you reach out to the new girls for me? Let everyone know that I will have this site taken down, permanently, by tomorrow night. It'll all be over soon.

I shut my computer and lay on the bed. There would be no sleep tonight. Just tossing and turning as I imagined gouging Chris's eyes out with my strong texting thumbs.

April 30, 11:11 p.m.

> **MARGOT:** who do you think is the worst person? Like ever? Hitler is obvious answer but i kind of think it might be leopold II or pol pot. Or like some ancient Greek who ate his children or something.

> **MARGOT:** chris heinz doesn't even crack the top ten. Which tells you how much evil there is in the world.

> **MARGOT:** I'm so fucking sick of him.

24

WE SHOULD'VE TAKEN
THE BUS

"Okay, do you both know what you're doing?" I handed Hoffman my dad's Dremel. Chugg had her dad's drill.

"Three holes through the center," Chugg said, then revved her drill for emphasis.

The Kelseys looked pretty confident and, unlike me, well-rested. I was tired and sporting some snazzy morning breath that they graciously ignored. I waved to our server, and she arrived with more coffee, having read my mind. Diners are the best.

P-Boy's parents were out of town this weekend, so the plan was for Chugg to wait until P-Boy left for prom and enter his house via a spare key the family kept under a statue of a toad. The Kelseys found out about this spare key via a stakeout (which I did not ask them to do, but was nevertheless helpful, and creepy!). P-Boy's house did have a security system, but apparently he never turned it on when he was the last to leave.

"Do you know how you're getting there?" I asked her.

"My sister's gonna drive me. She owes me."

"Did you tell her what you're doing?"

"No. She *owes* me." And I guess that was enough said.

Hoffman lived close enough to Kyle's to walk there. I had coordinated with Kyle's sister, Gia, to let Hoffman into Kyle's room while he was away. Gia was a fiercely independent, take-no-shit eighth grader who loathed her older brother even more than I did. According to her, Kyle got all the attention and kudos in their family for being a mediocre soccer player (and a below-mediocre everything else), while she was a straight-A student, a first-chair cellist, and a mathlete. Gia didn't require a reason to help us wreck her brother's computer. She loved any opportunity to prove she was smarter than him.

Once I zapped Chris's laptop with my electromagnet, I'd send a text to the Kelseys so they could move on their targets and do some drill-baby-drilling. Once all three laptops were destroyed, I would find a quiet place (likely a stall in the women's room) to do the ten-step verification process required to cancel the AWS account. At which point this whole sordid business would finally be over.[83]

We wished each other luck, then I left for the mani-pedi appointment my mom had insisted I make.

I let my manicurist pick out my polish color because I didn't want to waste my brain energy on something so tedious. Which meant she unloaded one of their least popular colors on me. An

---

83. Well, except for all the pictures and videos people downloaded on their phones and computers. But again, one "fuck me!" problem at a time.

hour and a half later (why, *why* does grooming take *so long*?), I returned home with nails I would call "tan" or "poop brown."[84] Oops.

I spent the rest of the day trying to commit all the verification questions to memory, in case my phone died or something. But my brain was such mush from not sleeping that I wasn't sure I retained everything. So I entered each of the ten things in like five different programs (an email draft, a note, an Instagram draft, etc.). I packed up the electromagnet in my purse, burying it under a generous pile of tampons,[85] and for the first time in months I blew my hair dry. (Also at my mom's insistence.)

I looked in the mirror. But instead of seeing my skin, I saw "Cujo." And "7981." I don't usually wear eye makeup, but I applied some to meet the occasion. I tried to focus on making a straight line while my brain said, "Powers." I tried to fill in my eyebrows all the while thinking, "Walt Disney Elementary." The result was that I looked . . . very bad. I normally rolled my eyes at girls who wore full faces to school. But now I had a hint of admiration for them. It turned out I didn't know the first thing about applying makeup, and it was not intuitive.

I decided to wipe off the eye makeup. But only my mascara was water soluble, so the rest didn't go anywhere. Smudge, smudge. I looked at myself. Somehow I'd ended up with a kind of smoky eye that I could never re-create if I tried, and I decided to just go with it. Sometimes you get lucky.

---

84. Though the color on the bottle read "Mystic Sand."

85. Feminine hygiene products will deter any chaperone who wants to inspect your bag. Use liberally.

Without thinking, I took a selfie and posted it. Highly unusual. But I guess I'm not above seeking validation. I wondered if anybody good would see my little thirst trap. I even refreshed my screen twice, but the only like I got was from Kevin Beane. I don't know what I was hoping for, but that was incredibly unsatisfying.

"Margot? Sammi is here," my mom called from outside the bathroom. Right. It was go time, and I was out of glam time. I tried parting my hair a little to the side, but that was a very bad idea. I shook it out, grabbed my clutch, and walked into the living room, where they were all waiting for me.

And I mean *all*. My mom, my dad, Sammi, Mrs. Santos, Sammi's aunt Juno, and also our sad neighbor Ms. Shultz from across the hall. (My mom got stuck talking to her this afternoon and accidentally invited her to come over for pictures.) Everyone broke into an overcompensating chorus of "Margot! My goodness!" "I love that dress!" "You look so cute!" etc. Because everyone was too nice or because it was so novel to see me in something other than jeans.

Meanwhile, Sammi seemed to escape the bulk of this pageantry. Which seemed unfair. Sammi looked pretty, too! He had on a suit and tie and some kind of product in his hair. It must've been Mrs. Santos's doing. It feels weird to say this because he's like a brother, but Sammi is handsome. He's got very good bone structure (I wouldn't mind having his cheekbones, actually) and big brown eyes. He'll have no problem getting a girlfriend in college.

We did all the stereotypical prom-picture things. We took

way too many pictures in a weird sort of hand-holding pose. Mrs. Santos and my mom cried, and Sammi and I scolded them. Then we had to retake all the photos because Sammi forgot to put the corsage he bought me on my wrist. Heaven forbid the photos didn't accurately represent that I had a corsage!

The whole scene felt unbelievably *normal*. Like we were a normal couple just going to prom together. Not like two weird misfits, one of us with an electromagnet in her purse. We smiled for the camera. We adjusted ourselves. My mom tried to get people to eat lemon squares. So very normal.

Once we had taken our corsage pics, followed by a round of "silly ones" (kill me now), Sammi escorted me to his uncle's silver Lexus, which he had borrowed for the night. I was starting to get a little nervous. A nice car. A corsage. Did Sammi think we were actually going to prom and not, like, "going to the prom" in quotes? I was not going to be a very attentive date. I was on a tight timeline. Sammi and I weren't going to be, like, dancing. Did he want that? Or more than that? The idea of him actually liking me, of me leading him on, gave me a hot flash. But then, right on cue . . .

"Sorry if the car is weird. I thought it would've been cool to just take a Lyft. Or the bus. That feels more . . . us." It did. And it would've been a baller move to show up to the North Webster Hilton on the M10 bus. "But my mom—"

"I get it," I said, needing no further explanation. Mrs. Santos was a hard woman to say no to.

I kept running over the plan in my head as Sammi got into the driver's seat, and I let myself into the passenger's. I fumbled through my clutch one last time to feel that I had everything I needed. I would've killed myself if I forgot my phone or the magnet.

"You okay?" Sammi asked as I rifled through my too-big clutch.

"Yep. Sorry, I just . . . wanted to make sure I . . . had my compact?" I responded, then quickly closed my purse so Sammi wouldn't see. He raised an eyebrow, rightfully suspicious.

"I won't go through your purse, if that's what you're worried about?"

"Sorry, I just . . . I'm nervous. I . . ." My brain was farting big time.

"You're nervous? Really?" Sammi asked, and I could've sworn he was blushing.

"Not because of prom. I . . . smuggled in some gin, and I'm worried it'll get confiscated." This was not a great lie. Sammi knows I'm as likely to get shit-faced drunk as I am to proudly wear flip-flops. Neither has happened or will happen to me. "When at prom, right?" I said, hoping that would end his curiosity.

"Totally. Sorry. I just . . . gin, huh?"

"Yeah . . ."

"I can get us more booze, if that's what you want."

"You can? Since when?" I blurted out, even though a smarter person would've been happy to move on from her terrible lie. I just couldn't help myself.

"Since—I don't know. I just can. If that's what you want. I can hook us up."

"Uh. That's okay."

"So you prefer drinking warm gin?" Sammi smirked.

"Yeah, I do."

"Can I have a swig?" Sammi said, now a little perturbed.

"No," I said coldly as I snapped my clutch shut, vowing not to open it again until I was inside the Hilton ballroom. "You're driving."

We drove in silence for a bit. Sammi tapped on the wheel, like it was a substitute for his impatient foot. Then he broke our talking embargo with a stern "I'm not buying it."

"Jesus, Sammi, what's your problem?"

"You? Gin?"

"I don't know," I snapped. "I'm trying something different. What, you can wear hats but I can't have gin? The gin is my hat, okay?"

Sammi nodded a stilted, frustrated nod. The kind you do instead of saying something mean. Finally, he said, "Yeah, it just kind of feels like . . . I don't know . . ."

My phone pinged. It was Chugg.

CHUGG: We have a problem. P-Boy armed the alarm.

Christ. There's always something. I wrote back:

MARGOT: K. Just sit tight. I'll think of something.

I closed out my messages and opened up my file on RB. I had a list of possible passwords P-Boy might use.

But then I noticed the car wasn't moving. We were stopped at a red light, and Sammi was just staring at me.

"What?" I snapped.

"What do you mean, what? We're in the middle of talking about something and you went to check your phone like I wasn't even here."

"I'm sorry, Sammi, I have . . . my parents had this mini-emergency and I just . . . have to text them back."

"That's another lie. What is with you, Margot?"

I glared at him. I didn't have time for Sammi to suddenly be so . . . pushy.

"Can you just drive the car? Please?"

The light changed. Sammi shrugged and revved the engine. I think he was hoping it would make a *vrrrooom!* sound to reflect his frustration. But because it was a hybrid, it only made a *mm-mmrrrrrrrrrrr.* He drove on.

I LOOKED THROUGH MY PHONE, BUT I DIDN'T HAVE ANYTHING I could give to Kelsey. No password or pin I was confident enough about. For some reason, I decided to check P-Boy's phone, which I could access via the TeddyFace app. I looked in his saved passwords, empty. I looked in his notes, nothing. Then I looked at his texts, and fortune smiled.

That very evening, around seven p.m., P-Boy texted his father, and the exchange went something like this:

P: Dad i forgot the password again is it 2113.

D: Jesus Peter. Call me and I'll tell you.

> **P:** dad your sick paranoid. Just y or n.

> **D:** Would you please call me before you set off the alarm and the police come to the house?

> **P:** Whatever i'm just gonna do it.

> **D:** No! It's 2131. Your birthday and your sister's!

> **D:** Don't just put in the wrong number!

> **P:** tight.

> **P:** wait what's Lucy's birthday?

And then he sent his dad a meme of Michael Jordan crying. I don't know why.

Anyway, with the correct password now safely in Chugg's hands, all was back on track. Great. I shoved my phone back in my clutch and turned to Sammi.

"Okay. So sorry about that, Sammi! Let's go prom it up." Sammi was slumped in his seat, looking somewhere between furious and very bored.

"Is that what tonight is going to be? You zoning out on your phone while I just sit here?"

I don't know. Maybe. What was with all the men in my life and their sudden neediness? "Sammi, I'm sorry. Something came up and I just needed a few minutes."

"Twenty-five minutes," he spat back.

"Sorry?"

"Twenty-five minutes is how long we've been sitting here.

Twenty-five. That's not including the eight minutes you spent on your phone while I drove us here. So that's thirty-three minutes of you just being on your phone not talking. Which is rude. Even for you."

I checked the time. The dashboard clock read 7:52. Huh. That was . . . pretty damn rude.

"I'm sorry, Sammi. I am. But I'm ready now, if you're—"

"What's going on, Margot?" Sammi said, pinching the bridge of his nose. "Is this a job? That I don't know about? The only time I ever see you get this focused is when you're working. Did you take a job? And . . . you don't want my help on it or something?"

"Sort of. It's complicated, but . . . can we just go inside?" Thanks to Chugg's PIN pad issues, I was running behind.

"So you *are* on a job. Right now? Okay . . ." Sammi nodded. I couldn't tell if he was relieved to have his suspicions confirmed or mad that I was working during our prom "date." "So what is it?"

I played out all my options. All the lies I could possibly tell him. But he clearly saw through me, and quite frankly, I was tired of lying. At this point, if Shannon found out I told him, it wouldn't matter. Because after tonight, Roosevelt Bitches would no longer exist.

I took a deep breath. Then I gave Sammi a complete overview of the case in the parking lot of the North Webster Hilton. I told him about my two-month odyssey to find RB's creator, only to discover it was Chris, with tech support from Kyle and P-Boy. I didn't go into all the details of the job, the dead ends of Jenji, Danny, and Harold. Or how dating Avery was a means to an end. Partly because I didn't think it mattered, but also because Sammi kept interrupting me. Interjecting things like "I'm sorry, who hired you?" and "Jesus, Margot," and "I can't believe you didn't tell me." Each interjection getting more terse and annoyed until he finally yelled, "Can you just slow down?" while grabbing my arm, which is something *no man should ever do!*[86]

"Don't grab me, Sammi—" I said, whipping my arm back.

"Sorry, but, Margot—"

"I'm serious. Don't ever do that—"

"I know, okay, but, Margot—"

"Sammi. Seriously. I know I'm your friend, but—"

"CAN YOU PLEASE JUST LET ME TALK? PLEASE!" he shouted as he laid on the horn. Which I guess is better than him grabbing my arm, but still a weird, aggressive choice. A couple walking near us turned to look, then saw Sammi's livid face and decided it was better to leave us alone. I was starting to worry about Sammi. He was not one for big angry outbursts. I hadn't seen him this mad since fifth grade, when he used to have LEGO tantrums if he realized he was missing a vital piece.

"Sammi?"

"Fucking Christ, Margot! How could you not tell me about this?"

"I told you. Shannon swore me to secrecy."

"I could've . . . Jesus . . . I could've—" He was choking on the words. I expected him to be upset that I hadn't used him for a job, but not this upset.

---

86. This happens in movies all the time. A guy, because he really needs to make a point or really needs to show how in love he is or how big his penis is, will grab a woman by the arm before declaring his . . . whatever. It's aggressive and not okay. *Use your words.*

"Sammi. I wanted to tell you. I really did. I could've used your help so many times these past two months. I was totally underwater. But tonight, finally, it's all going to be over. And then—"

"It's not going to be over, Margot. Your plan's not going to work," he said, glaring at me like I was the stupidest person in the world. "Because Kyle and P-Boy didn't design the site. I did."

And just like that, the world made no sense.

I'm not sure how I got there, exactly. It's possible I just ran out of the car. It's also possible I punched Sammi or slapped him and called him a traitor or something. It's all kind of a blur. The next thing I remember for sure is sitting on the curb, playing with the hem of my dress. A dress I bought so that I could go to Sammi's prom, so that I could destroy a laptop when no one was looking. But now it didn't matter, because there was a giant flaw in my plan: I hadn't actually found the creator of Roosevelt Bitches. It was Sammi. And a glaring, obvious friendship bias had hidden that from me. So now what?

"Margot?" I heard Sammi say as he took a seat next to me. His voice was quiet. I could tell he was no longer angry, just ashamed. "Can I at least explain?"

I shrugged, pulling at my hem with my dirt-brown-manicured thumb.

"I, uh, I have to go all the way back to winter break." He waited, but I gave him nothing. "You were visiting your grandmother in Florida. Remember?"

I couldn't look at him, let alone respond.

He finally continued, "While you were gone, I basically did nothing but play RPGs and listen to podcasts and eat mac 'n' cheese every night. And I was like, this is great. No Margot around to text me with jobs or whatever."

"Yeah, I really suck, huh?"

"No. It was just . . . relaxing. At first, anyway. But after a few days of basically doing nothing, I started to get anxious. I started to feel, like, crazy."

He paused. He didn't use that word lightly. "There was one whole night I didn't sleep. I almost went to the emergency room because I thought I was having a heart attack. And I realized that all this anxiety was because I don't have a life. Like, I have no friends. No job. Not without you." He was getting a little more animated. "So when you were gone it was like, shit. How is this going to work next year, when I'm at college and Margot is still here?"

"Okay . . ." I replied, not wild about the idea that this was in some way my fault.

"So . . . I was like, okay. I have to do something about this. So . . . I made a list."

I looked up at him for a split second and caught his eye.

"I know. It was very Margot of me. It was all like, 'try jogging,' and 'go to a party,' and 'talk to someone at school you've never talked to before.' Which, in my case, was everybody. But if I did it, hopefully it would get me to be . . . not so me."

I wanted to ask him if one of the things on his list was "ruin the lives of forty-five of his classmates." But I was too choked with anger to quip.

"Anyway, I did it. The whole list," he said with more than a little pride. "And I actually enjoyed most of it. Even going to parties. I felt like I was really changing. And to be honest, I was kind of surprised that you didn't notice. Not until I started wearing that stupid Yankees hat."

Right. Hatgate. That made more sense now.

Sammi shook his head. "You know, I always thought you were joking when you called me your 'most trusted associate.' But when you didn't notice, I was like, *Does she really think of me as her employee?* Because I thought you were my best friend. So . . ."

Sammi pulled his coat tighter. He suddenly seemed uncomfortable. "Do you want to get back in the car? We're getting kind of wet."

I looked at the wet pavement, my wet dress. The goose bumps on my arm and the splashing of raindrops, one after the other. Right, it was raining. How long had it been raining?

"No," I said with no inflection.

"Okay." Sammi nodded. "So one of the things on my list was to get a job. Like a real one. At Wellmans or something. But then . . . Chris saw me at a party and offered me a programming job."

"*That's* a real job?" I said under my breath.

"Just let me—Margot, I'm trying to tell you everything." He looked directly at me, and I could see the pleading in his eyes.

"Fine."

"Chris wanted me to make him a site. And you know I don't do that. I'm basically a script kiddie."

It was true that Sammi didn't normally build sites. He preferred to infiltrate existing ones.

"But I was like, I'm doing new stuff. Let me try it." He

continued, "And it turns out I actually like coding. I made a simple site, I showed Kyle and P-Boy how to maintain it (all they had to do was upload content), and I figured I was done."

"I have remote access to your computer. How come I never saw anything about RB?" I interrupted.

"Chris wanted me to build it on his laptop." Sammi shrugged.

"So you built the insidious revenge porn site on someone else's computer. Cool. Go on."

"No, Margot," he said forcefully. "*I didn't know what I was building.* They told me it was like a . . . secret digital yearbook. Chris said he was gonna upload pics from everyone's Instagram, and have people comment anonymously. Make up their own 'funny' superlatives. It sounded stupid. But I knew I'd make bank for, like, not a lot of work."

"You're saying you built the site and didn't know what it was for? I know I'm not as smart as you, but you know I'm not an idiot. Right?" I asked, a flush of anger coloring my face.

"It's true." He shrugged with a sort of defeated air that made me believe him. "I thought it was a fake yearbook. But then a couple weeks later, Chris shows up outside of Trinity Towers. With Kyle and P-Boy. They asked me if I wanted to go for a ride."

I scoffed audibly. Never let an assailant take you to a second location.

"Yeah. In retrospect, it was a bad move." He was quiet for a second before continuing, "Because once I got in, I could see they were mad. They said the site had been flagged on AWS."

"That was me. By the way."

"Yeah. Makes sense now," Sammi said, kicking the ground.

"Anyway, they were pissed. And they crammed me in the back of Kyle's SUV[87] and said: fix it. They said they wanted to pay me five hundred bucks a month just to make sure the site stayed up. And I was thinking about saying yes. Taking their money. But then I went to the site and I saw what it was . . ." Sammi wavered. His voice broke as he continued, "I felt sick, you know?"

Yeah. *I know.*

"Get to the part where you kept working for them anyway," I said coldly. I wasn't going to make this easy on him.

"Chris punched me in the stomach. In the back of the SUV. It scared the shit out of me." A tear rolled down Sammi's cheek, which he wiped away quickly with his French cuff. "There were three of them and they were blocking the doors. And . . . I don't know. After that, I said I'd do it."

Of course that's how they got Sammi to help them. With violence. And threats. I'm sure it didn't take much to break him. He's not a fighter.

"I got the site back up on Tor that night. I knew it was wrong. But I told myself it was just a prank. And pretty soon we were going to graduate, and we could start over . . ." He trailed off, wiping his face. Clearly, he knew *that* was bullshit.

"The girls on that site can't start over. Those pictures will haunt them for—"

"I KNOW!" he shouted. "I KNOW. Okay?"

Then neither of us moved. We just sat on the asphalt, side by side, getting rained on and staring at the dark, wet pavement as

---

87. Or REO Weedwagon, if you must.

puddles started to form around our feet. When I finally dared to turn my head and actually look at him, I could tell tears were lining his cheeks.

I knew what that punch did to him. In that moment, he reverted back to his old self. He was Sammi, nervous, shy, and afraid. The ten-year-old boy who could barely string two words together, looking down at my kitchen floor. I wanted to hug him. To tell him everything was going to be okay. To apologize for not being a better friend. And more than anything, I wanted so badly to tell him that this wasn't his fault.

But it was his fault.

I turned to him coolly. "Go home, Sammi. Take your uncle's Lexus and go home."

"Margot, I didn't—"

"Go home," I said. This was not a conversation. "And delete your backups."

"Okay, but—"

"You fucked up, Sammi. You so majorly fucked up. Go home and delete your copies of Roosevelt Bitches. All of them."

Sammi nodded, lifted himself up, and stumbled back to his car.

How was this possible? How could he have done this? How could I not know? I shook off these questions. They didn't matter right now. Sammi didn't matter, only the job did. I stood up and full-on slapped myself in the face. I think in an attempt to psych myself up. But it must have been damn hard, because Kara Michaels and Eric Gersen gasped as they walked by. "Jesus. Margot? Are you okay?"

"I'm great," I said. And I meant it. I truly didn't feel a thing.

"Are you sure? Your face is all red."

"Yeah. I'm great. Enjoy the fucking prom." I marched past them toward the entrance. Each *clip-clop* of my heels a war cry to take down Chris Heinz and all the people who propped him up. It's time for them all to burn.

May 1, 8:22 p.m.

MARGOT: IF YOU SEE THIS, I RAELLY WOULD LIKE IT IF YOU COULD WISH ME LUCK. IMMABOUT TO DO SOMETHIG A LITTLE CRAY

MARGOT: I LOVE YOU

MARGOT: EVERYONE ELSE IN THE WORLD IS GARBAG.

MARGOT: GARBAGE*

MARGOT: WISH ME LUCK.

MARGOT: IT'S A LOT OF CAPS BUT I SWEAR IT'S WARRANTED.

MARGOT: AHHHHHHHHHH

25

OPERATION SLEDGEHAMMER

My uncle Richard's desktop computer once caught on fire. They said the fans were clogged with dust, but I don't think we can discount the amount of malware he had unwittingly installed or the gazillion programs he had running. I used to think this was another example of what a loser my uncle was. But I now sympathized with Richard. Or, more accurately, I sympathized with his computer. Because now I was that computer. My brain was flooded with too many thoughts and overwhelming emotions. So many tabs open that I couldn't process: Roosevelt Bitches, Chris, the Kelseys, Sammi. Sammi, Sammi, Sammi. I was soaking wet, but my head was on fire.

I pushed everything down. Every feeling. Every bit of doubt. Nobody, not Sammi, not Chris Heinz, and not my overloaded brain, was going to stop me now. No distractions. Only Operation Sledgehammer was in front of me: *Find Chris. Kill his laptop. Close AWS account. Text the Kelseys. Done.* I had until ten p.m.

That's when prom was over. That's when everything was over. This would all end tonight.

I checked the time. 8:25 p.m. Shit, I lost a lot of time talking to Sammi. No more chitchat.

8:25 p.m. Approaching North Webster Hilton on foot. Limos lined up, unloading tipsy groups of teens. No sign of Chris, P-Boy, or Kyle.

Raining hard. Feet wet.

8:29 p.m. Entrance doors very heavy. Create some sort of wind vortex as I enter vestibule.

Dress sopping wet.

Imani Watkins (prom committee chair) manning the entrance and checking people in.

Give her my name. Not on list. Momentary panic. Finds me under Sammi's name. I guess he had to pay for my ticket or something.

Will reimburse him later. Don't need handouts.

Sammi. The little nerd I'd traded Halloween candy with. The quiet goofball who refused to eat orange foods until he was fourteen. How could he do this? How could he build a site that had hurt so many people?

Imani concerned. Asks if I'm okay. Guess I zoned out. Tell her I'm fine.

8:34 p.m. Mandatory bag check by Mr. Lumley. Examines bag. Suspicious, but won't dare touch tampons. Asks if I'm okay. I'm *fine*. Jesus.

8:38 p.m. Aggressive photographers refuse to take hint that I do not want prom photo. Evasive maneuvers.

Enter main ballroom. Refreshment tables by entrance. Mirrored wall to the left. Dance floor straight ahead. At far end of the room, a small dais set up for DJ, accessible from both sides via tiny staircases. Visual on Chris, aggressively bobbing head to his own music. As suspected, terrible DJ. (He never plays a song for longer than a minute, and raps over many of them.)

Chris. The human SOLO cup who made this whole thing happen. Who used Sammi. Who assaulted Beth and made her move away. I was so fucking sick of Chris Heinz. I wanted him canceled. I wanted him ruined. I was so tired of him being in my head. God damn it! Focus.

8:44 p.m. I station myself by the drink table. Spot Kyle dancing (badly) with Tiffany Sparks. Spot P-Boy returning from the bathroom, putting in eye drops.

8:57 p.m. Chris takes off headphones and . . . *leaves booth* in direction of bathroom.

Go time.

I reach into clutch, feel electromagnet. Phone is in my other hand. Browser open to AWS.

Winding through dancers as I approach stage. Will need to be quick and discreet, as I'll be in full view. I put my head down. And—

Whap.

Some jerk flails into me and knocks phone from my hand. It skids across the tile floor. I chase after it. Screen is cracked. Shit.

9:00 p.m. Phone won't turn on. Shit shit shit.

If my phone won't turn on, then I can't sign in to AWS. There's no point in destroying Chris's laptop if I can't kill the actual site. Do I go home? Or ask the Kelseys to do it? How? My phone isn't—

Phone reboots. It's working. Phew. Game on.

Chris returns from bathroom. Shit. Opportunity missed.

I reopen AWS on my browser. Go to delete account page.

Kelseys text again, I text back, hand is shaking again, tell them to stand by.

Run to bathroom to splash water on my face. Hand stops shaking. I catch Jenji Hopp in the mirror looking at me. Concerned or silently judging. I don't even let her ask. "I'm fine!"

9:21 p.m. Chris isn't leaving booth. Doing way too many call-and-responses with crowd. Getting late. Why is he showing more devotion to this than anything else he's ever done? Except RB.

Kyle and P-Boy approach stage. Talk for two minutes. Leave.

A girl I don't know approaches him. They talk for ten seconds. Chris leaves the stage. Now playing: a pre-selected playlist (Far better than his DJ-ing. Finally, some Beyoncé!).

I text Kelseys: **STAND BY.**

I reach into my purse and grab the magnet. The other hand grips my phone. I walk toward the stage. Might be shaking. Eyes blurry, for some reason. Take a deep breath.

Fifteen feet away. Ten.

"Margot?"

It's Avery. Standing between me and the stage. "Are you okay?" He looks concerned. Or worried. Or constipated.

Tell him I'm fine.

He asks again.

About to tell him to leave me alone. But for some reason I look at him. Right in the eyes.

THE ROOM CAME INTO A WIDER FOCUS. BEHIND AVERY, I SAW Claire Jubell standing by herself on the dance floor. I heard Imagine Dragons echoing around the room. I smelled that weird prom smell of food and perfume and body odor. I don't know why this snapped me out of my tunnel vision. Maybe it was the shock of seeing Avery and the look on his face. He was genuinely worried about me. He cared. I forgot how nice that look was.

I saw myself in the ballroom's tacky mirrored walls, and I finally understood why everyone was asking me if I was okay. My hair was a rat's nest. And I was low-key crying. The reason my eyes were burning was because of the mascara flowing into and right back out of them, raining down my face. Unaccustomed to wearing mascara and unaccustomed to crying, I hadn't attempted a "pretty cry" that would have saved my made-up face.

Instead, I looked like one of the losers on *Cheat Retreat* after they get booted from Cheatin' Island.

Also, there was a big splash of mud going all the way up the side of my dress. I . . . don't know where that came from.

Okay, so I might not look my best. I didn't care. Chris's laptop was unattended, so I had to move. I turned back to Avery, with every intention of telling him I was fine and, more importantly, that I was busy. That the attention he was giving me was *unwanted*. And that if he wanted to help, he should get the hell out of my way.

But when I opened my mouth, I said this: "Um. I don't . . . think I am . . ." And cried harder.

Avery put his arm around me and guided me to a banquette against the wall. I was curious if he was getting some sort of sick satisfaction from seeing me in my current state. Most exes would've felt a bit of schadenfreude. But I didn't see it. He just looked worried. And ready to listen to whatever I had to say. And honestly, hot. I suspected his tux was owned, not rented. It fit him perfectly.

I tried to get it together. But I couldn't. I told him everything.

"Sammi made Roosevelt Bitches," I said, not caring who heard me. "I spent months scouring the Register and banging my head against the wall and snooping on people's hard drives . . . and it was a complete waste of time, because it was Sammi!"

He managed to get out, "Whoa—" before I kept rambling. I couldn't help it. It was the purge my body desperately needed. I told him about Shannon and the Fury WhatsApp, and how before Chris I wasted all this time on Jenji, Danny, and Harold, and how Avery was my "in" to all of them. I told him about Mrs. Blye and how she's still cheating on her nice husband and why do people cheat and why do people lie and how did I manage to fuck this whole thing up and I'm a fraud and I have no idea what I'm doing. It was raw and probably incoherent, but after months of keeping it all to myself, I felt dizzy. God. What was it about Avery that made me talk like this? That made me feel safe and not judged? I looked at him, deep into his big brown eyes that were filled with so much . . . anger. Undeniable, seething anger? Uh-oh.

"Sorry. I . . . was your *in*? The whole reason we dated was so . . ." He trailed off, putting his hands to his head and almost pulling his hair.

Oh, right. So the only thing Avery really heard during my word vomit was *blah blah blah I was just using you and never really liked you blah blah blah*. Hence the murderous look he was now giving me. He was not having a catharsis like I was. He was in his own personal *Black Mirror* episode, just getting to the third-act twist.

"So dating me was just part of a job?" His eyes darted back and forth as he tried to make sense of it.

I waited as he collected his thoughts. Whatever angry tirade he was about to unleash on me was fully deserved. Avery was not an angry person, but everyone has their limits. And I was the shitty tour guide who had shown him his. I braced myself for maximum, emotional impact.

And then he looked at me. Right in my damn eyes. And . . . he . . . laughed. Not a real laugh. Or a crazy maniacal one. It was an "I give up" laugh. A single, sad laugh that comes when there's nothing else to say.

"Avery," I started, "I never meant to—"

"I hope you get the site down," he said, alone on the high road. "It's toxic. And it's hurt a lot of people. So . . . I hope you kill it."

He started to walk back toward Claire, who was patiently waiting. But then he stopped, turned to me, and casually unloaded an observation so rough that I'll likely talk about it in therapy years from now. "You really have no idea who you are, do you?"

And with that he left. Back to the dance floor. Back to Claire. My eyes blurred as I saw him disappear into the crowd.

You have no idea who you are? What the hell was that? Of course I know who I am. I started a company when I was fifteen! I pay taxes! I have a code! I'm Margot Goddamned Mertz! Why the fuck would he say that?

I spun around and faced the DJ booth, ready to murder the laptop.

But Chris was already back, picking up his headphones, asking the crowd if they were ready to "bring this bitch home." That was it. I'd missed my chance. Operation Sledgehammer was over. I had lost.

But I walked toward him anyway. I didn't know what my plan was. I was beyond plans. I was just going.

And then I was in front of him. Chris Heinz. Two feet of folding table separating us.

He looked up from his computer in disgust. "Jesus, Margot. You look like shit." He slid his headphones on. "If you're looking for someone to fuck you, I'm not drunk enough yet. Try me in a couple hours."

Fuck it.

I grabbed his laptop, wrenched it free of all cords, and in one fluid motion threw it to the ground. The music stopped. The promgoers all watched as I repeatedly smashed it with a nearby microphone stand. Over and over again, until the case cracked and the hinge snapped off. This had nothing to do with the plan. This wasn't going to erase the data stored in his hard drive. But I didn't care. In that moment, I just wanted to kill something.

"You crazy bitch!" Chris shrieked in the otherwise quiet ballroom.

"SHUT THE FUCK UP, CHRIS! FOR ONCE IN YOUR LIFE SHUT! UP!"

Blood rushed to my face. I was out of control. So unhinged that even Chris Heinz did the unthinkable and listened to a woman. I looked around. Saw my classmates staring at me. Waiting for me to burn them alive with my mind. I wanted to close with some witty remark. But I couldn't think of one. So I left.

Somehow I made it out of the North Webster Hilton and into the parking lot. It was still raining, which helped get more of the mascara off my face. That was about the only plus. I noticed my phone had six missed calls from the Kelseys.

I texted them that the mission was off. The Kelseys were, obviously, pretty PO'd. They had put a lot of effort and time and trust into my plan. But I just didn't know what to tell them. I smashed Chris's laptop, but who knows if I damaged the hard drive. I hadn't erased the site from AWS, and even if I had, I couldn't trust Sammi to destroy his copies of the site. There were too many contradicting thoughts bouncy-housing around my head. I sent one more text that said I'd call them tomorrow, and blocked their numbers.

I passed the empty parking lot of a Sam's Club and walked under the awning of Mel's Deli as I continued home. My head hurt so much from crying and from the hard work of trying *not to* cry. I felt drained, and nauseous, and suddenly cold. As I clutched my phone in my wet hand, I realized I had left my bag somewhere at the prom, while likely leaving my dignity somewhere nearby.

I fired off a text to Beth. Beth never judged, and I desperately needed some non-judgment right now. I sent off another. Then two more.

I tried to wrap my head around what happened. What went wrong? Was it all just too big for me? I thought I could handle it. But I'd never tackled anything of this scale. There were just so many culpable people.

Chris, Kyle, and P-Boy, obviously. They were the top of this shit pyramid. Then there was Sammi, who, however dubiously he got involved, provided the tech skills to build a functioning site. Without him, I'm convinced the site couldn't exist. And even though I knew there were good parts of him smuggled in among whatever bad parts did this job, it didn't excuse what he did.

I texted Beth again. It was almost a reflex. Like picking at a hangnail or bouncing my knee. *Tap, tap*, send.

I thought about all the guys who had sent in pictures of their girlfriends and ex-girlfriends. The assholes who uploaded pics of people they had hooked up with, kissed, fingered, etc. *Been inti-mate with.* Then betrayed.

I tried to picture every person who had visited the site. From the boys who went on it looking for some jerk-off inspo, to the guys (and some girls) who viewed it out of curiosity. Even some-one like Avery, who swears he only went on it once (and who knows if that's true?), was complicit. I mean, he didn't report it! Or try to take it down. So what does that make him? How the fuck was I supposed to clean this when everything about Roosevelt Bitches is so dirty?

I typed out one last text to Beth. A brief apology for the string I just sent her. My thumb was hovering over the send button, when I got lightheaded. I almost fell over. All the walking and crying and not eating since . . . breakfast? . . . was probably tak-ing its toll. I steadied myself against a parked car. Took a deep breath, tracing my thumb over my phone's cracked screen like a meditation exercise, when . . . the text screen disappeared. And I was suddenly looking at a picture of Beth.

It was shocking to see her. Frozen in our freshman year. Happy. Fun. Making a peace sign. I hadn't seen it in . . . months? Over a year? It took a few buzzes to realize what was happening.

She was calling me.

26

INCOMING!

"Hello?" I wanted to say, "You've reached Patrizio's Pizza," because that's how we used to answer the phone back in the day. But I stuck with hello.

I could feel her on the other end of the line before she even spoke. There was a nervous hesitation.

"Margot?" she said, and suddenly I was transported to seventh grade, when Bethany lived two blocks away and we'd hang out every day. It felt *so* good to hear her. To know that when I was truly in my hour of need, I could still count on her and that she would—

"You have to stop texting me."

Oh. Um. What?

I stopped walking. I was in the parking lot of a 7-Eleven, just a few blocks from Trinity Towers.

"Beth. Wait. I think maybe . . . you misunderstood a text or—"

"Margot. You have to stop. I didn't want to block you. I tried just ignoring all your texts but they've gotten so . . . it's just too much. Okay?"

I was trying to process what she was telling me. She *had* read my texts. All of them. And it turned out they were not keeping our friendship alive. I was not helping Beth by texting her. In fact, it seemed like I was doing the opposite.

"I know I texted way too much tonight."

"It's not just tonight. Margot, you text me like every other day and act like nothing has changed. I know we used to be, like, inseparable. But I haven't seen you in two years. Don't you think that's a little strange?"

I didn't know what to say. I was so tired and then shocked that Beth had actually called me, it took all my energy to give a barely audible "Uh-huh."

"I've worked really hard to put everything that happened behind me. But when you text me all the time, and when you talk about Chris . . . It's like I'm a freshman all over again. It makes me feel crazy . . ." Her voice broke. She was crying. I, her *best friend*, had made her cry. My stomach sank.

"Beth—"

"I can't." She continued, "I'm sorry, I just can't do this anymore. I mean . . . don't you have anyone to talk to about this stuff? Don't you have, like, friends?"

I paused for way too long before responding, "Totally. Yeah."

I DON'T KNOW HOW WE ENDED THE CALL. I MAY HAVE SAID GOODbye. I know that I wanted to tell her how awful I felt, but I don't think I said more than "Totally. Yeah." I think I promised to stop texting her, but I don't know for sure. Once I hung up I felt dizzy again, so I sat down. I don't know how long I was there or when I picked my wet ass off the pavement or how I eventually made it home. I was in a fog. I just kept hearing Beth's voice in my head. Shaken. Angry. Upset. Her voice that sounded exactly the same. But also completely foreign.

You text me like every other day and act like nothing has changed.

Don't you think that's a little strange?

No. I was trying to be a good friend! I was trying to keep our friendship going. I was trying to help you.

But also, yeah. Maybe.

Was I crazy? I had no social life. No hobbies. No friends. And the two people who considered me *their* friend, I'd exploited for . . . a job I don't even like doing? One that is morally . . . not great? Was that part of my code? To treat the people who like and respect me like garbage? Maybe Avery was right. Maybe I had no idea who I was.

I got home. I opened up the door and heaved myself into the foyer. I was soaked.

"Hello?" called my mom from the kitchen. My parents were not expecting me home so early. "Margot?"

"It's me," I called back, but my voice faltered. I wanted to sneak to my room and avoid them, but my feet took me into the kitchen. The second I saw them, I wept.

Both my parents stood up from their fancy-looking take-out mid-bite, and buried me in a hug. They didn't ask me what happened. They didn't try to fix anything. They just gave me the hug I needed. And for a while, we three stood there in the middle of the kitchen, my mom petting my hair while her chicken French got cold.

This is not me. I don't sob like this. I don't cry on prom night (cliché alert). And I don't let my parents comfort me. It brought out a side of them I hadn't seen in a while. They usually didn't have to "parent" me. But when they did, they were good at it.

Once I stopped sobbing, my mom had me change out of my (ruined) dress, and my dad made me some tea. I sank into the couch, and my mom looked at me very seriously and said, "Just tell us one thing. Are you safe?"

"Yes, Mom. I'm safe."

"Do you need our help?" my dad asked.

"I don't think so. I don't think anyone can help."

I bit the side of my cheek, trying to hold it all in—but in the end I looked at their faces, wanting the best for me . . . and I told them pretty much everything. Even though it meant telling them things about my business I'd rather they not know. Even though it would probably forever color their opinion of Sammi.

"I don't know if I should've gone through with it. I want to help the girls, and I want to see these guys pay, but I can't figure out how."

"That's not your job, bug," my dad said. He hadn't called me "bug" since I was maybe seven.

"Margot, you are the most capable person I've ever known," my mom said, carefully taking the snarls out of my hair. "Your father and I would love to take credit for you. But we can't. You've been this way since you were six. You are truly beyond us."

I could feel a "but" coming.

"But you're one person, and you can't fix everything."

"You're not a judge or a police officer or a social worker," my dad added. "And that's what these boys need."

"I can't go to the police. The police are useless when it comes to cyber-harassment. And you know the school isn't going to do anything." I told them about what happened at Wakefield, how no one there got punished. I told them about Shannon and how much she'd changed already, and how going to the authorities was the last thing she'd want. "I just want to think about it some more."

My dad nodded. My mom half smiled. They didn't push it. They didn't try to convince me. They just gave me the space to make my own decision. Which was in keeping with their parenting style.

"I think I'm gonna go to bed. Sleep on it for now."

"Good idea, honey," my mom said, and gave me my third giant hug of the night.

As I looked over her shoulder at their fancy takeout, now cold, I was struck by how cute my parents could be. They were using *candleholders* and *cloth napkins*. They must have been having a date night since I was out of the house.

"What's with the schmancy dinner? Is it your anniversary or something?" I asked, knowing full well it wasn't August.

"Haha," said my dad. My mom gave a polite laugh, too.

"Seriously? Is this how you guys *always* eat when I'm not here?"

Now they both looked at me, a little more concerned.

"Margot, it's Mom's birthday," my dad said.

And it was. It was May 1. Wow. Not only did I not get her a present, I also didn't wish her a happy birthday or *even remember that she was born.* Today was full of new lows.

"Oh my god," I said, my eyes welling up again. At what point would I run out of tear-fluid and just die of dehydration? "I feel terrible. I can't believe I—"

"Hey," my mom said. "Do *not* feel bad. You've got a lot going on."

"That's no excuse—"

"Margot, if I wanted your life to revolve around mine, I would've had a dog instead of a daughter."

Weird, but okay.

My dad jumped in. "I got your mom a cake from Jackson's. Let's all have it tomorrow and we can celebrate then, okay?"

They gave me one more hug, and I made my way to my room. My mom had been so gracious and obviously didn't want to make me feel worse. But forgetting her birthday was indicative of other issues. Another sign of my rampant self-obsession.

I got into my pajamas and hugged my Hemspillow. I felt so tired my bones hurt, and my cheeks felt stiff from crying. How the hell had I gotten here, so lost that I had to beg Mommy and Daddy to help me? Was this it? My last job? Was this the case that finally broke Margot Mertz?

Trudy Keene had a case that broke her. It was in the fifteenth and final book. The [ghost]writers decided a fitting end to Trudy's saga would be to give her one final case that broke her will. After that, Trudy retired, got married, and had a baby, "as every good woman eventually does."[88] She lived happily ever after, inspiring countless young women to give up on their dreams.

For me, that was the bleakest of all possible endings.[89] I'd rather Trudy drowned in a lake or got machine-gunned in a toll-booth stop. I couldn't go down like that, could I?

Going to the authorities was essentially admitting defeat, that the case was too big for me. But if I didn't, and RB stayed a secret, then so did the crime. And no amount of laptop-smashing would matter. If I really wanted Chris & co. to pay, I'd have to shine a light on the whole thing, not make it disappear.

But that was a lot to ask of the victims. The police would want them to press charges and give up even more of themselves: their time, their anonymity, their humiliation. Just to get some kind of half-hearted resolution. The pursuit of justice is thorny. Full of pricks that leave scars.

I was so tired of the whole thing that I *wanted* my parents to be right. I wanted to turn it over to someone else. I wanted to get out of the way.

I rolled onto my back and looked out the window. It was still raining, showing no sign of letting up. But I felt calmer as I listened to the sound of a gutter spout clicking against the building. It always does this, and usually I kind of hate it. The *pit-pit-pit* sound is an earworm, just out of rhythm enough that I can't stop thinking about it. But tonight, it was a relief. It was familiar, and

---

88. Genevieve Russell, *Trudy Keene Can't Have it All*. (New York: Chambers and Wythe, 1931), 263.

89. Don't settle. And if you start to think you might settle, I suggest reading *Revolutionary Road*.

more consistent than anything else in my life. I hoped it never stopped raining.

I WOKE UP THE NEXT MORNING WITH A SPLITTING HEADACHE. The kind that happens when I blow past my very necessary six thirty a.m. cup of coffee. I rolled over and looked at my phone. It was 2:35. *In the afternoon.* Wow. That's some good in-sleeping. Last time I remembered doing that was . . . never?

I walked into the kitchen, downed a cup of instant coffee (*gross*), and was ready to make up for lost time. But then I saw my parents sitting on the couch doing a crossword puzzle and I thought, screw it. Chris, RB, and my train wreck of a life would all be waiting for me on Monday. So I spent the day hanging with my family, eating day-old birthday cake, watching old movies, and even cleaning our bathroom. I simply existed as a member of the Mertz clan. I was a daughter, and a human being, and for one Sunday, like God herself, I took the damn day off.

27

I Hope You Like Your
Justice Served Cold

"What a bunch of assholes! *Ass-holes!*"

I've talked to a few lawyers in my life. Often under the guise of Melanie P. Strutt. Most were what you'd expect: polite, curt, professional. Caroline Goldstein was . . . something else. For one, she said "asshole" a lot.

"These assholes![90] This is so disgusting! Oh, god damn them! I'm gonna get these entitled little fucks!"

When I told my parents I didn't want to go to the police or to Principal Palmer, my mom suggested I talk to a lawyer she knew (from DanceLetics) who specialized in class action lawsuits. However, my mom's lawyer had little to no experience with these kinds of cybercrimes and so referred me to another lawyer, who in turn referred me to Caroline. Apparently, lawyers

---

90. See?

who specialize in online revenge porn are very rare. The internet happened so fast that laws are just now catching up. (Which sounds like an excuse to me. Make some decent laws already!)

I sent Caroline an email explaining the case with a link to RB and several screenshots. She called me within the hour. And the first words out of her mouth were, "What a bunch of assholes!"

"Oh yeah. These guys are definitely not allies," I said.

"Sorry, I know I'm coming in hot. But I'm looking at the site right now," she said. As she scrolled, I could hear her muttering, "Assholes. Assholes!"[91]

"So how many of the victims are willing to come forward?" she asked while furiously typing.

Come forward. Right. I was still hoping there was a way to charge Chris without getting the victims, Shannon especially, involved.

"Well, with all the evidence I have—the hard drives, the phone logs and stuff—I thought maybe you wouldn't need, uh, the girls to come forward?"

The typing stopped.

"Right. Here's the thing. Without victims pressing charges, we don't really have a case. You could, I guess, turn over your stuff to the police anonymously. But it was all illegally obtained, right? I'm guessing you didn't have permission to copy Chris's computer?"

I said nothing.

"Yeah. So that's not admissible in court. Sorry. But, if any of these young women are willing to press charges, I will represent

---

91. She was almost Hodor-ing "asshole."

them and make sure these assholes pay. And I'll do it pro bono. Which means I won't charge."

"Great!" I said, knowing full well what pro bono meant.

"Super. Aaaaand, shit. I have to be in court in half an hour. Once you have victims, call me, and we'll set up a meeting. Okay! We're gonna get these guys!"[92] And she ended the call.

My mom popped her head into my bedroom with a basket full of laundry. "How did it go? Does she know what she's talking about?"

"Yeah. I think so. She's intense. And a little scary."

"So . . . she's your new role model?" My mom smiled.

"Haha." I threw a sock at her.

SO I HAD TO FIND SOME VICTIMS WILLING TO COME FORWARD. I texted Shannon first, since she was the one who actually hired me. But after two unanswered texts, I started to get antsy, so I decided to reach out to the Kelseys. I figured if anyone was game for some sweet belated justice, it was them. I texted Hoffman first. Her response was:

> **HOFFMAN:** why would i trust you when you blew us off??

It appeared she was still pissed at me for bailing on Operation Failure.[93]

> **MARGOT:** Fair. But let me apologize? Feel like some Nick's?

---

92. Shocked she didn't say "assholes" here. Seems like a missed opportunity.

93. Guess I'm still workshopping names.

> **HOFFMAN:** Fine.

> **HOFFMAN:** Chugg is coming too.

The following night, over a "Nick's Plate," which is basically everything Nick has on the menu,[94] smothered in Night Sauce,[95] I apologized to the Kelseys for bailing on the plan. I tried to explain how Sammi's confession threw me into a tailspin. But Chugg wasn't buying it.

"That's not an excuse. You can't let these shitbags get away with it just because *your* friend was involved. That really sucks, Margot."

"I know that. And I'm sorry. It just . . . in the moment it threw me, okay? Sammi was kind of my only friend." My vulnerability seemed to quell the Kelseys for a moment. "But I agree, that doesn't excuse what he did. I don't want to let him off the hook. But that's the problem—what's 'the hook'? We were going to sabotage Chris, Kyle, and P-Boy's computers in secret and delete Roosevelt Bitches. Right? But by doing it in secret, it gives them all a free pass. I mean, where's the punishment?" The Kelseys nodded. I dipped an onion ring into a pool of Night/Nick Sauce before continuing.

"I talked to a lawyer who specializes in revenge porn cases like this. She's willing to take on the case and actually make these assholes—her word—pay for what they did. Including Sammi. But first she needs the people on the site to come forward."

---

94. Including lots of stuff that doesn't go together like spaghetti and hot dogs.

95. Night Sauce is just Nick Sauce from the breakfast menu, but now available for dinner. Nick is kind of a one-trick pony, but man! What a trick!

They sat there silently for a minute.

"I know it's a lot to ask," I said. "The lawyer said it could stretch on for months."

"*Months?*" Hoffman asked.

"Yeah. And everyone who comes forward would be questioned by lawyers, the police, not to mention maybe testifying if it went to trial or something."

"What if *no one* wants to press charges?" Chugg asked.

"Then that's it. I think. You can't bring a criminal to justice without a victim. So . . ." I bit a fry in half.

Chugg was about to ask another question when Hoffman cut her off with "Screw it. I'll do it."

"I don't want to pressure you into this," I said, making sure she really looked at me. "This trial could be hell. P-Boy's parents have money. And Kyle's dad is a lawyer—"

"Oh, fuck them and their money. I don't care."

Chugg gently reminded her, "When this whole thing started, you said your biggest fear was that other people would find out about it."

"I know." Hoffman shrugged. "But I'm over being ashamed. I'm just mad now."

I nodded, relieved. Chugg took a minute and drank a sip of her pop for courage before saying, "Me too, then. I guess. I only have one pic on there, and it's not that bad. But if it helps, I'm in."

Before I left Nick's, I gave them another chance to back out. But the Kelseys didn't blink. They were fed up and prepared to face this head-on. I paid the bill.

With Hoffman and Chugg on board, I felt a little more hopeful as I messaged the Fury chat.

> **MARGOT:** anyone interested in talking to a badass lawyer?

I went into more detail and explained everything I had just told the Kelseys. And at first, no one responded. The WhatsApp was—for the first time—as quiet as my econ study group WhatsApp (which consists of three messages about the loanable funds theory). But then Tatiana Alvarez responded.

> **TATIANA:** in

Their responses slowly started to stagger in. And as I expected, they varied.

> **JESS:** no. im sorry guys. no.

> **MICHELLE:** i need some time to think. this is kind of a major thing.

> **ABBY:** i read that lawyer's website. In.

> **TYRA:** thank u for trying but i'm a no.

> **SARA:** no way. My mom would def find out. It's too real i can't.

A few more said they were in, but got cold feet after a few days and pulled out. (I couldn't really fault them for not coming forward. They were still going to school and facing the world.

Just showing up is a kind of bravery.) By the end of the week, I had nine girls willing to press charges. Women who would put their reputations on the line to put a real end to Roosevelt Bitches.

But I still hadn't heard from Shannon. She'd been ducking my texts and DMs, and I was starting to get nervous. If she didn't want me to take the case to Caroline, I wasn't sure I could go through with it.

THE LAST WEEK OF SCHOOL, SHANNON FINALLY RESPONDED AND agreed to meet me at Greenbaum's. I offered her the choice of scone or muffin as she sat down.

"I'm not really hungry. Thanks."

Shannon looked about the same as the last time I saw her. Thin. Tired. I truly didn't want to make her life any worse, but I was starting to get almost *hopeful* about turning the case over to Caroline. I nervously ate both pastries as I gave her my best pitch. I told her about Caroline, the nine other Fury girls who were willing to press charges, and how I truly believed this was our best move.

"But," I said, making her look me in the eye so she'd realize how serious I was, "you hired me. And if you don't want me to do it, any of it . . . then I won't. I'll call Caroline and tell her it's off. I'll drop the whole thing."

Shannon continued to play with a sugar packet. From the way she was turning it over and over, I wasn't sure she really heard me. So I gave her a gentle "Shannon?"

She dropped the sugar packet. "Sorry. I . . . I'm thinking."

"Take your time," I said.

She rubbed her eyes before finally saying, "So two months ago you said you wanted to go to the police. And I said no. And now your solution is to . . . go to a lawyer? Who will then take this to the police?"

"I mean, she'll take it to the district attorney's office in Albany, who will coordinate with the police but . . . yes. Essentially, we are . . . right back where we started," I said, shoving more scone in my mouth.

She laughed. Then rested her forehead in her hands. Maybe she had been through too much. She had hired me to make the site go away quietly. She never asked for revenge, let alone highly public revenge. I was the one who kept insisting she deserved justice. Maybe she disagreed.

But then, with a swift hand-slap on the table she declared, "Yep. I'm in."

"You sure?" I said. "Because I just want you to be fully aware of what it will mean to come forward. There will be media and—"

"I know, Margot. Believe me, I've thought about it a lot." She seemed so sad. But also so tired of being so sad. "I thought if you made it go away, I could just move on with my life but . . . I don't think that's how this works."

"What about your mom?"

"I started going to a therapist. She thinks I should tell my mom. So I'm kind of getting ready to tell her anyway." She reached over and took a bite of the scone.

I tried to remain politely detached, but I really had no chill.

I may have even let out an audible "phew!" because Shannon laughed, saying, "What would you have done if I said no?"

"Honestly? No idea."

THE FOLLOWING WEEKEND, THE TEN GIRLS MET ME IN CAROLINE'S cramped office on St. Paul Street.

Caroline's office had a style that can only be described as "soon to be condemned." There were watermarks on the ceiling, and the window AC unit would occasionally start to clank, causing Caroline to kick it with her four-inch pumps. It gave me some confidence in my fictional Melanie P. Strutt character. (At least Melanie had stationery!) A quick look around the room told me that I wasn't the only one having second thoughts.

But then Caroline started talking about the case, and everyone relaxed. She was smart, direct, and had an encyclopedic knowledge of revenge porn laws. And best of all, she was angry.

"So the bad news is that prosecuting a crime with the word 'cyber' in front of it is always a pain in the ass," Caroline explained. "It takes persistence and coordination and patience. You have to explain to *everyone* why exactly this is a crime and not just, I don't know, a naughty meme or something."

The AC clanged, and she kicked it without missing a beat. Abby Durbin looked particularly concerned, I think because she was closest.

"But the good news is there is precedent. This type of revenge porn, even in high schools, is sadly common. Girl texts boy. Boy exploits image by sharing it without her consent and does irreparable harm. I go after boy 'cause that is a fucking crime."

Tatiana sat up in her chair. "So you're saying we have a chance?"

"Yup. Doesn't mean we'll convict. A lot of that depends on how old and tech-aware the judge is. But I'll do everything I can to nail these little shits. *That* I promise," Caroline proclaimed, slamming her hand on the desk so dramatically that Kelsey Chugg actually gasped.

"And is there anything you can do . . . like now? 'Cause I wouldn't mind having my naked picture taken down . . . like now?" Shannon asked.

"Totally. As soon as we're done here, I'm sending a cease and desist order to Chris Heinz, Kyle Kirkland, and Peter Bukowski. *And* I'm sending it to their parents. And then I'm calling their parents to let them know exactly what kind of trouble they're all in and that they're all pieces of shit.[96] You know, the whole fire-and-brimstone act. Of course there's no guarantee, but in my experience, that usually does the job."

With every question we asked, our group's confidence in Caroline grew. After months of being victimized, harassed, and shamed, suddenly everyone's power was being restored. These young women weren't gonna hide anymore. They weren't just going to hope it all went away. They were going to fight.

The meeting wrapped, and Caroline escorted everyone out of the office, except for me.

"So as I said before, the drive you gave me, it's incredibly

---

96. Caroline seemed partial to "shit" today, rather than her usual "asshole."

informative. But also, incredibly inadmissible." Caroline shifted her weight. "You said there was another guy who did the actual coding?"

"I did say that."

"Think he'd come forward? Implicate the other guys? It would help the case."

I shrugged. "No way to know. We're not speaking."

I walked to the door of her office half expecting her to stop me, but she didn't say anything else, and I let myself out.

The meeting had gone better than I expected. Caroline seemed competent and highly invested. And the ten-woman band of accusers seemed committed. I should have been full of energy. But I was stuck on Sammi. He was sitting on all the evidence Caroline could ever want, and he could deliver it legally. He might even earn a leaner sentence. I just wasn't sure he deserved one.

That night at dinner, I hardly ate and instead smooshed my mashed potatoes into a variety of shapes (a mountain, a mound, a shoe that looked like a mountain, etc. I guess I can only make mountains). It was an obvious cry for help. My mom finally said, "Anything you want to talk about, honey?"

I smooshed it up again and took a bite. Then I asked my parents what they thought I should do about Sammi. By giving him this chance, was I going easy on him?

"Possibly. But that doesn't mean it's not the right thing to do," my dad said with a mouthful of reheated meat loaf.

My mom chimed in, "If he testifies and cooperates, he'll help

build the case. And it sounds like these sexting…porn…cases…
whatever you wanna call it. They're hard to prove, right?"

"Yeah. I think you're right." I tapped my fork on the plate.
That would mean talking to Sammi. Which . . . I wasn't sure I'd
ever do again. But their logic was sound. "Huh. Why don't I ask
you for help with my cases more often?"

"Because you didn't want to tell us about your illegal part-
time job. Which we still need to talk about, by the way. Your
punishment and all that," my dad said, brandishing his nonthreatening butter knife at me.

"You could always keep me inside all summer and not let me
see any of my friends. Oh, how I'd hate that!" I said dryly.

"Uh-huh," my mom replied. I almost felt bad for them. How
do you punish someone who would prefer to be grounded all the
time? "We'll think of something. Trust us."

I lifted my hands up as I backed off, the infuriating way Avery
always used to do when he had won an argument. It was cocky,
but I couldn't help it. Damn you, Avery! Keep your mannerisms
to yourself!

After dinner, I called Sammi. I knew he wouldn't answer, so
I explained what I needed over a series of voicemails. Despite
his very, very bad choice, I was giving him an opportunity to *partially* redeem himself. Because it was the right thing to do. And,
maybe, because I still considered him a friend. Maybe.

He never called back, but later that night he texted:

> **SAMMI:** ok

28

ROLL UP FOR THE APOLOGY TOUR

It was the last week of school, and everyone was coasting through half days and early dismissals. And with Roosevelt Bitches in capable-seeming hands, my own hands were free to . . . do nothing, I guess?

But still I felt crappy.

I didn't like the way I left things with Sammi. I was glad I'd given him the chance to do the right thing. But still, something seemed off. I guess I felt sorry for the way I'd treated him the past . . . six years. Or more. I'd been a bad friend to him since long before RB was a twinkle in Chris's evil eye. And while I wasn't responsible for Sammi's extremely bad choices, I was responsible for how I had taken him for granted. And I'm person enough to admit when I'm wrong.

I decided to apologize to him. He was a shitbag. And he really let me down. But I couldn't control any of that. I could only control how I acted.

Sammi's preferred mode of contact was text. So I wrote him everything I wanted to say in little blue bubbles of remorse.

> **MARGOT:** I'm really sorry for how I treated you for the last, I don't know, 6? 10? years of our friendship. You have always been a good friend to me and in return I basically pretended you weren't my friend at all.

> **MARGOT:** Obviously I'm a little fucked up re: friendships and you have received the brunt of my fucked-up-ed-ness. I'm sorry I treated you like someone I could turn on and off like a video game. You're more than that. You've been my only real friend the past two years and I should've treated you like one and appreciated you. You deserve better.

> **MARGOT:** I am here if you ever want to talk.

I sent it and still felt . . . mixed. It's hard for your brain to hold two competing ideas at once. He was my friend, but he did a bad thing, but I've known him forever, but he aided predators, but he truly is a good person, but he made a bad choice, and on and on and on. It was complicated.

When I returned Jenji's computer back in March, I asked her about the "apology tour" she went on. The one she journaled about in her laptop. She told me it "changed her life" and made her feel "like her soul had been cleansed," that she "slept better than she had in years" and that she even "lost three pounds." So that's kinda what I was hoping for when I apologized to Sammi.

Some sweet peace of mind and, for god's sake, just a few hours of sleep! But that night, my soul still felt dirty, and I slept like I was trying to kick meth. Tossing, turning, teeth falling out, etc. Not the kind of sleep I was promised, Jenji!

But maybe that was because I hadn't done it enough. I mean, how many times had I ever actually said "I'm sorry" to someone? My normal instinct when I felt remorse was to aggressively defend myself until the other person apologized to *me*. Which, you know, isn't a great way to live your life.

I decided to go on an apology tour of my own. It would be a thorough cleaning of my conscience.

Once again, I found myself making a list. This time of all the people I had steamrolled, lied to, or hurt, be it inadvertently or . . . very vertently. I opened up the Register and started to scroll through the eleven hundred plus names. But as I looked at the pithy comments and mean notes I wrote about everyone, I realized that the Register wasn't helpful. It was full of judgments and generalizations. It turned my classmates into numbers, and I needed to see them as people. I deleted it.

So instead I just used the old noggin and made a handwritten list of people I'd wronged. And I got to work. I started with the Kelseys, who informed me that I had technically already apologized to them when I took them out to Nick's. They gave me shit about "double-apologizing" and "needing validation," which told me they were on their way to forgiving me.

Next was Beth. I drafted out the most eloquent apology my thumbs could type. I told her I was sorry for my nonstop texts to her. And for treating them like they were my diary. I told her I was happy she was moving on with her life. That I thought I understood where she was coming from. And at the end of it all, I wrote that this would be my last text to her.

But then I realized this was exactly what she asked me *not* to do. That sending long, intense, rambling texts, even apology texts, was exactly what was making her anxious and resentful. I tried rewriting it a few more times in a more chill, sparse way, but nothing felt right. I guess because it's not what she asked for. She asked to be left alone. And so I figured the best apology I could give her was doing just that.

I deleted the message without sending it. And I deleted Beth from my contacts.

I didn't need to have the last word. Not everything was about me. I let her go.

And you know what? Doing some personal inventory, deleting Beth from my phone, it actually made me feel . . . *so much worse*. Huh. But maybe that's not the point of apologizing. Maybe apologies aren't always supposed to make you feel better. They're just something you do.

Or . . . maybe . . . (hear me out) I just hadn't apologized to enough people yet? Maybe I wasn't getting the Jenji high/three-pound weight-loss bonus because I still had a lot of sorrys to give.

I charged ahead and started apologizing to everyone I could think of.

I apologized to Harold, Jenji, and Danny for hacking their computers. Jenji had heard about my attempts to take down RB and was largely supportive. Danny also took it pretty well.

(I think? He didn't say much.) But Harold was, of course, a real smug prick about it. He gave me this whole lecture about privacy and freedom of speech and how "Satan's work is done by liars" or something. I was a little distracted because he was basically *spitting* the whole thing at me. Plus I kept thinking about what a hypocrite he was. All the pictures he downloaded from RB, and the anonymous sexting thing he never got punished for. He eventually stormed off, threatening to get Palmer and the authorities involved and saying I should be worried because his dad is a Freemason. Sure.

Next, I was going to apologize to Mrs. Blye, but I realized I had nothing to apologize for. So instead, I donated the $300 in STFU money she gave me to Planned Parenthood. I felt absolved thinking about all the women who could get mammograms and birth control because of Mrs. Blye's affair.

Onward! I apologized to my parents for taking them for granted and for omitting certain details about my business. (They were still trying to figure out a proper punishment for me.[97]) I met my uncle Richard at Gaetano's and apologized for always being so cold to him at family gatherings. He surprised me with a sincere apology of his own for failing at the dry cleaning business. Apparently he's in recovery now, so he's kind of on his own apology tour.

And I could not stop. I apologized to a local barista for using the bathroom when I hadn't bought anything, to the school's Monday/Wednesday security guard for trespassing, and to my

---

97. By the time of publication, they still had not.

grandmother for not calling enough. I even apologized to Elysse Brown from Brighton for pretending to be her and starting a rumor that she had a UTI. Pretty much everyone's reaction was "Uh. Okay?"

And then, after a week of this, it became clear that all these low-level, nonessential apologies were actually helping me to avoid a big one. Avery. Out of all the people who deserved a mea culpa, he arguably deserved it the most. I deceived him, used his kindness to my advantage, and knowingly hurt him all because I was convinced that what I was doing outweighed his feelings. Or that because he was rich he could just buy new feelings. But clearly that wasn't true. I was just a shit, and he deserved a big freaking apology.

But I still couldn't do it. My aversion to him had gone from procrastination to pathological. *Twice* I took the bus to his neighborhood, walked by his house, and then . . . kept walking. Like I was your friendly neighborhood stalker. It was not like me to procrastinate . . . ever. I hate things that are a waste of time and procrastination is *literally* a waste of time.

Sunday morning, I boarded the M10 bus for the third time in forty-eight hours. The route to Autumn Hills, where Avery lived, is about a forty-five-minute ride. The bus pulled away from Trinity Towers, and I promised myself that this time, *this time*, I would apologize. There was no logical reason to keep avoiding it. The only thing I had learned from my twenty-two and a half apologies was that asking for forgiveness is not an art form. You simply say the words "I'm sorry," then explain why you are sorry, and however the recipient reacts is how they react. And that's it.

So why was I being so weird about it with Avery? Knowing him, he would likely forgive me because he's a good person, which I realize now is not a creepy or suspicious thing, but a rare thing. To be kind in a world full of so much awfulness is a strength to be celebrated. Not a weakness. So . . . he would probably be fine with my apology. Right?

And if he wasn't, if he *didn't* forgive me and said he never wanted to see me or talk to me again . . . well . . . I could live with that, too. I mean, yes, that would be rough. I have unraveled a bit since we broke up. But that's just because Avery had proven to be a pretty good friend. I mean, he made mini golf *fun*.[98] He definitely had an annoying habit of calling me on my bullshit, like when I was working a case and/or lying to him. But that's because Avery listens—like actually listens—when you talk. And that just makes you want to talk to him all the time. Also his muscles . . . are okay, I think. I know I kept saying he looked too bulky, but doesn't a fit bod just mean he's taking care of himself? And isn't *that* ultimately a good thing? Self-care? Is good? Right? And yes, I know that saying all this stuff sure makes it seem like I like him, but I don't. I'm only saying it because I like him.

Wait. What?

No I don't. That would be crazy. I just like that he's kind and gets me and challenges me and makes me laugh and also thinks I'm funny and cool and respects my work ethic, and also I sometimes fantasize about making out with him, and also doing a lot more than making out with him. But that doesn't mean I like him!

---

98. Mini golf is empirically *not* fun.

It does. It does mean I like him. That's exactly what it means. *I like Avery.*

Margot? What. In the hell. Is wrong with you?

I once again realized Avery was right. I truly didn't know who I was. At least not when it came to my feelings. I was practically in love with him, and yet somehow I had convinced myself that I detested him. Oh, woof upon woof. It was like a doorbell going off in my brain. DING DONG! WAKE UP, MARGOT. YOU LOVE THIS DUDE. I hesitated. Could I really go on with the apology given my newly discovered feelings or—wait. *Like a doorbell in my brain?* What kind of simile is that? That doesn't make any sense . . .

I was day-thinking again. I had somehow blocked out the bus ride and the walk to Avery's door. Also, I had apparently blocked out that I had just pressed his doorbell. Eep.

Through the opaque glass door, I saw an Avery-shaped blob approaching. Oh no. Not ready. *Can't sincerely apologize to Avery while simultaneously realizing deep-rooted love-feelings for him!* Emotions overload! Force quit! Force quit!

I had only a few options at this point: 1) Run, and hope he didn't see me. 2) Stand and stammer through an apology while trying not to think about how hot it is to have *a single dimple.* Or 3) Hide in the shrubbery.

I, unfortunately, chose option 3. And since I chose it too late to properly conceal myself, I was forced to duck into some (boxwood?) bushes that only came up to about my waist. It was not a good decision.

"Margot?" Avery said, very much seeing me.

"Uh. Yeah?"

"Are you okay?"

"Mm-hmm," I said, then awkwardly rose to my feet, dusting off the leaves and dirt from my shirt and looking not at all sexy.

"Did you fall or something?" This was Avery giving me an out. Or, possibly, he just assumed that's what happened, because why else would I be in his front hedgerow? Either way, I could have, and maybe *should* have, just taken this excuse. But I didn't want to lie to Avery anymore. That was my whole problem. So I went with the truth. The whole, humiliating, will-probably-keep-me-single-forever truth.

"No, I honestly came here to apologize to you. But then I . . . chickened out and thought hiding in your shrubs here might . . . make me invisible, I guess?"

Avery scratched the back of his head. "Okay."

I almost kept going and told him that I liked him and that I was overwhelmed by the feelings I had for him and also disappointed in myself that I hadn't realized those feelings before. But I didn't want to muddy the apology. I hadn't come here to win him back. I just needed to own my shitty behavior.

During the long pause while I weighed how much to tell him, Avery filled the dead air by saying, "Look, I actually have a couple people over. Could this, um . . . maybe wait?" I looked to Avery's feet and saw a bunch of shoes. I could hear voices coming from within and I realized that there were several cars parked in his driveway and in front of his house. In fact, I could see a couple people craning their necks to look at us through the front blinds. Cool. Cool.

"I'm sorry but—can I just say this? It will be quick, I promise. I've been here two times already this week." *Jesus, Margot. Why would you tell him that?*

"Okay." He shrugged politely, looking back toward his friends.

"I'm sorry I wasn't honest with you about why I wanted to date you. I'm sorry I used you for a job. It wasn't fair. You didn't deserve it. And you were right. I don't really know myself as well as I thought I did. But I'm . . . trying to work on that. I'm trying to figure out why I do things like that."

He looked like he might say something, but I went on.

"And I'm sorry for not going to your mom's gala thing! You asked me a bunch of different times, and I knew it meant a lot to you. I should've just gone." I was gaining momentum but losing any remaining filter. Nevertheless, I persisted. "I'm sorry for calling you Avery Ween behind your back in seventh grade. You're not a ween."

"Ween? Like—"

"Like a wiener, I guess? I don't know. I never really thought about it."

"Okay. Uh—"

"Oh, one more thing! I'm sorry for being creeped out by how nice you are. That says more about me than you. And I'm sorry for teasing you about being rich. That's not a thing you chose. I'm just jealous. Having an infinity pool and a fridge for just LaCroix sounds nice."

And then I lifted my hands in the air in an exaggerated shrug. "And that's it. I'm also very sorry for interrupting your party. Thanks for letting me talk. Sorry."

And with that, I quickly turned away and speedwalked the 1.2-mile trek back to the closest bus stop. I could not bear to hear his response, whether it was forgiveness or vindictiveness. So I just skedaddled. The apology tour was over, and my feelings were still decidedly mixed. Relieved, but sad. Happy it was over, but exhausted.

I did have a slight pang of unrealistic hope that Avery would catch up to me, spin me around, and tell me how much my apology meant to him. That he forgave me and still had feelings for me. And then, you know, there'd be kissing and laughing and, I don't know, slow dancing or something.

But of course none of that happened. I hadn't earned that ending. So instead, I took the bus home alone.

29

Margot Mertz Will Clean Your Literal Filth

Finals were done. The senior class, which included Shannon, Kyle, Chris, Claire Jubell, and Harold Ming, all graduated before anything about RB became public. Which sucked.

I'd had this fantasy of Chris getting arrested onstage at graduation. Right as he was handed his diploma, about to make some lewd gesture to the crowd, officers in windbreakers would swarm in and slap the cuffs on him. Chris's family would say, "What's the meaning of this?" and desperately cling to Chris as he was hauled out of the room. Then they'd come for P-Boy who, as a junior, would be watching from the audience. And that aggro plant-pisser would resist arrest, flailing his limbs and shouting something like *"Fake news!"* as he was thrown into the back of a police car. And Kyle—poor, weak Kyle—would cry. A loud keening so pathetic you *almost* felt sorry for him. The press would devour the whole thing. There would be a four-part deep dive in the *North Webster Gazette*, which would attract national attention. *This American Life* would adapt the story and I would be interviewed by both Ira Glass and Sarah Koenig, who would recommend me for an internship, which I would turn down. (Interns should be paid!)

And! One more thing. Everyone who uploaded to and/or downloaded from Roosevelt Bitches would have their names printed—in letters big enough to read—on the billboard by the side of I-490 right by Costco. This, too, would get national attention, leading to arrests, public shaming, and the revocation of scholarships! The pervs and violators would pay. And the community and school would heal and start to rebuild, and by the time I graduated, toxic masculinity would finally be over! Forever!

I mean, it's a nice fantasy.

"Margot?" my mom interrupted me. "Are you day-thinking? I thought you were going to peel the potatoes?"

I *did* say I was going to do that.

"Sorry! I'm on it!" I said as I picked up the peeler and got started on what would eventually be a "dish to pass" at my uncle Richard's Fourth of July B.Y.O.B.B.Q., which had been delayed twice and was now being held in August.

The actual resolution—if you can call it that—of RB was so much more complicated than my fantasy. And far less satisfying.

After several weeks of review and investigation, charges were finally brought against Chris, Kyle, and P-Boy. It will be months still before they actually have a trial (*if* they have a trial at all. Caroline thinks they will most likely settle). They probably won't face jail time (though I'm holding out hope Chris might get a few months, since he spearheaded the whole thing). And the punishments would be nothing like what I had envisioned, most likely probation and community service. *But* the administration did report the incident to Chris and Kyle's colleges and their acceptances were promptly revoked. It was a victory, but an annoying one, because it meant they would be hanging around North Webster next year with nothing to do. And I had already run into Chris once, which is one time too many.

I had my dad's car and was running some errands for him. I had just dropped off some dry cleaning. And as I walked back toward the car, I saw Chris waiting for me. As petulant and entitled as ever, but now with a disturbing accessory. A baseball bat.

"If you're looking for an angel investor for your next tech start-up, I'm afraid I'm not going to be able to help you," I said, digging for my mace.

"Look. I get it. I pissed you off with my fake yearbook." He walked toward me. "I get that you can't take a joke. But can you cool it with my fucking car?"

"What?" I asked, keeping my distance as I walked around my car to the driver's side.

"Every week, my tires are slashed! Or there's sugar in my gas tank!"

"I don't know what you're talking about," I said, so very confused.

"I have to drive my little sister to camp all summer. So when you mess with my car, you're actually hurting Madison!" *Sister? Oh, right. He has a sister.* It's so hard to imagine. But what I *can* imagine is him using this sister as a shield. I could just hear him say, "Your honor, as the brother of a sister, how could I ever be involved in a site like Roosevelt Bitches?" Vomit.

"I haven't touched your car, pervert. Now go home before your ankle bracelet goes off."

Chris's face flushed with anger. He lifted his bat, clearly ready for some caveman justice, when I whipped out my phone and started livestreaming.

"I mean, go ahead, Chris. Break my windshield on Instagram Live. Let's see how this episode affects your pending trial."

Chris lowered his bat, seething. "You're such a fucking [hateful word that only the worst kind of men use]." And then he walked away, bat dragging behind him.

I got in the car and took a breath. Why did he think I was vandalizing his car? (And also why *wasn't* I? I loved seeing Chris all flails and pissy.) Then I thought about who else liked seeing Chris this way. I hadn't gone on the Fury WhatsApp since graduation, allowing myself a much-needed mental break. But now I opened it. And what I saw was . . . glorious. Picture after picture of vandalism ranging from the innocent (smoothie poured on backpack) to the very badass (Chris's car keyed, Kyle's windshield smashed, and I think someone set P-Boy's gym bag on fire!). The thread had morphed from victims support group to full-on gallery of the guys' misery. They're like the Banksys of revenge. I laughed. I commented. I sent the video I'd just made of Chris. Good times.

• • • •

THERE WERE NO PICTURES OF SAMMI, WHO APPEARED TO HAVE escaped Fury's wrath. Maybe because he was cooperating with Caroline Goldstein's team. By turning over all the evidence he had, he pleaded down from a misdemeanor and got two hundred hours of community service. But Rensselaer rescinded his acceptance. Last I heard (from his mom), he was now thinking about going to community college for a year.

About a month after my apology texts to him, Sammi finally texted me back.

> **SAMMI:** thank you. for telling me to bring stuff to the lawyer.

It wasn't exactly an "I forgive you," but I felt like he wouldn't hate me forever. At least he saw that I was looking out for him. I had to be okay with that for now.

As far as the people who used RB, uploading and downloading pictures, most of them got off with little to no punishment. A few guys who had uploaded pics got suspended. While a couple of guys who downloaded and distributed pics got—wait for it—a lecture from Principal Palmer. But the vast majority suffered no consequences. This was particularly dissatisfying.

Oh, except for a sophomore girl who had downloaded a picture in order to bully another girl. She was expelled. I guess boys will be boys, but girls will be held to a completely different standard.

But, I'm happy to report Goldstein proved to be as good as her word. Aside from pressing charges and forcing Chris's crimes into the spotlight, she was also really aggressive about forcing the school to provide counseling and outreach to victims, both those who chose to come forward and those who did not. And next year, there's going to be an anonymous reporting program, as well as more education on sexting and consent. So . . . progress?

My involvement in the case had obviously lapsed once I turned things over to Caroline and the cops. So I was surprised when I got a phone call from an Officer D'Antoni. He asked me to come in for questioning because—get this—*I* had been accused of illegal behavior.

It turns out my good friend Harold Ming's rage-filled tirade wasn't just him blowing off steam (and spitting in my face), it was an actual threat that he followed through on. He formally accused me of tampering with his computer and wanted to press charges. My dad drove me to the precinct, where I calmly confessed to D'Antoni that I had indeed made a copy of Harold's hard drive. And also that Harold's computer was crawling with images of underage girls downloaded from RB.

The end result was that I now have to do forty hours of community service this summer. (And Harold has to do a hundred. But who's counting?)

And that was it. Case closed. Although not really, because this will likely drag on forever, especially if it goes to trial. But, you know, for now I get a breather.

Which took some getting used to. The last time I remembered having free time was freshman year. I was tempted to pick up some MCYF work just to keep myself sane. I was flooded with requests once Chris was charged and word got out that I was the one who spearheaded it. (And of course, Stanford wasn't getting any cheaper.) But I exercised some self-control and placed a moratorium on filth-cleaning jobs while I thought a little bit more about the ethics of it all. I attempted a little of the ol' introspection, which was tedious, but not altogether a waste of time. I journaled. I helped out more around the house. I even started going to the Trinity Towers gym twice a week and walked on the treadmill until my heart felt like it was about to explode (seven minutes). I'm a work in progress.

In August, I dutifully reported to the town hall to perform my "service," which I assumed would be reading to old people at a nursing home or visiting patients at my mom's hospital. Instead, I was told I'd be *picking up trash by the side of the highway*, which was not a great match for my skill set. Remember me on the treadmill? Imagine that but on the side of the road! With a trash bag. That is not a service to anyone!

They gave me some gear and a large neon vest, which made me look like both a loser *and* a traffic cone. I assumed I would be sent off with some other juvenile offenders, perhaps a pyromaniac. Or worse, Harold Ming! But to my surprise, most of the people there were not court-appointed. It was mostly just volunteers (a grandma and her grandson, a guy running for state legislature, etc.) who wanted to beautify their town. It was kind of nice, and I hoped I could blend in without telling anyone that I committed a misdemeanor.

They ushered us into a very beige conference room to watch a video called "Roadside Safety."[99] When it was over, they turned

---

99. It was as riveting as it sounds. I give it two thumbs up and jammed in my eyes.

on the lights and asked if we had any questions. Someone at the back of the room asked if he *had* to wear gloves, because gloves irritated his psoriasis and he had a note from his dermatologist, who was also his wife. I turned back to see what kind of nutjob would go into this kind of detail. It turned out to be an old man who, from what I could tell, did not have psoriasis. But he did have a pet bird sitting on his shoulder. And sitting next to him, also wearing a neon vest, was Avery Green.[100]

It seemed very random (or even suspicious!) that Avery was there. But *of course* Avery Green spends his free time picking up trash. *Of course* he would volunteer for a shit job like this and happily sit next to psoriasis guy. Avery lives for do-goodery activities.

He noticed me the moment I turned around and had an honest expression of surprise mixed with fear. He probably thought I was stalking him. As we filed out of the room, we were momentarily separated and loaded onto two different school buses. I thought maybe we'd even be driven to different stretches of highway. But I was not that lucky. The buses parked side by side in the stretch along I-490 where the shoulder widens. I would have to face Avery.

A lady was handing everyone bags, and when I went to grab one, I made eye contact with him. I smiled politely. He was a little guarded, but smiled back. (He couldn't let a smile go unanswered. He's Avery Green.) And then he broke the silence with the ever-popular icebreaker . . .

"Hi."

---

100. Yes, he was the only person in the room who actually looked good in a neon vest. Like it was a statement vest.

I responded with an equally inarticulate and awkward, "Hey." My pleasure in seeing him was surely visible across my face. My cheeks had been in a permanent blush since I first caught sight of him in the very beige room.

After an awkward silence that was probably only three seconds, but I swear to you was actually seventeen years, Avery said, "So what brings you to the cleanup crew?"

"Oh . . ." I said, stalling. Wishing I could tell him that I was there out of the goodness of my heart and not due to a plea bargain. But that would be a lie. "I'm doing mandatory community service. For tampering with Harold Ming's computer."

"Oh. That makes sense now."

We drifted to a patch of highway that needed attention and started picking up straws, cigarette butts, and pop cans. Avery got to work methodically stabbing stuff with a little poker, his arms flexing each time he did. I preferred just picking things up by hand. I honestly didn't mind it. There was nothing morally questionable about picking up garbage in real life. Litter is bad. And I was getting rid of it.

After a few minutes of garbage-picking, I turned to Avery. "I swear I didn't know you would be here. I'm not stalking you."

He laughed. "I have been doing this every Saturday morning since school ended. And *now* you show up? It feels a little stalker-y."

"Haha." I wished I could think of something clever to say, but my brain was just going, *Arms, arms, arms. Flex, flex, flex.*

"Margot?" He looked at me expectantly. Jesus, did he say something and I missed it because I was staring at his arm muscles?

"Yeah?"

"I said, that was some apology."

"Oh, haha, yeah. Well, I'm person enough to admit when I'm wrong."

Some guy found a wallet in a drainage ditch, and everybody crowded around him to see. But Avery and I stayed on our patch of highway, working our way forward. The more trash I picked up, the cleaner I felt.

"You kind of ran away after. I didn't really get to tell you how I felt about it."

This was true. And, in retrospect, pretty rude. I could've at least listened to his response. It probably would've been good for me to hear if he was angry or disappointed or whatever.

"I'll be honest," I began. "I was mortified. And just saying out loud how I treated you, it made me realize how . . . bad it was." I picked up a men's loafer and placed it in my bag. "But you're right. I absolutely should've let you respond."

"Yeah . . ." he said.

We kept walking.

"Yeah . . . I was mad," he eventually said. "For, like, a while."

Of course he was. I totally deserved—wait. *Was* mad? Like . . . in the past? Like he's not mad anymore? I looked up at his face. He was wearing (expensive) sunglasses. But even so, I could see his eyes. And he didn't look mad. Interesting.

"I wanted to keep being mad, but the more I thought about it, I mean, it was a pretty good apology. It was very honest. Possibly too honest . . . some would say exhaustive."

And . . . we've got dimple.

I smiled back.

There was a clump of newspapers that had gotten trapped under some brush. I grabbed at it with both hands and lifted it, trying to hold it away from my body. Avery intuitively opened his garbage bag so that I could just drop it inside. And even though it was only for a second, and even though we were both wearing gloves, we brushed hands. And I'm sorry to report that this only confirmed my worst fears. That whatever feelings I had for Avery had not subsided. If anything, they had grown.

My instinct was to keep talking, to fill the silence with my thoughts on community service, to apologize further and to share the results of my apology tour. To talk and talk until I eventually told him how hot he was and how, even in the least romantic place in the world, a trash-filled highway, I had the insatiable urge to put my mouth on his mouth.

But I didn't say any of that. Instead, I just asked him how his summer was going. And then . . . I listened. Because I'm trying.

As we walked the stretch of I-490 right by Costco, cars whizzing by us, Avery stopped.

"What?" I asked.

"Oh, right. Like you don't know about this?" Using his hands as a visor, he looked up at the giant billboard towering above us. "It was on the news."

I, too, craned my neck to look at the billboard, which contained the full name of every person who had uploaded or downloaded pictures to/from RB. In letters big enough to read.

I know it's a little petty. And it cost almost $400. But your girl isn't perfect. And with all my other good behavior lately, I think I earned it.

"You know that half the soccer team got suspended because of this."

"Oh, that sucks. I love sports. So much."

He smirked. "You're seriously telling me you had nothing to do with this? 'Cause this is such a Mertz move." He was practically shoving that goddamned dimple in my face.

I shrugged before finally saying, "Avery, I really don't want to lie to you anymore. So . . . can I just not answer the question?"

He nodded, maybe surprised by how honest I was being.

"Yeah. That works for me."

We kept walking. Him poking garbage like an Olympian. Me bending over like Quasimodo. The billboard full of perverts behind us getting smaller and smaller until all we could see was road and sky. And trash. So much trash.

ACKNOWLEDGMENTS

We would first like to thank Alli Dyer at Temple Hill for thinking this story might actually be a book. Without her feedback, guidance, hand-holding, and support all along the way, this would still be a one-page treatment for a screenplay no one wanted to make.

We would also first like to thank Kelsey Murphy (*can we have two first thanks?*) for her energy and efforts in editing this book. Kelsey's insightful, in-depth, sometimes intimidating notes are what drew us to our home at Philomel, and we couldn't be happier here. We've taken comfort in the fact that we have an editor who cares as much about our story as we do. (Maybe sometimes more?) Kelsey has helped enrich this story through every step of the process. She is a goddamn treasure.

We are grateful for our whole team at Philomel and Penguin Random House. Thank you to Jill Santopolo, Ken Wright, Liza Kaplan, and Cheryl Eissing for leading us through the process. And to all who had a hand in designing this very cool-looking book: Monique Sterling, Ellice Lee, Maria Fazio, Kristin Boyle, Deborah Kaplan, and a big thank you to Katie Carey for bearing with us. (If you haven't seen Katie's other work, do yourself a favor and Google her.) We must also thank our publicist, Ashley Spruill, and the extraordinary sales and marketing teams, who are so much better at promoting our work than we are!

Thank you to our copyeditors, Krista Ahlberg, Laura Blackwell, and Sola Akinlana, for looking up things like "*Cheat Retreat*" and "FAST-D." We were so impressed by your work. Even if we did push back on using capital letters FAR MORE THAN IS RESPECTABLE. We'd also like to thank our authenticity reader, Ronni Davis, for sharing your thoughtful feedback and candid personal take on this book.

To Julie Waters and the rest of the team at Temple Hill (including Alex Addison and all her marketing wisdom), we'd like to say thanks for partnering with us on this story. We're thrilled to be working with you. And shout out to Temple Hill's fantastic reps, Simon Lipskar, Cecilia de la Campa, Alessandra Birch, and the team at Writers House.

We'd also love to say merci, 감사합니다, Спасибо, obrigada, and thanks to our publishing partners abroad: La Martiniere, Moonhak Soochup, Eksmo, Nacional, and of course Hardie Grant.

And then there's Jeff Roberts. What would we do without Jeff? The answer is, embarrass ourselves. We know nothing about computers, "hacking," the "dark web," or coding. Carrie isn't even totally sure how browsers work. Thank you, Jeff, for consulting with us, for providing the technical details we needed so that Margot doesn't sound as computer illiterate as we are. And for your patience while you explained .Tor to us for the thirty-seventh time. Also for your seemingly immediate grasp on Margot's voice and what we were going for. You met us more than halfway.

Thank you as well to Johnathan Fernandez for being an early

reader of this book. Your feedback and insight helped us dig a little deeper into some of our favorite moments. And your knowledge of YA made us feel a little more confident as we headed toward publication.

And where would we be without the youth? Thank you to Sam Levy, Charlotte Sheffield, and Sophia and Gia Triassi for fielding our very random questions and helping us with our research into "how the kids are talking these days." We love you so much! But, jeez, get off our lawn already!

Thanks to our many friends in NY and LA (and Rochester and CT!) who have supported us as artists and people, reading our many scripts out loud over the years and encouraging us even when what we wrote was very bad. Ian thanks Brendan and Jason for writers' group, and for his playwriting career. We both thank Dave for the initial TH hookup (and for his friendship, I guess). And Isaac because he thanked us in his book. Carrie would also like to thank the incredibly supportive friends she met doing comedy in basements. And she would never have survived/written a book about high school without Melissa. To our families, our siblings, and our supportive aunts, uncles, and cousins. And Grandma! We wouldn't be here without you.

Thank you especially to Laurie Duncan, Karen McCrossen, and Paul McCrossen, without whose childcare we could never have written a book. How are we so lucky to have this much love and support from our parents? Even when we're fully adults and should be self-sufficient? It boggles the mind. But still, we are grateful. We love you.

Thank you as well to Caroline Cotter and Hannah Deboer,

both creative artists in their own rights, for watching Calvin while we wrote. He loved hanging with you.

And thanks, Calvin! For being perfect and spreading joy wherever you go. We promise our next book will be about trucks, per your many requests. We love you. We do.

Lastly, to our dear managers, Edna Cowan of Edna Cowan Management and Alex Platis and Kate Moran at Untitled, thank you for always being in our corner. And for being patient with us while we wrote a novel. Two actually. And to our hero, Jay Patel at Peikoff-Mahan, thank you for your time and wisdom. And for legally having our backs.

And for our second lastly, we should probably thank Lauren, our couples' therapist. If we hadn't worked with her, we never could've worked with each other.